I0681205

Trent Zelazny

Voiceless

Evil Jester Press

Edited by Shannon Giglio
Cover art by Gary McCluskey
Formatting and design by Peter Giglio

First Edition: October 2014

ISBN: 978-0692300626

Printed in the United States and the United Kingdom

For Warren Lapine,
who gave me the time of day,
and has been a great friend.
You da man.

"He who hides his madman dies voiceless."
— Henri Michaux

ONE

It was dreary and lonesome. And now, for Max Pendleton, it was also home.

Sueño Roto. A small desert town with a population of less than a thousand, rurally situated between Crownpoint and Twin Lakes, in the westernmost part of New Mexico. At one time, during the mining heyday, it had been a thriving coal camp. But those days were long gone. Sueño Roto was now largely abandoned.

The sun lanced everything, stabbed his eyes and belittled the sunglasses fixed to his face.

Camille pulled into the parking lot of the ramshackle grocery store. The other cars in the lot and the few people meandering did nothing to counteract the solitude.

It felt even emptier when he got out of the car and stretched. He rolled his shoulders and looked into the back of their car, a fairly recent Camry packed with the things they would need over the next twenty-four-or-so hours. The movers wouldn't be showing up until tomorrow.

Camille laced her fingers and pressed her palms to the sky. She sighed an exhausted sigh, which enshrouded a stymied moan, then dropped her arms and headed toward the store, not bothering to look at him.

Max stood there a moment and watched her walk. The hamlet's emptiness neither waned nor rose. It was all one hollow dimension with his wife walking away, if indeed it actually *was* his wife. For all he knew it was just her framework and nothing more. An animated container drained of compassion and weary of soul, void of emotion save for soft breaths of resentment and whispers of spite.

Max crossed the parking lot, wondering what he'd allowed himself to get in to.

The grocery store was dim and dank with a stale chill that somehow failed to contrast the outside heat. Some of the fluorescent lights flickered. The peeling linoleum floor sported interlocking squares, and any sheen it ever had was now scuffed and frayed away from years of treaded wear. A transistor radio behind the front counter played a soft and static-laced Glen Campbell song. It was a very small store, limited in its stock. Shopping from now on would take minutes or years.

Max kept several paces behind Camille, who picked a few things from the small line of produce. The air of her said *Don't follow me, don't leave*, the result being him standing like an awkward, pussy-whipped asshole.

Which he wasn't, but for all intents and purposes he might as well have been. One semester of Psychology ten years ago and suddenly his wife could analyze anyone, know exactly what made them tick. Words were often weapons to her. Dangerous weapons, her knack for finding a tiny nick and then exposing the wound to infection. Recently she'd been very acute to the fact that there's always contagion in a person's own weakness.

Humanity sprinkled a small pinch of folks throughout the narrow aisles. The low-rise shelving concealed all but the tops of their heads.

That's not fair, Max. You're just as acerbic as she is. Don't get all judgmental and pedantic when you know you're just as bad. Pointing a finger with three pointing back. Hell, at least she's got words to go with it. When was the last time the God of Articulation graced *you* with a visit?

"Go grab a basket," Camille said, veggies in her hands.

Max glanced at her expressionless face, then turned and crossed back to the front, where a small stack of blue plastic baskets stood haphazardly in a bent metal stand. He picked one up, folded the handles together then dropped the whole thing like a hot plate as a blur of movement shot across his hand. He shook his arm and the spider plopped to the floor then skittered away beneath a shelf.

"*Araña?*"

Max looked at the old man behind the counter. Hispanic, thin both in body and hair, a mustache that had probably been on his face since he was first able to grow one. He looked mildly amused as Max brushed off his hand.

"Health codes allow that kind of thing?"

"There's little we can do about it, *señor*. Other creatures, they don't care about our health codes."

It was a bit of a surprise when Max found himself smiling. He nodded, then bent down and picked up the basket. "Fair enough."

Looking down at the basket, he turned toward the produce and his shoulder collided with someone else's and a powerful shrug forced him back a step.

Shaking off his second surprise, he looked at the body into which he'd crashed. The man was large, probably over two hundred pounds and carrying most of it in his chest and shoulders. He wore a tattered flannel shirt with the sleeves rolled up, jeans and work boots, and his dark brown hair was an unholy mess. Surrounding the narrow-eyed glance he gave Max was an angry face that hadn't shaved in days. He looked like someone who had seen too many puppies die, but also like he'd probably been the one to kill them.

"*Joto*," the man said, then was at the front counter ordering cigarettes.

Max blinked at the floor. His brain stuttered a thought that quickly vanished. Then he turned and went to locate his wife. His heart rate was up as he walked through the aisle. Then the downcast look that Camille gave him iced the deplorable shit cake. It was confirmation that, in this very store, at this very moment, in the eyes of this very woman before him, he was less than a nothing.

He chewed his lower lip as she dumped the veggies into the basket. He felt the weight of them, felt their relationship to gravity. The squash and the carrots and potatoes were in cahoots with the earth's gravitational pull. A natural conspiracy conjured by the things that grow and the things that fall, and their primary objective was dragging him down.

Then he was in a different aisle and Camille weighted the basket down with a bag of white rice. There was also kale in the basket. He didn't remember her getting kale.

A minute later they were at the register and the old man was ringing them up.

"Passing through?" he asked, weighing the carrots on an ancient scale.

"No," Camille said, "we're just moving in."

"Oh? *En qué área*? Where about?"

Max watched his wife slap on a suit of thin veiled armor. She made a vague hand gesture. "Out that way," she said.

"No," the man said to the tune of "Hit the Road Jack". "*La casa asesina de Ortiz*?"

"Ortiz, yeah, that's the one."

"So, then, you know Frank Albertson?"

"Frank, yeah," Camille said. "He's my uncle."

"*Bendeciré los que hombre*," the man said. He looked at Camille. "Your uncle is a good man."

"He is, yes. Thank you for saying so."

"Well," the man said as he bagged the groceries, "welcome." Then he gave them their total.

Camille looked at Max, who took out his wallet, took out money, and gave it to the man. The man punched some buttons and a drawer popped out of the old-timey register.

"*Cuáles son sus nombres*?" Then he blinked and stammered and said, "I'm sorry, I mean—"

"That's okay," Camille said. "I know Spanish well enough." She tilted her head at Max. "He's the ignorant one. I'm Camille, and this is Max."

Max began to extend his hand. When he saw the man had no intention of extending his, he quickly redirected to picking up the grocery bag.

"Moses," the man said. "Nice to meet you both."

"Likewise." She turned to Max. "Let's go."

Outside, back in the bright, oppressive heat, Max, grocery-armed, trailed Camille back to the car. "What was that House of Ortiz thing?"

"The house and property were owned forever by the Ortiz family before Uncle Frank bought it from them."

"Yeah, I know that."

"Then why are you asking?" She unlocked the car.

"It just sounded like…" He looked at her looking at him, then shook his head and loaded the groceries. "Never mind."

She got behind the wheel. Her eyes were skewers through Max as he climbed into his seat.

***

It was an historic, secluded, off the grid

twenty-acre property, surrounded by large tracts of undeveloped land with gorgeous views of both public land and nearby mountain ranges. It was an old house but had been restored, powered by a solar PV system, with a well and propane to provide water and heat. The stone construction had been preserved while modern amenities had apparently been added. Stone and brick floors, the ceilings constructed of pine decking, supported by large pine vigas. Two stories, two bedrooms, two baths, a nice open floor plan. There were patios both in the front and back, the back patio large and with a kiva fireplace.

A couple of ruined structures stood haphazardly across the back of the property. Evidence that this had once been a busy place. Max stared out the kitchen window and drank iced tea.

"This would be a good place for a dog."

"You're not getting a dog," she told him. She was putting the veggies away in the fridge. "You like the idea of a dog but you don't actually want one."

"How do you know what I want and what I don't?"

She shook her head. "Skip it. You're not getting a dog, that much I know."

Max filled his mouth with iced tea. It didn't taste like iced tea. He grimaced and set the glass on the counter, and frowned as he watched Camille close the fridge. A lock of her disheveled beach sand hair clung to her cheek. She looked tired and irritated. Both of them were. They'd been driving for what seemed most of eternity.

It hadn't been, of course. Portland, Oregon to Sueño Roto was roughly a twenty-hour drive. Excluding rest stops and whatnot, over the course of the trip they'd probably conversed for about twenty minutes, the most interesting being a brief and shallow discussion of a song they both agreed on. That alone was a feat. They didn't agree on much, and seemed to agree on less and less with each passing day.

"I'm gonna take a little walk," he said.

"Take a bottle of water with you."

"You wanna come with?"

"No, I wanna nap."

"I wanna check out the area, have a look around."

"Help me blow up the mattress first."

"Doesn't it have an electric pump?"

"Max, I'm tired. Please?"

Tired, yeah. He was, too. They were both tired of the whole damn business.

***

Gentle drafts of dust caressed the stagnant terrain. Out of the dust bloomed malicious and moistureless air as the sun sapped the sky, and slapped the barren land with open-palmed fire. Aspen, ponderosa pine, piñon and juniper trees stood like disoriented chess pieces.

Max walked among it all, his head down. He'd grown up in Santa Fe; spent the first twenty-three years of his life there, before heading to the Pacific

Northwest, bouncing from Spokane to Seattle to Olympia, and finally settling one state down in Portland, Oregon, the City of Roses. The desert was no stranger to him; the two were old friends, though the friendship had grown stale with time and distance, and at the moment his footsteps were their only conversation.

Everything was a shambles, and now there was nowhere to go. In every direction lay a wasteland. Rough, but all of it was rough. It had been rough for a long time. It had been rough when they got married. It had been rough when she got pregnant. It had been rough when she went to the hospital, and devastating when the baby died.

Camille was two years older than Max. Thirty-one versus twenty-nine. Whether that meant anything or not, he didn't know. What he did know was they weren't a team. They weren't any good together. They had never been good together. And now they were worse than they'd ever been.

He stopped at what had probably once been a tool shed, now little more than a rickety frame, a skeleton composed of rotted lumber, strung together with cobwebs. The sun intensified, scorched the back of his neck. He scratched it, and kicked once at the dilapidated structure. The entire thing rattled, swayed. Above, he saw a bird glide a circle in the air. He unscrewed the cap from his bottle of water, drank a mouthful, then another.

Replacing the cap, it slipped, clinked off a rock

and rolled a few feet away. He stepped over and picked it up, blew on it, but the moisture held the dirt, lining it with mud.

Like he'd seen badasses do with cigarette butts in movies, he flicked it away, over a small rise and into a shallow ravine.

He heard it click. Then it clicked again. The third time it clicked it was fainter and had an echo to it. Same with the fourth time. Then it stopped clicking.

He mounted the small rise. Below was not really a ravine; it was more of an incline in the ground, sparse brush and stony, an earthen path to a darkened doorway. An imperfect black square framed by dried, cracked wood. The hole, worn by weather and time, was no more than four feet high, three feet wide, a decayed board fastened across it.

When Max reached the opening he got down on one knee. A simple chop would have easily broken the cross board. With eyebrows raised and eyeballs lowered, he studied the opening's hollow interior. Darkness was the best he could make out—empty, spatial blackness.

He located a hand-sized rock, gauged its weight, then tossed it in. It clinked, then clacked. He listened to the long descent, which ended with an answer of silence, thus giving him no answer. If the rock had hit the pit's bottom, he hadn't heard it.

***

The air mattress was on the living room floor and Camille was on the mattress, her right arm draped over her eyes. Max knew she wasn't sleeping. She'd pretend that she was but he knew that she wasn't.

He filled his empty water bottle at the tap, took a sip and grimaced. The well water was awful. He set the bottle on the counter and got a fresh one from the fridge, thankful for the house's already running power.

On the mattress, Camille shifted and turned to face away from him. Her brief movement seemed to eat all sound.

"There's a shaft out back."

Silentious mites feasted on the disquieted tension that pervaded the house.

"Looks like an old mineshaft."

"Well, this used to be mining country. Uncle Frank said there might even be dynamite left over in some places."

"Seemed bottomless."

"It couldn't possibly be bottomless, and you shouldn't be playing around stuff like that."

"Why not?"

"You'll fall in, or something."

"Thanks for the vote of confidence, Mom."

"Fine, your dog will fall in."

"Thought I wasn't getting a dog."

"Problem solved." She adjusted herself a bit on the mattress.

Max drank his water. It wasn't very cold but it was cold enough to awaken disturbances in his stomach and chest. The refrigerator made a tiny click and then hummed.

"I wonder if the dynamite would still be any good."

"What a thing to wonder."

"I mean, does dynamite go bad? Like, have an expiration date or something?"

"Who knows, who cares," she said. "I'm tired."

He was tired, too, but knew he wouldn't sleep. Naps were never something easy for him. Sleep itself was typically a task. Too much going through his mind, too much emotion. In this day and age, with all the cosmetic surgery and anti-depressants and the ability to grow a human ear on the back of a rat, it seemed like there should be a simple brain operation that could rid someone of emotions. Something for the people who the pills didn't work on. He'd tried all sorts of stuff. Some of the pills worked for a day or two, maybe even a week, but inevitably Superman gripped kryptonite and they lost all their power and it was back to Square One.

"I'm gonna head into town."

"What for?"

"To look around."

"You'll have plenty of time to do that. We live here now."

"All the same, you've been here before, I haven't. I'd like to check it out."

"Don't stay out too long."

"Why not?"

"You don't need to."

"How do you know?"

"Because I do." She shifted on the mattress again. "You shouldn't be wasting gas on pointless outings."

The tingling in his stomach and chest spread to his neck and shoulders. He drank another sip of water, watched the living room and the woman within. Then he was gnashing his teeth. He didn't like the implications of this.

He gave a helpless shrug, then left the house and went to the car.

TWO

The main street was less than a quarter mile strip of business. Conveniently it was called Main Street. The largest cross street was *Calle de la Basura*, which accommodated a few small businesses before transforming into residential homes and then petering out and extinguishing into dirt. Both streets were two-lane blacktop.

The intersection boasted a diner at one corner, a gas station at another, with an empty, dilapidated building and a rundown Dairy Queen completing the square. The diner was called the Silver Moon. The gas station was an Amigo Mart. Just past the intersection, not far from the grocery store, was Shiloh's, a cross between a log cabin and saloon but exclusively a bar. With just a little make-up, it would have been out of place, but the natural look allowed it to blend right in. There were a couple of cars parked in its small gravel lot. Early day drinkers. He imagined there was a lot of that here. Then he looked at the clock in the dash.

It was after five. A glacially slow day passing much too quickly.

So this was now home. This was where he lived.

Where do you live?

Sueño Roto.

Never heard of it.

Nobody has.

The handful of hours he'd been in town, he already wanted to leave. This wasn't a country getaway. It wasn't a small town with a steadfast community. Sueño Roto was isolation, a ghost town, a prison. He already felt stifled. Rather than peaceful openness, the barren land was smothering, suffocating him as he drove.

There weren't really any other options, though. At least he hadn't seen any, and Camille hadn't been apt to look very hard. For the last two years Max had been working at the McLoughlin Paper Company as a back tender. Not a very taxing job, operating drier and winding sections of both fourdrinier and cylinder machines to produce paper and wind it onto rolls. Monday through Friday, he observed charts and gauges, turned valves and wheels. Others worked with him but it was solitary business. At least it was for him. He kept to himself a lot. He always had, and the McLoughlin Paper Company, out in Gresham, a half-hour drive from their home, was not a very large company, their business encompassing the Pacific Northwest and nowhere else. It provided Max with ample room to work and think. For what it was, it had been a good job.

Then the rumors had started floating around. Cutbacks. Layoffs. More and more, everybody seemed to walk around in a daze. Then, in the blink of an eye, came the storm of pink slips. Sean Krasnoff, Max's boss, called him into the office and flat-out said, "You're one of the people that we gotta let go."

And that was it. No notice other than rumors, no warning, no severance pay. Two months later the McLoughlin Paper Company shut down completely, and so did everyone's finances. Camille worked in a coffee shop on Burnside. Without Max's income, it wasn't enough to get by.

Frank Albertson, Uncle Frank, was Camille's uncle, having married her Aunt Holly when Camille was a teenager. The marriage failed but ended on good terms, and it wasn't long after the divorce that Frank bought the Ortiz place. After several years he grew tired of living the life of a rural desert rat. He decided to hold onto the place, but moved himself east. He was somewhere in New Hampshire now.

When the McLoughlin Paper Company laid him off, and reality of their financial woes sank in, and no matter where Max applied he couldn't find work, Camille eventually called Uncle Frank. The same evening she did, she came to Max and told him, "We're moving to New Mexico."

"I grew up in New Mexico. I don't wanna go back."

"Well, I think you're gonna have to suck it up and deal with it."

Frank had said they could live in his Sueño

Roto home for free. He loved it but had no intention of moving back, and such a large house in such a small town, it was next to impossible to rent the place. He had also spoken with Peter Parsons, owner of the Silver Moon. Apparently all Camille had to do was mention Uncle Frank and she had a job. No talk about anything for Max, and now that he was here, his job prospects were cut to a fraction of a percent of what they'd been in Portland.

He drove up Main Street, figuring Frank must have been suffocating and dying here, and that was why he'd moved to the state where the motto was "Live Free or Die." Seemed very few people could live here at all.

Civilization petered out and was replaced by desert. Max pulled to the shoulder, waited for a car to pass in the oncoming lane, then made a one-eighty and headed back. He couldn't help the sigh that slipped from his mouth.

This was it. This was the whole town, apparently. *Paloma? El parasol?* What the hell was the Spanish word for small? *Pequeño*, yeah, that was it. The town should have been fucking called *Pequeño*.

The grocery store was just up ahead on the right. On the left, not much beyond, was Shiloh's. A beer sounded good. Maybe a couple. He clicked on his blinker, then turned into the lot. There were already more cars than when he'd passed by a minute ago. It looked dark inside, but all bars were dark inside.

He got out of the car, locked it, crossed the lot,

and opened the door to cigarette smoke and country music. People sat at tables here and there and the walls were decorated with neon beer signs and old hunting photographs. The music wasn't loud and conversations dropped to match it as the door closed behind him. He felt like an outlaw barging into a saloon, then almost instantly the feeling switched to that of a rabbit walking into a pack of wolves.

Blue smoke blossomed around him as he crossed to a table against the far wall and sat down beneath a photo of several men showing off a slaughtered deer. There was a TV on, behind the bar. It had a baseball game on it and the volume turned off. He didn't look around directly, but he knew there were eyes on him. There were eyes everywhere. They were in the walls and the doorway, every nook, crook and shadow.

"What're you having?" the barman asked. He was big and tall and bald, forty-something, dark beard contrasting his chrome dome. He absently wiped the counter with a rag. There was no waiter or waitress.

"What do you have on tap?"

The man rattled off a list. Max ordered a pilsner and clasped his hands on the table. He had little interest in baseball but he tried to watch the game. The Rangers were playing the Rockies, zero to zero, top of the third.

He looked at the framed photo near his head. Black and white, fairly old, a snapshot enlarged a bit more than it could handle, blurry and a bit smudged. There were two dozen or so beer cans scattered in the brush. The deer was as dead as Max imagined it could get. Its eyes were popped out just enough to notice, and its head, held up by two of the brave warriors, was turned at a near impossible angle in relation to its body. A couple of the men had marks on their faces, like some kind of war paint—possibly, likely, the deer's blood.

A pint of beer set on the table before him and the bartender said, "Four dollars."

Max took out a five and gave it to him, told him to keep the change. The man nodded and went back behind the counter. Awkward air condensed the cigarette smoke and made it almost opaque. So thick that it actually obscured the TV a bit.

Max sampled the beer; it was nice and cold.

From the corner of his eye he saw movement and turned. A man in a wife-beater, presumably a barfly, smiled and gave him a wink. He looked half-cartoon, like someone had shaved his head and then slapped some of the hair back on with glue.

With a sheepish smile, Max turned back to his beer. The cigarette smoke dissipated from opaque to merely smoky, and he could see the game on the TV clearly again.

He heard someone say: "Vince overreacted, I think."

"What happened?" someone else said.

"Shit, you know how Vince is about football? Goes all crazy even at his kid's pee wee games?"

"Yeah?"

"Well, he was at his kid's game, over in fucking, what the hell, you know, Gallup. Ref had just called some fucking penalty on some kid on the other team for some shit with Vince's boy. Vince got all pissed, and, I guess, charged out onto the field. Didn't even talk to the ref or the coaches or nothing, just charged over and tackled the kid."

"Fucking Vince."

"Yeah, and there was, like, less than a fucking minute to play in the game. Kid's jaw is all fucked up. Fucking McKinley County sheriffs were there at the goddamn game. Vince is fucking looking at goddamn felony child abuse charges."

"Stupid asshole."

"That's what I'm saying. Dumb-fuck loses his shit and goes after the kid, for fuck all's sake. Go after the ref, man. Kid's just a kid."

"Yeah, I bet the kid... ah, shit, what's the word...?"

"What?"

"Fucking, you know, made him angry. Did some shit."

"Provoked?"

"Yeah. Kid probably provoked him."

"He provoked him by tackling his boy, or whatever the fuck he did. If it'd been me, I would've just knocked the shit out of the ref. I'm sure the ref probably had something to do with it. I fucking hate refs."

The sound of glasses clinking and heavy sighs. Max brought his own beer to his lips and took a slow, savoring sip.

"Passing through?"

Max looked up. A man a couple of tables over, beer in one hand, shot glass in the other, bottle of rye between them, was looking at Max with one and a half eyes; the left one was closed part way. Late thirties, Max guessed, maybe early forties, lightly bearded, and his body displayed the sort of flab that had more than likely once been hard muscle. His blue-sleeved baseball shirt was dirty and pocked with small holes. The table itself had another table pushed close to it. Two younger guys sat at it, drinking beer. Neither of them was looking at Max. They were studying the drinks in their hands.

Max's ass squirmed. "My wife and I just moved here."

The guys who'd been discussing the crazy football dad looked at him now.

"Where from?"

"Oregon. I'm originally from Santa Fe, though."

"Never been to Oregon," the man said, and poured rye into his shot glass. "I heard it's green." He downed a shot and filled the glass again.

"Yeah," Max said. "Yeah, it's very green."

"What brought you out here?" one of the others asked, a lanky guy with a mustache.

"My wife. Her uncle. Her uncle has a house here."

"Who's her uncle?"

"I'm sorry?"

"You said her uncle. Who's her uncle?"

Max couldn't tell if these guys were being hostile, or if they were always hostile and trying to be nice. What he did know was that he was the center of attention, and it was in a way he didn't much care for.

"Uh, Frank," he said. "Frank Albertson."

The man in the baseball shirt's face went straight. His glassy, bloodshot eyes became the double barrel of a shotgun as he looked at Max. He poured another shot and drank, never taking Max out of his crosshairs.

"I remember Frank," one of them said, a husky guy with black hair, a green plaid shirt. "He's been gone a while. Where is he now?"

"New Hampshire."

"What's in New Hampshire?" the lanky guy asked.

Max picked up his beer, gave a little shrug. "Well... Frank is."

The statement quieted everyone a moment. There were six men total; seven if Max counted himself. Baseball Shirt had dropped out of the conversation, and the two sitting with him, who had never been a part of it, continued to study their drinks.

"Albertson," the sixth man said. He was a little guy, properly proportioned but small, a perfectly formed miniature human being. "People hear a name like that, they might think he's Jewish."

Max sipped his beer, then said, "He is Jewish."

"Sometimes people have names like that, and people just assume they're ethnic, like a Jew."

"He is a Jew."

"People might get the wrong impression because of his name."

Max wanted to ask in what way, but figured pressing the matter would be either pointless or stupid or both. He sipped his beer again.

"That's my uncle there," Plaid Shirt said, and pointed to the photo near Max's head. "Second from the left."

Max looked at the picture again. There was a clear resemblance.

"Nice," Max said.

"My Uncle Gene, autumn of ninety-seven. He killed more deer than anybody that season."

"Really, huh."

"Good times," Plaid Shirt said. "Never seen such a happy group of men."

"Well, nothing says photo op like a slaughtered animal."

Projectiles of silence ripped the smoke-filled air. The country music still played but the silence played over it. The silence was the room, and the silence was choleric.

Then, "Someone like that," the little guy said, "with a name like Albertson, people might think he's a Jew."

Max discovered that the beer was hitting him harder than he thought. He'd just come from about fifty feet above sea level to an elevation of nearly seven thousand. No wonder he felt lightheaded. He pushed the glass away. It was still half full. He slid his chair back and stood up.

"Nice to meet all of you," he said. He was aware there hadn't been any introductions.

He left and went to the car, and sat behind the wheel for five minutes before starting it. Within that five minutes he took out his cell phone, wanting, needing to hear a friendly voice. Just about anybody would do. All he needed was to know that the rest of the world was still out there. But scrolling through his contact list, he saw that the reception indicator in the corner didn't have a single bar. He pointed the phone in different directions. Nothing changed.

Frank had told them they'd need different cell phones out here.

Heartache poured into his lone cauldron of emptiness. He tossed the phone to the seat. His hands became fists and he raised them slowly, aimed them at nothing, then let them drop. He opened his mouth to shout something, but it wouldn't come. He took a few breaths, then drove out of the lot.

***

That night, he raised his head from his pillow and looked at the darkness around him. The house had the kind of quiet that made the whole world seem dead. The darkness was a blackboard, and as his eyes adjusted, light chalk sketches drew outlines of things. He turned his head and looked down at the moonlit drawing of his sleeping wife. The calm rise and fall of her chest, the childlike vulnerability almost everyone has when sleeping. There was nothing remarkable or unremarkable. She was what she was, just as he was who he was. Like always, questions dangled in front of him, but he was too afraid to look for the answers.

What the hell are we doing?

This was a question that went through his mind several times, every day. It was the question that was always dangling, the carrot on the stick and he was always headed toward it. The stick was implanted in his back and the carrot was always dangling. He could always see it but never reach it.

She shifted away from him. It wasn't like when she'd pretend to sleep. This time she really was sleeping. Even while off in a dreamland she still turned away from him.

He eased back onto his pillow. He stared up at the wood slats in the ceiling. He only knew about them because he'd seen them in the day. He was really staring straight into blackness. The night was still too thick that high up. He stared into it for a long, long time, before finally finding sleep, and just as he crossed the threshold into the dreamland, the obvious answer to the most prevalent question came to him. He buried it in dreams, however. It was safer making believe it wasn't there.

THREE

The movers showed up a little before noon. Twice Max offered to help, and twice Camille cut him down in front of the men, once telling him he wasn't strong enough, the other time telling him he was clumsy.

Fine. He gave up. He went out into the back and assembled the patio furniture, then moved one of the chairs over into the shade of a tree and sat down with a paperback. There was a light breeze today, hardly noticeable, but pleasant nonetheless. For a little while he felt peaceful, comforted in the world of the book he was reading. He forced himself to read slower, savoring the words, immersing himself as deeply as he could into the story.

Half an hour later Camille came out and an uneasiness took root inside him. It grew, sharpened, became acute as she walked toward him, her expression an amalgam of conceit and amusement.

"You gonna waste the day doing nothing?"

"I offered to help, a couple of times. Clearly it wasn't wanted."

"Well, trying to look manly in front of the guys isn't the only thing that needs to get done around here."

"I assume you can think of a million things."

"How about organizing some stuff, or unpacking one of the rooms?"

He shrugged. It wasn't much of a shrug; it was more of a sigh.

"Take some damned initiative, Max."

"I tried earlier. You shot me down."

"Then fucking take initiative again, and go find something else."

"I did. I came out here, set up the patio furniture, then sat down with a book."

"The patio furniture was a good, if not low priority, start. Why don't you go unpack the guest room?"

"What are you doing during all of this?"

Her mouth tightened. Her lips pressed flat against her teeth, then her mouth opened and her face reddened. "I'm keeping everything under control. That's what I do. That's what I always do. That's what I *have* to do, because if I didn't, you'd be cowering in a goddamn corner. You know damn well what I'm doing, and you know damn well that I do it everyday. And you wouldn't know what the fuck to do if I didn't."

He opened his mouth but nothing came out. He looked at her looking at him. And then Camille made it clear that she couldn't take it anymore.

She yanked the book from his hands and turned away, flipping the pages and moving toward the house

If he wanted the book, he had to play the game. He stood up out of his chair, crossed the patio like a forlorn cat chasing a ball with a dead bell. The bell didn't make a cute jingle; it clanged with ghosts, and Max was the one for whom the bell tolled.

He followed her into the house, and watched her toss his book as if discarding trash. Max chewed his lower lip.

Two of the movers were bringing in the couch.

"That goes in there, nonadjacent to the wall," she told them. "The entertainment center should be contiguous with the wall. And make sure there's a schism between the wall and the credenza, and set the couch at an angle so it also faces the fireplace."

Her own version of trying to look manly, flaunting a vocabulary, one that she didn't always use properly. She didn't notice the agitated look the movers gave her, or the look they gave Max.

He followed her up the open stairway to the second floor, and into what was to be the guestroom. He wondered what the point of a guestroom was. Odds were good that no one was going to visit them here. Who would want to? It didn't make sense, but then there were very few things in his life that made sense. Of course, lately, there was nothing that made sense at all.

***

As they didn't have a whole lot of stuff, it didn't take a whole lot of time to move everything in. By six o'clock the kitchen, master bedroom and bathroom were operational, if still a bit chaotic.

Max had suggested ordering pizza, and settling in with a movie. Camille told him there was nowhere to order a pizza from, adding that he should know that, given his "so desperately needed" exploration into town the day before. Instead she boiled some rice and steamed some vegetables and made her own unique sort of stir-fry, the veggies over cooked, the rice not cooked enough.

Then, poking at her food, Camille said, "I know this is difficult for you."

"Yeah, it's pretty weird." His voice sounded weaker than he'd intended.

Camille glanced at him, then back at her plate. "I'm glad we're here," she said. "Tomorrow, I'll go talk to Peter, over at the diner. Find out when I can start working."

"You're sure he's gonna hire you, just like that?"

She shrugged. "Unless I show up drunk, or covered in blood." She looked at him again. "I'll ask about you. See if they need a dishwasher or anything."

"Gee, thanks."

Her mouth tightened. Her mouth always tightened when she got angry, which was often. "Are you saying you're too good to be a dishwasher?"

"What? No."

"You've got to give up on this crazy self-serving pride, Max. You're never gonna get anywhere if you keep letting it get in the way."

Max poked at his food. He wanted to stab it.

Silence for a few moments, and then he noticed Camille staring at him.

"What?"

"If there's a dishwashing job, you'll take it. If there's a job scrubbing the bathrooms, you'll take it. I'm serious. You're not above anything."

"What are you talking about?"

"You're not better than me or anyone else. You're just another guy, and I'm not gonna carry you anymore than I already do."

Her words inspired a sense of fear. His thoughts and memories went back to other harsh times: the death of his father, the loss of his mother, the death of their baby. Their baby had been a girl. They'd planned to name her Kimberly. She'd died in utero. A part of Max wished he could chalk up Camille's dominant and controlling nature to the sad truth of Kimberly's stillborn birth, but he couldn't. She'd always been that way. He'd been somewhat blind to it in the early days, but Camille had always been a bitch.

There were so many things Max wanted to say. So many things he wanted to curse her for, each thing its own stack of bricks, so many piled that he couldn't find the breath to knock a single one off. There were so many things he needed to be free of, but he lacked the strength and courage to attack even the smallest obstacle.

"You're not eating," she told him.

He looked at the poorly prepared stir-fry. It looked like a maggot fest in a garden. He scooped out a heap and stuffed it into his mouth.

***

Max awoke from a fitful sleep when the scratching started downstairs.

He raised his head from his pillow and looked at the darkness. For a moment he thought he'd dreamed it. Camille lay beside him, sleeping, unmoving. The only sound was a faint reverberation; the fading, lingering echo of a noise now passed.

He looked at the doorway. He looked at his wife. She remained motionless, breaths deep and steady. The darkness all around him had a silvery hue, a trick of the moon or a glint of the stars. The ghostly carillon faded to silence. The air whispered nothing. A rustling of things with no substance in them flickered within the walls.

He eased his head back down on the pillow and closed his eyes.

The scratching came again.

He jolted his head and then sat up straight.

The front door. Insistent, frantic, frightened barks of dire desperation.

Max turned to Camille. She still hadn't moved. He eased out of bed, toes seeking his slippers on the cold stone floor. He wore what he wore every night to bed: boxer shorts and his extra large Trail Blazers T-shirt. He went to the window, squinted out and down. There was nothing he could see that shouldn't have been there.

The knocking ceased. He turned from the window, crossed the bedroom and stepped into the hallway. He walked to the stairs and stared down into the open darkness. He wondered if he should wake Camille, but knew that somehow, in some way, he'd wind up looking foolish.

He lowered himself down, two steps, then three. The fourth step was when the door began to rattle. Rapid, metallic clicks flitted as the doorknob jerked back and forth. Heavy knocks and scrapes interspersed with the clattering, and Max told himself to go back into the bedroom, that foolishness no longer applied. But rather than turning and heading back up, a step at a time, his body contradicted his thoughts. His feet carried him down. Then he reached the bottom and his feet continued walking.

The scratching and barking and rattling persisted. The acoustics downstairs altered the quality of the echoes, gave them a strange and itchy ricochet effect.

There was no peephole in the front door. The outside light was not turned on. His eyes were adjusted but everything was still so utterly lightless. The scratching stopped but the jerking and rattling continued.

Without thinking he reached for the knob. The vibrations in his fingertips when he touched it made him yank his hand away. He stared at the door and took a step back.

"Who is it?" he said, weak-voiced.

The clattering broke off and silence poured down. It crackled with intensity. Electric silence that tingled the nape of his neck, shivered down the track of his spine, and conjured a metallic taste in his mouth. He stayed where he was and listened.

In the dead stillness of the night, a sound emerged at his back. The stirring quietude seemed to absorb it, permitted neither echo nor resonance. It wasn't inside with him; it was somewhere out back, out in the night-infested wasteland. A voice. A desperate, pleading voice soaked in fear, tainted with anguish, though human or animal, he couldn't tell. He turned and stepped to the far end of the house.

He hadn't forgotten the sounds at the door — the tips of his fingers still tingled — but it seemed any immediate danger had fled. It had run to the back of the house, amidst the trees of the gloom-shrouded desert.

He looked through the windows but couldn't see a thing. He sidestepped, slowly, to the glass-paneled back door and then past it, eyes riveted to the darkness outside. No movement, no flutter of shadow, no flicker of light.

His foot tapped something. He knew without looking that it was the paperback he'd been reading. The one Camille had taken and tossed. It slid maybe two or three feet, and when it halted so did the cries.

The silence was ambiguous, like a ghost trying to speak. Everything had vanished. Max sidled to the door, unlatched it, opened it. He stepped outside, onto the back patio. Calm and quiet, the desert didn't move. It was voiceless and still.

For five minutes he stood there, watching, listening. Whoever it was, whatever it was, it didn't come back.

He went inside and closed the door, and made sure to lock it. He stood there another minute, waiting. Nothing came; nothing changed.

He tried to stifle a yawn but failed. He looked out into the night one more time, then turned and headed back up to the bedroom.

He didn't question his sanity. There was no debate over whether it was real or imagined. The situation had pumped him full of anxiety but it had also completely exhausted him. Halfway up the stairs he began to stagger. He fought tooth and nail to keep his eyes open, and to keep his mind from shutting off. On the bed he was asleep before he'd settled on the mattress.

FOUR

In a lot of ways the Silver Moon, with its appropriately garish décor, seemed a throwback to the 1970s. Wood-paneled walls, Formica counter tops and burnt-orange vinyl-covered chairs and stools. There were mirrors on some of the walls, and oddly placed green squares that covered large swaths of the ceiling.

It was 9:30 in the morning. They'd been sitting in a booth for five minutes, sipping coffee and watching the busy breakfast crowd. The sun had been slipping behind clouds off and on all morning. It was the first time they'd seen clouds since arriving two days earlier.

They waited in silence, both to place their orders and for Peter Parsons to come out from the back. Camille had announced herself to the waitress when they'd first come in. The waitress introduced herself as Danielle, and said that as soon as Peter was finished with whatever he was doing, he would join them.

If there was music playing, the diners and the hustle and bustle drowned it out. The clinking of glasses and the clanking of plates was the diner's current rhythm section. Max added more cream to his coffee. He wondered if it was always this busy. He didn't think there were this many people in the entire town.

"What were you doing last night?"

"Huh?"

It was the first exchange they'd had since they'd left the house.

"You were downstairs rattling things at, like, three in the morning."

It was on the tip of his tongue to tell her what had happened, but he held it back, washed it down with a sip of coffee as the sense of foolishness twitched his circuitry. The truth would be just one more thing for her weapons of mass demeaning.

"I just couldn't sleep," he said.

"So what were you doing?"

Another sip of coffee, he looked at her hands, solid and steady and resting on the table. Max always had a mild case of tremors. Doctors told him it was stress. His wife laughed and said he had nothing to be stressed about.

"I'd gone out for a little walk," he said. "The door was stuck when I came back."

Camille's eyes narrowed but before she said anything a man stopped at their table.

"Are you Camille Pendleton?"

He was a good-looking man, tall, with a thick neck and broad shoulders, close-cropped blond hair and a strong, squared jaw, his eyes a curious gray. It was near impossible to tell his age. Max immediately felt impotent in his presence.

"I sure miss Frank," he said. "He's one of the good ones. When did you guys get in?"

"Day before yesterday."

"Settling in well?"

"So far," Camille said. Then she cracked a tiny smile and shot Max a quick but piercing glance. "Max is finding it a bit rough adjusting, but he's not used to changes in nomenclature. He won't believe it's just a bunch of hyperbole built up in his brain. Sometimes I like to call him Hokum Head."

Max gnashed his teeth, then drank some coffee and picked up his menu again.

Peter and Camille talked for about five minutes. It was agreed that Camille would come in the following day for basic training and a short shift.

"I don't suppose you have anything Max could do?"

"Unfortunately, no. In fact, you're lucky your uncle called me when he did. It's rare that I need, or can afford, to hire anyone. The timing just happened to work out right for you."

Camille narrowed her eyes at Max again, as if the Silver Moon's situation was somehow his fault.

Business concluded, Peter took their order. Ordering concluded, Peter told them there would be no charge. "My way of welcoming you to town," he said. The smile he flashed was almost all teeth. His teeth were perfect. A silent communication seemed to pass between the two. Then Peter said it was nice to meet them and turned and disappeared into the back.

"That was a little rude," Camille said.

Max looked at her. "What?"

"He was talking to us and you totally blew him off, completely ignored him the whole time he was here."

"I didn't blow him off. And the conversation didn't include me, after introductions."

"You have no manners. Nor do you have any persistence."

"Huh?"

"If you spoke up a bit, maybe you could've convinced him to give you some work."

"Were you not listening when he said that wouldn't happen?"

"Whatever," she said, "forget it."

A waitress stopped by and refilled their coffee.

Max said, "Why do you do this?"

"Do what?"

"*This.* What you're doing."

"I'm not doing anything, Max. And neither are you, maybe *that's* the problem."

Invisible hands pressed a swelling cork into his sternum. "I don't get it," he said.

"Of course you don't."

A dry swallow got words stuck in his throat, or maybe erased them all together. He added cream to his coffee and stirred it. He watched his hand move the spoon around clockwise. A slight tremble in his hand created the tiniest ripple effect within the swirls. He couldn't put the words together but understood and felt their meaning. He continued stirring his coffee.

Eventually their food arrived. Max had corned beef hash with two scrambled eggs and a side of potatoes. Camille had an egg white omelet with veggies and whole-wheat toast.

"Don't you think you eat that too much?" she asked.

"It's one of my favorites."

"It's high in fat and sodium. Especially sodium."

"Yeah, I know, you've told me before."

"That, right there, is more than a thousand milligrams of sodium."

"What, did you measure it?"

"I don't need to measure it, I can tell."

He shrugged, "Okay," and picked up his fork. The prospect of arguing was as appealing as spoiled milk with bugs in it.

He opened his mouth only to eat.

When finished they pooled their cash and left a generous tip, then waited at the counter for five minutes until Peter was free long enough for goodbyes.

"So we'll see you at ten o'clock tomorrow?"

"I'll be here," Camille said. Then she shook his hand and turned and left with Max following behind.

The clouds had gone away. The sky was one giant mural of blue with the sun embedded like a flaming jewel. Its light dripped over everything, a blinding shroud of heat upon the parched earth.

Camille didn't want to drive. She gave the keys to Max.

Neither spoke a word the entire ride home.

When they got home they exchanged words of panic.

There was a rattlesnake coiled on the living room couch.

FIVE

Startled, the snake looked ready to strike. Most snakes will usually flee from humans if they don't feel threatened, but both Max's and Camille's reactions — especially Camille's — were enough to put the rattler on alert.

The unblinking eyes stared from its flat, triangular head. The tongue flicked out with near hypnotic cadence, and the rattling noise was like malevolent static. Coiled, the animal slithered upon itself. Max estimated its tan and brown patchwork body at about three feet in length — maybe a little more.

"Get it out of here, Max!"

"Open the back door," he told her.

He tasted vomit at the back of his mouth. Even growing up in Santa Fe, he'd never much considered snakes before. Spiders could give him a good jolt, but snakes were far less common in the desert day to day; at least they had been in his experience. The reality of what was curled a dozen feet from where he stood made him sick with fear. The shaking in his hands increased. His legs trembled. Perspiration cascaded from the bottom hairline in the back of his head.

And the snake hissed, rattled its rattle.

Camille opened the door. When it was open as far as it would go, she quickly moved away.

All right, Max said to himself. *Now what?*

He reached into his pocket and took out his cell phone. No bars, no reception. He hollered to Camille to check her phone.

"We don't get reception here," she said. "You know that. We need to get new phones."

He kept his eyes on the snake, and remembered reading that the strike of a rattlesnake is faster than the human eye can follow. And while a dozen or more feet lay between them, he also remembered reading that a rattlesnake might strike farther than you would expect. He wished he knew how much farther that meant.

The snake slithered and hissed.

He heard Camille, clear in the kitchen now.

As though injected with venom, his fear became a neurotoxin, encouraging numbness and paralysis. The taste of vomit returned. He swallowed, drew a breath and swallowed again, forcing himself to not be sick. It wasn't the snake that made him sick. Even standing there, half petrified, he knew that much. It was the *fear* of the snake. Fear and fear alone was affecting his nervous system.

Like a hinge, the snake's mouth opened wide.

He could just make out the large tubular fangs as the mouth folded out. Then it closed again. The rattle waned. The snake seemed to set into deliberate stillness. The rattling returned but, other than the tail, the serpent didn't move.

Then he remembered snake hooks. Pretty much just a pole with a hook on the end. The purpose of a snake hook is to catch and keep them at a safe distance. Some use the hook to gently pin the head of a snake on the ground and then grab the tail. The hook is then used to control the direction of the head.

The head. That's what he remembered.

"Camille?"

"What?"

"Is there a broom in there?"

"Um…" She clinked and clattered a few things. "Yes, it's here."

"Bring it to me."

"You come get it."

"I don't wanna take my eyes off the bastard. Just give me the broom, or throw it to me, even."

"How did it get in here?"

"I don't know. You wanna ask it?"

"Just get it out of here."

An invisible hand gripped his heart and squeezed it.

"Here." Camille took a couple steps forward then tossed the broom. Her throw fell short and the wood handle clacked on the stone floor. At the clack the snake stirred. It moved along the couch. Its head extended out over the couch's brink. Max picked up the broom and took another step back.

The snake slid and eased itself down from the couch.

Watching, Max couldn't help admiring how gracefully it moved. The graceful, sexy slither of a dangerous, venomous snake, no longer on the couch but on the cold stone floor. It coiled up for just a moment, then unraveled and moved. It was horizontal in his line of vision, movements undulating like ocean waves. Initially it seemed to head straight for the open doorway. Then it detoured toward Max but stopped almost instantly. Its rattle began shaking again. Its head rose up and it showed him the inside of its mouth.

Slowly, Max took a step back. The snake hissed. Max poised the broom, bristle end downward, ready to spear it, knowing it would do little or no good.

Then, without explanation, the rattler thrashed. It didn't strike, just flailed about, as though it was caught on the end of a stick.

Max white-knuckled the broom handle. The blood seemed to drain right out of his body. The snake twisted and wrenched and spiraled in on itself, then jolted out of entanglement and bolted right for the door. It hesitated at the threshold, then crossed it and curved and went out of sight.

Max pushed the door closed. As he let out a breath his whole body started shaking. The adrenaline that had thickened in him was now breaking up. He went to the kitchen, opened the fridge, and took out a bottle of water.

Camille went into the living room. She opened the back door and then closed it again.

"It really went out?"

"It really went out."

"Where did it go?"

"It had a bus ticket for Phoenix."

"Oh, shut up. How did it get in?"

"It's the desert. Sometimes things get in."

"I know the desert, Max. Probably better than you."

He wanted to laugh. He wanted to mock her. But he already knew that he wouldn't dare.

SIX

That afternoon they drove forty-five minutes over to Gallup and went to Southwest Mobile, the only cellular service with good coverage in Sueño Roto.

Not quite destitute but certainly not doing well, financially, they got the cheapest phones that they possibly could: basic flip phones with virtually no features.

They ate a late lunch at Jerry's Café and then spent a few hours browsing stores and window-shopping. In spite of Camille's dominant personality, Max felt more open and relaxed. The town pushed a small breath of life into him. Just a little one, but things seemed more real than they had since they'd left Portland.

This and the incident with the snake had apparently shifted things, at least for the moment. More than likely it was temporary, but while the shift was here, Max relished it. Camille still had a domineering vibe, but she spoke little, as though she might have actually been a bit humbled by the situation. Just a little, and it wouldn't last, but it was still a pleasant change from the norm.

Conversely, inside of Max, someone had struck a match of confidence. He also spoke little, but he was aware that he carried himself with more backbone. The rattlesnake had scared the living hell out of him, and though he couldn't take an ounce of credit for getting it out of the house, he took pride in the fact that he had faced it. Stood and faced a venomous viper, while Miss Keep-Everything-Under-Control had cowered in the kitchen.

***

That evening, back at the house, they tested their cell phones by calling each other. The connection wasn't perfect but it was better than nothing. Max was more pleased than Camille was. For him it wasn't just a phone; it was a communicator to a world that had become unreal in just a few short days. A world that, in spite of traffic, crime, higher taxes, homeless people, shitty people, pollution and noise, was also a sort of paradise. He looked forward to hearing its voice.

Camille wouldn't sit on the couch until Max had thoroughly checked it, and even then Max had to drape a blanket over it.

They snacked on fruit and cheese and watched a movie. An old black and white with James Cagney and George Raft called *Each Dawn I Die*, about a reporter unjustly thrown in jail and who then befriends a famous gangster.

Max loved old movies. James Cagney, Humphrey Bogart, Fred Astaire and Ginger Rogers, Bette Davis, Grace Kelly and James Stewart. The stories, the intricacies of the dialogue, the depth of morals and the quality of acting, the uniqueness of the people and ideas, all of it created a timeless magic. Max loved all movies, but there was something extra special about the old black and whites. An additional layer of wonder that no amount of special effects could duplicate. Camille typically thought the classics were boring.

It was still early when the movie ended. Night had taken the land into its mouth but the clock hadn't yet ticked past nine.

"Bedtime for me," Camille said with a yawn, then stretched her arms above her head. She stood up and looked down at Max. "You're coming to bed soon?"

"Maybe," he said. "I'm gonna stay up and read for a while."

She yawned again. "Okay."

Then she did something so unexpected, Max didn't know how to react. She bent down, put a hand on his cheek and kissed him. A quick kiss, but it was tender and sweet. The subtlest hint of a smile etched into her lips.

"Don't stay up too late," she said.

"I won't."

She went to the kitchen and got a bottle of water. Then they said good night and she went upstairs.

Max got up from the couch and crossed over to where his paperback was still lying on the floor. He picked it up and found his page. Then he looked out the window at the desert night, silent and still, majestically dark. Somewhere out there was the rattlesnake. Out there were a lot of things. Over the mountains and far away was an entire world, rich with culture and diversity, rattlesnakes and spiders but also teddy bears and ice cream. A world where you could do any number of things. Where you could sit in a coffee shop all night, go through a revolving door without having to push, sing the national anthem with a big crowd, or eat a free sample of something you had no intention of buying. Other than the snake, Max worried the most interesting thing in Sueño Roto would be when dust collected and got so big that he could pick it up with his hand.

He took the book over to the couch, sat down and read. It wasn't long before the house grew silent. It was a serene sort of silence. Comfortable. There had been a lot of silence in his life, but very little of it had ever fallen under the category of contentment. Growing up, he lived in a house that consisted of four people in four separate rooms, and most of the time the doors were closed on those rooms, and more often than not those doors were locked.

Silence was a very common thing when he was young, and usually the silence wasn't by choice. His father had been a self-employed architect. Around the time that Max was born the attached garage was converted into an office. It was down a few short steps and had two doors separating it. His father spent almost all of his time there.

Clear at the other end of the house his mother essentially lived in the master bedroom. Up until Max was about ten, she rarely ventured beyond the kitchen, and after that point she was either in the bedroom or out somewhere. Cell phones were not yet common when he was a kid.

Two preoccupied parents connected by an invisible thread, and Max was one of two caught and tangled in its web. The other was Jeremy, his older brother. Four years older. Where Max had inherited shyness and sensitivity, Jeremy had inherited irritation and rage. He had a short fuse, and could explode without explanation. His humor was that of a trickster, and the punch lines often left Max in tears, and usually left something he held dear destroyed, or left him curled in a ball, clutching his stomach or holding his head; wherever Jeremy had decided to hit him.

Both the pranks and the rages occurred regularly, like a syndicated TV show. Max spent a lot of time locked in his room, afraid to go out, knowing what could—and very often did—happen. Knowing that he was outsized and outgunned, and knowing that, while curled and crying somewhere in the house, or just outside it, there would be no one coming to his aide. No mother, no father. Neither of them cared. They were too busy doing whatever they were doing. So he'd entomb himself behind his locked door. What he learned was that going out got you hurt, even if you were just going out for a cookie and a glass of milk.

Books were an important escape for him. He could open a book and disappear into it. In many respects it was the only way out of the house. It certainly was until he got a bit older. When he got his own car and he didn't have to be there so often; and then when he finally got his own apartment. The independence was great, but also rather harrowing. He'd never held a steady job before. He had to learn responsibility on his own. Locked away so often, he didn't understand simple daily tasks, like how bills worked, or how to fill out a W-2 or any number of other forms. He didn't even know how to fill out a deposit slip. There were a lot of everyday things he'd never even been told about. He learned by trial and error, often with error.

Then his father died when Max was eighteen. Max had only been living on his own a few months, and with the passing of his father the loneliness increased. A few months after that, his mother disappeared. She was later located in Honduras, and she and Max had one brief phone conversation in which it was determined that the best thing was to no longer speak. They hadn't since.

Jeremy took all of this harder than Max. Though Max didn't choose rage as a means by which to live, in some ways it seemed as though the two of them switched places. Jeremy shut down. He hid as much as possible, and his anger and fear of the world coalesced, driving him first to religion, then to booze, and finally into hardcore drugs. A couple times in jail, court-appointed rehab, and then, like his mother, Jeremy vanished from the radar. Max hadn't seen nor heard from him in several years now.

He read the last page and then closed up the book. It was almost ten-thirty. He rubbed his eyes. His vision was a bit blurry, but he wasn't at all sleepy. If he went up to bed now he'd be staring at the ceiling for hours.

He stood up and took the book over to the shelf, still empty but with two open boxes in front of it. The boxes were filled with paperbacks. Crime novels, mysteries, science fiction and horror stories. Escapism was what many of his friends called it. To Max each one was a life preserver. A reason to keep from throwing in the towel. To him the word "Escapism" was a term used to coincide with a pretentious and uninformed attitude. Arrogance was something he truly detested, and it was something that had hovered in the social circles of his life for as long as he could remember. Even the hint of arrogance in someone else often caused him to want to shut down. To him it was an unwarranted dismissal of things that helped to shape each person as an individual.

Not that he was extroverted when thinking such things. Very few times had he ever truly spoken up when it came to his opinions. Typically he allowed other people's opinions to dominate things, resulting in him constantly wanting to scream. He was afraid to scream, however. He was afraid of what would come out.

With his eyes and his fingers he scanned the

books in the boxes. They appealed to him as a whole, though none of them appealed to him individually. The idea of sitting on the couch lacked appeal. The idea of sitting in the house at all lacked appeal. A comfortable house with modern amenities and the confined, suffocating feeling of a dungeon.

Taking his eyes away from the books and looking around, the walls and floors and ceiling, the furniture and windows and everything else became repellent. Toxicity pervaded the air, and a sudden and desperate need to get out swelled within him. Even though he now had a phone and it was an hour earlier in Oregon, like the paperbacks, not a single person jumped out at him. And he knew that, right now, a phone conversation wouldn't be enough. The air would still drip with antagonism.

He looked up the stairway and trained his ears. All the lights were out up there, and not a sound was stirring. He couldn't help the adolescent feeling of the trouble he might get in as he crept to the door, eased it open, and slipped out into the night.

SEVEN

Shiloh's was busy. Busier than the day they'd arrived and he'd first stopped in.

The air was thick with smoke. Ceiling fans he hadn't noticed before whirled, churning carbon dioxide and carbon monoxide with liquor fumes and body odor. It was hot and stale and stuffy. Mild trepidation coursed through him as he negotiated his way to a table in the corner. Trepidation, hesitation, but there was also nowhere he would have rather been. Shiloh's was a stifling wheeze of fresh air.

The same man was working the bar. Max wondered if he was Shiloh.

Unlike his previous visit, there was a waitress making the rounds. She was a stunning woman. Long jet-black hair and burnished brown eyes perfectly complemented her smooth caramel skin. She worked fast and kept a smile on her face. A minute later she was at his table asking him what he wanted.

Max ordered a pilsner and watched her turn away.

The music was louder than last time, likely to compensate for the cacophonous crowd. This time it was pop music. Max thought he knew it but wasn't quite sure. Aguilera or Beyoncé or Lady Gaga or someone. Like the Silver Moon this morning, he couldn't believe there were this many people in town, let alone consolidated to a single bar. He looked around at the buzzed and laughing, drunken faces. Watching them, he felt an oppressing mixture of hostility and merriment. Late night bars were often surreal; have your beer and a smile and shut the fuck up.

Then he saw him through the swarm of people. Baseball Shirt was sitting at the same table he'd occupied last time. He had a beer and a bottle of rye before him. He still wore his blue-sleeved baseball shirt. The other two guys were also there, studying their drinks, just like before. He wasn't staring at Max, though he cut him cross glances every so often.

The waitress brought his beer. "Four dollars," she said.

"Can I start a tab?"

"Sure, I need your card."

Max gave it to her.

She went away again.

He picked up the beer and sipped it. It was ice cold and delicious. He sipped it again. He glanced at the man in the baseball shirt. The man gave him a glare. Max produced a sheepish smile, then looked down and studied the foam in his glass.

"Guy from Oregon," someone said.

Max looked up and saw the husky guy with black hair. The guy Max didn't know as anything other than Plaid Shirt. He wore a plaid shirt again, but this time it was red and white and black, rather than green. He appeared to have accumulated new flesh beneath his eyes, and the addition made him look a bit like a hound dog. Like the old cartoon character Droopy. He set his beer on Max's table.

"How you doing?"

"I'm okay, I'm okay," Max said, and accepted the man's handshake. "How are you doing?"

"Good, good." He looked around the place, then at the table and the drinks upon it. "May I join you for a minute?"

"Sure, yeah, have a seat."

The man sat down across from him. "I'm Alejandro, by the way."

"I'm Max."

"Matt?"

"Max."

"Max?"

"Yeah."

"Nice to meet you, Max."

"Likewise."

They each drank some of their beer. The rhythm of the music thump-thumped and the volume of drunken conversations rose.

"How are you liking it so far?"

"I'm sorry?"

"Here. How are you liking it here?"

Max shrugged. His head bobbed without

intention. He clasped both hands on his pilsner glass. "It's all right, I guess. Doesn't seem there's a whole lot to do." He glanced to the side. Baseball Shirt was talking to his two sullen companions.

"Yeah," Alejandro said. "I don't imagine there would be much here for a city boy like you."

Max didn't know what to say to that. He drank his beer. He looked up and watched a ceiling fan slice at the fog. Then he looked and saw Baseball Shirt and his two *compadres* watching him. He finished his beer and looked for the waitress. Suddenly one beer felt like enough.

The lanky guy and the little guy appeared. They looked half wrecked.

"This is Mike," Alejandro told them, pointing to Max.

"Max," said Max.

"Mike, this is Alton"—the lanky guy—"and Armando," he said, indicating the small one.

"Albertson, right?" Armando said. He had a faded Polo shirt and khaki shorts.

"No, but yes, we talked about that."

Alton's smile was all mustache when he nodded acknowledgement and greeting. He wore work pants and sneakers and a Pittsburgh Steelers sweatshirt with the sleeves rolled up. Both men had bottles of Budweiser.

"Sit down," Alejandro said. "Alton, find a chair."

"Actually," Max told them, "I was just gonna leave." He began to rise but protest from the men became awkward chains and uneasy shackles, keeping his ass tethered to the rickety chair.

"You can't leave yet."

"Stay for a beer."

"Another ten minutes won't kill you."

Max remained seated, hands clasped on his empty glass. It was interesting, the need to get out and the fear of going out. It was a precariously conflicted coin balanced on its side, wobbling and teetering; and until it landed on heads or tails with a metallic, thrumming onomatopoeia, he was the monkey in the middle of a charged and emotionally contrary indifference. It was surreal.

"Well," he said. "All right, maybe one more."

Alejandro got the waitress's attention, ordered a round. The waitress had a different demeanor now that the three men had joined him, as though an ounce of life had been drained from her. She nodded and went away.

"*Quiero cogida que culo duro*," Armando said.

The three of them watched her ass as she headed to the bar. Max watched it too. Then the crowd moved and swallowed the sight, and Max saw the TV screen for the first time. It was showing motocross. A rider crashed over a bump; he was on his feet before his bike stopped rolling.

"That was very good," Armando said.

"Looking at Selena is always good," Alejandro told him. "I'd give up a lot to get my dick inside her."

"Like what?" Alton said.

"Huh?"

"You said you'd give up a lot. What would you give up?"

"More than you could afford," Alejandro said.

Alton didn't persist. The conversation was dropped. The three of them looked at Max, who struggled to keep from twiddling his thumbs and to keep his hands from trembling. Their eyes were like polished needles.

"You settling in okay?"

"Yeah, fine, thanks."

Selena brought their beers. She made eye contact with Max, then went away again.

Alton said, "You don't sound as though you like it too much."

"There's not enough for him to do here," Alejandro said. "He's used to the big city. This is a shit hole compared to Portland, isn't it, Mike?"

"Max... and no, I wouldn't say that."

"Say you come from Portland," Armando said, "people might get the wrong idea."

"What do you mean?"

"People might think you're queer."

"I'm not," Max said. "I'm married."

"I'm just saying, is all. San Francisco, Portland, they've got a lot of gays. Lot of gay people live there. Lot of gays in Portland. People might think you're fagging, you say you come from there. I'm just saying."

"You're the first person I've ever met who's said that," Max told him.

"I'm just saying, is all."

Max almost asked why it would matter, then decided he'd rather not continue that thread of conversation. He picked up his beer and brought it to his lips, took very slow, very small sips, hoping to run out some clock without having to open his mouth for more than air.

"Too small for you, huh?" It was Alton this time.

"It's not too small," Max said, then paused, then said, "Well, it is small, I guess. Very small. But that's not what I was saying."

"You said there wasn't nothing to do," Alejandro said.

"Yes I did, but I've only been here a couple of days."

"Where's your wife?"

"Excuse me?"

"Where's your wife right now?"

"She's at home."

"Doing what?"

Max's mind did a backward somersault. "When I left, she was sleeping."

"There's not a lot to do here," Alton told him. "At least not like in a big city. But you can find things to do, and make things to do."

"There can always be something to do," Alejandro said. He looked even more like Droopy than before.

Then the table was quiet and around them was noise. The three men lit cigarettes, offered Max one. Max declined with a thank you and a shake of the head.

"I'm just saying," Armando said. "Lot of gays out that way."

Max looked to the side. Baseball Shirt and his friends were gone. Glasses and beer bottles stood on the table but the bottle of rye was no longer there. Likely it left with its drinking buddy.

"This, uh," Max said, "this used to be mining country, didn't it?"

"Oh yeah, from the 1800s all the way into the late fucking fifties. I don't know how this isn't all Indian land. We have pueblos on all sides of us, you know?"

Max nodded, and noted how few American Indians he'd actually seen since he moved here.

"Coal, mostly," Alejandro said. "Or maybe silver. Maybe uranium. Yeah, no, I think coal." He shrugged. "Doesn't matter. It's all closed down and done with now."

They all sipped their beers simultaneously. Max decided on another strategy, and took an extra big gulp. The smoke irritated his eyes and was starting to irritate his lungs and throat. The situation irritated him. The three men, the three A's irritated him. But most of all, above anything else, Max irritated him. He wondered where the guy from just that morning had gone. The Max who stood up to a poisonous snake. The Max who confronted a ghostly rattle at the door, who investigated the sound of an unseen voice at night.

"There was a mine way out where you live," Alejandro told him, "in the mountains that way. Blowed the shit up with dynamite, ran it for about six months, and then said 'Fuck all' and ditched it."

He wanted to leave. Get up and leave the bar. He wanted to go home. Except that he didn't. He didn't want to. He was afraid to. The coin of extreme indecision spun. The need to get out and the fear of going out. Agoraphobia of some kind or other. But unlike the fear when he'd faced the rattler, or even in the days when he'd faced his brother, adrenaline didn't pump. His senses weren't sharp. They were blunted, wrapped in a transparent but foggy curtain.

"*Tengo ganas,*" Armando said. "*Quiero comer Selena el coño.*"

"Maybe she could eat yours," Alton said.

"*Chingate,*" said Armando. Then he looked at Max. "What does your wife wear when she sleeps?"

"That's none of your business."

Alton smacked Armando's arm.

Alejandro rolled his eyes.

Max drank some more beer. He was almost finished with it, and when he was, he could be on his way. They'd asked him to stay for another beer. He knew he hadn't actually been, but he'd felt strong-armed into having this one. So now he was having it. And soon he would have had it. He would have held up his end of the bargain, and unless there was some fine print that he hadn't noticed, didn't get to read, he was then free to vacate the table, free to vacate the bar, free to even vacate himself should he feel the need, or deem it necessary.

He looked down into his glass. Two, three gulps tops.

"*Quiero coger a su esposa.*"

"*Que ni siquiera han visto a la mujer.*"

"*No importa.*"

Max always felt uncomfortable when people who spoke English opted not to in front of him.

He took another gulp. He definitely had a buzz. Had situations panned out more as he'd hoped he would've been feeling pretty damn good right about then.

"Do you like being married?" Alejandro asked.

Max sloshed the remainder of his beer around in the glass. "Sometimes."

"Only sometimes?"

He shrugged. "Everything has its ups and downs."

"Maybe marriage is like Sueño Roto to you. Not a lot to do after you've lived in the city."

He feigned a smile. "That could be, I guess."

"You go to an amusement park, you want to go on all the rides. If you get there and everything but the kiddie TumbleBug is broken, you ride it, but you also get bored. All around, you see the Drop Tower and Water Ride and the roller coasters, but you have no choice but to stay at the TumbleBug."

There was truth in that. Max didn't like looking at it in quite that way, but he appreciated the merit within the man's analogy. Probably even moreso because of the state his marriage was in. The state it had always been in. Doomed from the start. Doomed the first time they'd ever said hello.

He drank the rest of his beer and pushed the glass to the center of the table. "Well," he said, "I'm gonna get going."

"You're leaving already?"

"Yeah, I gotta go."

"What's the big hurry?"

"No, no hurry. I've just stayed longer than I'd

planned. Time to head home."

"Are we not good company?"

"It's not you, you're fine." He pushed back his chair. "I've got things to do tomorrow, and I should be turning in."

"*Cree que somos pendejos.*"

"*Callar.*"

"Stay for one more," Alejandro said.

"No, really, thanks. I, uh, I need to get going." He was on his feet now. "Nice to see you all. Thanks for joining me." He cleared his throat and scratched his nose. "Have a good night, guys."

The ceiling fans mixed a seemingly hostile vibe to the air, which vibrated with a strange, fierce pressure. He was sweating. He didn't know if he'd just started, or if he'd been sweating for a while and hadn't noticed until now. Shiloh's became like the Amityville horror house — *Get out* — as he floated through the scattering swarm of drunkards, reached the front door, opened it, and stepped out into the night.

It was very warm but felt like winter in contrast to the stifling smoke-filled bar, crisp and clear, fresh air with the dry smell of desert. He sucked a few deep breaths, coughed, spat. Then the door opened and a woman's voice said, "Sir?"

He turned around. It was the waitress. Selena. The outside lights made her eyes sparkle.

"You forgot your credit card."

Embarrassment plumed from Max's stomach and up into his face. "I'm sorry," he said. "I wasn't trying to skip out on my bill."

"I know," she said. "Leaving your credit card

would have been the stupidest dine-n-dash ever." She held it out to him.

He took it. "Thanks."

"You're welcome." She smiled; she had a sweet smile. "Don't worry about those guys," she said. "*Borrachos*. They're alcohol crazy. They drink so much it makes them seem dangerous. I think it's permanently damaged their brains."

"That's comforting."

"They're harmless, just stupid."

"Thanks for letting me know." He looked at her, smiled, and stuck out his hand. "I'm Max."

"Yes, I know."

"You do? How do you know that?"

"It says it on your credit card."

Another rush of blush flushed his face. "Yeah, that's right."

"I'm Selena."

"Nice to meet you."

She really did have a very sweet smile.

"Well, back to work for me," she said. "Have a good night, Max."

"Thanks, Selena, you too."

She turned to the door. Max turned toward his car.

"I didn't charge you for your beers."

He stopped, turned back. She had her hand on the door handle and her head over her shoulder and her eyes were sparkling again.

"Well," he said, "I'd be happy to pay, if you—"

"Welcome to Sueño Roto," she said. "Just tip me extra next time."

He smiled, nodded. "You got it."

"Good night."

"Night."

The door opened and she disappeared into it.

Max turned and walked to his car. The gravel crunched beneath his feet. The moon was a glowing scimitar. His hands went into his pockets. His left found the car keys and jingled them. It no longer felt like winter outside. It was oppressive heat amidst sweltering shadows.

His body felt lighter. He had a sprightly step that hadn't been there before.

Selena the waitress. He liked her smile. He liked her voice. He liked Selena.

At the driver's side door he stopped, extracted his hand and his keys from his pocket. For a split second he was more aware of the sound they made falling and hitting the ground than he was of the fact that he'd been slammed against his car. He bounced back and would have fallen on his ass except that hands and arms kept him upright. They used momentum and slammed him again. Then a hand on his shoulder spun him around. He would have fallen on his ass but his car was in the way. Then, like an improvisational, propless version of the medieval rack, he had a man on each arm and they were pulling them outward. His arm muscles stretched, excruciating fire in his deltoids and subscapularis. For a moment he thought he heard popping noises. Snapping cartilage or ligaments or bones.

But it wasn't his body pulling apart. It was other feet walking on the gravel. A light clicked on, bright and powerful, some kind of high-intensity flashlight. It shined right in his eyes with remorseless cruelty.

"What the—?"

"Shut up."

The light was blinding, so painfully bright.

"What have I done?"

"I said shut up." There was cold and calm bitterness in the voice.

"Whatever I've done," he said. "Whatever it is, just tell me and I'll stop doing it, okay?"

"I told you to shut up."

A hand struck his face. The tension on his arms increased. Max wanted to cry out but didn't. Or couldn't. Instead he made murmuring weepy sounds.

"Just cancel that shit, right now."

Max's lips quivered but he kept his mouth shut. He kept his eyes shut, too, but the beam penetrated his eyelids and he couldn't help wincing. He smelled liquor, which came as no surprise.

"You know Albertson," the voice said. Then a pause fleeted. The hand struck him again, two, three times, not hard but strong. "Frank Albertson, you know him?"

"Yes."

"How do you know him?"

"My wife."

"He fuck your wife, that how you know him?"

They pulled harder on his arms. This time he thought he *did* hear something pop.

"Uncle."

"They won't stop the draw and quarter

because you cry Uncle."

Teeth clenched, he sucked in a breath. His spit made slobbering mucus-like sounds. "He was her uncle," he said through burning pain.

"What do you mean, *was* her uncle? How do you be a *was* an uncle?"

"He's her uncle, goddammit."

"And where's the fucking hebe now?"

The pain in his shoulders was becoming too much. He started to moan.

The hand struck him again. His cheek stung.

"Where the fuck is the kike-ass hymie?"

Max tried to get his breath. Once more the pause was fleeting. The hand hit him again. "Dick skin faggot, I asked you a question. Where the fuck is Frank Albertson?"

"I don't know!"

The light still blinded him. His arms still pulled, but the hitting stopped.

"Far as I know, he's very far away."

"Far away where?"

"Somewhere in New England, I think. I *think*."

"Where in New England?"

"Hey!"

The light clicked off and Max was dropped to the ground. Conveniently, his hand landed right on his keys.

Footsteps running. Three sets away, one set approaching. Max was on the gravel on his knees, crying. He tried to fight the crying but it came out just the same. A moment later a man was helping him up.

"You okay?"

"Yeah," Max said, his voice a cross between panic and whining.

"Goddamn drunks," the man said. "You know who they were?"

"No," Max said. He was trying to keep the crying at least out of his voice but knew he was failing. "I don't know who they were."

But he had a pretty good idea. So far there was only one person he could think of who'd have the heavy smell of rye whiskey on his breath.

EIGHT

He was dreaming that he was in a cave swarming with bats. There were others with him, a famous country singer, a professional ball player, and a couple of people he didn't recognize. The cave had no opening, at least not one they could find. There were so many bats above that it was like an upside down insectivore ocean. Darkly surreal, but with all of this he also had an odd sense of something *Scooby-Doo*. There was a Hanna-Barbera quality to the whole thing.

"Get up."

The bats made squeaking sounds. Their black shadows above thickened, coalesced. They flapped and fluttered, nocturnal mouse-like mammals sputtering among the stalactites.

"Get up."

Circles of light flickered and wavered around them. Yet there was no gleam, no shadow. The ball player shrugged and said, "What do we do?"

"Get up, get up."

He could smell them, the bats. They smelled like nothing he knew. It related to nothing in his senses; hence, bats smelled like bats.

"Get up, get up, get up, get up."

He opened his eyes. Camille was standing at the foot of the bed. Her hands were on her hips. He blinked several times then rolled over. He preferred being trapped in a cave with bats.

"Come on, Max, get up. It's time to get up."

"Why?"

"Because it's morning."

"So?" His throat was dry. Minor dehydration from the beers last night. And the heat. The fucking heat. His arms ached, and his first fully conscious thought was whether or not he had a bruise on his face. He buried his head in his pillow.

"So it's time to get up. Come on, get up."

"What time is it?"

"Almost eight-thirty."

"Oh, for fuck's sake."

"Get up, get up, get up."

"I will when I'm rested."

"You gotta take me to work."

"You don't have to be there until ten."

"Come on, get up."

"Cut it out!"

Tension sucked the air out of the room. Unspoken exchanges passed between them, varying in subject and intensity. Birds chirped morning music outside.

"Asshole."

She left. Slammed the door.

Lying there, still half in dreamland, his hands clenched into fists. His teeth gnashed. He drew a deep breath, held it a while then let it out and looked through the bedroom window. The sky was a blue canvas smeared with fingers of flame cast by the morning sun.

A ferocious thunderstorm surged in his chest. His shoulders tensed, igniting the pain from his role in last night's drunken tug-of-war game. Every muscle was taut, and the wiring in certain parts of his brain seemed to momentarily go haywire.

He thrashed. Like having a temper tantrum. Then he drew another breath and it insulated the marred wiring in his head, and his muscles, while still tight, dispensed a little slack. His internal storm diffused to a light precipitation. He rubbed his eyes with his knuckles.

Downstairs things clanked and clattered. The passive-aggressive hullabaloo of an owner whose dog won't obey. A fairly common occurrence ever since they'd moved in together three years earlier. It wasn't just her, though. He was just as guilty of this behavior as she was. But with her there was more. Camille had what could be referred to as an uncertain temper, as Dickens had put it. A polite euphemism for a demeanor that was certain to make everybody around her more or less uncomfortable.

Okay, maybe in some ways he was a bit of a namby-pamby. He hated the thought but the Mirror of Truth was right in his face, showing him facts he would have rather not seen. It showed this to him even when he closed his eyes. But Camille, she was a control freak, with limited ability to modulate her impulses. Her odious mimicry of the world's most obnoxious alarm clock was a perfect case in point, as was her reaction when he wouldn't tolerate it.

He touched his left cheek. It was tender. It might have a bruise.

Outside the car started. Camille was leaving early. Taking the car with her. His punishment for not getting out of bed. For not obeying her aberrant whim. He eased off the mattress, bypassed his slippers and went to the window. He watched her drive away, dust pluming in her wake.

A mixture of rage and relief poured through him. A part of him said *Don't leave it like this*, while another part said *Sayonara, bitch*. He watched until the Camry was a speckle of dust, then went into the bathroom and showered.

He didn't have a bruise on his face.

*****

An hour later he was putting things away. The paperbacks were on the shelf, alphabetical by author. Linens and things were stowed. Artwork and photographs hung on the walls. The movers had left behind a dolly, and he used it to help him move larger and heavier things from one place to another. Then he went upstairs and made the guestroom adequate for those who wouldn't ever be visiting.

It was while organizing the closet that he found the box. A small metal box with a hinged lid, charcoal gray, about three inches deep, maybe five inches wide and ten inches long. It was a steel cash box, with a click-snap key lock. He didn't have a key but found he didn't need one. It wasn't locked.

Initially its contents made him want to laugh. A purple hand towel had been folded and fit into the bottom. On the towel was a pink vibrator, and beside it was a remote-controlled vibrating egg with a textured jelly sleeve, also pink. Though it didn't materialize, the potential laugh inside him had been ignited by the thought that maybe his wife would chill out a bit if she'd actually use these from time to time. The laugh was stifled, however, and never came to be. He didn't care that she had these things, but the sight of them caused him to think about their sex life. Their nonexistent sex life. Last time they'd even had a quick roll in the hay was back around when the McLoughlin Paper Company went under. And even then it had been like fucking a corpse.

Long and short of it, he didn't satisfy her. Not just in life but also in the bedroom. That's what the evidence here suggested. While in turn he felt the same about her. To him, anger and scorn lost its charm pretty quick. No amount of make-up could make hate attractive. He closed up the box and put it to the side.

It would be expensive as hell to get a cab from here into town. Come to think of it, did Sueño Roto even have a taxi service? Probably not. Nor did it much matter at the moment. Where was he gonna go? Hang out at the Dairy Queen? Go back to Shiloh's, where twice he'd been uncomfortable and once he'd been threatened? He knew the real answer, but didn't want to think about it. Or maybe what he wanted was someone, anyone, to pick him up and take him out of this place. Anywhere, as long as they took him away from empty, desolate Sueño Roto. As long as he could get away from Camille.

Maine came to mind. He'd never been there but it looked lovely and it was very far away. Even the smallest island would at least have some life in it.

Get away. That would be nice. It would also be impossible, as well as impractical. He tried to erase the idea from his mind with thoughts of other things. He left the guestroom and went downstairs and made himself a tuna sandwich. He couldn't eat tuna when Camille was in the house. The smell made her sick. He ate it at the kitchen counter, and looked out through the window over the sink. It still wasn't noon but he hadn't had breakfast, only a couple cups of coffee.

Everything outside was sun-gilded. The sky held streaks of a few latent clouds. The desert looked even lonelier than normal. He hadn't seen any footprints—tracks left by someone other than himself, Camille, or the movers—but he also hadn't really looked. Whoever had been at the door the other night, whoever had been crying and screaming—or barking—must have left tracks.

He chewed the last bite of his sandwich.

The strangest thing about two nights ago was that he had no doubt of its authenticity. Its sublunary absoluteness was as tangible and believable as the bread and tuna he now chewed in his mouth. Conversely, he had no doubt that it was all an illusion. Not in any sort of feebleminded way, but the knocks and rattles and shakes and cries were just as likely something phenomenal, completely abnormal. Something otherworldly, spectral, yes, something supernatural. Or maybe preternatural. But it was just as real as the corporeal presumption.

At the time his knees had been knocking. He'd wanted to run and hide and live an unassailable life of insipid incontinence. But then when it was over he had pretty much just tossed it aside. It became something that had merely happened, like a fender-bender or a flu shot, and then on with life we go.

An unknown entity trying to open a door in the fabric of the night?

Why not?

He washed his hands at the sink.

NINE

Max squinted. His sunglasses did little to assuage the flaring needles of sunlight stabbing from the sky. Trees, dirt, weeds and sagebrush. The dilapidated structure he'd kicked the other day seemed even more decrepit than before. The silence made the entire barren property surreal, almost illusory.

He roamed the landscape with his eyes. A few animal tracks, his own tracks from the other day, but that was it. No indication that anyone else had been out back here. No physical evidence to support what had happened the other night.

His eyes closed momentarily. His ears attuned to the nothingness. The faint buzzing of insects. Even their reticent sounds were merely faded, fizzled whispers.

He opened his eyes. The sun seemed even brighter than before. With slow deliberation, he walked along the dirt and undergrowth. In times like these a song usually entered his head, but not a single rhythm or melody came.

A snake-sized hole in the ground. He knew that snakes were incapable of making any kind of hole. Mice or squirrels or something else could have created it. But he also knew that snakes often occupied holes created by other animals. Utilized them for shelter, food, or egg laying.

Nearby, almost right beside the hole, was a decent-sized rock, maybe double the size of a basketball. Heavy but manageable, he raised one end then let it drop onto the hole, sealing it off. A sudden posse of spiders skittered around and he jolted back. He didn't know what kind of spiders they were, nor did he care to investigate. He turned away and moved on, wishing he'd brought a bottle of water with him. Once upon a time he'd been used to the heat. Not anymore. Not heat like this.

He walked another minute then crested the rise and looked down the incline to the darkened passageway. There was a rabbit near it, and when it sensed his presence it raced off. The pathway down was like an old cobblestone road reduced to rubble. He tried looking down into it again. Like before, he couldn't see down more than a few feet. It was like Poe's chamber door: darkness there, and nothing more.

With both hands he took hold of the cross board, gave one hard tug and the wood snapped in two. The splintered planks popped from the jamb and he tossed them aside. He looked for dangling spiders at the top, then stuck his head in, and peered down into the lightless cavity.

The silence became absolute. He was on his stomach with his head over the edge and he remained that way as his eyes adjusted. But they never did. It was a void, a black hole, with no gleam or glint or glimmer. He pushed himself up to hands and knees then got to his feet.

The rabbit was there again, less than five feet away, nose bobbing. It seemed to be watching him, no longer afraid of his presence or size. He took a step toward it and it didn't move, as above him a bird sliced circles in the air.

The rabbit hopped once, not away but to him. No more than three feet between them. He was certain the animal watched him now. The bird above descended in a spiral, then flapped and took flight and glided away. Max took another slow, cautious step, and this time the animal fled. It bounced up the incline then vanished from sight, and Max became aware of the tenacious sunlight trying to fry him.

He went up the small hill and then back to the house. He splashed cold water on his face, then took a bottle of water from the fridge and drank it, took another, sat down and sipped it and thought about the rabbit. Then he thought about the snake. Snakes eat rabbits.

When he'd cooled down he went to the small utility closet, rummaged through a couple of boxes until he found a flashlight. A green Economy flashlight with dead batteries and gunk on the lens. He set it aside and scoured the boxes and found a package of Energizers, size D. He took the old batteries out and replaced them with new ones, then clicked it on and the utility closet brightened. He clicked it off again, went to the fridge and got another bottle of water, then left the house and returned to the shaft in the back of the property.

He didn't see any rabbits this time. He set down the water and got on his knees. He turned on the flashlight and aimed it into the hole.

Maybe four by four feet, probably less, the walls were hard packed dirt and rock. About four feet down, on the wall opposing the opening, decrepit wood planks had been rigged horizontally, a single makeshift pillar running down vertically in their center, composing a primitive, simpleminded ladder. While clearly it was all very old, doubt that this had actually been a mineshaft grudgingly wove through his mind.

Mines themselves were typically vast systems of tunnels, and while some were so narrow and low that workers often had to stoop as they worked, something about this shaft made him think it wasn't a mine at all, at least not in any professional capacity. With the flashlight in his hand he extended his arm down as far as he could. Darkness swallowed the light's beam without revealing any of the passage's mystery.

As he withdrew his arm something gentle scampered, ruffling some nearby brushwood. It was a rabbit. It looked like the same rabbit, same size, same markings. Its nose bobbed with the grace of a hyper finger puppet. It came out of the brush and stopped two feet away and stared at him.

"Can I help you, little guy?" He clicked off the flashlight.

The rabbit simply stood there, egg-shaped body motionless, though whether tranquil or terrified, Max didn't know. He wasn't a zoological empath. He wasn't an animal mind reader; but he liked that the rabbit was there with him. Nature's version of a security blanket, or a stuffed toy.

Maybe there were some more holes in other areas. Tunnels leading to rooms, and somewhere another shaft leading down into the mine, entirely separate from the main shaft. What was it called? An airshaft. An enormous fan in the top of the shaft, which pumped air down into the mine. If this hole *was* part of a whole mining operation, it was neither the main shaft nor the airshaft.

So what did that leave? *The Treasure of the Sierra Madre*? *Treasure of Tayopa*? *The Bad Men of Tombstone*?

"You're over thinking this," he told himself, then looked at the rabbit. "Aren't I?"

The rabbit just stood there.

"Is this your burrow? Your rabbit hole? Would I enter Wonderland if I went down it?" He shifted and the rabbit bolted away. He also knocked the flashlight over the edge, into the shaft. It made a reverberating clack. Then another. He put his head back in and turned an ear downward, listening.

Finally, a hard crack echoed up the tunnel. Max hadn't been counting, but estimated six, seven, maybe even eight seconds passed from the time he knocked it over to the time it landed. He considered the rock he'd tossed in the other day.

He'd never heard that land.

Seven or eight seconds, okay, how did that work? Say seven seconds, for argument's sake. There was some sort of empirical equation to figure out how deep a pit really was. The free fall equation. He couldn't remember how it went. He used to have a friend named Christel, a real physics whiz who once at a party had explained it. Now, all that remained from that drunkenly intellectual soiree was that you're supposed to start counting at zero, not at one. "If you hit 'go' on a stopwatch, the timer first has to count up to one from zero," Christel had said. Max remembered nodding when she said this. He didn't remember anything else.

All right, so you count how many seconds it takes for you to hear the thud and multiply that by something and get the velocity, and you calculate it and multiply that by something, making sure you've made the proper adjustments to compensate for wind resistance and so forth, and there you have a rough estimate of the depth of the hole.

Doing these things with the scientific mind of an inebriated imbecile, Max determined the hole to be, as Newton might have said, pretty fucking deep. Hundred feet at least. Probably more. Strange such a narrow tunnel could go down so far.

Curiosity needled him, injected itself into him. The desire to climb down that rickety ladder was strong, almost overwhelming. He became flooded with all the curiosity and wonder of a little boy.

And yet an inhibitor of rationality somehow implanted itself in his brain. He knew how foolish it would be to go down there, especially with no one else around, no one even knowing what he was up to. If he fell, or something else happened to him, his body might be down there forever.

A fleeting satisfactory thought crossed his mind of dumping three bodies that reeked of beer and rye, seeing that baseball shirt dwindle into darkness, swallowed by the blackness of this earthen mouth. That would never happen, but the thought was fun while it lasted.

He went back to the house.

He took out his laptop, untouched since they'd arrived, opened it and turned it on. He wanted to know more about this property, maybe learn what the true purpose of the shaft originally was. But when he tried to get online he couldn't. It took him a prolonged moment to remember that they hadn't set up internet service yet. Hell, he didn't even know where you could *get* internet service out here, *if* you could get it all. But it didn't currently matter any which way. There would be no research today, no email check, no Facebook or Youtube or Hulu or Bing; again, he felt the icy hands of isolation grip him. Another way he was cut off from the world. He shut down his computer, closed it up and put it away.

***

He was reading when Camille got home. The couch still had the blanket on it, which had fallen from the back cushion and draped over his feet. He hadn't noticed until he heard her come in. He hopped from the couch and went to meet her. She had a single bag of groceries in her arms.

"Here, put these away."

"How was the Silver Moon?"

"Fine. A job." She tossed the car keys in the dish beside the door.

Max set the bag of groceries on the kitchen counter. One upside to Sueño Roto, there weren't any health food grocery stores. He had nothing against health food per se, but back in Portland Camille refused to shop anywhere that didn't have the vibe of a dirty hippie. She once got mad at him when she found out he'd eaten at McDonald's.

He began unloading the bag. It was a pseudo nonconformist's *work with what you got* assortment of items. Had they still been in Oregon, he was sure she'd now be a part of the booming gluten-free trend, which, consequently, would mean he was, too.

"Did you have fun being stuck here all day?"

Here we go, he thought. "Yeah, I did. Unpacked some stuff, hung up some of the artwork."

"That's a terrible place for your Mondrian." She was pointing into the living room.

Years ago, Max had found a framed print of Mondrian's *Broadway Boogie-Woogie* in a thrift store for ten bucks. It was his favorite piece of art he owned. The first time Camille ever saw it she laughed. Said it looked like something she'd played on an Atari 2600, said that geometry was not art, said a five-year-old could fill a page with squares.

"What's wrong with there?" he asked.

"It makes the wall look diseased. How about hanging it in the guestroom?"

"It'll hardly ever be seen in the guestroom."

"Precisely."

Like a blood red camera flash, his mind turned crimson. He drew a deep breath and attempted creative visualization. He imagined breathing in an ocean, and, after a moment, his anger cooled down.

"Let's leave it there for now," he said.

"I just don't wanna feel like I'm trapped in a world of Pac-Man or Missile Command every time I'm in the room."

"I like it there."

"Obviously, or you wouldn't have put it there."

"Well, we'll see. Maybe I'll move it later."

"The house would be happier if you did."

He sighed. "All right. I'll move it into the guestroom."

"Good. Then only visitors will worry about contracting tapeworm."

That was a drawback to breathing in the ocean. It also caused you to drown.

***

They spoke very little the rest of the evening. The house had a quiet like the inside of a corpse:

deathlike silence with occasional glissading verses of worms crawling in and crawling out.

Camille sat on the back patio with a glass of wine. Max sat on the couch with his book. His eyes scanned each word individually, though his mind didn't take any of them in. He thought about the Mondrian up in the guestroom, Camille's reference to tapeworm and the snide smirk on her face as she'd made it. He thought about her fear when they found the rattlesnake on the couch. He'd liked that she'd been afraid, though she'd never admit she was. Vulnerability and weakness were things on which she piled emotionless bricks. But everyone has a mouth, and everyone has an asshole, and most everything you swallow and pile up inside eventually comes out the other end.

He wondered if the snake had even crossed her mind, while pouring her wine, or passing through the back door, or settling down in the patio chair. If it hadn't crossed her mind, would she suddenly freak out if it did?

He bookmarked his page with an old business card, then set the book aside, stood up, and crossed the room to the windows, then to the glass-paneled door. The sun had just recently set. The sky was a beautiful violet, with streaks of orange and yellow in it. The way Camille sat, she had her back to him.

His fingers found the lock in the doorknob, turned it. He took a step back, as if the door had grown teeth, and stared through the glass at the back of his wife, who was transforming into a silhouette. He crossed the house to the front door, and locked it as well. Then he went upstairs, stripped out of his clothes and took a shower. He'd taken one that morning, but with his adventures outside and the building stress since Camille got home, he felt he needed another.

As the warm water cascaded over his body, his heartstrings uncovered an On/Off switch. Maniacal breeds of satisfaction one way, then the switch would flip, and worrisome electrons of guilt would charge. And the invisible hand in control of the switch had serious obsessive-compulsive disorder. He held his head at an angle so that the water muffled his ears. This always relaxed him.

When he turned off the water he heard knocking at the door. He took his time toweling off, then put on the same clothes. With hair still wet, he made his way downstairs. The invisible obsessive-compulsive hand stopped questioning and held the switch to guilt. Currents of it surged through the remorseful conductors of his bloodstream. The pounding at the door grew angrier when he reached the bottom step.

He'd already devised his half-assed response of how the door must have locked behind her. He turned into the living room then stopped. The knocking had ceased. A vacuum sucked out his guilt and a blanching plenum replaced it. The sky was a deeper and darker purple. The orange and yellow streaks were now amethyst, burgundy and amaranth, and the black silhouette of Camille was still sitting in the patio chair.

Speechless, baffled, he crossed the room and unlocked the door.

TEN

The next morning Max drove Camille to work. Like every preceding Sueño Roto day, the sun was ablaze and piercing. Gilded hills and trees and strips of the broken lane divider grew then swept behind them.

"I don't like the Mondrian in the guestroom," he said.

She sighed. "I don't like the Mondrian at all."

"I want it somewhere where I can see it."

"You can hang out in the guestroom."

"I don't wanna hang out in the guestroom."

"Is this really how you're gonna start my day?"

"It's my day, too."

"Not to me it isn't. I'm the one who has to go to work. Maybe if you get a job we can discuss it being your day, too."

Max chewed his lower lip. His hands gripped the wheel. A million things he wanted to say. A million things he could have said. His teeth let go of his lip and he drew a breath and said, "Fine."

A half-sigh-half-chuckled came out of her. "Complaining over superficial crap first thing in the morning is both moot and exasperatingly vexatious," she said. "Spend some time today ruminating on what's a relevant and viable point before you try to express yourself."

"What?"

"Think before you speak."

They pulled into the parking lot of the Silver Moon. It looked busy inside.

Camille opened her door, "Be here at four," and climbed out.

"See you later."

She closed the door.

Max sat there a minute and watched her go in. There had been a time when he'd liked the way she walked. The swing of her hips. The step of her feet. The way her ass moved. It did nothing for him now. If anything, her walk was, to quote the woman of whom he spoke, exasperatingly vexatious. Then she entered the Silver Moon and was out of sight. But not out of mind.

He wished there was a correction fluid for the past. Then he looked out at Main Street.

Traffic was sparse and sporadic. It would take nothing to go to the house, grab a few things, pile them in the car and head out of town, while Camille took control of things at work rather than home. It would be so easy to do. The car was registered in his name. The insurance was in his name. She could report it stolen but it wouldn't do any good. If they pulled him over they'd realize the car belonged to him, and he'd be free to go on with his day. On with his life. Back to Portland, maybe, or back up into Washington. Even back to Santa Fe, or, hell, someplace completely different. He wasn't too far from Utah, or Colorado, and he was a stone's throw away from Arizona.

Or maybe it was time to check out the east. He hadn't spent enough time in the east. He'd been to Maryland a few times. Maryland was nice. Or he could drive all the way to New Hampshire, see if he could find Frank, ask him if he left Sueño Roto because the town was a depressing flyspeck, or because there were people in town who wanted his head. Or was it a combination of the two?

It would be so easy to just drive away from it all. He imagined Camille's face, the way she'd react when he didn't show up to get her at four. By four he could likely be in California.

He rubbed his eyes. He wanted coffee, but didn't want to get it at the Silver Moon. There was the Amigo Mart and the Dairy Queen. Chances were their coffee would suck, but the Silver Moon's coffee was nothing special. He wondered if Shiloh's was open this early.

"Yeah, right," he said. "Next thing you know you'll be a drunk."

He pulled out of the lot and went to the grocery store. He remembered seeing a self-serve coffee counter there. Why this had any more appeal than the other places, he didn't know. Nor did he care. He parked and got out and went inside.

It was hard to tell if the store was stuck in the

forties or the seventies. Not that Max had been alive during either decade; but for some reason the fifties, sixties, eighties and nineties didn't seem applicable to the market's atmosphere. He didn't know why. He watched the sheenless linoleum squares as the radio sputtered and crackled Steely Dan's hit "Do It Again." The small orange counter with the coffee dispenser and cups and things was stained with coffee rings. Shredded remnants of sugar packets, plastic stirrers, and empty little creamer containers littered it like a snack bar junkyard.

He took a cup, and blew into it out of some old habit.

"Spider-Man." It was the old man with the mustache. He had a tooth-filled smile that his dark skin made extra prominent. "*Cómo estás?*"

"Morning," Max said. He set the cup under the coffee spigot. Other than Max and the old man, the store was empty.

"You settling in good?"

"As good as good can be, I guess."

The old man chuckled. "You don't sound *satisfecho*."

Max shrugged.

"That coffee is shit," the old man said. "I know. I make it."

Max regarded his cup. "Why do you drink it, it tastes like shit?"

"I don't drink it," the man said. "I make it, but I don't drink it. *Diablo con eso*. I have a little room, in the back of the store. There's a Mr. Coffee just for me, where I make real coffee. Colombian coffee. Any time I drink that piss there, I always say *Qué chingados es eso?* What the fuck is that? Because I know it is not coffee."

Max picked up a couple sugar packets and flapped them back and forth. "You're not very good at selling your merchandise," he said. "If anything, I thought you'd try to get me to buy a larger size."

"Most of the people, the ones who buy the coffee, they are either drunk or drugged, or *un burro sabe más que ellos.* They are just stupid, or in a hurry and they don't care. Do me a favor, *señor.* Don't drink that. Let me go into the back and make you a real cup of Colombian coffee."

"I'm sure this will be fine, thanks," Max said, stirring now.

"I tell you this because you are new. You and your wife."

"Well, thanks."

The radio transitioned from Steely Dan to Santana. "Black Magic Woman."

"I forget your name."

Max was taking a test sip. The man was right; it was crap. He swallowed it down and said, "I'm sorry. Max."

"Hello, Max."

"Hello. I don't remember your name either."

"Moses," the man said.

Max took another sip of coffee.

"Tastes like shit, doesn't it?"

"To put it mildly, yes. It's kind of like licking a hot cinderblock."

"You really should let me make you a cup in

back."

"No, really, that's very kind, thank you, but I don't have a lot of time this morning."

Moses nodded and smiled. "I understand. Some other time."

"Yeah, how about a rain check?"

"Yes, of course. Anything other than the coffee this morning?"

"I think that'll do it. No, wait, I'm sorry, I'll also take a pack of cigarettes."

"What kind?"

"I dunno. I don't smoke very often. Something that isn't menthol."

"How about Camel?"

"Yeah, that'll be fine."

"You don't look like a smoker."

"Well, I'm not, really. But I can just tell, you know. I can tell it's gonna be one of those days."

Moses nodded, closed his eyes as he did. "I'm not a smoker," he said, "but if I was, I'm sure I would have many of those days."

Someone else entered the store.

"*Buenos días*, Peter."

Peter Parsons, owner of the Silver Moon, Camille's boss, was the someone who entered. His broad shoulders were extra prominent in the tight gray T-shirt he wore. Like a comic book superhero out of costume.

"*Buenos días*, Moses. How fare thee?"

"No complaints, but it is still early."

"I hear ya. Just ran out of staples, believe it or not."

"That is truly astounding," Moses said. "You

know where I keep them."

"Yes I do." Peter gave Max a cursory glance but didn't actually acknowledge him. Then he vanished into the aisles on his early morning staple hunt.

Moses turned back to Max and gave him his total. "I'm only charging you for the cigarettes," he said. "It is bad enough you are drinking the coffee. I cannot take your money, too."

Max smiled.

"You're Camille's husband, aren't you?"

He turned and saw Peter Parsons, who now stood beside him with two boxes of staples in his hand. He was larger than Max remembered. Like if GI Joe were a real person, he and Peter would be about the same size, Max figured, fully aware of the strange comparison.

"Yes," he said. "Yeah, yeah I am."

"Mark, is it?"

"Max."

"Max, that's right, sorry."

"That's okay."

"You're getting coffee here?"

"Yeah, you know, I wanted, well, I wanted to get something else, too, so…"

"Cause, you know, coffee's on the house, anytime you like, over at the Moon."

"I appreciate that, thanks."

"Sure, my pleasure. Didn't know you smoked."

Max looked self-consciously at the cigarettes. "Oh, only from time to time."

"Can't imagine someone like Camille would

like that."

"No, she wouldn't."

"Well, no worries, I won't say a word. That'll be our secret." He turned to Moses. "Can you just bill me for these, hombre?"

"Sure. How many, two?"

"That's the number. Gotta run." To Max: "Your wife is good. She's driven and commanding."

"That's an understatement," Max said, opening the cigarettes. He preferred to call her conceited and demanding.

"Well, good to see you again, Max."

"You too."

Peter headed for the door. "Thanks, Moses."

"You're welcome. *Vamos de nuevo.*"

"Yeah, right, okay."

The door closed.

Max was putting a cigarette in his mouth.

"Your wife is working at the Silver Moon?"

"Yeah, she just started yesterday."

"Sorry, you can't smoke in here."

"I'm not, I'm gonna smoke when I get outside. Oh, right, I need a lighter, too."

Moses turned around to a small cardboard lighter display. "Any particular color?"

"Not really."

"How about orange?"

"Fine."

Moses took his money and gave him the lighter. Max clicked it a couple times, making sure it worked.

"May I ask you something, *señor*?"

Max put the cigarettes in his pocket. "Sure."

"It is none of my business, so feel free to tell me to v*ete a la chingada*."

"I wouldn't say that," Max said. "Hell, I don't even know *how* to say it."

"It is not my place to say, really, but you, what's the word? Radiate. You appear to radiate *derrota*.

"*Derrota*?"

"Defeat."

A solid tingling emerged in his chest, like he'd swallowed a dozen oscillating bricks.

"Your wife, she is very headstrong. From just the couple of exchanges we've had, I can tell she really does not like it when things don't go her way."

Max didn't know what to say to that, so he said nothing.

"I am sorry. I know I am out of line. It just seems that she, that Sueño Roto, that she and Sueño Roto, are crushing you."

"I don't see how that's any of your business," Max told him.

"It's not, it's not, and I am sorry. I am sorry for saying anything. Sometimes I say things I shouldn't. I don't always think before I speak. It's just that, sometimes, I sense things. Some of my friends, sometimes they call me *La Mística de Sueño Roto*. Do you know what Sueño Roto means?"

"Guess I never really gave it much thought."

"Broken Dream, señor. Sueño Roto means Broken Dream. My friends, they are kidding me when they call me what they do, but I've had experiences. I've seen things. Things in people.

Maybe I am just good at reading people, I don't know, but I have been right more often than I have been wrong. And if there is anything to what my friends say, then I do not like it. I do not want to be a mystic of broken dreams."

Okay, this all just took a turn for the wacko. Max was half-tempted to make a joke involving the man's name, broken dreams, parting water or something. Before anything cohesive formed he already knew it was both inappropriate and not even a little bit funny.

Instead he asked, "There a lot of crime here?"

"It's a very small town," Moses said, and a couple people entered the store. "There is very little work. The most popular place is a bar, and drugs are not hard to come by. So, yes, you could say there is a lot of crime here."

"What about the mineshaft on Frank's property?"

"Sir," a woman said, "there's a small colony of hairy brown spiders living over in the bread section."

Moses sighed and rolled his eyes. "I hate those *pendejos*."

"Get rid of them."

"Yes, ma'am." Moses walked out from behind the counter. "Arañas lobo," he told Max. "Wolf spiders. The fuckers can jump. We will talk later. Have that coffee."

"Sounds good."

Moses followed the disgusted woman into the aisles. Max went outside and lit his cigarette, both appalled and snickering at the first time they'd interacted and the man had said that other creatures didn't care about health codes. No reason they should, really. The other creatures didn't even get a say when people moved in and tore up their homes.

And on the subject of health, he coughed hard with the first drag from the cigarette. He'd been a smoker at one point and had been able to kick the habit without any difficulty. Now he only smoked on occasion. When life seemed in the shitter.

He took another drag as a battered old SUV pulled in. What paint remained on it was a dark army green. Sun bleach and rust had done a number on the body, and the windows were tinted near black. The engine idled like an angry bull and then shut off, leaving a trail of fading clicks behind. The man who got out was skinny but strong, build like a professional swimmer. Black hair pushed back and draping to his shoulders. He gave a cursory glance and then studied his Doc Marten feet as he went into the store.

Max smoked as he walked to the Camry. He put it out as he unlocked the door. He climbed in, started the engine, and pulled out of the lot. The oscillating bricks inside him crumbled. Their bits splintered and quivered and gyrated.

The man in the SUV was one of the two who hung out with Baseball Shirt.

***

There was sunlight on his left arm and on part

of his lap. The road intersected and Max slowed just enough to take the corner without losing control. He ascended into rocky hills above the desert plain, a narrow and winding route, forcing him to reduce his speed.

He paid no attention to the details around him. His awareness of the few distant and remote houses was far removed from his genuine focus. The washboard road surface made everything rattle, tried to shake the suspension apart, but it was merely the buzz of a household appliance to him. His anger and his fear were too opaque, and everything else glided in the shadows with only the faintest imposition.

He crested a hill. There was a turnout at the top of it. He swung in and braked. Plumes of dust clouded the car. There was no guardrail. Just a steep incline of rocks and shrubs and occasional trees. Max reversed the Camry into the road, cut the wheel, put it in Drive, then tapped the gas pedal and eased the car up to the cliff's edge, stopping with maybe a yard between the front tires and the drop off. He put the car in Park and pulled up the emergency brake, then slumped in his seat and stared out at the magnificent view.

Sueño Roto was down there to his left. Farther left still, he could just make out the Ortiz property, or the Albertson property; whatever the hell it was; it would never be the Pendleton property.

He ground his teeth.

It would be so easy, he thought. It would be so easy to just release the brake and put it in drive. Wouldn't even have to touch the gas. The car would just carry itself forward. Just bounce wildly, hurtle down the slope, crash through brush and rock, then get tossed about violently, bump around, smash through branches and dirt, and finally land with a splash, and come to rest. All of this could go away as quickly as that.

He took out a cigarette, got it alight, and rolled down the window.

It would be so easy, he thought.

A morbid yet funny sense of satisfaction came when he thought about how dying this way would screw Camille out of having a car. For whatever reason this became so funny that he laughed out loud. And with the laugh came a morbid yet funny sense of elation. His anger dissipated and a muzzle slapped onto his fear. A snippet of goofy music, like Thelonious Monk scoring a TV game show, twiddled through his mind.

"Your wife, she is very headstrong," he told the desert in a terrible Hispanic accent. "She really doesn't like it when things don't go her way."

His laughter turned chuckle turned snicker turned silence. The music in his head used the classic fade out. For a moment, the idling of the Camry and the sight of the desert were the only things in the world. Then a voice very much like his own asked him if he really planned to spend his life this way. The jaws of fear tore apart the muzzle. As much as he wanted to give a certain, straight, solid answer, he couldn't.

The caterers had been late for her wedding reception. It was *her* wedding reception, and she'd made sure that Max was aware of that. She'd been angry with the caterers the entire night.

He looked over the wheel and over the dash, as far down the slope as he could. There was no reason to stay married. The only reason Max could think of was fear. Just where in the hell would he go, and what the fuck would he do? At one time there had been a reason, if honor was worth its weight in spit. Honor, trying to do the grown-up thing, trying to take responsibility, even if it meant allowing yourself to be crushed further into oblivion with each passing day. Isn't that what honor is, though? Maybe. What the fuck *is* honor, really?

Whatever it is, whatever it was, it wasn't there now. Kimberly was dead. She never even got to see her parents' faces. Max never got to see her, alive or dead. The idea of that still terrified him. Kimberly had potentially been the glue, and when she didn't adhere there was no other form of adhesive between them.

He wondered what his daughter would be like. Then he screamed and forced the wonder away. His hand had dropped to the emergency brake. Tears filled his eyes then poured out. They funneled down his cheeks. His breathing came in quirky gasps. He lifted his hand from the brake and wiped his face, then asked himself why he'd come up here. It hadn't been to plummet to his death, had it? No, it had been to get away, simple as that. Get away from everything, even for a short while.

The quirks of his breathing quibbled and

steadied. He closed his eyes and tried to relax. He remembered the rattlesnake. His position, the snake's position, Camille's position, a three-way stop on a two-way street. He was just as capable of driving as she was. He needed to get that through his thick skull. Maybe he wasn't as aggressive, but he was just as capable behind the wheel.

He put the car into reverse, took hold again of the emergency brake, looked once more out to the sprawling desert, then released the brake and backed into the road. He was more aware of the washboard surface, the remote houses, the general desert wildlife. His descent was leisurely, unlike the climb. He reached the highway that would turn into Main Street, and headed to town.

Then he made an abrupt right turn onto a small dirt road. He had to at least investigate. The sign at the corner said *Dogs For Sale*.

***

It was ten minutes after four when Max pulled into the parking lot of the Silver Moon. Before he'd come to a complete stop Camille came out the front entrance, looking half-bored and half-angry.

"You're late," she said as she climbed in.

"Sorry."

"Just go."

"Home?"

"Where else?"

"You look like you could use a drink."

"A couple," she said.

"Long day?"

"No, it was zip-a-dee-fucking-doo-dah."

"Sorry. Wanna stop and get a drink?"

"There's wine at home." She brought a hand to her head. Then the air in the car suddenly charged with electricity. "What the hell are you doing smoking?"

"Smoking?"

"I can smell it, Max. Shit, you smoked in the car."

"Just one."

"Yeah, I'll bet just one. Peter said he saw you buying cigarettes."

So much for trusting that guy.

Camille's hands were on her thighs now. She was looking at him.

"Where are they?"

"What?"

"The cigarettes."

"In my pocket."

"Give them to me."

"No."

"Yes."

"Why?"

"I'm not gonna let you spend my money that way."

"What do you mean, *your* money?"

"It is my money, and I'm not paying to give you cancer."

"Okay, then what are you paying for?"

"Do you really wanna get into this?"

He sighed. He did not. In fact, he wanted to get further out of it.

"How about we stop and have a beer," he said.

"Cool down a little."

"Where, at Shiloh's?"

He shrugged. "Be good for us to get out a bit."

"We can't afford to go out."

"We can afford to get a beer."

"I don't want to get a beer. I wanna go home."

What he really wanted was to get drunk. Get drunk and get her drunk and fuck her goddamn brains out. Not because he wanted her, per se, but because he was so completely stressed out. He really, truly needed to get laid. He thought of the vibrator in the box.

"I could use a beer."

"There's wine at home."

"Not much."

She stammered. "How much?"

"A glass, maybe two."

"Were you at home drinking while I was at work?"

"No, I don't even like wine."

"Then how did we get that low?"

Another shrug. "Maybe you're drinking more than you think."

It seemed the first time in centuries that she didn't have a quick response. Though he may have just—in some very minor way—put her in her place, he didn't feel good about it. He felt no personal achievement whatsoever. Instead he awaited the backlash. Their mutual energy pressurized the air. A stealthy, invisible valet conducted them through dark and intricate passages of silence, helplessness, hopelessness, and, above all, contempt.

"You want me to turn around and go to the store?"

"No. Just go home."

"We could get some wine and some beer. Then everyone would be happy."

"You don't get beer. You lost that privilege when you decided to smoke."

"I lost my privilege?"

"You're throwing them out when we get home."

"Why does it bother you so much?"

"Because you shouldn't be smoking."

"Okay, then what, exactly, should I be doing?"

"You could drop the condescending tone. Find some vicissitude, make an effort to get something going for yourself, stop being so reliant on me and on others."

Had he been looking at his knuckles, he would have seen how white they were, hands gripping the wheel. He wanted to ask her if he was so lame then why didn't she just get rid of him? If he was such a baby and needed so much attention, then why didn't she just kick his ass out the door?

A part of him knew the answer to this. A tiny part peeking through a shadowed perforation. He couldn't release it into his mind and down to his heart, but he knew it was true: she needed him worse than he needed her.

The remainder of the drive was silent. The silence facilitated his anger. His cheek twitched. A smirk jounced. Then his teeth were grinding again.

They pulled up to the house and he turned off

the car.

When they got out she said, "Gimme the cigarettes."

"Let it go," he told her.

"I will when you do."

"Whether or not I smoke is none of your business."

"It's completely my business."

"Why?"

"Because I'm the—" She caught herself. "Because I don't wanna watch you kill yourself."

He looked at the ground. "You can consider it part of my pending vicissitude." He turned away and went to the door. He wondered what she was thinking, and wondered what she would think. He unlocked the door and went inside. It was unnaturally quiet. A quiet with more life in it. He went to the fridge and got a bottle of water as Camille came in, fuming.

The moment she entered the quiet life died. Already the walls were closing in again. Whatever courageous beast he'd been conjuring outside now shriveled up and ran to hide in the corner. The outpost at which he'd begun to take a stand was now aflame and reducing to cinders. He just wasn't strong enough to confront his adversaries. Only strong enough to passively stand by as his fortress crumbled and diminished to ash.

"I'm sorry," he said. He didn't want to say it. He didn't mean it. But he said it just the same. Invisible hands tied knots in his stomach.

"Does that mean you're through?" she said.

His sigh contained a defeated chuckle. He

couldn't look at her, wouldn't look at her. All he could do was grip the bottle of water and say, "You think you're pissed *now*…"

Though he wasn't looking, he knew her hands had set on her hips. "What do you mean? What did you do?"

Still shriveling, shrinking, the beast had gone limp. Words wouldn't come. He went into the living room and sat on the couch, exhausted, so exhausted. He was ready to cave in and give her the cigarettes. He was ready to curl up and join the beast in the corner.

Camille joined him in the living room but didn't sit down.

"Why am I gonna be pissed?" she said.

As if on cue, the golden retriever ambled into the room, smiling as only a dog can smile, tongue lolling out and dripping with spittle.

New monthly cell phone charge: $65.

Average charge at Shiloh's: $10 and some medieval torture.

Look on your wife's face when she says no dog and you bring home a dog: priceless.

"And who is this?" Camille said with an up-tilt in her voice. She crouched down and scratched the animal behind the ears.

"His name is Granger," Max told her. "He's about two years old."

"Granger? Is your name Granger?" she said in a little baby voice. "What kind of a name is Granger?"

"The people named him after Danny Granger."

"Am I supposed to know who that is?"

"He's a basketball player. Played for the Indiana Pacers and now for the Los Angeles Clippers, played college at UNM."

"You wouldn't know that unless they told you." She continued petting the dog.

"Well, obviously they told me."

"He's adorable," she said. Then her voice went back to baby talk. "Too bad we can't keep you, Granger. Yes, it's too bad. You're so cute and I'm sure you're very loveable, yes, but this can't be your home. No, it can't." She looked up at Max with haughty derision. She rubbed Granger's head a little bit more, then rose up.

Her mouth tightened.

"You got a fucking dog?"

Max hung his head. He didn't want to, it just happened. There had been a moment there when he thought she might actually go for it.

"You got a dog and didn't check with me?"

Granger sat on his haunches, panting with joy.

Max chewed on his tongue.

"Remember what I said the day we moved in?"

"You said I liked the idea of a dog but didn't actually want one."

"I said you can't even take care of yourself, no way you can take care of a dog."

"I don't remember you quite saying that."

"I do."

"I remember asking how you knew what I did and didn't want, and I remember you telling me to skip it." He stood up and looked at her, unable to make eye contact. He looked at the dog, handsome with his sleek coat in varied shades of gold, his smiley dog smile. "Granger there doesn't look like the idea of a dog. In fact, I'm pretty sure he's an actual dog."

"He'll die within a week if you're taking care of him."

It came out before he could think. "Is that what you said to the mirror when you were pregnant?"

She slapped him. Hard. It felt like the skin had been peeled from his cheek. He deserved it, though. He knew that. He'd asked for that one. He regretted saying it but he couldn't unsay it.

The charge in the air was now worse than in the car. The slap to his face had energized it with vehement hostility, induced a venomous haze that carried a mild metallic pulse.

"Asshole."

She turned away, walked past the dog, up the stairs, and slammed the door.

***

Half an hour later he knocked.

No answer, he knocked again.

"Camille?"

Nada.

He gently opened the door. Camille was face down on the bed, head resting on her crossed arms. She wasn't crying. If she had been, there were no traces of it now.

"Cammy?" he said. He hadn't called her Cammy in ages, and self-consciousness swallowed any desire to again.

"Leave me alone," she said. Her voice was just

above a whisper, the result evoking an even heavier silence.

"I came to say I'm sorry."

"Okay, you said it."

Max approached quietly. He sat on the bed. His hand fell onto her back.

Camille reached out, took his hand. She clutched it tightly, then flung it away.

"Just get out of here, Max. I don't want you here." She rolled away from him. "Go play with your fucking dog."

Reluctantly, Max stood up, drifted out of the room, and closed the door.

***

Twilight expunged the late afternoon, turning the sky a silken purple with flecks of gold. Granger was exploring the house while Max sat on the couch with a book.

The bedroom door opened and Camille came down.

"I'm going to the store before it closes," she said, "get that bottle of wine."

"All right. I don't suppose you could get me a six-pack of beer?"

"I could, yes, but I'm not going to."

Max drew a breath and looked at his book. A moment later the door opened, then closed. After another moment the car started, and shortly after that, it drove away.

ELEVEN

Shiloh's was surprisingly quiet. After the other night he assumed it was always hopping. The apprehension of coming here after what had happened last time vanished with his first beer. Baseball Shirt wasn't here tonight, nor were either of his cronies. This didn't, however, keep him from flicking a paranoid eye at the entryway every so often.

Alejandro, Alton and Armando, Triple A, sat at a distant table. They'd hardly given Max a glance. The TV had some old eighties movie on it.

It was late. Maybe the rush had come and gone. Max had waited for Camille to fall asleep before coming here. She'd returned from the store with two bottles of wine. She'd finished the remainder of what had already been there, then consumed one of the two fresh bottles in its entirety. That should be, he hoped, enough to keep her down for the count.

He was finishing up his second beer, thinking

about the mineshaft out back of the house, when Selena appeared.

"Ready for another?"

Max looked at her. He couldn't help smiling.

"I dunno," he said. "Two's usually my limit."

"Do you always limit yourself?"

It was a friendly witticism, just the kind of sprightly comment that a waiter or waitress makes in the short span of conversational time they're allotted with each patron. Be that as it may, it became a profound and troublesome question in his mind.

He looked up into her shimmering brown eyes. "Yeah, all right, I'll have another."

She smiled at him. She lingered there a second longer than was customary, then turned and went to the bar.

Taking out his cigarettes he fired one up, puffed it a couple times and then held it in front of him. He stared at the burning tip. Smoke slithered upward, twisted and curled in on itself. He didn't much want it, really. Just the few cigarettes he'd had that day had already taken their toll. His lungs felt itchy, his throat felt scratchy; he almost snuffed it out. Almost. Instead he put the filter end back between his lips.

Selena brought him his beer.

"Good day?" she asked.

Max felt his flesh and blood squirm in his skin. "Good is sort of a relative term. I'm still alive."

"That's good. I would be scared to learn I was serving a ghost."

"Yeah," he said. "I imagine that would be

creepy."

She smiled again.

"Selena, *cerveza, darse prisa!*" It was someone from the Triple A.

The waitress left and was at their table in the blink of an eye.

Max sipped his beer and smoked his cigarette. He hoped Granger was okay at home, essentially alone in a new place he didn't know. Poor guy was bound to be a little freaked out, trapped inside that foreign world. A world where Mondrian was restricted to the guestroom and dogs were half forbidden. Poor pooch. He'd take him out for a lot of play tomorrow. Somewhere, packed away, he had a can of tennis balls. He'd find it tomorrow and they'd play fetch.

He watched the soundless movie on the TV and only just became aware of the soft-leveled country music humming through the place. A female singer. He didn't know whom.

His eyes flickered down and he saw the bartender watching him. His beard seemed darker and his head had an extra shine to it, likely just the way the light was catching it.

Self-conscious smile, self-conscious nod, Max extinguished his cigarette and stared into his beer. Then he heard the door open. He jolted as if to a gunshot, and saw that no one had come in, but rather people had left. It was after one a.m. He went back to his beer.

"Settling in okay?" It was the bartender.

"Yeah, sure, I guess so."

"Can be difficult, coming here from a real

place."

Max liked the way he phrased that.

"You're not from here?"

The bartender shook his head. "Tucson."

"Arizona?"

"Is there another one you know of?"

"No."

For a moment it seemed the conversation was dead. The barman took a sign from Selena and drafted a beer. As he did he said, "Been here ten years. Don't ask me how I got here."

"Is this your bar?"

"Yup."

"Are you Shiloh?"

"Nope."

Again it seemed the conversation had died.

Max put a cigarette in his mouth but didn't light it.

"No, I bought this place about eight years ago. Shiloh, I think, was six owners ago. 1952, this place opened. Before your time, before my time."

Max guessed the man only smiled about once annually. He took the cigarette from his mouth and returned it to the pack.

"*Quieres mi verga por tu culo.*"

"*Chingate, estás borracho.*"

"*Tengo ganas. Tienes ganas?*"

Max looked over to the Triple A table. The little one, Armando, had his hands on Selena. While Alton was amused, he was also trying to pull the guy off, though in hardly even a half-assed way. Alejandro just sat there, cussing at Armando in Spanish.

Selena got hold of Armando's wrists and twisted them. The little man's face seemed to pop like a jack-in-the-box. His mouth sprang open and his tongue shot out. His eyes doubled in size and his nostrils expanded to twice what they'd been.

"*Cagaste y saltaste en caca, hijo de puta,*" Selena told him, then spat in his face, shoved him back, and walked away.

Max looked at the bartender. The bartender shrugged, and went back to cleaning a glass.

Max took this all as his cue to vacate. He gulped down a mouthful of beer and stood up, took out his wallet, and saw he only had six dollars in cash. Plus tip, he owed more than double that. So much for drop the money and run.

"Hey, Oregon Guy."

Pins pricked all over his skin.

"Join us for a beer."

"Not tonight, guys. I gotta get going."

"Come on, *ese*, just one drink."

"Alé," the bartender said, "it's time for you guys to leave."

Max looked around. Selena was nowhere in sight. Actually, there was nobody else in the bar.

"Come on, man, we haven't done anything. Just want Dave to join us for a drink."

"He said not tonight. He's going home. You guys should, too." He looked at Max. "Your name's not Dave, is it?"

"No."

"Didn't think so. Twelve dollars."

Max gave him his card and then signed the slip. Remembering what Selena had said last time, he wrote in a 60% tip.

"Tell Selena thank you," he said.

"I will." Then to Triple A: "C'mon, you guys, pay up. Time to go."

"When do you close?" one of them asked.

"Now," the bartender said. "I close now."

"Thanks," Max said, and headed for the door.

"You don't close yet, Carl," one of them said. "You don't close until two."

"Well, tonight I'm closing now."

"You can't do that."

"Sure I can. It's my bar."

"You didn't even do Last Call."

Then Max was outside. Again, he hadn't realized how stifling the air was in the bar until he got out of it. There were five cars in the lot. The night sky had a fairy tale quality, a painter moon, a wheelwork of stars; they breathed radiance on the ground in a gentle, comforting sparkle. He walked slowly to his Camry, wanting to get away but reluctant to leave.

Then he jolted when the tavern door opened behind him. Without thinking, he picked up his pace. They weren't hostile, but the drunken mumbles and grumbles became pressure on his back, pushing him forward, toward his car.

"Hey, Dave?"

He stopped. He didn't want to but he stopped, and turned around. Alejandro and Alton had their sailor legs on. They went to a modest yet sparkling sedan. Alton fumbled with a set of keys.

"It is Dave, right?" Alejandro said.

"Max," said Max.

"*Max?* Shit, where did I get *Dave* from?"

"I dunno," Max said. "A lotta people are named Dave." He felt a tremor in his neck. It spidered into his shoulders and his skin became hot, as though he was about to spontaneously combust.

"Do we scare you, Max?"

"No, you don't scare me. Why would you scare me?"

"That's what I was wondering. If we scare you, we don't mean to scare you."

"No, no, you don't scare me."

"You sure?"

The tremors had spread down his arms, down his spine, and were currently invading his stomach and hips.

"Sure, yeah. Of course I'm sure."

"Good." Alejandro put a hand on his shoulder. "Be good." He patted his shoulder, then turned around. "We'll talk to you soon, *hermano.*" He climbed into the car, a Chrysler of some sort.

Max stepped back. He watched them reverse out of their space, drive around the lot, then get onto Main Street, at which point the accelerator was tromped and the car zipped away at an alarming speed. He leaned against the side of his car and waited. Knowing they were drunk and seeing how they drove, it felt safer to give them a couple minutes head start.

But that's not the only reason you're waiting. You're conjuring something but it's only in your head. Maybe there are an infinite number of universes, but you only exist in this one, and all you can do is occasionally catch a flickering glimpse of action or emotion in another. It's nothing tangible, and there's nothing you can do to manifest it here.

He looked at the bar. He was tired; he yawned. He took out his keys and turned to the car.

The tavern door slammed open again. Armando half stumbled, half flew from the entryway. Max saw Carl's silhouette and then the door closed, bolted with a loud snick. Armando kept on his feet, staggered, swayed, did a childish sort of skip, and finally went down, face first into the gravel lot, no more than a dozen feet from Max.

A heavy increase in his heart rate, his body moreso than his mind conflicted between whether to challenge or flee a perceived threat, Max unlocked the driver's side door and opened it, his entire anatomy a broken faucet of adrenaline and cortisol.

Then he stopped, looked at the tavern, looked at the man sprawled on the ground. Inside the bar the country music elevated, bled through the nooks and crannies and gaps. Crank it up for closing time.

He still didn't know who was singing.

Like a warm towel after a cold swim, his conscience wrapped around him. He drew a deep breath of the fresh night air, and, leaving the car door open, walked over to the inebriated man, whose breathing made awkward whistles in the crushed rock.

The rattlesnake, he reminded himself. This is

nothing compared to that.

"You all right?" he said.

"*Joder, mi cabeza.*" The man's arm twitched. He grumbled. Then he slunk back and forth in the gravel, hands striving for base support. When he found it he pushed himself upward. Crinkles surrounded his eyes when he looked and saw Max.

"'Sup, bro?"

Max leaned a little and put out his hand. He knew the guy was drunk, but he seemed much worse off than his friends. This meant nothing, of course — people out-drink their friends all the time, and this was the guy who'd made inappropriate advances toward Selena. Selena had made it clear she could take care of herself, and the way the bartender had flung him out the door, and given the man's small size, Max was unable to rule out physical injury. He found himself looking for evidence of this. There were dark glistening splotches on his face, but they were clearly the result of his plunge to the ground.

With some effort he got Armando to his feet.

"Which car is yours?"

"The Nissan." He pointed at a white sedan. "That one there."

Max held him up and they headed to the car. Twice Armando almost fell before the absurdity of what they were doing hit Max. No way was this guy getting behind the wheel. Max didn't want to drive him, but there was no way he was going to let this man even attempt to drive. Alejandro and Alton shouldn't have been driving, and this guy was much worse off than either of them had been. This guy would surely kill himself or someone else. Tired as he was, frustrated as he was, scared as he was, Max couldn't let this guy out on his own.

"Where are your keys, Armando?"

"Huh?"

"Your keys. The keys to your car."

"Pocket, *bolsillo*, my pocket, pocket."

"Can I see them?"

They were now at the back of the Nissan.

"Armando, can I see them?"

"See what?"

"Your keys."

"Why for?"

"Never mind. How about we go over to my car? I'll drive you home."

"I'm fine. *Muy bien*. I can drive."

"No, man, that's a bad idea."

"The fuck, *culo*? Get away from me." For a little guy he was surprisingly strong. He broke Max's hold and shoved him away.

Max took three steps back before regaining his balance. The increased heart rate, the jacked up intensity of his nervous functions, these were reactions to the "fight or flight response" encoded in every human being. The pendulum had shifted and made its choice. He stepped toward the drunkard again.

Armando had staggered to the driver's side door. His keys were in his hand and he was searching for the proper one, using the car to keep himself upright.

"C'mon, man, you're wasted." He closed the gap between them, uncertain what to do but having to do something. As the physical gap closed he saw a gap of opportunity. By the light of the moon the keys balanced on fingers like a cluster of jagged metal tightrope walkers.

Max's arm became the rattlesnake. He struck faster than the human eye could follow. And then he held Armando's keys.

For an inebriate the man's reaction time was sharp. Max felt the elbow slam into his gut and he instantly tasted vomit in his throat. He doubled over but didn't collapse, and managed to hold on to the keys.

"Vete a la verga culero."

A metallic slicing sound and the moon winked upon a whirling cutlass. The casing that housed the blade became the handle of a knife. A butterfly knife.

There is no living thing that is not afraid when it faces danger. The Great Oz said this to the Cowardly Lion. But afraid was not a big enough word now. The sensation of fear was so strong, such overwhelming frantic anxiety, extreme but perfectly consistent with his current animalistic fight-or-flight reaction

Again, as drunk as the man was, his dexterity was amazing. Using this blade must have been second nature.

Max backed away as quick as he could as Armando advanced.

"Cago en tu leche."

One thing people don't often consider: the

potential insanity that can manifest when the mind is inundated with liquor.

Frenzied, Max's foot clipped the Nissan's rear tire. He fumbled alongside the hood of the trunk as the talons of gravity gripped him. The keys fell from his hand; and as he fell from his feet his legs collided and tangled with Armando's. The Nissan's bumper hooked his shoulder, jammed into him hard as Armando went down, first smacking against the side of his car. Max's shoulder let go and both men hit the gravel and crumpled like dying spiders.

Hot pain seared his upper back and shoulder. He winced, squeezed his eyes shut, opened them, and looked up at the winks and twinkles of stars.

Armando was half on top of him, twitching. Through the ringing in his ears Max heard subtle gurgling sounds. He drew a breath, drew another. It was a hot night, but suddenly he was cold, the ground a block of ice on his back. He closed his eyes again, saw crimson and black, then rolled the man off him and sat up. He shook his head, hoping to clear it, then looked at the drunk, now sprawled on his back.

The moon was spreading its light on Armando, who no longer twitched, no longer moved. His eyes were wide but expressionless; his mouth was agape. The butterfly knife and the blood both sparkled, reflecting the moon and the stars at his throat, where through odds Max couldn't comprehend, the blade had penetrated straight into his trachea.

Absently Max noted Brad Paisley was singing,

first song he'd recognized all night.

No coroner was needed. Even in the heat of everything, Max knew the man was dead, and a copious debate yammered in his head as to whether or not he'd killed the man, or if the man had killed himself.

Shaking worse than ever, Max got to his feet. He wanted to run to the bar. He wanted to pound on the door, scream for Selena and the bartender, Carl. He wanted to get in his car, drive home and pretend he'd never come out. Pretend that he still hadn't yet *been* to Shiloh's. But each impulse to run was also a straight stare into Medusa's eyes. His body got heavier and the weight got denser. There was fight or flight, yes, and there was also fight or flight or freeze. He wanted to move, begged himself to move, and the more he wished it, the less likely it seemed.

There's a dead man at your feet. It's almost two in the morning, you're outside a bar and there's a man with a knife in his throat at your feet. No, you didn't kill him; or if you did it was an accident; it was self-defense. If he didn't kill you he would have hurt you, and bad. It would be you on the ground right now, dead at *his* feet. But if that were the case he wouldn't just be standing here. Drunk or not, he wouldn't freeze up. He'd move. He'd be moving. Except he's not moving. Because he's the dead one. He's the dead one and you're the live one. And now you've got a situation on your hands. A very serious situation.

The police will wanna talk to you. Whatever you say, they might not believe you. Armando's reputation might cause no surprise to anyone that this happened. Maybe everyone knew this would happen, some day, eventually. But then again, that might not be true. And small towns like this, people stick together, whether they're a community or not, and if that's the case, then you're the outsider. You're the one they'll narrow their eyes at. *You.* People will narrow their eyes at Armando, too, but that'll be as he lies on a slab and they cut him open. You're the one they'll be questioning, and it'll be up to them, thumbs up or thumbs down, like a Roman emperor. If they don't like you, you're as good as dead. And when you're dead you'll have to have an explanation for Armando. I'm sure he'll wanna talk to you.

And what about the two in the bar? Would they help you or hinder you? What the hell happened when he was thrown out? Other than behaving like a douche, had he done something else? Or was it simple douchebaggery? Chances are they'll believe you, based on your behavior and based on his. You're bigger than he is — was, is? — But you're also the namby-pamby. Clearly the pussy. And that could work *for* you or *against* you. You wanna take that chance?

Still standing there, motionless other than uncontrollable shakes, if he didn't do something, if he didn't move a muscle, he knew he'd have no chance to take. There weren't really any other options. He had to move, one way or the other. He was the living one. His was the body still animated; ergo he was the one who had to move.

Finally, he moved his face. His eyes squeezed

shut. There was still crimson and black inside them, but when he opened them he released a valve of tension. Just enough so that his muscles worked again. Just enough to break down the paralysis, and exercise the wound-up strain, anxiety, and nervous tension that roared and accelerated throughout his body.

A breath shot out of him. A long-held breath as though he'd almost just drowned. He stepped away from Armando's corpse. A warm breeze arose and then pumped into a short gust of wind, startling a night bird out of a tree, its sudden flutter startling Max.

He turned and stepped over to his Camry. The driver's side door was still hanging open, the interior dome light weak but glowing.

Crickets chirruped.

As he placed his hand on the door, nausea belted him. Dizziness swayed him. The recent on and off acid reflux, the vomit he'd tasted now expelled itself in a single bitter mouthful. A couple spoonfuls at most, but it watered his eyes and burned up his nose and flared in his lungs. His stomach tightened and twisted and he clutched it. Gasped. Everything bobbed like driftwood, shifted, sank into despair then broke into oblivion, straightened out, then things cleared and evened and the sickness and dizziness vanished.

He turned around. Armando was still there. He was still sprawled in the gravel. He still wasn't moving. He was just as dead as he'd been before.

Max slung a glance at the bar. Something had to happen before one of them came out and saw him. The urge to flee revved up inside him. The music was loud enough that they probably wouldn't hear him drive away. He could drive out with the headlights off, wait until he got onto Main Street before turning them on. He'd been the first to exit the bar. If Selena or Carl had seen Alton and Alejandro's headlights, they might have assumed it was him. If he left now and they didn't notice, they might think an altercation arose between the three, and that Max had already been on his way home.

There was a chance they'd assume this. There was also a chance that they wouldn't. When Carl had flung Armando out through the door, what had the man seen? Had he seen Max standing there? Had he bothered to look at the parking lot? And if he did, had the darkness revealed anything? If the police pressed him to think long and hard about it, a sliver of memory might come to him. Even if he hadn't consciously taken it in at the time, or even if the memory was somehow manufactured, it could very easily place Max at the scene.

Running could bring him safety for now, but that safety might not even last an hour. The moment Selena and Carl saw the body — which could be any minute — the eruption would start. There would be knocks at the door. Knocks with people behind them. Knocks with police and detectives behind them. Or the sheriff. How did that work? Sueño Roto didn't have a police station, nor did it have a sheriff's office. McKinley County sheriffs would likely and logically be the first ones involved.

So what are you gonna do? What could you do and what can you do?

The moment Selena and Carl saw the body the eruption would start. Any minute. Hell, any second. Time wasn't waiting for him. Time was a perpetual motion machine. It could change, but he couldn't create it and he couldn't destroy it.

Any minute.

Any second.

He had to do something. Fight or flight. But he couldn't freeze. Time wasn't going to freeze, so he couldn't either. He could drop to his knees, bring his hands to his face and cry. A part of him very much wanted to do that. Or to simply curl up into a ball and spend the remainder of his life muttering incoherently. But he knew he couldn't. That would be the equivalent of freezing. And time would continue on. It could do what it wanted. It could speed itself up, or slow itself down, but the latter wasn't likely. Time was the only master of time.

He turned back to his car, depressed a button on the inside of the door. There was a soft but hearty *ka-chunk* as the locks on the other three doors disengaged. He opened the rear door and a second dome light lit up. There were still things strewn along the back seat. Useless things. Trash. Empty paper cups. A filthy baseball hat. A stale half-eaten muffin haphazardly wrapped in cellophane. CDs without their cases. A hodgepodge of junk and garbage.

Another short burst of wind. Just the whistle of

it terrified him.

He couldn't put Armando in the back seat. He'd bleed all over it, and there were too many random things capable of leaving evidence on. An old coffee cup with a single particle of skin could be enough to burn him alive. Even if he then cleaned out the car, there would still be a stray hair, or a blood droplet. He'd still leave behind some bit of trace evidence, and Camille would raise an eyebrow in wonderment as to why he'd suddenly decided to clean it. He'd seen enough episodes of *CSI*.

So what, then? The trunk? There was just as much crap back there.

"You're wasting time," he said aloud.

He reached back into the front and pulled the trunk latch. Another soft but hearty *ka-chunk*. He closed the rear door then lifted the trunk lid. There was crap here, too. The spare tire was here, not properly stowed away. But there was room. There was plenty of room for Armando. Plenty of room in the trunk for a body.

"Shit."

Brad Paisley was finished. He didn't know who was singing now.

He turned and crossed back to the Nissan and the dead Armando beside it. Nothing had changed. The knife was still lodged in his throat. Near the rear of the car Max caught a glimmer: Armando's keys. He swooped and picked them up. They jingled. They felt like icicles. About to stick them in his pocket, he froze. A dead man's keys. A dead man's car. This wasn't a movie or a

James Cain novel. He was holding a dead man's keys. He shuddered, then shook himself out, then quickly went through the keys and found the obvious one. He unlocked the Nissan. The dome light came on. The interior was immaculate. Not what he expected. It looked and smelled like it had just been detailed. Other than common wear, the car was pristine.

He went under the wheel, found the proper lever, and popped the trunk. He closed the door and locked it, then went to the back of the car. The light in the trunk was incredibly dim. There was a small Coleman cooler, a Coleman propane stove, a blue sleeping bag stuffed perfectly into its compression sack, a rolled-up sleeping mat, and a cylindrical nylon pouch with a label explaining that it contained a two-person, two-pole tetragon tent. There was also a camouflage rifle scabbard, no doubt containing a rifle. Max remembered the picture on the wall. These men were hunters.

A single clack sounded. It came from the bar. Max spun and looked but there was nothing to see. And there was no time for deliberation.

He reached in and pulled out the sleeping bag. It might be noted as missing later but time and options were shrinking. He closed the trunk, stuck the keys in his pocket, then looked at Shiloh's again. Nothing had changed.

He pressed the button on the sleeping bag clasp, zipped it out along the nylon strings and pulled out the bedroll like a kid tearing into his presents on Christmas. He dropped the outer sack and hoped and prayed as he sought the zipper and dragged it through the teeth. He opened and spread the bag as quick as he could, and laid it on the ground, right beside Armando, opposite the Nissan. He was thankful for the sleeping bag, but horrified at what he was doing.

Tension. A whole other level of tension gripped him, as though his body was actually *striving* for tension. Nervousness fizzed like exploded champagne. Maybe a part of him *did* strive for tension. He was always high strung. On some level anger was a character flaw. It must have been for him to repress it so much, to seethe rather than face confrontation. But at the moment he had to embrace the tension, because right now it was a survival factor. He'd started to fight, and now he had to see it through. No flight, no freeze. He stepped between the Nissan and Armando's body.

Passive aggression. That was his thing. Seethe with anger, and fear to burst. It builds and slips out. Eventually the levees start springing leaks.

He crouched down. The moon reflected off the knife.

Now he had to touch Armando. Touch a dead body. He put one hand under the dead man's hip, the other under the dead man's shoulder. He expected the body to be stiff but it wasn't. Time was flying, but it couldn't have been more than two or three minutes since they collapsed on the ground together. Even less time since Armando stopped twitching. He heaved and rolled the man onto the bedroll.

And now I've disturbed the crime scene.

He pulled up the edge of the sleeping bag and pressed it against the dead man. He hefted and rolled him, then rolled him again, making Armando a dead man burrito.

Another gust of wind. Another frightened night bird.

Max stepped one foot over the bundle, crouched again, got his hands under it, and hoisted. For a little guy he was heavy. Max understood the meaning of "dead weight." He couldn't carry him, as he'd hoped. He swung a leg around, shifted and put strain on his back. He almost fell backwards, almost lost hold of the bundled body, but kept his footing, gnashed his teeth, and waddled to the Camry, dragging Armando over the gravel. He almost dropped him again as he loaded him into the trunk. The Camry bounced when the body rolled in, but the sound was gentle.

About to close the trunk he halted, spun back, and picked up the sleeping bag's outer sack. He tossed it in the trunk then closed the lid, then climbed in the driver's side and closed the door. The dome light shut off. He started the car. On instinct he almost switched on the headlights but managed to stop himself. There was nothing he could do about the reverse lights. He just had to hope that neither Selena nor Carl saw them.

He backed out and put the car in drive as fast as he could, and fought the urge to peel out and race away.

From what he could tell, the drag marks in the gravel weren't very obvious, and if everything were okay, two more cars would be driving over them.

He drove slow but not too slow. At Main Street he looked both ways. Far as he could tell, the coast was clear. He made a left onto the road, pressed the accelerator, and as soon as he passed Shiloh's he switched on the headlights and his foot added pressure to the pedal.

He knew he was heading home. He didn't know where else to go. The big question was what he would do when he got there.

TWELVE

Not a single light glowed in the house. He killed the headlights before he stopped, and switched off the engine as quick as he could.

Silence rained down. Not a mere absence of noise; the desert seemed to withdraw from noise. Retreat in a roaring assertion of scorn. Thunderous quietude. Reticent tempest. The quiet was an absolute judgment. It watched him with furious eyes. Its scowl suffocated the air, muffled and swallowed and hushed all sound.

His presence had done it. His and Armando's. It had silenced the crickets. Silenced the coyotes and rabbits and snakes.

Max brought up a hand, pinched the bridge of his nose. He could hear things in his ears but they didn't exist.

The drive home from the bar had been surreal. Glacially slow passing much too quickly. Time was not on his side, any which way. Nothing was on his side, it seemed. Sueño Roto had already lived up to its name.

He compressed his eyelids as tight as he could, but the tears leaked out anyway. Drool seeped from the corner of his mouth; mucus trickled from his nose. Both hands covered his face now, and the palm of each was drenched. He drew a breath and dropped them, then looked through the windshield.

The moon was still bright but had begun its descent. He didn't know what time it was; he hadn't looked at the clock in the dash, and he wasn't gonna turn the key again. In fact, he yanked it from the ignition. He wanted to throw them but instead he clenched them, and jagged metal bit into his skin.

He couldn't indulge in his tears. He needed his strength for what still lay ahead.

"Okay," he said, and his voice was clear. It was breathy and scratchy but clear as a bell. His breathing slowed, finally. It had still been holding hands with his relentless high tension, shallow and fast to keep up with his heart. Now it was fading. Instead of racing through the circuitry of his nerves, it floated.

"Okay," he said again, and focused on his breathing. "Now what?"

He looked at the house again. Just the sight of it made him sick. Knowing what was inside it made him sick. Almost as sick as what was in the trunk.

But I got myself a dog. Got myself a mutt and now I got myself a corpse. Both in one day. Good show.

He sucked in a breath as deep as he could. With it came the rematerialization of sound. There wasn't much, but it was crisp. He released the breath, and with it released more tension. He still needed the tension, but his lungs were a basin and his throat was a spigot, draining the tension from his body as his skin and muscles absorbed exhaustion. Layers of black film coated his eyes, and a stifled yawn was plotting escape.

"Not yet," he said. "You're not done yet."

He looked at himself in the rearview mirror. His eyes were as black as he thought they'd be. Another deep breath and he opened the door. The air was no different than inside the car. He stretched his back, rolled his shoulders. The tension was leaving aches in its wake. Gently as he could, he closed the door. Then he patted himself, found his cigarettes, got one going, and thought about things.

Why'd you get the dog? Why'd you get Granger? Did you really want a dog, or was Camille maybe right? Maybe it's an idealization; the solution to fixing a problem that simply can't be fixed. Like ruined couples having children. People feeling a loss of connection and love in their marriage, so they create this fantasy that if they have a kid or two, everything will go back to being okay. And what does that do? Where does that get them? It damages more. It opens all kinds of new doors of destruction. All these new complications pile on. And now they've brought a kid in to damage as well.

He shook his head, then dragged on his

cigarette.

If something's broken and can't be fixed, what's the point of trying to fix it?

He shook his head again, jostling his thoughts, rifling his brain as if panning for gold, searching for a nugget of the proper focus.

You got the dog because you wanted the dog. You've wanted a dog for a long, long time. Someone who'll actually put up with you. Because humans are very conditional; but the love of a dog is unconditional. There's something about a dog that can teach you more about being human than actual humans ever could.

The moonlight made the desert glow gray. It was almost ethereal. If not for the house and the trees and shrubbery, the land could have passed for a moonscape. And there was a lot of land. Certainly enough to hide a body.

Was Armando a Sueño Roto native?

There was bound to be a shovel *somewhere* here. But a search at this hour would be both taxing and risky. Just going back into the house would be risky. The wine had helped knock Camille out, but it didn't guarantee *keeping* her out. She'd often heard him when he was sure she was sleeping. This would not be the time to risk waking her. Even less so to stir her curiosity.

The biggest problem Max saw was that it wasn't flatland. Twenty acres, and other than right up to the house, the car couldn't go anywhere. He didn't wanna turn the car on again, but he also knew the strain of hauling Armando. Dead weight really was quite heavy.

Okay, so, well, he wasn't gonna leave him in the trunk. He didn't wanna touch him again. The thought made him sick. But he couldn't leave him in the trunk of the car.

So where was he gonna put him, and how was he gonna get him there? Even if he had a shovel, chances were that the tension, which was already petering out, wouldn't last long enough to dig a hole—

Correction, wouldn't last long enough to dig a grave.

The mineshaft. The imperfect black door into nothing. At least a hundred feet worth of nothing. It wasn't very far from the house. Far enough, though, and it couldn't be seen from here. Even if you stood on the roof, likely you couldn't see it.

Okay, he thought, you can drop him down there. But then you've got a corpse in a hole, and it's a hole you can't fill up. You won't be able to bury him. And you certainly won't be able to pull him back out if you change your mind or get a better idea. It's better than a corpse in the trunk, however. And you know you can't get rid of him in a Jeffrey Dahmer fashion...

The mineshaft is the best option. Maybe later you can conceal the opening. But for now you can dump him, then work on figuring out what else you gotta do. Sound good? No, of course it doesn't. None of this is good. Every option sucks. But you gotta do what you gotta do. And what you gotta do is get rid of Armando.

All right, the mineshaft, fine. Now how you gonna get him there? You know you can't carry him. You might be able to drag him, but can you drag him that far?

No, probably not. Certainly not.

Then he remembered the dolly. The movers had left that dolly behind. He'd used it the other day to move some boxes from one room to another. When he'd finished he'd put it outside, beneath the kitchen window. He blinked several times, then went up to the house.

It was there, right where he'd put it. The moonlight was briefly like a spotlight upon it. Metal screeched against rock when he pulled it from where it leaned against the wall, and its handlebar felt like ice. He braced it in one hand and brought it back behind his shoulder. There was a brief flare of pain, then a persistent dull ache where the bumper of the Nissan had hooked into him. He winced once, then carried the dolly over to the car.

Surreal. That was the word for this. Other than terrifying, ridiculous, implausible and impossible, surreal was the other word to fit what was happening.

He set the dolly down, fished out his keys, and opened the trunk.

Armando's keys jingled out and fell to the ground.

The blue sleeping bag filled up most of the space. Actually, it wasn't so much the sleeping bag as what was rolled up inside it. Armando was a small guy, but he was still big for a trunk. The only good thing he did was cover up all the other shit thrown in there. But if everybody used corpses to conceal unkempt habits, the entire world would smell like crap.

Max put out his cigarette.

He reached in and found the outer edge of the sleeping bag. He pulled it tight and then slid his hands under the bundle, and felt the pain in his shoulder and the strain in his back as he hefted the dead man upward. This time he was more prepared for the weight, but when he had the body halfway out, it slipped from his hold, and hit the ground with a solid thud, missing the dolly by mere inches. That would have been a noise he didn't want.

He closed the trunk, looked at the house, looked at the body, the dolly, then looked at the house again. Granger was apparently not much of a barker. With a dog's acute hearing, Max had no doubt that the animal was aware of the frenetic chaos happening out here. If the pooch took it upon himself to speak up, the likelihood of Camille coming to would pretty much be a sealed deal.

He looked again at the bedrolled Armando. The bundle was thick, the wrapping a haphazard muddle at best. The dolly stood about four feet high. Armando was small but he wasn't *that* small. Especially with the sleeping bag wrapped around him, it was gonna be harder than hell to keep him on the metal platform.

But the more he considered things, the fewer options he saw. He could tuck the body away in a nearby crevice or something, wait for Camille to go to work, then try to deal with the situation after she'd gone. There was a lot of appeal in this idea. It would give him some time to think, to consider some other avenues. He would be able to do things he couldn't do as long as she was here. He could make noise, for example, and not concern himself so much with potential prying eyes.

No, he wanted to get this over with. As much as he liked the idea, he knew it would only prolong the inevitable. Armando would keep asking him what he planned to do. His mind was already a shambles, stir crazy ants inside of a jar. The more he put it off, the more his own hands would jostle the jar, scramble his thoughts, and shatter his options into questionable fragments.

The time to do this was now.

Did they have any rope? No, not as far as he knew. Neither of them had any need for rope. A lot of people kept rope around, just in case a task called for it. Neither Max nor Camille was any of those people.

He was wasting time again.

Okay, no rope. So, then, what? He bet that if he'd searched Armando's trunk further, with all that camping stuff, there would have probably been something. Some straps or bungee cords. *Something.*

He scanned through the database in his head. Some bungee cords would have been great. Ideal, really. Better than rope. But nowhere did he recall they had any.

"Fuck it," he said, and looked at the house once more.

It remained dark, no glowing windows.

Nothing had changed.

He grabbed the handlebar of the dolly and brought it down onto the dirt, setting the metal framework at a near horizontal angle. With a sigh he shook out his hands, and gently rolled his shoulders. Then he crouched down, scooped the bundle, and winced once again at the physical strain and the fact that he was handling a dead man. He dragged and heaved the bedroll onto the dolly, pain spidering down his back and up into his neck. The caddie barely accommodated the cadaver, but it *did* accommodate it. His lips curled back as he put one hand on the bundle and the other in the gap between handlebar and frame.

He lifted.

Physics, though he wasn't an expert, now seemed to work with him. He got himself mostly upright, a little bend in the knees, a little slouch in his back. Bracing the body with his left hand, he removed his right from the gap. The whole thing wobbled but he gripped the handlebar and got it steady. He moved it forward and back, testing the wheels. It seemed to roll okay.

Above him, the stars were beginning to retreat into the penumbra of sky. Dawn was fluttering its eyes, and it wouldn't be long before it started its approach.

Again, he looked at the house. Then he took a deep breath and stepped backward, pulling the caddie with him. He covered ten feet before it wobbled again. It tipped to the right but his left hand kept the body steadfast, and the threat was short-lived. He remained in control.

He continued moving, through dirt and brush, rock and shale, up inclines and down them, around trees. In some places the soil was hard, in others like beach sand. Numerous near occurrences of lost balance or grip, he somehow managed to keep the thing upright.

A gentle breeze carried whispers of contempt. It rose and faded, dwindled away, rose and faded, rose and faded, dwindled, dwindled away.

His back, his shoulders, his neck, the muscles were harrowed and taut, straining and ready to unravel like string. There were moments when he wanted to cry out, but he forced his voice down as far as he could, afraid of making too much sound, and trying to keep the storm inside. The storm kept the tension up, and without the tension he'd likely still be back at Shiloh's, or maybe in jail by now.

He hefted up the final small rise. Breaths were a tuneless music in his ears. He eased the caddie down the incline, and right at the bottom was when he finally lost balance. He stumbled back and hit the ground hard, the impact knocking the wind out of him. He heard the dolly scrape the dirt and rock, the body thump and roll.

For a time he remained on his back, gasping for air. His eyes filled with tears but it was a physical reaction, rather than emotional. The moon and the stars wavered in water. As he sucked at the sky he became aware of how thirsty he was. All of this stress and exertion, and nothing but beer preceding it. And when he inhaled he was collecting more dust. He would have killed for a drink of water.

Okay, bad choice of words.

His body calmed as oxygen returned to him. He sat up, brushed off his hands and then wiped off his face. He blinked hard, looked at his feet, drew up his knees. Then, with a little effort, he got himself up. For a second he worried his back was cramping. He twisted one way, then the other, and it loosened rather than stiffened. He laced his fingers, pressed his palms toward the moon. When he unlaced them and dropped his hands at his sides, he experienced a head rush, but it quickly passed.

He turned and regarded the hole. The square-like opening stood out in the lunar-platinum umbra, its blackness so solid, so absolute. From where Max stood it didn't look hollow, nor did it appear to have tangibility. Just darkness. Blackness. A quadrangle utterly exempt from space, exempt from substance, and thus, in effect, exempt from time.

A few feet away, Armando had partly unwrapped himself. One foot hung out at a crooked angle, pants leg pushed up and displaying a white gym sock with a stripe at its top. Max stared at it and wondered with morbid curiosity if the appendage was going to move.

You're wasting time again.

He crouched once more, reached down and took hold of the sleeping bag—the opening was only a dozen feet away; the dolly was no longer needed—gripped it tight in two places near the head, and dragged the cadaver along the stony earthen path. The body had put on weight again.

At the opening, he stopped to catch his breath, and quickly scrolled through his options, making sure this was the best one.

You could leave him right here, he thought. You already know that this place can't be seen from the house. There aren't any roads back here, and unless somebody trespasses for a leisurely hike, no one's gonna see it. No one but the rabbits and spiders.

Even so, Max knew he couldn't take the chance. One trespasser was all it would take to render everything he'd done useless, to put an end to his life, or what little he had of one.

For the final time he crouched down. He gripped the sleeping bag and heaved the body over the edge. Dirt and rock crumbled, boards splintered. The sounds all had a reverb effect. A breeze whispered, though whether outside or inside the shaft, he didn't know. He listened as the collisions and ricochets grew fainter. And when all was silent he continued to listen. Silence, stillness, emptiness. Nothing.

He stood up and experienced another head rush. He staggered a couple of steps, as if drunk, closed his eyes, saw splotches of crimson and black, then walked over to the fallen dolly.

Somewhere out here was the rattlesnake. The one that had been in their house. The one that had both instilled fear, and at the same time had given him the strength to face his fear. There were other rattlesnakes out here, too, but somewhere out here was the mystical one. *There is no living thing that is not afraid when it faces danger*. The Great Oz had said this to the Cowardly Lion. *The true courage is in facing danger when you are afraid...*

He carried the caddie up the incline.

So that's where Armando is now. In a deep black hole. A deep, dark, dismal black hole.

It couldn't possibly be bottomless, and you shouldn't be playing around stuff like that. You'll fall in, or something.

He cringed at the sound of her voice in his head. If he'd had more strength he would have flung the dolly in rage. But he was too tired. Exhaustion fluffed pillows in his bones. The tension had been diminishing since he got to the house, and while electric frenzy still charged his nerves, fatigue had been fighting to take the throne, and now it was time for the coronation. Hands of slumber pressed down on his shoulders, tugged down his eyelids, and tried to compress his brain from a horrid and frightened pebble of coal to a single diamond of dreams.

His feet ached. In his mind they had no flesh, were simply skeletal remains stuffed in shoes. With every step he took, he staggered a bit more, and his arches threatened collapse.

But for now it was done. There wasn't anything else he could do at the moment. Nothing but sleep; but he wouldn't sleep. He knew he wouldn't. As much as it tempted him now, he already knew it would remain elusive. Sleep was almost always a task for him—too much going on in his mind. The events tonight had most certainly done nothing to temper the thoughts racing round in his head.

Yet he was exhausted. He couldn't wait to lay down. And he had to do it soon, or his body would do it for him. While at the same time the thought of entering the house—as it had often been in Portland as he got home from work— kindled within him an angry fire that started in his sternum and burned up into a scowl on his face. He knew that the moment he stepped through the door, even if she was still asleep, a barrage of oppression would bombard him. A frustrating, sickening thought, the worst part being that, for the most part, he was accustomed to it.

Fuck it. There was little he could do. For now he had to simply grin and bear it.

He schlepped the dolly down the final hill. Like the night-world around him, the house was a spectral construction of darkness. It was in plain sight now, and it watched him with judgmental windowpane eyes, and smirked and sneered with mouths that hung on hinges. The platinum-hued back patio was an especially lonely sight. Maybe it was the way the furniture was arranged. As though people had just been sitting there in discourse and the residue they'd left behind now augmented the solitude.

When he got there, he gently set down the caddie. And when he did, the frenetic tension wound up again, the kinetic wiring kicking back into gear. On the other side of the house the scratching knocks' reverberations were thin and crackling, as though bleeding from an old radiograph. But they were there. They were solid.

154 | Trent Zelazny

Real.

He didn't have a key for the back door. He wasn't sure there was one. He had to go around to the front.

Fear charmed his adrenal glands. Not only was he afraid of stopping dead in his tracks, he was afraid of complete paralysis. And yet he moved. He walked. Each step was like pushing through a viscous seizure. But his feet rose up and set back down, one at a time, carrying him forward.

He reached the side of the house. More shadows here, and the acoustics made the knocks thump right in his ears. Then rattling, someone jerking on the handle.

He saw the Camry, the front patio. He rounded the corner into the front. He couldn't see the door. Shadows spread over the entryway, shrouding the door and the porch and the short awning in blackness.

Then the shadows lightened in texture. The shapes of things grew clear. The door jerked and rattled, but the knocking had ceased. There was nobody standing there. The striving soul was *inside* the house, trying to get *out*.

With jittering hands he pulled out his keys, jingled them as he found the proper one, then scraped it on the door and on the bolt, before finally inserting and turning it.

As he did, the jerking stopped.

The bolt disengaged. He eased the door open and stepped inside. There was the pitter-patter of Granger coming over to greet him. And a click and a buzz as the fridge revved itself. The air was tuneless. There was nobody here.

Didn't dogs usually sense odd things? In horror movies, wasn't it usually the dog or cat that reacted first? Barked at the invisible? Hissed at the fluttering curtains?

Granger sniffed his crotch, whimpered once, then fell in step beside him as he quietly searched the downstairs darkness.

Nothing. If there was something else here, it was unknown, or unknowable, and the after effects of his nightmarish pilgrimage sputtered, opened, embraced him. Whatever it was, there were too many other things on his mind for him to worry much about something like invisible knocks and unseen whimpers, or possible early onset dementia. Really, that could be all that it was. So much stress that it was screwing his mind. Chronic stress causes brain damage, and he'd had stress in spades.

He went into the downstairs bathroom and turned on the light. Other than toilet paper, hand soap, and a tattered old towel, there was nothing in it. He turned on the sink, splashed water on his face, rubbed his eyes, then put his mouth under the faucet and drank. The well water was utter crap but he didn't care. He drank until his stomach ached, then sat down on the edge of the tub, and tried to sort his thoughts.

Granger came in and looked at him.

Max lowered his head, dropped elbows to knees. Coherency was shredded. His entire body quaked. He felt like a wrung out sponge.

All right, now. All right. Okay. So all that

happened. Now what?

He looked at Granger, half expecting the dog to tell him. Granger cocked his head, as though expecting the opposite. Being here such a short time, the dog already seemed pretty well adjusted. Not quite lovey-dovey yet, but comfortable. Max wished he could say the same about himself. He wished he'd stop shaking.

Why can't this all just be a dream? Right here, right now, can't this not be fucking happening? Hell, not just now, not just tonight. It's been a bad dream for so fucking long, could it please just be time to wake up already? Time to wake up, to get up, get up, get up, get up? Goddamn!

He had no choice but to seethe; he was too tired to do anything else. Granger's paws made clicking sounds, thick nails scraping and tapping. He maneuvered in and placed his head in Max's lap.

Hasn't even known me twenty-four hours, and already he gives me more love than I'm accustomed to.

He straightened up a bit, scratched the dog behind the ears. He'd been told that pets can help lower blood pressure and lessen anxiety. Stockbrokers with high blood pressure who adopted a cat or dog had lower blood pressure than did those without pets. Maybe this was why he'd wanted a pet all along. Something for the people who the pills don't work on. Not a brain operation, just a furry friend. He'd tried almost every pill on the market, and while some worked briefly, they inevitably lost their mojo.

His friend Melissa, back in Portland, who

worked for Assistance Dogs of America, once told him that during stressful tasks, people often experienced less stress when their pets were with them, even moreso than when a supportive friend or spouse was present. This had to be at least partially due to the fact that pets don't judge; they just love.

And right now it was clear—Granger didn't judge him.

It all came crashing down right then. He sniffled, sobbed, then burst into tears.

THIRTEEN

At eight o'clock in the morning he was sitting on the couch, staring out the windows. The sun had risen, and brought with it a dreamlike reality, a new angle from which to experience angst.

He hadn't slept a wink. The tremors of fear had been replaced by tremors of exhaustion. But the fear was still there. He still heard a trembling noise inside him. It was the sound of his own breathing, the sound of his distress, the sound of despair.

Granger was curled up at his feet.

As a flock of birds crossed the panorama he heard Camille shuffle into the room and he closed his eyes.

"What're you doing?"

Max bit his lip to keep insanity's laughter from escaping. She had no idea how big that question was.

"Just sitting," he said.

"Have you been up all night?"

"No, but I didn't sleep well at all."

"You're still wearing the same clothes." She turned and went into the kitchen. "You didn't even put on a pot of coffee."

Max looked down at his clothes. They were filthy. He was covered in dust, like a wimpy cowboy. His left sleeve...

It was the first time he'd really looked at himself. There were a couple of little brown splotches on his sleeve. Very small, but noticeable. All this time and effort to get rid of evidence, and yet he walked around with it on him. Like looking for your glasses when they're on your face — or trying to hide them, or something. *Stupid idiot.*

From the kitchen Camille said, "Will you stop going for walks at night if it makes you forget how to use a fucking door?"

Max had nothing to say to this. Suddenly all he wanted was to get out of his shirt. He closed and opened his eyes. Fibers with spotty refractions of light drifted over his vision. He stood up quickly, startling Granger, crossed to the stairs and made his way up them.

He peeled off his shirt and threw it into the corner that currently functioned as a hamper. A head rush and a bout of nausea hit him. He steadied himself, drew a deep breath, then sat on the bed. The spell only lasted a couple of seconds, though the idea of lying back on the bed was more than a little appealing. Instead he rubbed his eyes and stood up again, went to the dresser and pulled out a clean shirt, a basic royal blue thing he'd picked up at Target, sometime back in

Portland.

With the change of his shirt, he decided to change the other things, too. Fresh underwear and socks and a clean pair of jeans. A shower would have been a good idea. The sound of water rushing in his ears almost always relaxed him, and his body ached from exertion and lack of sleep. Yes, a hot shower would have been good. Help rid of other evidence he might not be seeing. But it also might be the thing to finally knock him out, and he needed sleep badly. At some point today someone would be contacting him about what had happened last night. He had to be well rested when that happened. His mind had to be sharp. He couldn't afford to trip up on his thoughts.

But he also had to take Camille to work. He could argue with her and be ditched again, and maybe that wouldn't be such a bad thing, but having the car was a good idea, whether he used it or not. He had to keep as many doors open as possible.

He thought about the drawstring sack the sleeping bag had been in. He knew it was still in the trunk. He kicked himself for not taking it when he should have; it should have been in the shaft with the body.

Not that Camille would find it. He was certain she wouldn't. That wasn't a concern. The thing to do was to take her to work, then rid of it as soon as he returned. He could burn it, or simply throw it down the hole.

Down the hole. He'd thrown a dead body down a hole. He'd been there the moment a human life had been reduced to a lump of flesh and bone. He'd been there when his father had died; that was *nothing* like this. This was completely different.

He crossed the hall and went into the bathroom, splashed cold water on his face, brushed his teeth, shaved, and put on deodorant. The bags under his eyes were two full sets of luggage, and swollen blood vessels made his eyes red. A quick search and he found some eye drops. The redness vanished almost instantly, though little else changed.

Camille made noise downstairs.

Max cringed. They were the angry noises of spiteful breakfast preparation.

Not ten minutes and he'd already pissed off his wife.

He told himself to forget it. He tried to forget it, but knew it would be useless until she was at the Silver Moon.

She *was* working today, right?

A sinking sensation of dread came and went.

Yes, she was working today. She'd been pounding it into his head that she worked. She worked, and he didn't. She was the master, the one in control, and he was a good-for-nothing waste of air. A freeloader, in her eyes, in spite of the fact that he'd always made more money than she did. He'd always had a job as she'd bounced around from one thing to another. Never mind that she'd been out of work half a dozen times, and he'd had to cover everything himself. This was meaningless in her mind. Meaningless, or maybe nonexistent altogether.

It amazed him that he wasn't a drunk. A lot of people would have been, in this line of life.

He splashed more water on his face. He looked at himself in the mirror. No different than when he'd first come in. Same weak and tired Max. Same pussy-whipped Max who didn't get pussy. He sighed and splashed his face again, then pressed his face into a towel and went back downstairs, desperately wanting a cup of coffee.

The pot had just finished brewing. He stepped around Camille and found a mug, filled it, then drank down a big burning gulp. For a second it was as though he'd just consumed fire. In spite of everything else, Camille knew how to make coffee.

"Are you ignoring me now?"

"Huh?"

"Pouting child, giving me the silent treatment."

Max had another sip of coffee. "Whatever," he said, and went to the living room.

Granger cocked his head at him, then rolled onto his back. Max wanted to crouch down but was too sore. His body was an abundance of aches. He sat on the floor and sipped his coffee and rubbed the dog's belly. Granger smiled, four legs in the air, and panted the happy pant of a contented dog. Man's best friend. Unconditional love. Max felt closer to the animal than he'd felt to anyone in quite some time.

"What the fuck?"

He looked up at Camille, who stood just inside the living room, one hand holding a cup of coffee, the other hand set on her hip.

"What?"

"Where do you get off thinking you're King Shit? Acting like a spoiled kid. When are you gonna wake up to reality, Max?"

"Reality?" He couldn't help the bitter chuckle that swelled in his chest.

"Yes. Welcome to the real world. This isn't a playground and we're not on vacation. This is *real life*."

Granger winced at the tone of her voice. Max continued to rub the dog's belly, looked at the retriever's golden coat, studied the animal's vulnerable position. A full-blown expression of complete and utter trust.

"Honey," Max said, still petting the dog, "I think it's time to say this just once. Shut your fucking mouth."

"*What?*"

"Leave me alone."

He continued petting Granger. He was too tired to listen to her shit. Too tired, too run down, too fed up. She had no idea what his real world was.

A couple heavy breaths sucked and blew through her nose. He heard her turn and shuffle back to the kitchen. Heard a drawer open, slam shut. Something smacked hard on the counter. The kitchen was a clinking, clanking, clattering collection of caliginous wrath.

Max closed his eyes. He tried to block out her anger, take an emotional step away from it. It was too much to take on her shit, too, but it was there, in the forefront of his mind, consuming everything else he had on his plate.

A torch of rage ignited inside him, waking his nerves, setting him atremble. He swallowed a dry swallow, then swallowed some coffee. Drew deep breaths in hopes of putting the fire out. This was not the time to get caught up in this. There were much bigger things going on than what she thought of him. But, still, he couldn't temper the stirrings inside.

He couldn't put out the torch, but he did finally manage to turn it around. The rage sweltered and flared in his sternum, and began to spread. He caged it, put a lock on the cage, then closed the door. The tremors increased, and now he wanted to sleep. Exhaustion was a part of it, yes, but the true want came from a need to escape. A need to lock himself up in his room, to keep away from the words and the fists that hit him, the belittlement and judgment for walking around, for breathing, the air filled with absence, filled with hate, the scorn that bit him and scorned him for hurting. That was Max Pendleton's real world.

And yet he wanted to apologize. Wanted to tell her he was sorry. One time he'd said he was sorry in junior high soccer practice; another kid said that he was always sorry. Max said he was sorry for being sorry. Then he'd been sorry all over again.

Another clank, another slam, then something smacked and shattered on the floor. Max jolted and looked back to the kitchen. Granger jerked and flopped over and got to his feet. A moment later Camille went upstairs and slammed the bathroom door. A moment after that, the shower was running.

She didn't like it when Max barked back.

FOURTEEN

At nine-thirty Max drove her to work. Palpable silence rose from the floorboards, dripped from the ceiling and emanated from the seats and the doors and the dash.

Camille had turned on the stereo. Belle and Sebastian sang. The volume was low.

Neither spoke a word the entire drive.

Max pulled in front of the Silver Moon and Camille climbed out, shut the door behind her, and entered the diner without looking back.

Max turned off the music. He'd wanted to bring Granger along. The dog already felt like a bit of a lifeline. But something told him that if he had, in one way or another, he would have regretted it.

He made a left onto Main Street and drove to the grocery store. A part of him tried to avoid looking at Shiloh's as he passed it, but he couldn't help it. Of course he had to look. He didn't know why he even tried to fight it.

The Nissan was still there. The rest of the lot

was empty. It was a lonely, haunting sight. If suspicions had been raised, it wasn't enough to issue a state of emergency. Seemed in a town like this, it would be fairly common for cars to be left at the bar. Little else to do, so why not get drunk?

He put on his blinker then made a left at the grocery store, found a space near the front and parked. He wasn't sure why he'd come here.

The sun was bright and hurt his eyes. His sunglasses felt useless, but he kept them on and sat there, looking at the storefront.

A woman and child went in; a man came out. A tanker truck drove down Main Street and he felt the first pangs of a headache coming on. He closed his eyes as a light blanket of sleep spread over him. He had to sleep but knew he couldn't. Needles of pain stabbed at his neck and shoulders. He shook his head, which stirred and roused the oncoming ache. With a sigh he switched off the engine. Another sigh and he opened the door, stepped out. He stretched hands over head, then brought them down and locked the car. There'd been a body in the car, a dead body in the trunk. In the very same car, not a dozen hours later, he'd taken his wife to work, and now he was running errands.

It's how you have to play it. Business as usual. You don't play it business as usual and you're sunk. Too damn small of a town. You can't afford to act guilty, especially when you're the new guy, the unknown stranger who's come into town. People are already looking at you. They always study the new folk in towns like this. It's part of the nature of things. Start acting eccentric in any way whatsoever and they'll think you're a witch and burn you at the stake.

He went into the store.

The transistor radio sputtered Tommy James and the Shondells. "Crystal Blue Persuasion." The man, Moses, was behind the counter.

"*Buenos días.*"

"Morning."

"*Me lleva la chingada.* You look exhausted."

"I have insomnia," Max told him, then yawned, then said, "Do you carry dog leashes?"

"Yeah, there's a pet section in the back corner."

Max thanked him, yawned again, and headed to the back.

"Maybe today you need some *café Colombiano*?"

Wanting to respond, Max found he was too tired to piece the proper words together. He located the pet section. It was limited but adequate. A small assortment of flea collars, chew toys, food dishes, and various treats. A couple of leashes hung from a peg. Nylon, four feet long, they were all the same, save for the color. Max took down the red one in front.

A wave of dizziness passed over him. He closed his eyes and pinched the bridge of his nose and an involuntary shudder convulsed him and he dropped the leash. He reached down and picked it up. Rising, he found someone else in the aisle, watching him.

An exhausted but lively frenzy rippled through him. He didn't know how much more he could take. Another jolt of his nerves and he worried he'd explode.

Black hair pushed back, Doc Martens on his feet, a T-shirt for a monster truck rally, the man didn't so much watch him as give him multiple hurried glances, as though he wanted to get Max's attention, but didn't quite know how.

A heavy moment passed. Then the man went into the next aisle.

Max let out a raspy breath and made his way back up to the front. There was a small boy browsing the candy rack. He had a *Toy Story* shirt on, Woody and Buzz Lightyear. The contemplation on his face, it was clear what a momentous decision this was.

Moses leaned on his crossed arms on the counter, smiling at the sweet innocence of the child. "Remember those big decisions?"

"Vaguely," Max said. He set down the leash.

Moses lifted himself from the counter, punched buttons on the old-timey register. "You don't sleep good?" he asked.

Max shook his head.

"I'm sorry, *señor*. That cannot be fun. Everyone needs to be able to sleep. People can survive longer without food than without sleep."

Food. Max's stomach growled. He hadn't eaten either. He had a queasy feeling in his stomach. The dizziness had mostly subsided, however, but only for the moment. It would return, no doubt about it.

"So you have a dog?"

With a tired breath, Max said, "Yeah, just got

him."

"Ah, *felicidades*. What kind of dog is he?"

"A retriever."

Moses beamed a little. "Good for you, señor. Good for you."

Max thought about how the man had shrewdly observed and inappropriately talked about Camille, how she was headstrong, and apparently just from the couple of exchanges they'd had, he could tell she was someone who really didn't like it when things didn't go her way. And how he'd said that he could tell that both Camille and Sueño Roto were crushing him. But now Max had Granger, and for whatever reason, this appeared to make Moses quite happy.

"There is a story," Moses said. "About a man and a dog."

"I'm guessing there are a lot of stories about that," Max said as he twitched with a back spasm.

"This man, he got lost in the wilderness. He was far away and hungry, and had little strength. After a while a dog come along. And the man, he tells the dog that he is lost and hungry and scared." He paused to scratch his mustache. "A monster then came, a *soportar*, a giant bear, and the man, he thinks, 'Oh, no, I shall be eaten and never get home. I am to die right now.' But the dog, the *Gran Perro*, he come and steps between man and bear, and the dog shook himself, and began to grow until he was five times the size of the man. He sprung at the bear, and he killed him, and then when the bear is dead, the *Gran Perro* shakes himself again, and grows smaller and smaller." Moses smiled and nodded. "Yes, señor. Dogs are protectors. And this is also why we call them Man's Best Friend."

"But the man was still lost and hungry," Max said, though he was too tired to care about any of it.

The man in the monster truck shirt got in line behind him.

The smile swept off of Moses's face. "Anything else for you?"

"I think this will do it for now," Max said.

"Five thirty-nine."

Max pulled out his debit card.

The man behind him cleared his throat.

"*Cómo estás*, Wayne?"

"Good," Wayne said.

Moses ran Max's card and handed it back. Max entered his pin and then got a receipt. The man hadn't touched him, hadn't said a thing to him, yet his presence loomed like a giant, stealthy spider. Like Max, the guy was clearly shy. The way he'd studied his drinks at the bar. The way he'd been more interested in his shoes back in the aisle. Being an introvert made him no less frightening, however. Often it was the quiet ones you needed to watch out for.

"Thank you, *hermano*," Moses said. "We'll see you soon."

Max nodded, took the leash, and left the store. He'd hung his sunglasses on his shirt collar, and they fell to the ground when he unhooked them. He staggered a step, then reached down and grabbed them.

"Hey, bro?"

It was the man, Monster Truck, Wayne, apparently, stepping through the doorway and opening a pack of cigarettes.

Fight or flight or freeze, Max stood there with his heart thumping. He knew this was one of the two men who'd tried to pull his arms off.

He heard himself say "Yeah?"

"You're Albertson's kid, huh?"

"No, I'm not related to him at all."

"But you know him."

An acidic burn danced in the back of his throat, which he cleared. Then he said, "What's this all about?" His bottom lip quivered. "What do you want from me?"

"Money," the man said, and lit a cigarette. "It's all about money."

"I don't have any money. I could barely afford this leash." A wash of the acidic burn trickled through his chest.

Wayne smoked. He seemed incapable of making eye contact. "Chill, scrote. I'm not gonna hurt you."

It was neither relief nor tension that enveloped him. Rather it was a flat out knowledge that this *was* what worried him. His physical sensations didn't alter, but there was something gained by naming his immediate fear. And there also had to be something gained by not being readily willing to believe him.

"However you're connected to Frank," he said, "uncle or whatever, shit. You know him, like... like, you know, shit, you know what I mean..."

"No, no, I don't know what you mean."

"You got a phone?"

His inflamed chest felt raw. "Yeah."

"What you gotta do, you gotta fucking call Frank. Shit, you gotta call him and tell him you met Ivan."

"Ivan, the, the baseball shirt guy?"

"Your Frank—"

"He's not my Frank."

"—owes Ivan money."

"I don't... I don't see how that's my problem."

"Doesn't matter if you see or not, scrote." He puffed his cigarette. "Shit, look, I'm trying to help you. Call Frank, tell him you met Ivan."

The faltering conversation dripped with apprehension, resulting in a distressing moment of awkward silence.

"So, then, what? I just tell him that I met Ivan and, what, *poof*, everything's magically fixed and better?"

"That part's up to Frank."

A woman came out of the store with a bag in one hand and the little boy's hand in the other. The little boy had a Twix bar and looked happy as a dog with two tails.

Wayne tossed his cigarette down and crushed it. "Shit, man," he said, smoke puffing from his face. "You don't wanna listen, that's up to you. I'm just trying to help, that's all."

"Why?" Max said. "Why do you wanna help me?"

"Because it's not your problem, but it is. You seem like a stand up guy." He shook his head, took out another cigarette, lit it. "See you around, *cabron*." He stepped away and got into his SUV.

Max watched him drive off. Whether or not he should believe what the man had said was a giant question mark filled with smaller ones.

He yawned. He coughed once and it burned. Seemed pointless for the guy to tell him what he did unless there was truth in it. To say what he did and then to simply leave, there was no logic unless he'd meant what he said.

Max rubbed his eyes and saw black. It was a deep, complete black. A whirl of colors came in, then rippled away from the tumultuous sight pool. The black held for an immeasurable time, then he opened his eyes and was back in the parking lot. His legs trembled. His body wanted to shut down. He couldn't wait until he fell asleep.

Then he laughed without sound.

That was a joke. As though sleep was simple and came naturally. Like all he had to do was put his head down and close his eyes and sleep would come automatically. It was downright fucking comical, really. Kick you in the crotch hilarious. Every damn night he debated with sleep, debated and argued until it finally just knocked him the fuck out, which was usually around the time the sun got started. That was how he slept; that was his sleep; and tired as he was, that would more than likely *still* be his sleep.

He unlocked the Camry, wished he could inoculate himself from either sleep or wakefulness. Either/or, the current state was nothing but a hindrance.

The sleeping bag's drawstring sack was in the trunk. When he opened the door it seemed to call from the trunk. For whatever reason, it sounded like Beaker from the Muppets.

He put on his seat belt and started the engine. The nylon sack gave a final *meep*, then quieted.

"Now what, cowboy?" he asked himself.

Another large truck passed by on Main Street.

Go back to the house. Get rid of the sack. Try, man, *try* to get some sleep. If what Monster Truck Wayne told you is true, you might consider calling Uncle Frank. Tell him you met Ivan. See what happens. See what he says. But rest first, man. You're not yourself. Of course, after last night, you'll never be yourself again. Shit, you've *never* been yourself. You don't know who the fuck your *self* actually is. You never really had a chance to learn that, did you?

He reversed out of the parking space, put it in drive, pulled onto Main Street, and headed back to the house of affliction.

FIFTEEN

There was a great stillness about the place. The whole panorama suggested a picture rather than an actuality. Sparse white clouds sailed about the sky, and birds sliced through it.

Max walked over dirt and the parched brush toward the almost void-like opening, the blue nylon pouch in his hands, fingers playing with the drawcord toggle. Low vibrations emanated from somewhere in his chest. Ominous vibrations, scattered particles of torment that structured a cordon of uneasy fervor.

Granger was a hundred yards off to the left, smelling things and chasing things, marking territory every so often.

The heat had gathered its morning force, and now it discharged in rippling waves, greasing Max with perspiration. His shoeprints and the dolly tracks were hardly visible. With only a few exceptions, they were surprisingly nonexistent.

He crested the mound of earth. Ground

disturbances were clear on the incline. Shoe impressions, disrupted dirt where he had fallen, where the dolly had slid, where Armando had landed. He looked down at the brush and stones. The clearing was rocky enough to keep whatever evidence of this early morning's activities to a minimum.

He looked at the opening. The imperfect square, black upon black.

He plodded down the hillside.

The curtains of shade drew back on the hollow black box showing muted rocks embedded in dirt. He moved closer, looked down. The sun stretched and composed light-hued etchings of the top ladder plank, but the light was a pencil-sketch gray, and the little detail inside the anthracite hole was reminiscent of a black and white comic book panel.

Granger mounted the hill and stopped. He stood there a moment, panting. Then a whimper escaped him, followed by a growl. Another whimper and he panted again, seemingly uncertain of things.

Max stepped to the precipice and tossed in the sack. It fluttered, wavered, then disappeared into darkness.

Down there was Armando. Down there was a dead man. No matter what lay ahead, Max couldn't change this. He couldn't bring Armando back to life. Neither anointed nor eulogized in Max's world, Armando was still the son of somebody, maybe the brother of somebody, a cousin, a father, possibly, maybe a husband or lover. Now the man was reduced to an incriminating corpse. A burdening lump of flesh, down a deep black hole.

Max was crying. He hadn't realized it but it was as though he'd been crying for hours. Both for the dead man and for himself. He wished he could take back last night. He wished he hadn't gone out. That he'd taken Camille's anger with a smile and just sucked it up and not tried to run. He wished he'd never come to Sueño Roto. He wished he'd never married that nasty bitch. Wished he'd never fucked her. Wished he'd never met her. Her and her goddamn domineering temperament. Her condescending, belittling malevolence. Her and her goddamn concealment of the fact that she was bleeding. Her refusal to acknowledge the bleeding that had started during the third trimester. The rare but devastating condition, fetal vessels crossing in close proximity to the inner cervical os. The blood vessels running through the umbilical cord, then growing out of the cord and into the placenta. The warning sign, apparently painless, and she'd dealt with it just as she'd always dealt with it. With a tampon. There'd been blood in her panties but she'd said it was nothing. The shameless and ignorant act of thinking nothing was wrong. The arrogant belief that she was above others. That she was above such harm, and so blowing off the most common symptom of rare but dangerous vasa previa: painless uterine bleeding. And then the day came when her water broke, and the unsupported vessels both in and around the umbilical cord tore. The result was their unborn daughter's death. Baby Kimberly's death from blood loss. Because Camille knew best. And even when her child died, she still knew better than the doctors did. Her unshakable belief of personal ability, insane delusion of infallibility. Her refusal to admit failure or even error. Her personal opinions unquestionably correct. Her delusional belief of omnipotence, when in fact she was nothing but a self-important, arrogant bitch who refused to be wrong about any fucking goddamn thing in the world.

He kicked at one of the rotted planks that framed the shaft. It cracked and splintered. Little shards of wood rained down into the hole. Tiny rivulets of sand drizzled in. He turned and saw Granger, still standing on the rise, tail and ears down, head lowered, back arched.

Max called to him, drummed a brief beat on his thighs. The dog took a step forward then stopped again, ears going up then dropping back down, a single whine escaping him. Then he stepped backward a couple paces, watching the opening.

Max turned back to the shaft. There was nothing new and unusual about it.

Maybe Granger sensed the corpse? Dogs have acute senses beyond our comprehension. They sense odd things, bark at the invisible, howl at the moon, whimper at the unknown, possibly somehow known to them.

Then he heard the light rustle in the shrubbery. It was just up the incline, to the left of the pit. It sprang from the brush then froze, ears raised, chin forward, tail up. Just a rabbit. Looked like the same rabbit he'd seen the other day. It thumped its foot and then bounced off into a new copse of shade and brushwood.

Granger whimpered again. Licked his nose. His tail and ears were still down, and his head was still lowered.

Max stifled a yawn and then rubbed his eye with his palm. And as he did, another flutter issued from the underbrush, where the rabbit had retreated. It didn't poke its head out, didn't reveal itself again. But it was there, no more than a dozen feet away, invisibly present. Granger growled and then left, and went off in search of something else to do, leaving Max alone where he stood.

Didn't dogs chase rabbits? Seemed that they did. Of course they did. Hunting dogs, right. Dogs chase rabbits.

Of course the rabbit may have had nothing to do with the mutt's sudden unsettled demeanor. A rabbit's just a rabbit, like Peter Cottontail. Peter Rabbit. Thumper. Little Bunny Foo Foo.

Something about the hole, or what was inside it. *That's* what got the dog squirming. The hole was an enigma. An abandoned mineshaft that wasn't a mineshaft, a body resting down at the bottom.

Max turned and headed back to the house. Granger was up ahead, sniffing things, tail wagging. The sun throbbed above, pulsing swelters and scorchers and blinding eyeshots. Max watched his feet. They didn't look like his feet. They looked like stop-motion clay figurines.

Granger was just outside the patio, by the side of the house, eyes glittering. He made thin mewling sounds as his paws tromped unnaturally on the ground. He tottered like garbled skeletal framework, on which flesh and fur was plastered, constructing what suddenly passed for a rickety dog.

"What's gotten into you, Grange?"

As though his question was the crack of a starter's pistol, Granger shot to his feet and dashed away to the front of the house.

Max shook his head. The headache was getting worse, ready to explode with debilitating pulses. He closed his eyes, drew a breath, then rounded the house to the front and went inside. First thing he did was kick off his shoes. The leash was in his pocket. He removed it and dropped it to the floor, just inside the entryway. Blurry pools kept rinsing his eyes. He crossed to the stairs and went up them, pausing a couple of times to battle with vertigo. He went into the bathroom, started the shower and stripped out of his clothes. Then he looked at himself in the mirror. The redness had returned to his eyes. The flesh of his face was slack. All the trouble he always had sleeping, and yet he couldn't function without the stuff. He chewed his lower lip, then tested the shower water and climbed in.

For the first time in what seemed eternity and a day, a vague sliver of something resembling calm peeked out from tiny fissures in his nervous system.

He needed to be sure that he'd covered

everything, hadn't left any traces behind. He needed to figure out what he was going to tell the police when they came, whenever that was. They *would* come, however. He knew they would, and he needed to make sure that he had his story straight. A logical story that would fit with anything Carl or Selena might have seen.

He couldn't deny being at the bar. Camille would just have to accept that he went out. Hell, if the cards were dealt right, maybe she'd never even have to know that. Maybe a few simple questions and that would be it.

Whatever, whatever, he was getting wound up and not thinking clearly. Relaxation was trying to ally with him, and he needed to let it. He closed his eyes and let the water run over his ears.

He stayed in the shower until the hot water was gone. Then he toweled off, left his clothes on the floor, crossed the hall to the bedroom and flopped on the bed.

The sheets smelled like Camille and he contorted his nose. It wasn't a bad smell; rather it was an unpleasant sensory trigger, firing off instants of memory, and fragments of abstruse emotion. Somehow, however, exhaustion's blanket was heavy and opaque enough to eradicate these thoughts and feelings, which skittered away, like frightened spiders.

Sleep, in the long run, Blackwood had said, *proves greater than all emotions.*

And sleep's comforting nectar poured through him, seeped into the rifts and splits of his heart, his body, and finally pooled and filled his mind.

The vision behind his closed lids was a thinly hued and heavily veiled scatter of garbled images. They drifted and bobbed in a sea of black ink, submerging and then reemerging as something completely different. A rattlesnake swam through it all, mimicking a water moccasin, keeping its head elevated above the black lacquered fluid. A rabbit splashed in, then tried to splash out but was snatched and gripped in the snake's jaws. The strike was faster than his mind's eye could follow. The snake walked its lower jaw over the rabbit as its backward-curving teeth clenched the animal. One side of the jaw pulled in while the other side moved forward, crushing the rabbit and pulling it deeper into the serpent's digestive tract.

The rabbit twitched and shuddered. Its legs jounced with nowhere to go. Its nose no longer bobbled and its eyes swelled and slowly poked from their sockets.

He recoiled and tried to step away. But being in bed, his attempt created a falling sensation.

He rolled over and buried his face in the pillows. He gnashed his teeth. He tried to relax, tried to force himself back to his near-sleep place.

Outside, Granger barked. The dog had been off gallivanting in the wasteland and hadn't come into the house when Max did. Now he was barking at something.

Max rubbed his eyes and sat up. The bedroom materialized around him. His shoulder spasmed and then throbbed. He slid to the far edge of the bed and looked out the window. Granger was below, not far beyond the Camry, looking down the timeworn dirt drive. Far down it erupted tiny plumes of dust. Then little flickers as the sun reflected off the car's roof and hood.

Max's stomach sank. His heart picked up a pace, and frustration at not getting any rest set in. He was all too aware that his mind wasn't functioning properly. That he was still, after all this, going without sleep.

The dust clouds drew closer. The sound of tires crunching dirt crackled into his ears, muted slightly by the window glass.

It wasn't a car. It was a van, a utility van, white. Max watched it roll up, slow down as Granger accosted it, then stop a dozen feet behind the Camry.

Max squinted at it. Certainly wasn't the police. Not a sheriff. On the van's side was a composite of colorful wavy lines and smiling people, and stenciled around the image were the words "Wavelength Connectivity."

A minute passed and the van just sat there. Granger spent the first half-minute sniffing around the thing, and then lost interest and was off to the side, pissing on a bush and then sniffing other things.

Wavelength Connectivity was a retailer for Internet service. He remembered them from Santa Fe and they'd also been up in Portland. Max knew that he hadn't ordered Internet service or cable or anything, and it seemed unlikely that Camille would have done so. If she had, she would have made sure to let him know, for no other reason than to tell him he'd better be home when they showed up, and the typical time window for such things was usually somewhere around twelve hours. Expect them between eight and eight, or something like that.

Max went away from the window and located clothes. New, clean clothes. The other clothes he'd been wearing were still in the bathroom but he'd put them on only earlier that morning. They were still clean enough, but for some reason he felt he needed fresh stuff. He pulled on a pair of boxers and then a pair of khakis and then he heard one of the van doors close.

He grabbed a tawny crewneck shirt and carried it with him back to the window. A man was standing outside the van. He wore matching navy blue pants and collared T-shirt, and held a clipboard in one hand and a cell phone in the other. The cell phone was pressed to his ear.

Max pulled on his shirt, then rolled his head and his neck made popping sounds.

The man below remained on the phone, tapping the clipboard against his leg.

Max stepped away, watching the man through the window. Then he turned and went into the bathroom, went into the pocket of the crumpled jeans on the floor, and took out his own cell phone. He dialed Camille.

It rang a few times and then went to voicemail. Max knew she would give him shit later for even leaving a message, so he disconnected. He scrolled through the numbers stored in his phone. He hadn't yet added the Silver Moon.

There was a knock at the door. He knew it was

coming, but he still found himself startled. His shoulder muscles clenched and his toes curled. There was some lag time and then another series of knocks, a little sharper than before. None of these raps were at all reminiscent of the ones he heard at night.

His shoes were downstairs but his socks were up here. He pulled them on, went into the hall, then made his way down the stairs.

He expected the man to knock again before he made it to the door, but he didn't.

He slipped on his shoes. He reached for the knob and then stopped.

"Who is it?"

"Wavelength."

"Who?"

"Wavelength Connectivity."

There was no peephole in the door. For all he knew the man was waiting on the other side with a knife, or gun. The deadbolt wasn't engaged, and there was no security chain. His fingers moved toward the deadbolt latch.

"What's Wavelength Connectivity?" he said. His cell phone was in his other hand.

"Internet service," the man said. "An order was put in a few days ago. Installation is scheduled for today."

The apparitional syringe that injected him wasn't so much filled with trepidation as it was with confusion.

"Sorry," he said. "We haven't ordered service with you guys."

Another time lag, short and befuddled.

Max said, "Who ordered the service?"

The pause was even shorter.

"Albertson," the man said through the door, his voice now twinged with impatience.

Max wasn't expecting that. Had Frank arranged to have Internet installed for them? Understanding what they were going through, was he really going out of his way, and doing whatever he possibly could to help out? It was possible, he supposed. As if a free home wasn't enough. A free home, even if it *was* in Sueño Roto.

With hesitation, Max opened the door.

The man was stocky and brusque and likely coming off of a hangover. His eyes were a stoned type of bloodshot, but there was no doubt he was acutely aware. Wavelength Connectivity was embroidered on the breast of his shirt, along with the wavy-line logo, sans the smiling people. He held the clipboard in both hands now. The cell phone was now in a holster on a basic, minimal utility belt.

"Ordered by Albertson?" Max said.

"Yes, sir." The man looked at the clipboard. "Frank Albertson."

"From where?"

"Excuse me?"

"Frank Albertson from where?"

The man's glassy eyes jiggled for a second. "I don't know what you mean."

"From where did Frank Albertson order the service? Frank Albertson doesn't live here."

The man's face tried to match the bloodshot shade of his eyes, but didn't quite succeed. "I don't know. The order just says Albertson, Frank."

Conundrum upon conundrum tumbled in upon conundrum in his head. On one hand it seemed too convenient, like a set-up from a bad crime movie. On the other hand it seemed quite possible that Frank might be kind enough to do something like this. Far as Max was concerned, Frank was a pretty good guy. There was something on the other-other hand, it seemed, however, and something else still on the other-other-other hand, but before he could consider them, Granger charged in, bumping and startling the man, who dropped his clipboard. The dog went into the kitchen.

As he watched the man bend down and pick up the board, Max told himself to keep natural. If Frank had indeed ordered them Internet service, then there was no point in raising suspicions of any sort to some working class dude who just happened to come out to do a job.

At the same time, if Max's paranoia was more than the simple act of letting his imagination run away with him, turning the bad things that had happened into everything that happens, and indeed the guy had some link to Baseball Shirt or the Mafia or whoever, it wouldn't currently do him any good to act like the crazy freak he was. If such a situation presented itself, maybe he'd get lucky, and be able to bust out his craziness at an opportune time. Employ the raving loon inside him when the opportunity of fight or flight or freeze arose.

"May I see that?" Max said, and gestured to

the clipboard.

The man shrugged and handed it over. He seemed anxious to simply get on with his work.

Max read the order. Certainly looked official enough. Wavelength Connectivity letterhead, more than one person's handwriting on the order. On the second line from the top, right next to where it said Albertson, Frank, was a phone number, area code 603. Max scrolled through the phone book stored in his cell phone, found Frank and selected to "view info." Frank's number came up. The area code was 603. The two numbers matched. Max beeped off his phone and handed back the clipboard.

"Sorry," he said. "We just really weren't expecting you." A brief and awkward, stumbled upon pause, then Max stepped aside and invited him in. "Can I get you something? Coffee? Water?"

"No, thank you," the man said. He looked briefly around the house, and furrowed his brow at the kitchen floor.

Max looked and saw a shattered mug. The thing Camille had smashed this morning. He'd forgotten all about it. He almost tried making up an excuse for it, then decided to let sleeping dogs lay. Wait, lay? Lie?

Damn, he needed sleep.

Over the next ten minutes Max kept an eye on the man—whose name was Michael—and although sleep kept pouring into his eyes, he took advantage of the time to cuddle and play with his new dog.

The animal was truly lovable. A very well mannered, intelligent dog, with great charm and great patience. Gentle, energetic, self-assured, and he was already well trained in obedience and such. Granger was, Max decided, exactly why he wanted a dog.

During this time Max also took advantage to caffeinate himself, drinking three cups of coffee. Three cups in ten minutes, possibly a new personal record. If sleep wasn't going to cooperate then he had to tell sleep to fuck off. He knew he'd regret it, but he couldn't spend the day cranking wheels without grease, and if they weren't going to come to a complete stop, then he had to get them moving faster. He couldn't afford to simply clunk along.

After the ten minutes Michael went outside. The inside of the house was not set up for high-speed Internet, and the man had to locate the exterior cable box.

Max felt more comfortable with the man outside. Though he struggled, he refused to worry that the man would find the shaft, even less so Armando.

He cleaned up the shattered mug in the kitchen. It had been one of his favorites. It had Marvin the Martian on it, with his Illudium PU-36 Explosive Space Modulator and ACME Disintegration Pistol. As he swept the pieces into a pile, he considered Camille's wish for him to read less fiction, and concluded that the types of books he read was completely irrelevant to her actual wish. What he read had nothing to do with it. It was just another case of her needing to tell him what to do. He could've been nailed to a cross with thorns crammed into his head, bleeding profusely, and his wife would have told him that he would do better atoning for humanity's sins by making a figure eight.

Another ten minutes went by and then Michael returned.

"Doesn't look like you'll have Internet today."

"Oh? Why's that?"

"There's no exterior box. One's gonna have to be installed, and routed to the next nearest one. This is a large property, but there might be one just down the road. Looks like we'll have to lay down at least several hundred feet of cable."

What normally would have been disappointment was instead a blasé feeling of indifference.

"Do you know about how long before that can be done?"

"Probably about a week, give or take."

"Okay, that's fine." A tiny bit of disappointment did enter here. It wasn't because he couldn't check his email, or check Facebook or stream Youtube or any of those other time-wasting things. It was that he still wanted to see if there was any information about the Ortiz property online.

"I'll have to put in the order. You might want to call us in a day or two, check on the status. By then, we'll be able to tell you when they can get started on that."

"I appreciate it."

"Here's a card with the number to call. Also has your order number on it."

Max took the card. "Thank you."

"Have a good day."

"You, too."

Max closed the door. He watched through the window as Michael walked to the van. At the front of the van, between it and the Camry, the man stopped. He stared at the ground, then crouched down and picked something up. Whatever it was, it caught the sun and showed Max a white flash. Michael stood there a moment, holding the thing. One of his legs seemed to inch toward the house while the other appeared edging toward the van. Before the man had made any full-fledged movement, something blasted and scattered shots of panic into Max. He quickly went to the door and opened it.

Upon hearing the door, the man looked over at him. "Lose a set of keys?"

Each shot of panic exploded a little.

"My wife misplaced a set," he said.

Michael's expression bordered uncertainty. After a second of this, however, he made his way back to the house. Max moved out and met him part way and the sun was a bitch. The man handed him the keys. Armando's keys. As he did, the uncertainty turned scrutiny, though no words were spoken.

"Thank you," Max said.

Michael gave a small nod, then turned and went back to his van. Max stood there and watched until the van turned around, drove down the dirt road, and disappeared.

Max went back inside. The keys. The fucking keys. Someone now knew he had them. And that someone had likely noted the Nissan key. And noted there wasn't a Nissan in the driveway. Sometimes speculation and hearsay are all the mob needs to lynch you. He had to get rid of the keys, had to toss them.

First, however, it was time to call Frank.

SIXTEEN

Third ring:

"Hello?"

"Hi, Frank?"

"Yes?"

"Hi, it's Max."

"Hi, Max. How you guys doing? How's the place?"

"Oh, it's fine, it's fine."

"Camille start at the Silver Moon yet?"

"Yeah. Yeah, she seems to like it."

"Good. Glad to hear it. What's up?"

Max was on the back patio with Granger. He held Armando's keys.

"Well," he said, "I was actually wondering. Did you put in an order to have Internet installed here?"

"I did."

"Oh, okay."

"Why, is there a problem?"

"Oh, no. No, not really. I just didn't know, and

was a bit confused when the guy showed up, that's all."

"Thought it would be a nice surprise. Guess I didn't really consider that one of you would need to be there."

"Oh, that's okay. I was here."

"So, you all set up now?"

"Well, no. They need to install a cable box, somewhere outside. Probably take about another week."

"Crap, I'm sorry."

"Oh, no, no reason to be. Hell, it's appreciated more than you know. I just wanted to confirm that you had really put in the order."

"Yes, don't worry your pretty little self, Max. I'm the man behind the scenes."

Though Frank was a nice guy, he still had his own subtle backhanded ways of belittling Max, which flipped a dim anger switch inside him.

"Could you tell me something else?"

"Sure."

"Okay, uh, well…"

"What is it, Max?"

"What, uh, what happened with Ivan?"

Electric silence crackled.

Then, "Ivan?"

"Yeah, big guy, likes rye whiskey?"

Another static-laced pause.

"I'm trying to think who Ivan is."

"Apparently you owe him money." Max was surprised that he was so assertive on the matter.

A little silence, but less than before.

"I don't think I owe anyone in Sueño Roto

money," he said.

"Are you sure about that?"

When Frank spoke again, his voice was ensconced with annoyance. "What are you getting at, Max?"

"Just that a guy named Ivan said you owed him money. He was kind of a dick about it, too." A part of him wanted to tell him about Wayne. Moreso, a part of him wanted to tell the tale of being stretched and smacked and threatened, but his assertion didn't go that far. Exhaustion and all the coffee had him encased in a bizarre, perpetual state of dreamlike anxiety.

"Sorry, Max," Frank said. "I don't know what you're talking about."

"You sure?"

"Max, don't go getting accusatory on me. I've done a lot for you guys. I've given you guys a home, got Camille a job; I'm even setting up the goddamn Internet for you."

"I'm not accusing you of anything. Jesus, the guy was just a dick and that's what he said, that's all. I'd rather not have to deal with something like that again."

Another silence, even less than before.

"I gotta go, Max."

"So you really don't know what I'm talking about?"

"Tell Camille to call me soon. Love to you guys."

He hung up.

***

Granger wandered but stuck closer to Max than before.

Max walked toward the hole. There was nothing special about the keys. No novelty trinkets, no tiny flashlight attached to the key ring. The only thing setting them apart from a billion other sets of keys was the story tied to them. A story that only Max and Max alone knew.

He stopped and looked down the incline. The earth was still disturbed in all the same places, undisturbed in the rest of it. The keys jingled in his shaky hand as his stomach growled. He needed food.

Stepping down the incline, he stopped and stood at the opening. He looked into it, could see the top ladder board. Then he looked around the brush, his ears homed for rustling rabbit sounds, of which there were none.

Granger trotted down the incline this time, no whimpers, no raised ears, just a happy dog joining his new best friend.

Max wanted to berate himself for dropping the keys in the driveway and even moreso for forgetting about them, but he couldn't. Not right now. He couldn't even allow himself to worry about the fact that Michael had found the keys. Unless Armando's disappearance made the news, and that he drove a Nissan was specifically mentioned, Michael from Wavelength Connectivity should have no reason to wonder for even a second. Right? A part of him didn't quite believe it. But, for now, he had to believe it.

He tossed the keys into the pit, then scratched Granger behind the ears, and the two of them made their way up the incline.

SEVENTEEN

There had been very little food in the house, so Max had grabbed the leash from by the door, loaded Granger into the Camry, and was now parked across from the Silver Moon in the lot of the Dairy Queen. There were outside tables and Max tied Granger up at one of them before heading inside.

Despite the rundown exterior, the interior was nice and clean. And air-conditioned.

He was craving a hotdog. It was rare that he had such cravings, but he was having one now. The level of shit he would get if Camille even knew he was here almost made him laugh.

It was a young girl behind the counter. A teenager, short and incredibly thin, eyes like blunted needles waiting to be sharpened. There were a few people dining inside. Max hadn't given any of them a glance. He ordered two hotdogs, fries, and a large Coke.

While he waited for his order he looked out at

Granger, who sat on the dining patio, tethered to a seat, seemingly contented just to be there.

"*Buenos días.*"

Max looked at a nearby table. With fast food wrappers crumpled on a tray, Selena, the waitress, sat, sipping on a soda. Already a stunning woman, daylight seemed even kinder to her.

"Hi," he said.

"Here you go, sir." It was the teenager, sliding a food-filled tray across the counter in his direction.

"Thank you." He looked back at Selena.

"Would you like to sit down?"

She had beautiful eyes. He glanced down at his tray of hotdogs and fries, then looked out the window at Granger, then beyond Granger to the Silver Moon.

"Is that your dog?"

"Yeah."

"He's beautiful."

"Thanks."

"Wait, he or she?"

"He, you got it right."

"I assume you don't want to leave him alone too long."

"Well, I just got him recently. Still working on building trust. Leaving him out there alone too long might not help very much."

"Well," she said, "I could join *you*."

"I suppose you could."

"That is, if you don't mind."

All of a sudden, Max's face felt funny. He'd forgotten the sensation that came with smiling.

"No, not at all. Please do."

Selena stood up and disposed of her trash. She refilled her soda then followed Max outside. She set her drink on the table then crouched and started rubbing and petting Granger, making the cutesy noises people do with dogs.

"What a sweetheart. *Ángel de un perro.* What's his name?"

"Granger."

"Hello, Granger. You are a beautiful dog, yes you are. *Hasta que uno ha amado a un animal, una parte de su alma permanece dormida.*" She looked at Max and blushed just a little. "Something my mother used to say. 'Until one has loved an animal, a part of your soul remains asleep'." She rubbed her forehead against Granger's, then touseled his ears, rose up, and took a seat at the table. She lifted her soda, and stuck the straw between her lips.

Max was adding mustard and ketchup to one of the hotdogs. "So," he said, "you doing all right, today?"

"Yeah, I'm fine," she said. "Should I not be?"

Max shrugged. "Well, just given what happened last night..." He stopped there, afraid to say anything more.

"What, Armando?" She rolled her eyes. "*Borracho estúpido.* It's not like it was the first time he was a *baboso.* A fucktard. I've gotten kind of used to it."

"Seems like kind of a shitty thing to have to get used to."

"Yeah, well, it is what it is. Show me another

job in this shit hole and I'll gladly take it." She drank more soda, swallowed. "What do you do?"

Max stuffed a napkin into his lap. "Trying to find that other job in this shit hole."

"What does your wife do?"

"What?"

She gestured to his hand, his finger, and the wedding band wrapped around it.

His hand tucked like a bird's head under wing beneath the table.

"Sore subject?"

"I'd rather not talk about it."

"Okay."

A car drove along Main Street with another car tailgating.

"How long have you been here?"

Selena rolled her eyes again. "Too long," she said.

"Yeah, me too."

"Didn't you just move here?"

"Few days ago."

"Already too long, huh?"

"Much too long."

She laughed. It wasn't a humorous laugh. "*Pudrete en el infierno*," she said. "That's what I'm doing. I'm sorry it's already happening to you."

"I don't speak Spanish," he said. "What did that mean?"

"Rot in Hell."

"Oh." He shrugged and brought the hotdog to his mouth. "Seems to kind of be the long and short of it." He took a bite.

"It's Max, right?"

Max nodded. Finally, someone remembered his name.

"Do you know what Sueño Roto means, Max?"

Mouth full of hotdog, Max bobbed his head. "Doesn't it mean Broken Dream?"

She nodded. "It's a fitting name, really. I don't know any dreams here that aren't broken, in one way or another. This whole town, it's like a small room made entirely out of unbreakable windows, and the windows are always closing in. You can see this vast world out here" — she gestured — "but the windows are always moving closer to you. They never quite touch you, but they're always there. The only time you touch them is when you forget about them, and the contact only lasts long enough for them to remind you that you're suffocating."

Another sip of soda; she cleared her throat.

"You stand there at the windows, looking out upon the desert, seeing the mountains, the blue of the sky, the trees, the birds, hearing their noises, the noises of nature. Sometimes all you want is to be a part of it all. You want to get some of that life, get in on that activity out there, whatever it is. You don't really care all that much what it actually is. All you know is it's something alive. Good or bad, it's full of life, and you want to go out into it. But the windows remind you, they tell you that you can't, they insist that you can't, and they make you afraid of even trying to go out."

Max nodded. He understood this. Understood it well. In the two minutes they'd been sitting together, already Selena had named the prescription of the lenses Max was looking through. The realization brought on more fright. He wiped his napkin across his mouth, and, with his eyes closed, envisioned a stagnant progression of nothingness. The town was a prison that offered nothing, and the reinforcement of this knowledge made him shiver, swallow his bite of hotdog hard, almost choking on it.

"I gather you wanna get out," he said.

"I gather you do, too."

Max shrugged, but he tried to make it a warm and communicative shrug, as though to indicate yes.

"What did you do before you came to Broken Dream?" she asked.

"Worked as a back tender at a paper company."

"What's a back tender at a paper company do?"

"Not very much. Operate a few machines, wind paper into rolls. Look at charts and gauges and stuff, turn valves and wheels. Press buttons."

"So what happened to your job as a back tender at a paper company?"

"Like everything else these days, it closed down."

"I'm sorry."

Another shrug, leaving out the warmth.

"Where was that?"

"Oregon."

"So why Sueño Roto?"

He held up the hand with the ring on its finger.

Selena nodded and looked down at her drink.

Another car drove by on Main Street.

"What about you?" he said. "How did you wind up in Sueño Roto?"

"You don't wanna know."

"Of course not. That's why I asked. I like to ask questions when I don't want an answer."

"Well," she said, "I've learned that, often, people ask questions just to let the truth fall on deaf ears."

"I'm genuinely curious," he told her.

Her finger flicked at the tip of her straw. "I was born in Roswell," she said. "Demi Moore was born in Roswell, you know."

"I did not know that."

"Yeah, so I was born in Roswell." She stared at the straw but clearly wasn't seeing it. She was somewhere else, in a pocket of herself. "I lived there until I was fifteen. I didn't like Roswell. Or maybe I should say I didn't like life in Roswell. Soon as I could drive, I left."

"And you came here?"

She shook her head. "I went other places. I didn't *choose* to come here. Very few people *choose* to come to Sueño Roto. But sometimes, in a crapshoot, you end up with crap. Colorado, Utah, Arizona, I've done all the Four Corners. Then I managed to get here, and before I knew it, I couldn't manage to get out." She put the straw between her lips, drank, then said, "I don't wanna talk about that anymore."

Max gave a solemn nod and ate his hotdog. A light breeze picked up, warm and dusty. Granger stood up and put his head in Selena's lap. Selena smiled and rubbed the dog's head.

"*Hasta que uno ha amado a un animal, una parte de su alma permanece dormida*," she said, then looked at Max. She was still smiling, blushing a little. "That's the same thing that I said before, about loving an animal."

A single breathy chuckle and Max smiled back. It was foreign to him, but also very appealing, seeing his dog and this beautiful woman together, and the loving camaraderie that had already developed. It was one of those moments in which he realized what could be, or at least what could have been.

He drank a bit of his soda then said, "You know Moses? The guy at the grocery store?"

"Yes. Nice man."

"He started telling me a story about a man and his dog earlier. He kind of left it on a bleak note. I don't think he was finished, just got interrupted."

"What was the story?"

Max told her about the man lost in the wilderness, and the dog, how the dog shook himself and grew into a giant, and killed a bear, then shook again and returned to regular size.

"Ah, yes," she said, "*El Gran Perro*. Yes. That is a folktale, but in a way that really did happen, a long time ago, here in Sueño Roto."

"A dog blew up to the size of a Buick and took out a bear?"

She giggled. "Of course not. But the end of that story is, after the dog saved the man's life, the man petted the dog and thanked it, and said if he could get home, he would give the animal respect and love and many treats. And so the dog shook again, and at once grew bigger and bigger and then picked the man up in its mouth and set him on its back. The man held on and the dog leapt over trees and hills, over rivers and in between mountains, and after a very long time, the man saw his village in the distance, and the closer they got, the smaller the dog became, so that the man had to walk on his own for the last part of his journey." She smiled, scratched Granger behind the ears. "Some say when you hear the howls of animals at night, it is the song of the dog they are singing. The song of the man's best friend."

Max nodded, finished his hotdog. Now having the rest of it, at least the man wasn't still screwed.

"You said in a way that really did happen? How so?"

"You wanna hear it?"

"No. As I said, I like to ask questions when I don't want an answer."

Her smile broadened. There was something about her energy, positive and warm. In a way she almost seemed to glow.

"From what I understand," she said, "it happened about forty or fifty years ago. The man's name was Joe. He was out hunting by himself and somehow managed to get turned around and lost. For two days, I think, he wandered, trying to find his way. His canteen was empty and he was dying of thirst."

"So far it sounds pretty similar."

Selena nodded. She was still glowing. "From out of nowhere a dog appeared. A friendly dog. I do not know what kind but he immediately licked Joe's hand, and even though he was lost and heading in the direction of death, Joe was happy to at least no longer be alone.

"With gentle jaws, the dog tugged on Joe's sleeve, as if to say, 'Come on, follow me,' and he followed the dog to a freshwater lake.

"After Joe had drunk all he could and refilled his canteen, the dog tugged him again, and Joe followed him for hours. The dog led him from nowhere right into Sueño Roto. The dog left him close to his house and then disappeared. Joe never saw him again. But after that, from time to time, Joe heard ghostly knocking and howling, as if the dog had returned, though there was never anything there when he opened the door."

Max had picked up a French fry at some point, and now it was mashed between his fingers. "And that's a true story?"

She shrugged. "As far as I know. Weirder things have happened."

He nodded in agreement, thinking about the knocks and scrapes and barks he'd heard outside the house, on more than one occasion. A spirit dog? Maybe yes, maybe no. This was the mystical New Mexico desert, yet Max was hesitant to believe it. Not because it wasn't possible — as Selena just said, weirder things have happened — but because if that was all to the story, was it actually a happy one? The dog vanishing on its own but then returning as a ghost or some such thing at night, trying to get into the house? What did that mean? Happy or haunting, a good omen or bad one?

"So that is the story of Joe Ortiz," she said.

Max physically froze as his insides flared into discombobulated distress. Ortiz? Any chance that Ortiz was related to the House of Ortiz?

"Max?" Selena looked at him with concern. "You okay?"

The paralysis vanished quickly. "Yeah," he said, a little embarrassed. "Yeah, sorry. Just visited another world for a second."

Granger had been licking Selena's hand but now moved to search for Max's. A couple seconds passed as an unseen animal ululated somewhere in the hot summer air.

Then: "I should get going," she said, and stood up. "Nice talking with you, Max."

"You too, Selena."

She smiled at him, smiled at Granger, then turned to the parking lot. "Enjoy your other hotdog."

"Thanks. And for what it's worth, I find you far more interesting than Demi Moore."

She turned back and smiled again, gave a little wave, then went to her car — a battered old Subaru Legacy, dark blue where paint still remained. It made a metal on metal scraping sound when it started, and it did a lot of sputtering and coughing. He watched her pull onto Main Street. She gave a jaunty double honk as she passed. Then she drove away, out of sight.

Max opened condiment packages and added said condiments to his hotdog. He looked at Granger, who was also smiling.

"Yeah, I know," he said. "You like her."

Granger's tail wagged.

"All right, okay. Fine, yeah, I like her, too."

He alternated between stuffing his mouth with hotdog and stuffing it with fries. As his blood sugar rose and his stomach filled, dizziness came back and muddled his mind. He placed his elbow on the table, placed his head in his hand, and stared across at the Silver Moon. The sense of what could be was already fading, the warm image of Selena and Granger drifting away. When he saw Peter Parsons step out of the diner, it all faded just a little bit more. And when he saw Camille trail out behind him, smiling like a smitten schoolgirl, it vanished altogether.

A part of him wanted to go over to the diner, find them outside, wherever they'd gone, and then act like he'd been out and decided to take Peter up on one of those free cups of coffee. A part of him wanted to do this—a big part, but the other parts overruled it.

Instead he drove back to the house. He sat on the couch to try and think things over, but the energy the food had given him had been energy channeled into sleep. He'd barely been home five minutes when his eyes involuntarily shut and he finally entered Dreamland.

EIGHTEEN

There was a telephone ringing somewhere. He wished it would stop. He was so tired and it was bad enough that he was in a cave, with an ocean of bats overhead. He remembered a cave he and his childhood friend Rick had found, down in an arroyo, not too far from Max's house. They'd turned it into a sort of fort. They'd probably been about twelve years old.

It had been a small cave, nothing like this one. They'd camped out overnight in it a few times. They'd never heard any phones in their fort.

One time, while camping out, they'd gone off, making the twenty-minute trek into town. They hadn't realized until they got to a Seven-Eleven that it was a little past two in the morning. It was called Seven-Eleven but open twenty-four hours. They'd bought Slush Puppies, and Rick, being the more brazen of the two, asked the guy to sell them a pack of cigarettes. The guy didn't think twice, just asked what kind they wanted.

Rick said Marlboro.

The Seven-Eleven's phone rang just then. Then man answered and gave them their cigarettes. The phone never rang in their cave. There was no phone to ring in their cave. There was no phone in this cave either, and yet, somewhere, there was.

He wondered what Rick was doing now. They'd had a lot of good times together, but the friendship had petered out and they'd lost touch. He hoped he was doing well.

The damn phone must have been at the other end of the cavern. Such a gigantic place, might as well have been at the other end of the world. Unless this was the world. Land of stone, stir of echoes, sky of bats. But if this was the world then how did they get to the Seven-Eleven?

Who on earth would be calling? He was tired and the phone was invisible and the cave was plenty big. Big and dark and swarming with bats. Why call anybody here?

The country singer wasn't with him this time. Neither was the ball player, or any of the other people. He was standing alone in relative darkness, and somewhere the phone rang with no one to answer it.

There were hieroglyphics on some of the walls. Not the standard image of Egyptian picture-writing one usually imagines when the word comes to mind. Runes, maybe? No. Etchings? Not really. Cave paintings was maybe the best choice of words, but it wasn't quite right. If chalk and a blowtorch could be constructed into a writing implement, it would have likely been the tool used to decorate these walls. The images were abstract but somehow very personal to him. They reminded him of things. Made him think of things. Too many things at once. And everything had a Huckleberry Hound, Quick Draw McGraw, Top Cat, Jonny Quest sort of feel.

The bats were squeaking overhead.

The stupid phone still rang.

Then came thunderous footsteps, followed by a loud but harmless click. A deep, booming voice like an assertive British Yogi Bear said hello from someplace unseen. A moment after that the voice sounded more like Orson Welles and told Max that the call was for him, and an old rotary phone materialized, mounted on a short, blunted stalagmite.

Max picked up the receiver and said hello, and inside the phone was the ringing of a phone. And the cave went away as Max opened his eyes.

He was flopped on the couch. The ringing was coming from his pocket. His cell phone.

He felt drugged. He didn't know how long the thing had actually been ringing; he was still so tired.

He sat up, rubbed his eyes with one hand and took out his phone with the other.

How long had he been asleep?

"Hello?"

"Ever plan on picking me up?"

"What time is it?"

"Four-thirty."

"Shit." He rubbed his eyes again. "I'll be right there." He beeped off the phone without saying goodbye.

Granger was curled up on the floor, by the windows, in the sun.

Well, at least he'd managed a couple hours worth of sleep. Hopefully it was better than nothing. Sometimes a little sleep was worse than getting none at all. His head felt ten times heavier than it had, his mind ensconced in cavernous shadows. Blinking several times, then several more, the shadows fluttered but others overshadowed them.

He sat up straighter, rubbed his eyes more thoroughly, yawned, tilted his head, and popped his neck. As he worked on coming to, he found that the sleep had neither helped nor hindered. He was still exhausted — but at least he was no more exhausted than he'd been before.

Did he ever plan on picking her up? Sort of, but not really.

Did he want to pick her up? Not at all, actually. The idea of seeing her bitchy face, of having to listen to her bitchy reprehension made the thought of taking a hammer to his skull all the more appealing.

But you're not gonna do that. You can't do that. What you gotta do — you know what you gotta do…

He got up from the couch, went to the kitchen sink and splashed water on his face, drank a couple of foul mouthfuls from the faucet.

Granger was in the kitchen now, looking at him.

"Probably better if you stay here," Max said.

"You wanna be outside or in?"

Granger licked his own nose.

"Better if you stay in, I think."

Granger closed the distance between them, turned sideways, and leaned with considerable weight against Max's legs.

Full-blown trust. Unconditional love.

Max patted the pooch's side, told Granger he was a good dog, warned him about throwing a party in his absence, then went out, locked the house, and went to the car. The sun had put on a translucent jacket, muting the shine but still burning bright, like a naked woman in a see-through raincoat.

"How very French New Wave," he said, and got into the car.

NINETEEN

Camille was standing outside the diner when he pulled up. She looked annoyed, but it was like she'd exchanged one form of annoyance for another. She got in the car without saying anything; the air churned about in erratic unknowing.

They waited for a car to pull out of a space in front of them.

Camille cleared her throat, waited. Then she said, "Wanna get a drink at Shiloh's?"

Butterflies fluttered in his stomach, found insect-sized shovels and started digging holes inside him. Why now? Why now, of all times, did she present the idea of Shiloh's? She'd had no interest yesterday. The very mention of it had seemed to bother her. But now she suggested it. Now it was her idea. Maybe it was as simple as that. She'd wanted it to be her idea.

"Not sure I'm up for a drink," he said.

"Well, I could use one."

"You still have wine at home."

She sighed. "Good. Then there's something for when I get home, too."

Max didn't want to go to Shiloh's. But as he pulled on to Main Street he told himself it would be all right. Maybe he could figure out what was going on... if anything.

He drove the short distance and pulled into the gravel lot. The Nissan was still there. Other cars were there, too, including a modest Chrysler, and a battered army-green Ford Bronco. Max pulled in alongside the Bronco and switched off the engine. Camille was climbing out before Max had unbuckled his seatbelt.

For a moment he sat there, reassuring himself, telling himself that everything would be okay. He jumped when knuckles rapped on the window. Camille looked down at him, a glare that asked him what he was waiting for.

He got out of the car.

The warm, dusty breeze was a bit heavier than it had been earlier. Max didn't know if it had gone away and come back with reinforcements, or if it had been whisking all along, maybe getting annoyed that no one was paying attention to it.

He followed Camille toward the bar. There was something different about the way she walked. Her movements held a simultaneous mixture of both liveliness and defeat, sprightly circumvention in each step she took.

His own heart pounded. He forced himself to breathe. He watched her open the door. Watched plumes of smoke drift out. Watched her step into the fog.

He looked around the small lot again. There was no battered Subaru Legacy. For whatever reason, this brought a minor sense of relief. He took the next few steps and then he was inside.

Carl was behind the bar. When he saw Max he nodded. Max nodded back. On the stereo Roger Miller sang "The Last Word in Lonesome is Me." Camille went to the far corner table. She sat down with her back to the wall and looked around the place. Max kept his head down, as though his forlorn slump would somehow render a cloak of invisibility.

"Hey, Mitch."

Max pretended not to hear Alejandro's voice. He sat at the table, across from Camille. His eyes were on his hands but his ears were on the table where Alejandro and Alton sat. He prayed no one would mention last night to him.

"Mitch," Alejandro said again.

Max still refused to acknowledge him.

Then, from the bar, Carl said, "What y'all having?"

"Pilsner," Max said. He looked at Camille who was looking at Carl.

"I'll have a Nut Brown," she said. Then she clasped her hands together and set them on the table and then she looked at Max. "You gonna smoke?"

"What?"

"I didn't think you could smoke in bars anymore. All the second-hand we're getting, you might as well, if you want."

"I might, we'll see."

Carl arrived and set their beers on the table. By nature it seemed that Carl was an off-putting fellow, but his looming presence added additional fright and tension today.

"Nine dollars," he said.

Camille took out a large wad of ones and gave some of them to him.

Carl went away.

Camille looked around the place again. "Love the décor," she said. It was a snide observation and Max had no response. He lifted his beer and drank, cut quick glances around the place.

Alejandro and Alton occupied the same table they had last night. It looked especially empty without Armando there. Empty and less safe. Max's glances were fast enough that they didn't see him seeing them. They seemed to have lost interest in getting his attention.

At another table across the way sat Wayne and his nameless counterpart, minus Ivan and his rye whiskey.

Max kept his head down and his hands on his beer.

"They apparently like hunting," Camille said.

Max kept quiet, stared at his beer, watched the little bubbles inside it.

"Only a coward would kill a helpless animal with a gun," she said. "I mean, how is that fair? It doesn't show any type of skill."

Now Max wanted her to shut up.

"Humans clearly have the advantage. I mean, like, in an age where wild animals are increasingly becoming endangered, and food is so easy to get at grocery stores, hunting for sport is just an example of mental deficiency and torpid minds that know nothing other than murder."

While there was a part of Max that agreed, Shiloh's was the last place he could think of to voice such opinions, especially on a very first visit. And when Camille felt opinionated—which was often—she was also loud, and inconsiderate of the people around her.

Max chewed his lower lip.

"Few, if any animals are killed for survival purposes."

His eyes did a lightning quick scan of the place. Several sets of eyes were on them.

"Could you keep your voice down?"

"Why? Am I embarrassing you?"

His hand brushed air in a forget-it gesture.

"I have the right to say what I think, and what I believe in, even when it is not the overall popular opinion of those around me."

"And while I won't argue that," Max said, and lowered his voice, "sometimes it's just not a good time to share what you think." He used his eyes to try communicating to her that they were being scrutinized, and that much of the scrutiny came from likely hunters.

Camille's voice lowered. A smirk sneered her face. "You worried what others here think?"

"No, I'm concerned that your self-importance, morally justifiable or not, is gonna get the shit kicked out of us."

"You *are* worried," she said.

"Only that you're lacking common sense," he told her.

Her eyes narrowed. Her mouth tightened. "You're about two seconds away from walking home, Max."

One by one, he popped the knuckles of his right hand. "Well, Sweetie, it pains me to say that your threat doesn't hold an ounce of weight." He drank some beer. "Unlike me, I know you won't find any reason to kick yourself, but that's an idle threat when there's only one set of keys for the car, and I currently have them."

Her lips turned white and her face turned red. The smirk was now a grimace.

"Would *you* like to walk home, Camille? I'd be happy to leave *you* here."

The last part of his sentence overlapped with her action as she grabbed her glass of Nut Brown and threw it in his face.

Several people in the bar laughed. A few were simply shocked.

Max stared at her, pain and rage mixing like hot and cold water, bringing his emotions to a tepid indifference. He reached across the table and picked up the napkin her drink had been sitting on. He dabbed it at his beer-drenched face. He crumpled it into a wet ball, then drank some of his pilsner.

She set her empty glass down hard and stood out of her chair, knocking it over. Then she walked through the bar and out the door.

Hank Williams was singing now, having replaced Roger Miller, but the tense, smoke-filled silence in the bar almost completely drowned him out.

Max took his own napkin and wiped his face some more. Then he took out a cigarette and got it alight. He sat there, smoking and drinking his beer, looking at the beer spilled across the table, running over the edge and cascading to the floor. He felt the coldness on his shirt, the stickiness on his face.

A moment later Carl showed up with a couple of rags.

"You all right?" he said.

Max blew out a stream of smoke. "My wife," he said.

Carl mopped up the beer. "She's a charmer," he said.

"She is, isn't she?"

"You all right, Mitch?"

Max turned and looked at Alejandro. He looked at Alton, then Alejandro again.

"Is that your wife?"

Max said nothing, just stared at the man.

"She's feisty. You're lucky. I like 'em feisty."

Max continued staring, smoking, holding his tongue. The table was cleared and had a fresh napkin on it. Carl went back to the bar. Max sipped his beer and set it on the napkin. He smoked, then cleared his throat.

"You know that's not my name," he said.

Alejandro looked confused. Alton did, too.

"What's that?"

"You heard me."

Max finished his beer and stood up. He

snuffed out his cigarette, and made his way to the door.

"Mitch, don't be like that."

He passed the table where Wayne and the other guy sat. Wayne kept his head down, facing his drink, but his eyes flickered up, corneas like needles darting at him.

"Mitch!" Alejandro said.

Max opened the door and stepped outside.

Camille was nowhere to be seen. He was pretty sure he knew where she'd gone. It would take less than five minutes to walk to the Silver Moon. The question in his mind was whether or not to go after her.

He was still pondering when the blue Subaru Legacy pulled in and parked a couple spaces away. Time ticked off a few, then Selena climbed out, raven-wing hair catching a glimpse of the sun, which was moving toward slow descent.

"What happened, Max?"

His shirt was still wet and his face was still sticky, the gummy beer-based gelatin also likely catching the sun.

"I came here with my wife," he said, as though this explained everything.

"*Perra,*" she said. "You okay?"

"Oh, fine. Just debating whether or not I wanna go after her."

"Do you know where she went?"

"The Silver Moon." Then he added, "That's where she works."

A pause, and then, "She's the new woman at the Silver Moon?"

Max nodded.

Selena rolled her eyes. She bit at her lower lip and closed her car door. Then she let out a sigh.

"What?" Max asked.

"*Perdóname*," she said. "I guess I hadn't made the connection that she was your wife. I guess I should have, but I didn't." She looked down Main Street.

The wind had eased up. The sun had dimmed a shade.

"Nothing wrong with not knowing that," Max told her. "People don't usually just magically know things."

She looked up at the sky, then down at her shoes. She looked at Max and then back at her shoes.

"I need to get in to work," she told him.

"Wait," Max said, and took a step toward her. "Is there something you wanna tell me?"

She sighed. "Probably wouldn't be anything you don't already know."

"What does that mean?"

She wouldn't meet his eyes now. She seemed to be trying but couldn't quite do it. "*Qué chingados*," she said. "Okay, without being too inappropriate, and forgive me if I am, but your wife is not a very nice person."

Max couldn't help but chuckle. "Well, yeah, that much I know."

She took a step toward him. This time she was able to meet his eyes. "You are a good man, Max. I hope you'll be good to yourself, but also be cautious."

Max almost laughed but didn't. In the past sixteen or so hours, he didn't know the meaning of much other than caution. But he sensed what Selena was getting at. As the sky bent in on itself, and the breeze whispered secrets in a hushed flurry, tossing its arms about him in confidence much too late to ever bring peace of mind, he had a good idea of what she was telling him. But, on the other hand, as he'd just said, people don't magically know things.

"What do you mean?" he asked.

Selena looked down again. "I just wouldn't trust her," she said.

"Well, I guess I already don't," he said, and allowed himself a shrug.

"Good." She put a hand on his shoulder, squeezed. "I have to work now," she told him. She let go of him, then walked away.

He watched her walk to the bar and then disappear inside it. It was true: Looking at Selena was always good.

TWENTY

The sun sat atop a mountain range, getting ready to dive down and splash up the night. Max had located the tennis balls he'd had packed away, and he stood out back of the house, throwing one of them and letting Granger fetch it. He'd washed his face, and changed his shirt back to the blue one he'd put on that morning.

Throwing the ball revitalized the throbbing pain in his shoulder. For a while the pain had seemed to nearly disappear altogether. He definitely felt the strain but decided that, unless something was torn (which was unlikely), the movement and exercise would probably be good for it. Hopefully keep it loose. Maybe he was wrong and doing more damage, but it seemed like he was doing the right thing.

It had been a mental and emotional debacle, but Max had decided to leave Camille, and let her do whatever the hell it was she'd decided to do. Let her correct someone else's grammar. Let her tell someone else they didn't know what they meant. Let her ridicule and mock and talk down to someone else. Max didn't so much mind that she thought he was stupid as he minded her *talking* to him like he was stupid. So let her be mad. Let her go do her thing, whatever it was. She could do it without him.

There was little doubt it had something to do with Peter Parsons. That was at least a part of what Selena had been getting at, he was sure; and although it was upsetting, he also knew, with a vague indifference, that he simply didn't care. Maybe he just couldn't care anymore. Maybe he was beyond caring.

He threw the ball. He watched it land and bounce and watched Granger chase it, snatch it in his mouth, then turn and race back and drop the ball at his feet. Max scooped it up and threw it again, and watched the dog repeat what he'd only just done.

There had been chemistry between Camille and Parsons. Max had seen it right from the start, right from the moment the guy had introduced himself at the diner, the morning they'd first had breakfast there. There had been tension right from the get go. Not the sort of tension Max had been experiencing. Not the self-preservation kind of tension. Not survival tension. It was the kind of tension that would happily put Camille on her back. The kind of tension that would happily spread her legs.

Infuriating, and yet, whether he liked it or not—and what was not to like? —he just didn't much care. It was probably something that had been going on for a long time. Not with Peter Parsons, but just a thing. A somewhat common occurrence. Long before they'd even come to Sueño Roto. It had probably been going on back in Portland, and the temptation to feel like a sucker arose. But he couldn't be sure. He couldn't be sure and there was no point in letting his imagination go any further than it already had. He didn't currently need to toss anything else into the jumbled mix of crap in his brain.

He threw the ball again, watched Granger fetch it.

The hills and mountains seemed to roll into one another; then vast open space, a shell of a land that once breathed would emerge, a taunting glimpse of a route of escape, before more hills rippled, and rose into view. It was sparkling and surreal, a trick of the light.

He couldn't see the mineshaft from here—though he was sure it wasn't one, he'd settled on calling it a mineshaft—but he could see the dilapidated structure. The one that had probably been a shed. It seemed to tilt with the descent of the sun. If Max wanted to, he could have allowed the thing to have eyes, could have allowed it watch him, let it judge him, scrutinize him. Instead he took the ball from Granger, now slippery with spit, and allowed the shed to be nothing more than the battered old thing that it was. Because, really, that's *all* it was.

Again, he threw the ball. This time when he threw it, he started walking. When the dog brought the ball back to him, he threw it again. Then he walked some more. He stood near the shed for a couple of throws. The structure didn't move but it made gentle creaking sounds.

The tension in his shoulder seemed to be loosening. The throb began to mute. Then he walked again, throwing the ball, until he'd finally gone far enough that the ball went over the earthen mound behind which was tucked the shaft.

Granger scrambled up the incline. He took a couple of steps down and then stopped. He whimpered, then barked.

Max neither stopped nor picked up his pace. He just kept walking, easy, steady. Granger no longer made any sound, just stood atop the mound, staring down below.

Max reached the knoll and climbed it, and stood beside his dog. The tennis ball was settled in a gap in the rocky floor below.

"Go on," Max said. "Go on, boy, go get it."

But Granger didn't move.

The sun lanced streaks of light through the sky. Each streak blazed in varying colors. Max took two steps down then stopped. He didn't know if he chose to stop or if something had stopped him. A swarm of cold needles prickled his flesh. His spine turned to ice. His sternum started turning, spooling his muscles and nerves, tightening everything, stretching every neuron and contractile filament. Cranking round and round, creating such tension that he feared he'd crack and implode upon himself.

He stepped back up. He was glad that he could — at least he could move. The spool was still cranking, still turning inside him. But at least he could move his legs.

Granger whimpered again.

"Forget it," Max said. "There are more balls at the house. We can come back and get this one later."

He turned on his heel and went down the slope and started heading back toward the house. Granger kept close beside him as the air seemed to thicken with something unknown.

As they passed the dilapidated shed, it made more creaking sounds, like a rocking chair swaying on a splintered wood floor.

He was tired. Too tired. His body stifled sobs at being so tired, but also at being so tightly wound up. The beer he'd had at Shiloh's had done little to affect him, but his footsteps staggered, almost like sailor legs.

Tired as he was, though, he'd tossed out the entire idea of sleep. He was lucky to have gotten what he did. At some point he'd get more, but that time was not now. He knew that if he closed his eyes, he would find himself in a deranged and sleepless darkness. Already, no matter where he went, he was in a timid sort of darkness, but if he closed his eyes and tried to conjure Mister Sandman, the darkness would become an inconceivable geography of utter madness. And the darkness would be full of fallen shadows, full of failures and regrets and bereft self-loathing. Memories would choke on senselessness. Short lifetimes of memories and remorse would explode, embrace him in their malevolent tears and pus. It sounded crazy, but he somehow knew that that's what would happen, if he made the simple but foolish effort to lay down in an attempt at sleep. His mind wouldn't shut off; it would multiply; and with its multiplicity would also come intensity. *Sleep*, Poe had said. *Those little slices of Death. How I loathe them.* Only in Max's case, it wouldn't be slices of death. It would be snippets and ribbons of insanity.

Too many things had happened. Even awake, staggering like he was, all that had happened, not just today, not since yesterday, but all of it, everything, his entire life, from the moment of his birth to this very second, every bit already choked on senselessness. There had to be reasons for all of it. Reason existed somewhere in there. But reason was a tattered dishrag in a dark, dusty corner, where maniacal mice and furious spiders roamed. On which reprehensible vermin gnawed. Reason was in there, somewhere, but it was hidden and injured and frightened.

He went into the house and got Granger's leash.

TWENTY-ONE

The sun was gone but the sky still sparkled. It pulsed with crystalline color. A sort of rainbow dusk. A prismatic, spectral dusk, with all kinds of colorful smears in it. Jagged mountain peaks quivered with black and pink and orange and sapphire.

People came and went at regular intervals. Max sat there, regarding the place. He wondered if Moses ever had any back up, or if the guy was a perpetual solo act.

He cracked all the windows then climbed out of the car, leaving Granger inside. He locked the car, simultaneously loving and loathing the sky, then went into the store.

There was a line at the counter. People with carts and baskets and little patience. Moses was alone, ringing things up. Through the cacophony the radio sputtered what Max guessed to be the Kingston Trio, though he could have been wrong.

He spent a few minutes browsing the aisles. In

one of the aisles he stopped, and recent memories assaulted him. He didn't shiver, didn't tremble. He blinked at the floor.

The downcast look that Camille had given. It became the cortex of his mind. An image layered over everything else. It was the very moment in this very aisle when confirmation that he was less than a nothing had officially arrived. When it spit in his face and cut off his dick and sang the song they sing on the Loser Train. It was evidence that a new world, a new environment, didn't change a damn thing. It hadn't changed him and it hadn't changed her. The truth within the old adage, Wherever you go, there you are. And the truth was she hated him. The truth was she had never liked him, never loved him, and like a blood brother handshake, sliced hands, bleeding palms, blood intermingling, blood into blood, soul into soul, truth into truth, he had never loved her either. He'd been so lonely, so desperate for love that he'd taken the first thing that came along. Even if what he'd embraced was a snake. A venomous viper that, when it wasn't biting, was hissing and spitting and thrashing, rattling its rattle, waiting to strike.

He left the aisle.

There was still a line when he returned to the counter. He went to the side and leaned against it. Moses flashed him a look then continued punching buttons on the old-timey register.

"Evening, *señor*."

"Hey," Max said. He shifted his weight from one leg to the other. Words tumbled upon each other in his head. He managed to snatch a few, and said, "I was hoping I could talk to you."

"*No ahora, señor. Ocupado como el infierno* right now." He made a quick gesture to the impatient line.

"Could I maybe come back later?"

"*Sí*, yeah, sure, come back later. But if it stays like this, I'll be busy all night."

"I'll stop back by," Max told him, and rose from the counter, turned, and went outside.

The sunset a dwindling kaleidoscope, he went to the car, reached into his pocket and took out the keys. They jittered in his hand, jingled like a weary Christmas bell. He stuck the proper key in the lock and turned it.

"Did you call Albertson?"

Max looked one way and then the other, and then he saw Wayne, standing a dozen feet away, smoking a cigarette. Even though it was hot out, he had a green army jacket over his monster truck shirt. He stood with a bit of a hunch.

"Ivan," Wayne said, blowing out smoke, "he's at the bar now."

Max stared at the man, hands clenching and unclenching at his sides. "I—I don't really know what to do with that," he said.

"Did you call Albertson?"

His breath seemed stuck. "Yeah, I did." His lungs relaxed, then tried to seize up again. He kept them moving by speaking. "He said he didn't know who Ivan was, and that he didn't owe anybody here any money."

Wayne dropped his cigarette to the asphalt,

crushed it underfoot. The crystalline colors were starting to mute. Wayne ran fingers through his long black hair.

Max removed the keys from the car door. His right hand made a fist with them.

"Are you following me?" he asked.

"Maybe."

"Why?"

Wayne shrugged. "No real reason."

Time gobbled a bit of itself. There seemed to be more cars on Main Street than usual. The parking lot they stood in was busier than normal. It seemed something had fucked the town and spawned things. Malicious things, expressionless things, it wasn't really clear; but there *were* more things. Sueño Roto almost felt like an actual living place.

This surreal moment, however, was gone in the blink of an eye.

"I got no reason to follow you," Wayne said.

"Sounds to me like you do."

"You wanna get a beer?"

Max shook his head. "No, no, I don't. I really, really don't." He opened the car door. "I gotta get going, is what I gotta do." He climbed in and then reached for the handle to pull the door shut.

"Do you think we don't know where you live, scrote?"

Max froze. The sternum spindle cranked again. He looked at the ground and then looked at the man, who lit another cigarette and puffed up clouds.

He should have known. It should have been

common sense. Yet he hadn't considered it until right now. And there was nothing to consider. It was a cold hard fact. Of *course* they knew where he lived. They knew Frank Albertson; they'd know the Albertson place. Formerly, once upon a time, the Ortiz place. Currently but never to actually be the Pendleton place. Why *wouldn't* they know where he lived? Why wouldn't *everyone* in town know right where he lived?

"*Everybody* knows where you live, man." He puffed more smoke. It danced above his head and disappeared.

Silence poured down in droplets, then sheets. And in the silence he felt close to exploding. Nothing in the world existed but silence. Dangerous, shrieking, overwhelming silence, so loud that it ate through space and time, its only purpose to rip him apart.

Max let go of the door handle.

"Tell you what," he said, hoping his words would chase the quiet away. "How about I give you Frank's phone number?" He reached into his pocket for his cell phone. "How does that sound?" He extracted the phone. "I'll give you his number, then you can deal with him directly." The phone was in his hand now.

Wayne placed his cigarette between his lips then held out his hand. "Lemme see that," he said.

"What, my phone?"

The man nodded.

"Why don't I just give you the number?"

Wayne beckoned with his hand. From where Max was, sitting in his car, the guy was ten feet tall.

"I'm not gonna give you my phone," Max said.

The colors in the sky were wilting to black. Wayne stepped closer, his hand still out.

Max swallowed a heavy gulp of air. He wanted to cover his face with his hands, hide himself under the covers from the bogeyman. If he could only bury himself in dreams...

But he couldn't. Light on or off, Wayne was still there, and he wouldn't disappear with a shut of the eyes and a wishing away.

At the same time, the guy also wouldn't vanish if Max gave him his phone.

It was too late to shut the door, however. Too late to shut it and lock the guy out. Too late to entomb himself behind a locked door. Max had learned long ago that going out got you hurt. Going out made you the subject of irritation and rage. It could leave you in tears, leave your things destroyed, leave you curled in a ball, clutching your stomach or holding your head. Going out could kill you, and, knowing this, Max had still chosen to do so.

Last night's scuffle speared through his mind. The moment he fell and his legs tangled with Armando's; the hot pain that seared his upper back and shoulder; the winks and twinkles of stars; the drunk man sprawled on his back; the blade of the butterfly knife jammed in his throat.

Wayne took another step.

Max battled between the forces of fight, flight and freeze. The one thing he was certain of: he wasn't going to allow the same results as last night. There would be no more death, this way or that way. Whatever happened outside this grocery store, Wayne would still be alive. And he would be, too.

"Lemme see your phone," Wayne said.

Tremors had been with him the entire time. Now the oscillation increased. His heart rivaled a jackhammer. Invisible insects swarmed his neck and skittered down his back. Sitting in his car, he was vulnerable, without enough room to even close the door. Granger stood on the back seat, making mewling sounds.

Max clutched the phone in his left hand as his right hand moved up to the ignition. He slid the proper key into the slot.

"Why do you want my phone?" he said. The head of the key positioned between his thumb and forefinger. He was ready to crank the engine. What would happen after that, God only knew.

His tension became fear, and his fear became a neurotoxin, encouraging paralysis. He tasted vomit at the back of his throat. Like the rattlesnake, the guy standing before him with his hand extended scared the living hell out of him. It wasn't the man who made him sick, however. That much he knew. It wasn't the man. It was the fear. The fear of the man. The fear of the snake. It was fear and fear alone that disrupted his nerves.

But he had faced the snake. He'd stood there alone and faced a deadly viper. He'd done it. He'd proved he could do it. Proved he could detour from the track that had been embedded inside him. The track that went round and round in one small circle. He'd broken away from it before, and the result had been astonishing. And now Wayne, standing there, wanting his phone, telling Max that everyone knew where he lived, the fear recreated all over again. Max regarded the man with terror, but also veered to the track's outer edge, and additionally regarded him as a touchstone against which he could test for a trace of the courage he'd shown only days before, in the face of a serpent.

His fingers pressed to turn the key.

"I told you, you can have his number," Max said.

Wayne didn't smile. He didn't frown. He held his hand out, and smoked his cigarette.

"Beautiful dog," he finally said.

"Thank you."

The grocery store door opened. A couple stepped out. Wayne's extended hand dropped. He took a step back. Max's fingers relaxed on the car key.

The couple, each carrying a bag of groceries, moved toward them. They had the Honda parked to the right of the Camry. A swanky, new upscale thing. They were laughing about some inside joke. It was clear they didn't live here.

Wayne took another step back. His boot tapped a bottle cap, sent it clacking along the asphalt. The fire in the sky continued to wilt; had actually reduced to mere embers glowing on the mountaintops. Max gnashed his teeth then chewed his lip.

"Look," he said, then swallowed dry

nothingness. "Just—just leave me alone."

He closed the car door. He turned the key and the engine revved up.

Wayne's expression didn't alter. He took another step back.

Max switched on the headlights and put the car in reverse. He backed out before the swanky Honda did. He fought the impulse to run Wayne over. He drove through the lot and stopped at Main Street. He looked at the gauges in the dashboard. Half a tank of gas. The Amigo Mart was a stone's throw away. He could fill up and simply hit the road. Head over to Arizona. Head back to Portland. Head any fucking where he wanted. He could stop at the house and grab a few important things, then head out and hopefully never look back. He could take the Mondrian out of the fucking guestroom.

He was sure Camille wouldn't be there. Why would she be? Why should she be? And yet fear plucked notes on his strung out nerves. A fear of what would happen if she *was* there. The garbage compactor of defeat that would compress and oppress him. The fervor, inspiration, the willingness to try and live a life, all of it would crumble in her very presence. Just the thought of her made it all shrink a little.

Was there anything he really needed at the house? There were things he liked. The Mondrian, for example. But he could find another print of *Broadway Boogie-Woogie*. The paperbacks he loved could be replaced, and family heirlooms and mementos were few, if any at all. His laptop was the only thing he could think of that would be of any real use to him. But again, there was nothing on it so crucial that it justified the tiniest risk of coming face to face with Camille. The thought of confrontation with her was very dreadful. Dreadful enough that he feared going home. If the urge to escape wasn't so strong, he could resign himself to her soul crushing, spirit breaking supremacy. He'd spent a long time now, resigned to it. Seemed he'd pretty much thrown in the towel before the first bell had ever rung.

He looked at the store in his rearview mirror. He couldn't see Wayne but it was really getting dark.

The Honda drove by on Main Street. It had taken a different exit from the lot. Wayne was most likely still back there, somewhere. Danger doesn't usually just decide to walk away. But whether it was gone or not, Max was caught in a trap. A bear trap called Sueño Roto. A deadly version of the TV show *Cheers*, where instead of everyone knowing your name, everyone knew where you lived, and instead of jokes and merriment, it was threats and hostility.

He pressed the accelerator. After less than a minute he pulled into the Amigo Mart.

TWENTY-TWO

Filling the gas tank, he stared across at the Silver Moon. He glanced at the Dairy Queen but kept his focus on the diner. Like the rest of the town tonight, it seemed to be hopping, almost like a raucous party instead of people dining. He had little doubt that Camille was in there. And if she wasn't, he guessed Peter Parsons wasn't either. They weren't the only two people who worked at the Silver Moon.

The nozzle made a *ka-chunk* and the gas stopped pumping. Max removed the nozzle and hung it up, then capped the tank. Then he just stood there for a time, staring at the diner.

A part of him expected Wayne to emerge from out of some dark corner. The thought made him feel more ridiculous than afraid. It was all ridiculous, really. Every bit of it was ridiculous, in one way or another.

He got into the car. Then he sat there, still staring at the diner. His jaw tightened. Then, abruptly, he looked down at his dashboard. His headlights were on. He didn't recall turning them on. He looked at the diner again, then started the engine.

A cold, wet nose touched his neck. He turned to Granger, who licked his face. He rubbed the dog's head, said, "*El Gran Perro*," then put his hands on the wheel.

Across the way, where the empty, condemned building stood, was a car. He didn't recall it being there a minute ago, and it was just too dark to see if anyone was in it. It was motionless and its headlights were off. It was in the building's lot, though parallel with the street. It was a dark-colored car and his own headlights didn't hit it, restricting detail, keeping information to a scant minimum.

"Ridiculous," he said, aware of where his mind was trying to take him.

He pushed paranoia away, and looked both ways down Main Street. To the left was the fifteen-minute drive to the house. To the right was desolate road that would eventually lead to the highway, which would eventually lead to freedom, eventually lead to light, eventually pass through the gates that would release him from sorrow. But either direction, as it currently stood, was asphalt-floored cloying blackness. Night was here. It covered floor and ceiling and every wall. Traces of sapphire still streaked like contrails, but darkness had now taken control. The moon was still tucked away somewhere in the hills.

He looked left, looked right, afflicted by

distress. His heart began thumping against his breastbone, knocking breath out as he tried to inhale.

"Shit," he said. It was useless to resist. No choice but to submit. Refusing to submit, as tempting as it was, as much as he wanted to, much as he needed to, he couldn't simply run away. And fleeing town now, he'd be more than a suspect. He'd be convicted without giving his side of things. A killer on the loose, on the run, driving along a disambiguated road to nowhere.

He went left.

Moving at a good speed, he felt he was going at a mournfully slow pace. The broken yellow line was faded and chipped. He turned on the stereo. Belle and Sebastian came on, and with their music came a bitter cold that flowed up from somewhere in his sternum. It frosted up his back and when it reached the base of his skull his entire body felt contaminated. The chill lingered, and with it came the intense feeling of a presence, right there with him, as though someone or something malicious and malignant was in the back of the car, alongside Granger, ready to grab him by the chin and slit his throat.

He turned off the music but the chill didn't leave.

There's nothing here with you. It's you and Granger and no one else. You're tired and stressed. You get weird when you're tired, and it's the most stressful tired you've ever experienced. Hell, why shouldn't it be? Nothing that's happened has been a day at the beach. You're just weird when you're tired and weird when you're stressed and you're paranoid. Good reason to be but that's all that it is. Paranoia. Your brain's not working right.

The chill shuddered away. Exasperated with himself, he checked the rearview mirror.

His breath caught in his throat. His heart slammed against his sternum. There was a car behind him. Right behind him. It didn't have its headlights on. He checked the road ahead of him, blinked, then looked back into the mirror. The black shape was right on his tail. He looked back to the road and tromped the accelerator.

The shape took form as it shrank. Definitely a car, but it wasn't in pursuit. At least it wasn't now. Max eased his foot from the gas pedal. Back behind him, a good distance now, headlights winked on then off, and a second later, dim hazard lights blinked. It's headlights winked again. Then came the distant, echoing sound of the horn, two blasts.

Max applied the brakes, stopped in the middle of the road. He waited, watching the mirror, watching the hazards blink on and off.

The headlights flashed again. If this was real trouble, why did they have their headlights off?

Max let off the brake. The Camry slowly inched ahead. The car behind him seemed to have come to a stop.

Its horn sounded again.

It's a trick. No two ways around it. People just don't behave that way on the road. Even if you're drunk, that's not what you do.

His cell phone rang. The sharp digital ring startled him. He pulled alongside the road and answered.

"What are you doing?" It was Camille. She didn't sound angry. She sounded weepy.

"That's what *I* should be asking *you*," he said.

He looked in the mirror. The car was still there, hazard lights blinking.

"Are you at the Silver Moon?"

"I'm at the fucking bar," she said.

"You went back to the fucking bar?"

"Yes, I'm back at the fucking bar. What do you think I mean when I say I'm *at* the fucking bar?"

The hazards went off. He saw the shape moving in the darkness behind him, like a stealthy predator stalking its prey. With the distance and the darkness, he couldn't tell what it was actually doing.

"Come pick me up."

He heard the words but they didn't register. The car behind him didn't move like a car. It was more organic than that. It moved like a graceful black panther, creeping through the night.

"Max?"

Then he saw the red glow of brake lights. The car had turned around. The lights went out and the shape eased away, back towards town. Granger was now propped against the back seat, staring through the rear windshield.

"Max, are you there?"

"Yeah," he said. "Yeah, I'm here."

"Come get me."

He almost asked why, but didn't. He beeped

off without giving her an answer, and tossed the phone into the passenger seat. His eyes were still fixed on the rearview mirror. On the black panther of a car which dwindled, dwindled, then faded away. Max was parked alongside an empty stretch of road, and other than his dog, he was all by himself, which was nothing new. He was almost always by himself, ever since he was a kid.

He sighed, then made a one-eighty, and slowly went back into town.

TWENTY-THREE

It was now riotous party fun inside Shiloh's. Several hours had passed since Camille had thrown the beer in his face and stormed out, though it felt like the blink of an eye. The music was more energetic. Bob Seger, it sounded like "Hollywood nights." Smoke plumed and twisted up into the ceiling fans, where it whirled and scattered.

Armando's Nissan was still parked outside. There were a lot of cars parked outside. Only now was the unusual liveliness of Sueño Roto understood. Max just snapped to the realization that it was Friday night.

He maneuvered his way through waves of liquor-tainted patrons, searching for Camille in the cacophonous crowd. There was a gap at the bar and he fit himself into it.

Carl mixed drinks and drafted beers. His lips had a slight downward curve. Max turned and leaned his back on the counter, dissonant thoughts and feelings churning as he scanned the throng of carousers, looking for his wife, hoping to avoid being discovered by other parties, which were very likely still here. Or here again.

His place at the bar felt relatively safe. He watched people drink, laugh, and dance in the limited space where there was no dance floor. Everyone seemed to talk at once. He saw Selena work her way through a few times. She didn't seem to notice him.

The longer he stood there the more anxious he became. He was sick of being anxious, but it was becoming as though he didn't know any other way to be. He was sure that any moment Alejandro would spot him, or Alton or Ivan or Wayne or the other guy. He turned back to the bar to get Carl's attention. In hindsight, he was shocked that he'd come here so willingly. Each time he came here it felt more like a prison. A prison within a prison—one that served drinks, yes, but a little more dangerous with each visit.

Finally, Carl caught sight of him.

"Pilsner?"

Max shook his head. "Gimme a double scotch."

"You want the well?"

"What's the well?"

"Scoresby."

"Fine."

Carl set a glass on the bar. He poured a generous double shot. Max took out his card. Carl brought up a hand and waved at it.

"On me."

"You sure?"

"Yeah."

"Why?"

"No reason," Carl said with a tiny smile, then moved on and helped someone else.

A hand clapped hard on his back.

"Max." It was Alejandro. Alton stood behind him.

Max was starting to feel like a celebrity in town. Sadly, it wasn't in any good way. He said nothing. Just sipped his scotch.

"*Perdóname por sonar como un idiota,*" he said, "but you wouldn't happen to know the whereabouts of our friend Armando, would you?"

Max drank more scotch. "Your friend Armando?"

"Yeah."

"Little guy?"

"Sure, yeah, Armando *es pequeño.*"

"No, I haven't seen him."

"Because his car's outside but no one has seen him."

"Huh," Max said.

"In fact," Alejandro went on, "his car's been parked there since last night. He was supposed to meet with us earlier today, but he never showed up."

"Maybe he's really hung over," Max said.

"He's not at home," Alejandro said. "And it seems he hasn't been home."

Max felt the spindle crank. He brought the glass to his lips and swallowed what remained. "Sorry," he said. "I haven't seen him." He set the empty glass on the bar.

"You sure about that?"

Max swallowed again but there was nothing to swallow. "Sure I'm sure."

"Because you were one of the last people to see him last night."

"I was?"

"You were."

Max looked at the empty glass. The scotch was starting to hit him. "Why didn't you ask me when I was here earlier?" He regretted asking the question as soon as it came out of his mouth. It was a question that put him on the defensive, and he didn't want to be defensive, couldn't afford to be defensive. "That is," he added, "if you've been wondering this whole time."

"Carl said he threw him out last night."

"Well, he was kind of being a jerk, don't you think?" He felt himself starting to tremble. He imagined he'd hung a darkened neon sign reading "Guilty" on his head, and all he had to do now was turn it on.

"So you haven't seen him?"

Behind them, over Alton's shoulder, Max saw Camille.

"You saw me leave last night," Max said. "I was out of the bar before you guys were." He glanced back at Camille. She looked annoyed and sad. "Now, if you'll excuse me, I need to collect my wife."

Neither man tried to stop him.

Max wove through people. Camille was standing by the portrait of the group with the slaughtered deer. When she saw him she walked to him, then walked past him, and Max understood he was supposed to follow, which he did. Another glimpse of Selena, another quick glimpse of Alejandro and Alton, he didn't see Ivan or Wayne or the other guy, but, again, he felt like a pussy-whipped asshole.

Seeing them approach, a man with a bottle of beer in his hand opened the door. He smiled at Camille, then looked at Max. The sparkle in his eyes condensed into blades and his jaw set tight. He stared at Max, and it was not a friendly or even curious stare. The man holding the door was Michael, the installation guy from Wavelength Connectivity. The man who'd found Armando's keys in the driveway. Too late to act like he didn't know him, Max nodded and walked through the door.

"Good night," Michael said.

"You, too."

The door closed behind him. The music and voices muffled into a soft rumble of gibberish.

"Where'd you park?"

"Right over there."

They went to the car, not saying a word. Granger was curled on the back seat. He sprang to his feet as Max unlocked the door, and Camille sighed at the sight of him.

Max got behind the wheel and started the car as Camille settled into the passenger seat. He reversed and listened to gravel crunch under tire. He had questions for her, but didn't want the answers. At least not right now. He drove out of the lot and got on to Main Street, and found his eyes roaming for suspicious cars.

When the town was behind them and the world was nothing but walls of night, Camille said, "You ditched me."

Max chewed his lower lip. It was as though the rattlesnake was in the seat beside him. It turned up anxiety's volume, but he was starting to build immunity to this type of venom. The neurotoxin no longer had the numbing strength it did before. It upset him, yes; it disrupted his nerves; it filled him with a disgust that could easily mature into nausea, but freeze did not seem to be an option. Fight or flight, but to hell with freeze.

"I didn't ditch you," he told her, and gripped the wheel. "You threw a beer in face, stormed out and disappeared. *You* ditched *me*."

"Oh, Christ, Max."

"You *insulted* me, *shamed* me, then walked *out* on me."

A moment of silence passed. It was an awful, repulsive moment of silence. Max kept flicking his eyes to the rearview mirror, but as far as he could tell, there was nothing there that shouldn't be.

"You were being a prick," she told him.

He gripped the wheel tighter. "How?"

"You know."

"That's right. I love asking questions I already know the answers to."

"You've been a prick since we got here. You were being a prick back in Portland. A spoiled little brat. You refuse to grasp the real world and it gets exhausting. You want everything for nothing, and you're mad that it doesn't work that way."

He tapped the brakes, tapped them again, and then slammed them down as hard as he could. The tires screeched and they shot forward in their seats. Granger stumbled off the back seat and into the floor.

"The fuck is wrong with you?"

Then time took on its own paralysis. Nothing moved. Nothing breathed. Max stared out at the two cars parked across the road.

One was a gold colored, stretched sedan. A Grand Marquis or a Crown Victoria or something, with heavily tinted windows. The other was a battered army green Bronco.

"Shit."

The sight injected more of the neurotoxin. Only moments before, freezing had not been an option, but it was pouring through his veins now, trying to overwhelm him, trying to immobilize him from the top of his head to the tips of his toes. He trembled, almost shook violently, but otherwise he was unable to move.

"What's that?" Camille said.

Max couldn't speak. Invisible cats had claimed his tongue.

"Who are they?" she said.

Max found nothing in his arsenal but wordless sounds.

"What do they want?"

He both felt and heard his heartbeat pounding.

Then her next question managed to break the spell. "What did you do?"

He shot her a glare, then looked back at the cars. "What did I do?" he said. "I agreed to move to fucking Sueño Roto, that's what I did."

Lights suddenly flashed behind them, winked on then off, on then off. It was a third car, likely the one from earlier. The Bronco flashed its lights. Then the gold car did. All three flashed their lights at varying intervals, on and off, on and off, like an angry stroboscopic junkyard disco. One of the two cars in front of them honked. Then the one behind them honked. Then the other one honked. Flashing lights and now a horn blast game of stationary Marco Polo began.

"What are they doing?"

"They're fucking with us."

"Make them stop!"

"Sure, how about I just get out and ask them to quit? Or better yet, you're the one who keeps things together. You take care of everything. How about you go out and tell them to quit it?"

His ears filled with the din of honking horns and Camille's panicky whimpers. Granger started to bark and howl. All of it was hurricanes breaking in his eardrums. The flashing lights assailed him from both front and back, and reflected back to front in the rearview mirrors.

Max squeezed his eyes shut, opened them, and looked to his left at the oncoming lane. He looked in the mirrors, and tried to gauge the position of the car behind them.

The lights kept flashing. The horns kept honking. And cutting through all of this, engines started revving, like a screwball Grand Prix of maniacs. Max didn't know what their plan was, but it wasn't to simply let them sit here.

From right to left, he studied the road. He cranked the wheel left as fast as he could, and stomped the accelerator. A very short stutter and then the car whipped around, bouncing in the shallow off-road trench. He held the pedal down, grappled only briefly for control. The single car behind them, now in front of them, moved into their lane, crosswise, at an angle.

Max didn't ease up. He kept his foot on the pedal, kept steady in the lane, headed straight for the front end of the car, which no longer flashed its lights but left them off.

"Stop, Max!"

But he didn't stop. The Camry picked up speed. The broken yellow line whipped faster and faster. With two dozen feet between them, Max cut to the right, onto the road's shoulder. The driver of the other car anticipated this and moved forward. Max kept right as much as he dared. Dirt and rocks spat up. The front of the two cars met and they clipped each other. There was a crunch of metal on metal, fiberglass scraping. A quick burst of sparks. The black car shot back with its hood crumpled up. The Camry fishtailed.

Camille screamed. Max kept his foot down on the pedal. Held the wheel as tight as he could. The car weebled and wobbled, then straightened out.

Two sets of lights had already blasted to life behind them. In the rearview mirror the silhouette of the car he'd hit appeared stuck where it was. Max darted his eyes front and kept them steadfast to the road. Another minute or two and they'd be back in town. But as far as he knew, this town had no law. There was nothing saying they'd give up the chase when streetlights appeared. There was nothing saying that people would even think twice if they saw what was going on.

"Call nine-one-one," Max said.

The car moved well enough but pulled hard to the left. Black tree shapes loomed and flashed by them. Absent surprise that the airbags didn't go off whirled to consciousness then flew out again.

Up ahead he saw the intersection. The main intersection. The only intersection. *Calle de la Basura.* The streetlight ahead turned orange. The automotive predators had never fully caught up, and were still a good distance back. He held his foot down as hard as he could.

There were cars waiting to cross at the intersection.

Max gnashed his teeth.

The light turned red.

They were just outside the intersection.

Cars began to move crosswise.

Gripping the wheel with his left hand, he slammed and held down the horn with his right. They raced into cross traffic. Other horns blared. Camille screamed again. Max feared he was gonna scream, too. Electricity fluxed and rippled his spine. Someone shouted something but he couldn't hear what.

Then, in the blink of an eye, they were on the other side. They'd managed to make it through. The rearview mirror's reflection showed that the pursuers hadn't.

"Call nine-one-one," Max said again.

They shot down Main Street, past Shiloh's, past the grocery store. A few more seconds and there was no one behind them.

Camille had managed to take out her phone.

Max powered the Camry down the road, eyes trained on the right. Dumb as it might be—possibly beyond dumb—he knew where he was going.

"Someone's chasing us," Camille told the phone. A pause and then she said, "Main Street. On Main Street… in Sueño Roto. County? What county, of course McKinley County. Where the hell else would Sueño Roto be?"

Max saw the turn. He clicked the headlights to exterior taillights without the main lamps, and used the dim orange glow as his only guide.

"No, I don't know where we are," Camille told the phone. "Just please send somebody." Then she screamed, "Fuck!" and slammed the phone into the floor. "We got cut off!"

They ascended into rocky hills, along the narrow and winding route. The washboard surface made everything rattle, tried to shake the suspension apart. Max didn't know what the damage to the car really was.

Shadows glided within shadows as they crested a hill. He found the turnout, swung into it, braked, turned off the engine, and got out of the car.

Camille got out as well. "What the fuck is going on, Max?"

Max found his cigarettes, lit one and smoked.

"Your Uncle Frank," he told her, "is a

dickhead."

TWENTY-FOUR

The moon lay half-cocked upon the mountaintops. Darkness held dominion over the arid desert, while stars twinkled with smirking faces, and the faintest breeze whispered empty words through shadows wrapped in crystalline lightlessness. Max looked out over the night-swathed precipice. From up here the world was a breathing cipher, containing nothing but occasional flickers, which vanished quicker than they appeared.

He took out his phone. No signal. Thank you, Southwest Mobile, the only cellular service with good coverage in Sueño Roto.

"Check your phone," Max told her.

She went into the car and retrieved it from the floor, flipped it open, pressed a button. "It's flickering between one bar and no bars."

"Try calling Frank."

Granger had remained in the car. Now he hopped out and wandered, whimpered, keeping in close proximity to them.

"Max," Camille said with a spoonful of strength. "Stop trying to pin this all on Frank."

"None of what just happened would—"

"So you're blaming him for all of this. The man who gave us—yes, *gave* us, *blessed* us, with a place to live, who hooked me up with a job…"

"Stop being so fucking daft, Camille."

"Daft? Oh really?"

"Yes, Keep-it-Together Camille, stop being so fucking daft."

"You're preposterous. This is just like you, you know that, Max? Something goes awry and you refuse any responsibility. So everything is suddenly Frank's fault. A convenient scapegoat, all things considered, don't you think? That's right, Frank made that whole thing just happen."

Max heard his teeth scraping inside his ears. Scapegoat. That was the perfect word. The perfect word for what Max was. The word summed up his marriage. It summed up his entire life. *Max* was the scapegoat. He'd always been the scapegoat.

"If I'm so preposterous, then take the car and go on back down there. Go locate those guys. Find out for yourself."

The land was quiet. The scattered houses were distant. The breeze stopped whispering. Max and Camille were alone in this bone-dry, darkened wasteland.

"Call him," Max said.

With sheets of night between them, Max could still make out her expression. It was the same one she'd given him at the grocery store, only lacking the assertion it had previously carried. The downcast look that confirmed her true feelings about him. It didn't press him down, however. This time his anger and frustration found a small opening, and though much of it wasn't willing, some of it slipped out.

"If you're so certain that I'm making it up, then call him. Embarrass me, if that's what you need to do. Shame me, fine, I'm used to that. I'm more used to shame than you know. But by not calling him, you're being fucking daft."

"You're an asshole, Max."

"I'm a scapegoat, Camille."

"*You're* a scapegoat?"

"Just fucking call him!"

She cursed silently, lifted her phone, pressed a couple buttons, stared at it, sighed, then closed it and let her hand drop to her side. "No signal now."

"Great."

"So what are we gonna do?"

"I dunno. For now, we're gonna wait."

"What, wait and hope it just magically goes away?"

Max searched but could find no words for a reply. That last question clamped him like a razor-sharp bear trap. It was both the best and worst question she'd ever asked him. It cracked him like a hammer to the skull. Not consciously, but it was a painful reality suddenly bubbling to the surface. It was something he did. Not something he wanted to do. He would have given just about anything to not have this hindrance as a part of his being, but it was, and it had been there for as long as he could remember. Wishing fear away. Locking himself behind doors, knowing and aware of the danger lurking outside, hoping, praying that the danger would get tired and simply leave. That it would grow weary of pestering him, get bored and figure he wasn't worth it, and simply move on, go away, and find someone else to harass.

He hated that she said this. The question literally made him sick. A part of him wanted to drop to his knees and heave, and if anything came up he already knew it would be darkness. Black exhaust fumes full of dead spiders and swarming with flies and the shells of other insects, dirt and grime and staples and tacks, and the rotted flesh of diseased corpses.

The question made him think that maybe she knew him better than he thought. That through everything, while maybe not knowing a single other thing about him, she had still managed to grip a very central, core part of his being. There were too many things in his life that he hid from, and too many ways by which he hid.

His anger vanished. Now he was disgusted with himself. Then the disgust twined with anger, then with both self-pity and self-loathing. The result was a barrage of disappointment, as well as a need to not wallow.

He bit his lower lip. He checked his phone again. Still no signal.

His head slumped. He tossed his cigarette to

the ground and went to the front of the car to check the damage. The driver's side headlight was shattered. He hadn't been aware of that while driving. To his surprise, though, there was less obvious damage than he'd expected. Probably one of the reasons the airbags hadn't deployed. A smashed headlight, clear body damage, but overall the car was more together than he thought it would be. He looked down, ready for the front tire to be flat, but it wasn't.

"Honestly," he said, "I don't know what to do." He ran his finger along a crumpled spot near the smashed headlight. Paint or something flaked off. "I wish I knew, but I don't." He stood up. "I just don't." Then he looked at her. "Do you?"

"No," she said.

"Okay, well, at least we're on the same page about something."

Granger circled him, leaned against his leg.

Good dog, sweet dog. In spite of how pathetic and lost he felt, the golden retriever, who'd been in his life for such a short time, still trusted him, still loved him. Everything he knew was an upheaval of chaos, topsy-turvy emotion, unbalanced, unfocused thoughts, and through all of it Granger still snuggled him.

"Maybe we should just wait here a while," he said, and patted the dog's side. "*Not* wait and *hide*, but just wait. See if either of us can come up with a good idea. Let whatever that was back there cool down a bit." He raised his shoulders, lowered them. "I wish I had a better idea. I really do, but I just don't."

The darkness became slightly less oppressive. The breeze whispered again, but its words were still unintelligible, yet suddenly, the emptiness wasn't quite so empty.

Camille sighed. The exhale seemed to expel some of her anger. She took a step toward him.

"Okay," she said. The way she stood made her look deflated. "But we can't just sit up here all night."

"We could leave town," Max said. "Head over to Gallup and get a motel, maybe."

"Leave town?"

"Just a thought," he said. "If we're not gonna just sit up here all night, then we need to figure *something* out. You working tomorrow?"

"I'm supposed to."

"What time?"

"Ten."

"All right." He was still holding his phone. He put it in his pocket. He was still shaking. He was always shaking; he wished he could steady himself but it simply wasn't in the cards life had dealt him.

Heading to Gallup had its appeal. It was a real city, over twenty thousand people, and it wasn't very far, all things considered. Safety in numbers, it would be easy to hide and be anonymous. But even though the damage to the car seemed less severe than he'd expected, he had no real knowledge as to the actual extent of the damage, and couldn't escape the thought of breaking down on the way there. Being stuck on the side of the road, spending the night in the middle of nowhere, wide open and vulnerable to anything that might happen to come along.

Of course, they were vulnerable up here, but at least being tucked in the hills had an illusion of safety. And town was close. Probably no more than a fifteen or twenty minute walk from here. Or maybe a ten minute run.

"Well," he said, "you should go to work tomorrow."

"Well, that's a big old duh."

"Yes, thank you, hon, that's very helpful."

Camille kicked at the ground but didn't say anything.

"I don't like the idea of going home. Not tonight."

"Going to Gallup isn't going to solve anything," she said.

"I know."

"And neither is sitting up here."

"Okay," he said, "so, then, what do we do?"

"I wanna go home."

"Bad idea. They know where we live."

"How could you possibly know that?"

"Well, you refuse to hear anything about Frank, so there's no point in going into that. But one thing I can tell you is I know they know."

"Stop talking about Frank."

"I have. That's why we're not getting into it. You want something else, anything else, so long as it doesn't affect the way you see things. But just like you said, hoping it magically goes away isn't going to make it go away. It won't change what he did or didn't do. But there we have it. So what do we do?"

"Fuck," she said. It was almost a whisper. "This sucks."

"It's another part of the real world," he told her. He heard traces of condescension in his tone. He didn't mean for it to be there, but with it his words sounded stronger than he'd expected them to.

A minute passed. Far off in the sky, a shooting star sailed, descended, disappeared. The breeze blew in and out, a flickering susurration, draining, returning. A mumble, a rumble, a murmur, then hushed whispers fading, departing, silence, silence, then all coming back again.

"Okay," Camille finally said with a sigh. "Tell me about Frank."

TWENTY-FIVE

They remained parked in the turnout until about midnight. After Max had told her everything he knew, and Camille had finally listened, they'd both sat on the trunk of the car and watched Granger wander around. They spoke very little. The night was quiet but seemed to know things. Max hadn't said a word about Armando, but the man was always a lingering image behind his eyes.

Eventually they got back in the car and drove back down to Main Street. The road was empty. For a short time the town seemed devoid of life, but this sense was eradicated as they drove past Shiloh's, where it seemed every car in town must have been. They both looked hard, searching for a gold Grand Marquis or a green Bronco, or possibly a black sedan with a crumpled hood, but there was too much traffic, both in the lot and all around the place, and with it also being night, there was no way to tell unless they wanted to stop. And neither of them wanted to. They were heading home. An unnerving prospect, but after much deliberation, home seemed the best option—the only option, really. Hopefully enough time had passed for the guys to give up for the night. Hopefully no one would be lying in wait when they got there.

They crossed *Calle de la Basura* without incident. When they came to the spot where the confrontation took place, Max felt a shiver ripple his spine. With apprehension, they both studied the scene, but there was no scene to study. They didn't even see evidence of their collision. The only viable substantiation was in their memory imaginariums.

Nothing jumped at them from out of the darkness.

The house was just as ominous and lonely as before, ergo it appeared unharmed, both outside when they pulled into the driveway, and inside when Max unlocked the door.

Granger went straight for his water dish.

The instant Max crossed the threshold, the severe exhaustion that had plagued him all day returned with full force. His eyeballs throbbed and his lids grew heavy; his legs went rubbery; his back and neck ached, and his shoulder pulsed with a dull pain that made his muscles twitch. He stumbled to the living room and sat on the couch, a merry-go-round of shadows and specters spinning round and round in his head. He heard Camille close the door and lock it. The sound made him cringe, and he wished to hell and back he could fucking stop trembling.

Camille sat down next to him. Her posture was rigid, her expression forlorn. She looked like the odd kid left out of a ball game. She looked like a sad mannequin. Even though the emotion was distant, Max couldn't help feeling sorry for her.

He looked around the living room. Black windows and rundown furniture. The spot where his Mondrian had briefly hung. The ceiling with its large pine vigas. The worn-out shelves of paperbacks. The couch they both sat on, upon which had writhed a snake. This wasn't his home. In no sense of the word was this his home. It never had been and never would be. It was a truck stop on a road to nowhere. A rest area attached to a dead end.

"I'm going to bed," he said, and struggled to get himself up off the couch. A dizzy spell hit him as he got to his feet. He wobbled, swayed, then steadied himself and walked to the stairway. He placed a hand on the banister. Ribbons of sleep fluttered in his eyes. His solar plexus felt cramped, and the rest of him was stiff and sore. His feet were lead weights as he climbed up the stairs. It took longer than forever to reach the top.

He stumbled into the bedroom. He didn't turn on the light. He located the bed and eased himself onto it, kicked off his shoes, then let gravity pull him down. His body sank into the mattress. Then his mind sank into dreams.

TWENTY-SIX

Someone was screaming.

He didn't move, just listened. Shrill shrieks of horror, tormented and relentless, as if the business of each wail was to crush and shatter all silence forever. And yet the screams were distant, a far away sound, echoing and hollow and pouring right in his ears. Bloodcurdling, loud, yet abstracted, sequestered, and soft. Long and tedious, an endless string of cries. It wasn't so much frightening as it was tiring and strange.

And the voice reverberated, as though carrying through long hallways, seeking destinations it would never reach. Crushing the silence while simultaneously being swallowed by it.

It was hot but he felt chilled. He wondered why Granger hadn't barked, or wasn't barking now. Dogs and cats were acute to these kinds of things, weren't they? At least they were in movies.

He'd fallen asleep atop the covers. He slid off of them now, and brought his feet to the floor, where they blindly sought his slippers and then eased into them. He stood up, still lightheaded. He placed one foot in front of the other, then did it again. After a couple repetitions, he was standing in the hall. Then, he was at the top of the stairs. Then, one by one, he descended them. He couldn't see a thing. His eyes refused to adjust to the darkness. But he moved mechanically, somehow knowing where everything was and what movement was required of him to maneuver about it all.

The screams had given way to pleading cries. Cries and whimpers, fainter now, but no less present.

As he reached the bottom of the stairs, Max crossed the house to the back door. His eyes were adjusted now, and what he saw was night. Desert and night. A star-speckled wasteland. A thinly angled scythe of moon aloft what was both majestic magic and moistureless nightmare.

He placed his hand on the doorknob.

The cries petered out. Whimpers now. Whimpers and sobs. They were out there in the night, and they were also right in his ears. He stood right beside them, through those trees and over those hills. He was right next to them, all the way over there. Time and space seemed infinitely finite. For a single breath he was here and there at the same time.

He knew the voice was lost. He didn't know how he knew, but he did. The voice couldn't find its way.

His hand moved up from the knob to the

deadbolt thumb-turn. Then he stopped. Exactly what did he expect to accomplish?

He let go of the thumb-turn. He took a step back.

Whimpers and sobs. Whimpers and sobs.

The night remained night. But like always, the night held secrets. The night knew things that the day did not. Instead of daylight with its crevices, nooks, and crannies, the night was one giant rift, with infinite crevices that split off into infinite crevices, and few shadows existed because the night was made of shadows. And it kept its secrets. It rarely articulated more than a breathless wind of the secrets it held. The night knew things that only the night knew. And night and night alone had say in what was and wasn't revealed.

He took another step back. He closed his eyes and tried to wish the voice away, but it wasn't that simple. It wasn't as simple as wishing. Wishes were merely acknowledgements of hopes. He hoped it would go away. He wished it would go away. But the fact was it wouldn't go away. Not by simply wishing and hoping.

The whimpers had dropped a decibel. Max wondered if he should go back upstairs and put on his shoes. Or maybe go back upstairs and pretend this wasn't real. After all, maybe it wasn't real. Max had no evidence that a single sound he heard out there was anything more the conjuring of his own freakish mind. Same with the banging and scratching on the door. From outside every time, except for once, just after he'd dumped Armando down the shaft. The knocks had come from inside the house that time. What proof did he have that he wasn't making it all up? What proof did he have that all of this wasn't simply the result of stress and an overactive imagination?

Zero.

And still, there was whimpering.

He flipped the thumb-turn on the door, opened it, stepped out, eased the door shut, took a couple steps…

The whimpers grew quieter. Still there, but softer now. Softer and starting to sound familiar.

Max crossed the patio, and then his slippered feet were on dirt and, mechanically, one foot went in front of the other, through dirt and rock and brush as time ran like an ethereal stopwatch. He walked by the rickety shed. Then he was stepping over a large rock. Then he was walking around a tree, then up a slope, down an incline.

There was the tennis ball, sitting comfortably between rocks.

But, still, there were sobs. Weaker, less desperation and more defeat, as though the closer he got, the more he oppressed them.

Dirt climbed into his slippers as he descended the hill. The opening was sheer blackness; it wasn't opaque. He saw the dirt and stone, the ladder plank. A part of him asked again why he hadn't even tried going down into the hole, but the answer was obvious. And he wasn't going to climb down it now. Not with what he knew about it. Not with what he'd done to it.

The sobbing stopped. For a split second all sound sapped away. Max briefly thought he'd suddenly gone deaf. Then he heard voices. The words were unintelligible, sexless, and their sound reverberated. Voices at the far end of a long, echoing tunnel.

He didn't even think about it when he said, "Hello?" But his callout altered nothing. The talking continued, obscure and unlistening, soft, so soft, like wilted flowers speaking of death. And though sound was gone, an energy lingered. It radiated from everything, a cold energy, icy and electric. It washed over him like a breeze, and then it was gone.

***

"Get up."

His eyes fluttered open, closed again.

"Max, get up. Get up, get up, get up."

He opened his eyes. Out the window sunlight shimmered, bright as hell. It hurt to see it. He shut them again, and turned away from it all, pulled the blankets tight over his head.

"Max, c'mon."

"What time is it?"

"Just after nine."

So she was still a morning bitch, but at least she'd let him sleep in a bit later than usual. He was still exhausted. His body ached. His head felt like a bucket of stones.

"Is there coffee?" he asked.

"Yes."

"Gimme just a minute, then."

Without a word, she left the room.

A few minutes later he was downstairs, drinking coffee. He'd washed his face and brushed his teeth, taken a couple of ibuprofen tablets. His shoulders were rock hard with tension, and his back and neck were stiff.

Camille was sitting on the couch. Max joined her.

"So, what's the plan?" he asked.

She shrugged. The movement was emotionless. "I'm going to work," she said. "I'm gonna serve coffee and rattle off specials and act like nothing happened." She drank some coffee. "What about you?"

Granger was curled on the floor. Max couldn't tell if he was asleep or not.

"Remember the day we got here, and you and Moses spoke at the grocery store?"

"Yeah?"

"Do you remember what I asked you when we got outside?"

"No."

"I asked you what that House of Ortiz thing was. You told me something I already knew and then blew me off."

"What does that have to do with anything now?"

"Because I'm curious. Moses said more about it than it was simply the property owned by the Ortiz family."

"So?"

"So, what did he say?"

Camille drank more coffee. Then she sighed. "I didn't tell you because I know how you are."

"What does that mean?"

"You're a daydreamer."

"Huh?"

"You indulge in reverie. You let yourself get swallowed by fantastic, impractical ideas. You live in an absent-minded fool's paradise. Castles in the air, reveries, daydreams that will never come true, that hinder you, inside and out."

She got up from the couch and went to the kitchen.

"So," Max said, "there's something you won't tell me, basically, because I have an imagination."

"You should take me to work now," she said, and he heard her rinse her cup.

"Just tell me." He got up and went to the kitchen. His wife looked annoyed. She also looked scared. "You're outright keeping something from me. Even if it's trivial, this is the kind of thing that solidifies the fuckedness in our marriage. If you won't even tell me this, what else is there you're not telling me?"

She shot him a glare. "Fine," she said. "If it's really *so* important to you."

"Yes, it's really *so* important to me."

"*La casa asesina de Ortiz*," she said. "The murderous house of Ortiz." She went to the front door, opened it. "Can we go now?"

TWENTY-SEVEN

They didn't speak a word the entire drive to the diner. The radio was off. The car pulled to the left but it wasn't as bad as Max had expected it to be. There was obvious damage to the front of the car, but he seriously doubted the other vehicle would report it. The engine also made a clicking sound he didn't much like.

They pulled into the lot of the Silver Moon. Everything seemed to be business as usual. Camille opened her door and climbed out.

"You'll pick me up at four?"

"Barring unforeseen circumstances, yes."

Not another word. She closed the door. She turned away and went into the diner.

Max removed his sunglasses and rubbed his eyes. Achy, he still felt better than he had in some time. He knew he hadn't gotten enough sleep, but he'd gotten more than he'd expected to. A little more coffee would be nice.

He looked at the diner again. Then he put on

his sunglasses and drove out of the lot. He made a left onto Main Street, and a few moments later made another left at the grocery store. It wasn't nearly as busy this morning. He parked, got out of the car, and went inside.

First thing he heard was the transistor radio. Marty Robbins, he was pretty sure. Whoever it was who sang "El Paso." The light inside had a tint of gloom, and the air had a stale, unnatural chill to it. These things were always present here, he was just currently more aware of them.

Moses was behind the counter, putting up packs of Salems. "*Cómo estás, señor?*"

"Hey."

"You look like you got some rest."

"Yeah, some."

"*Bueno.* Good."

Like other mornings, the store was empty.

"I was wondering," Max said, "if maybe I could take you up on some of that, uh, Colombian coffee."

"Ah, ready for some *café Colombiano*, eh?"

Max nodded.

Moses smiled. He laughed a little. "Now that you are rested, forgive me, it seems a little *irónico.*" He laughed a little more. Then he cleared his throat. "I'm sorry I was so busy last night."

"I'm glad you were," Max told him. "Means business is good."

"You very much looked *hombre curioso*, like a man with something on his mind."

Max looked at the floor, looked at his shoes. He felt an acidic kind of burn in his throat and his chest. Still looking at the floor, he said it.

"What can you tell me about the murderous house of Ortiz?"

***

Max was surprised that Moses actually closed the entire store. In the front door he hung a cardboard picture of a clock with adjustable hands that said "Back in..." and set it for fifteen minutes in the future. They went into the back office, which was not much larger than a cubicle. There were several pictures of women in bathing suits taped to the walls, and a desk cluttered with papers and lacking a computer. The desk chair must have dated back to the Carter administration, and there was an ancient end table in the corner with an old Mr. Coffee machine, a stack of paper cups, and a ceramic container with an airtight gasket and the Juan Valdez logo.

"It is not Juan Valdez," Moses said. "This is *suprema de café*. Real coffee. Any time I drink that instant piss out there in the store, I always want to vomit. It is not real coffee. *This* is real coffee." He pointed at the coffeemaker, which made bubbly percolating sounds.

Max nodded. Moses offered him the office chair and he took it. It was rickety and squeaky.

"The murderous house of Ortiz," Moses said. He was staring at the coffeemaker.

"Is that a common name for it?" Max asked.

"Not so much common as simply known," Moses told him. He took two paper cups from the stack and set them upright on the small table. "Your wife did not tell you?"

"My wife doesn't tell me much, other than what's wrong with me."

Moses nodded. "Yes," he said. "I don't really know her, but she is strong-headed."

"She's a control freak and a bit of a snob," Max said. He wasn't sure why, but he almost immediately regretted having said it.

"I would not argue that, *señor*. But it is not my place to pass judgment. Do you take cream or sugar?"

"Any which way is fine," Max said.

Moses removed the coffeepot and filled the two cups. "Cream and sugar are out in the store."

"Black is fine."

Moses handed him one of the cups. The coffee was decent. Certainly better than anything else he'd had since moving here.

"You are shaking."

"I have tremors."

"All the time?"

"Pretty much."

"I see."

"So what is it that's simply known?"

"*Perdón*?"

"Ortiz, the house."

"Oh, yes, of course." He sipped his coffee. "Forgive me. Sometimes my mind scurries like a frantic spider."

"It's all right. What can you tell me?"

The room had a single fluorescent tube in the ceiling. It flickered every now and then.

"Emilio Ortiz," the man said. "He is the man Frank Albertson bought the property from. Emilio, he grew up in that house, as did his father. Grandfather had it built in the early 1900s, I believe, when mining was *una cosa maravillosa*. A big deal. A wonderful thing. Truth be told, *hermano*, I am not entirely sure about that part. Maybe it was his great grandfather. I met Emilio when he was still a little boy. I was between his age and his father's age. His father, Joe, was the local handyman. Anyone in town needed something fixed, or built, Joe was the man you called."

He sipped his coffee again. Joe Ortiz, the man in the real-life *Gran Perro* story.

The fluorescent light flickered, steadied.

"Joe died of an aneurysm in 1992, I think it was. He was spackling a ceiling, apparently said his head hurt, then dropped his spackle knife before dropping off the ladder. Emilio inherited the house after that. Overall, Emilio was a good man. He and his wife Estella, they were both well respected. They were devoted to each other, active with the church and the community. Everybody liked them."

Max nodded, drank a bit of his coffee. For the first time in a while he wanted a cigarette.

"About ten years ago," Moses went on, "Emilio's cousin, Hector Archuleta, and his fiancée, Anita Calderón, they came from Pagosa Springs for a visit. Couple of weeks, *más o menos*." He shook his head, began picking at a loose piece of tape on the wall. "I met them. They were nice people. From what I heard, Hector was a very reliable man. He had a good employment record, he was very religious. He seemed helpful and very friendly. Had a smile for everyone. He seemed a completely normal guy, better than normal." He shook his head again, drank some more coffee.

Max noticed the distant look in the man's eyes. As though the man had been there. As though he were reliving what he was saying.

"The four of them stopped here on a Saturday evening," he continued. "They did not need to tell anyone they had been at Shiloh's. It was clear as day, the way they moved, the way they giggled, the way they slurred their speech. They bought a case of beer and a bottle of scotch. I would not have sold it to them, but Hector appeared to be quite sober. The designated driver, you know?"

Max nodded, drank coffee.

"I watched them through the window as they got into their car, pleased to see Hector get behind the wheel. Had he not been acting like his normal self, I either wouldn't have sold to them or I would have called the sheriff. But the man seemed straight as a die. Sober as a judge. As long as one of them was being safe and taking care of things, there was no reason to concern myself with it. Would you like more coffee?"

"Sure, thanks."

Moses removed the pot from the coffeemaker and refilled both cups.

"So they left. I assume they went home to continue their party. I thought nothing else of it. I finished up the night and closed the store. Went to the Silver Moon and had a late dinner. Back then, the Silver Moon was open later than it is now. I had my dinner and did one of those Sudoku puzzles. I was never any good at those.

"Next morning, I come in and open the store. Within twenty minutes, *hijo de puta*, a man comes in, asks me if I heard about what happened at Emilio and Estella's last night. 'No,' I tell him, but I remember the night before and know whatever it is that has happened, it cannot be good. The man—I forget his name now—he tells me that someone went *loco* at the Ortiz place. Estella was dead, as was Hector's wife, Anita. Emilio and Hector, they were both injured. Turns out that Emilio had been stabbed several times, just like his wife, but he'd managed to survive. Hector was curmudgeoned."

"Curmudgeoned?"

"Is that wrong? *Mierda*, you know. Hit a lot, beaten."

"Oh, bludgeoned."

"Yes, that is it. Hector was bludgeoned, but also still alive. Unconscious. Both men were taken to the hospital in Gallup." Moses leaned against the wall now, looked deep into his cup of coffee. "Estella and Anita were pronounced dead at the scene. Two dead, two injured. There had been nothing at all like this in Sueño Roto in decades. It is a depressed town, there is a lot of crime, but not usually so violent, or maybe sadistic is a better word. Gruesome, maybe."

"How was all this discovered so quickly?"

"*Perdón?*"

"I mean, it all took place between the time you closed the store and the time you opened it the next morning."

Moses nodded. "*Sí*. Emilio, stabbed, wounded, but not dead, he got to the phone and called the police. He called them at some point very early in the morning, because people were already talking about it when I opened the store."

A shiver coursed through Max. He sipped his coffee but it didn't chase the shiver away.

"Hector died a few days later in the hospital. Blunt force trauma, I think is what they called it."

"And Emilio?" Max said. "Did he ever say anything to Frank about all this?"

"I do not know, *señor*."

"But Frank must've heard about it. Someone told him or he figured it out somehow."

"That is between Frank and what Frank knows," the man said. "Once Emilio had healed, he put the house up for sale. He did not want to live where so much horror had taken place, where he had seen his wife murdered in front of his very eyes."

"So," Max said, "does anyone actually know what happened?"

"Oh, yes. Emilio's wounds were bad but not fatal. Still in hospital, he told police what happened." Moses paused, drank some more of his *café Colombiano*.

Max figured the fifteen minutes the cardboard sign had indicated were either up or about to be.

"Apparently," Moses said, "they had been at the bar. Just out for the evening, having a few drinks, having a good time. Hector, charming as always, was not having as good of a time as the others. People who saw them at the bar that night said he was still polite and friendly, but that he seemed more *hosco*, sullen, more morose than usual. Not angry. More uncomfortable, and sad. I had not noticed this when they came into the store. I do not know how drunk the other three were, but was just pleased to see that one of them was sober.

"Emilio said they got back to the house and everything was fine. They left the scotch on the kitchen counter and took the case of beer into the living room, and set up a board game."

Moses sighed, drank some coffee, went on.

"At some point, Hector said something to Anita about how she was looking at someone in the bar. Sexy looking, you know? Giving sexy looks to some guy. Apparently it escalated into an argument, and Hector got up and walked away to cool off. They stopped playing the game at that point. The three of them just sat on the couch, drinking beer.

"Shit. After a few minutes Hector came back to the living room. Emilio said the man had clearly been into the scotch. He also said that he saw it too late. Hector lifted an eight-inch chef's knife and plunged it down into Anita's back. Emilio said it happened so fast, he didn't understand what was going on. Before he knew it, Hector had stabbed him too, and while he was still reeling from the pain, he saw his wife collapse down to the floor, knocking the game off of the coffee table. He said that much of it was a blur after that. Anita tried to escape out the back door but she was having some trouble walking. Apparently Hector did not go after her right away. Instead he stabbed Emilio again, several times. Emilio was still conscious but couldn't move much, and he watched as his cousin stabbed his wife repeatedly, until the floor was a pool of blood and she no longer moved."

Max shifted uncomfortably in the chair. The chair squeaked.

"He then watched Hector head over to his fiancée, just before she reached the back door. He stabbed her many multiple times. And then, with *carnicería*, with blood and bodies on the floor, Hector went outside and began to scream.

"While his cousin was gone, Emilio strained and fought to move. He made it to Estella, but she was already dead, and he knew that he could not do anything to help Anita. He was not sure he could do anything to help himself. On the floor, in a pool of his and his wife's blood, he crawled. The telephone was in the kitchen, which, in his state, *señor*, was very far away. He dragged himself a body's length and had to stop. Somewhere, far off, he could hear Hector screaming. He listened in fear, and tried to think what to do. And then the screaming stopped."

Moses finished his coffee. He crumpled the cup and threw it into a small wastebasket.

"Lying there in both his and his wife's blood, Emilio discovered he was not far from the fireplace. On the *bonco*, the lower ledge of the fireplace, there stood a foot-high bronze statue of

Saint Michael. You know who Saint Michael is, *hermano*?"

"Yeah, sure."

"Saint Michael, the Archangel," Moses said. "Emilio crawled, dragged himself across the living room, over to that fireplace. There were no fireplace tools because they never built fires in it. And he knew, since the man outside had stopped screaming, it would likely not be long before Hector returned to the house.

"With all of his strength, Emilio pulled himself up to his feet. He lifted the statue and held it, both prepared to use it as a weapon and also praying to it. He said it was the heaviest thing he had ever held in his life, or maybe he didn't say that and I just believe it was, and that he had never had so much trouble staying on his feet.

"He waited, hidden off to the side. When Hector finally returned to the house, he was crying. He said to himself, 'It's finished,' over and over again.

"Emilio managed to slam Saint Michael over Hector's head. The two of them collapsed. Eventually, after much struggle, Emilio was able to drag himself to the kitchen, and was able to get to the telephone. He called *la policía*."

Max crushed his own coffee cup. He had a sensation of bugs crawling on him. "That's fucked up," he said.

Moses nodded. "At some point during that night, Hector must have suffered some kind of a complete mental breakdown. Went fucking *loco*, crazy." He moved away from the wall.

"Police found the bottle of scotch had *not* been opened."

Max scratched the side of his nose. The tiny room filled with a new sense of quiet.

"Hector, he was unconscious most of his time in the hospital, but after about a day he did come out of it for a short while. Said that, as he stabbed the three of them, he knew what it was that he was doing, that he didn't want to hurt Emilio or Estella, but he had no control. He wanted to stop but had no control of his body, and all he wanted was to kill Anita. That he had become fed up with her. How she was mean, how she was *obseso del control*."

"Control?"

"She was a control freak, and apparently very nasty to him. Everyone in Pagosa Springs, where they were from, they said she enjoyed making him look stupid, enjoyed making him look weak, small. She nit-picked him, and apparently really liked doing all of these things in public, *echar sal en las heridas*."

"Huh?"

"Salt. Rubbing salt in his wounds. She liked being in charge, and also liked beating him down, and that day, here in Sueño Roto, in Broken Dream, the man had simply had enough. After two days in the hospital, Hector finally died."

Someone knocked at the front of the store. Moses moved and exited the tiny office, slowly made his way to the front. Max followed him. Moses opened the door to a woman who slightly resembled a cat, and was oddly in need of cat food and cat litter.

"I must get back to work now," Moses said.

TWENTY-EIGHT

Outside, Max lit a cigarette. The smoke tore at his throat, like he'd swallowed razors and chased them with sand. There were several cars out on Main Street now, but the rush passed as quickly as it came.

People here and there, doing this and that, but they were characters out of a silent movie, and there was no piano or organ music. Just the sound of a very small town. A rural desert town smack dab in the middle of nowhere. Just like the day they arrived.

So, there were questions and answers. But there were no dividends in the answers, only more questions, and the questions were recondite at best. This Hector Archuleta goes crazy, and tries to kill everyone in the room. He only wanted to kill his fiancée but tried killing everyone in the house. Do the details really matter? No, not especially, because what it amounted to was that some crazy-ass violent shit happened in that house. The way

Moses told it, sounded like the guy just went crazy. Just *whoomp*! Snapped. Does that happen, out of the blue like that? Or was there more to it? Was there something standing right in the middle of the blue?

There was no appeal in his cigarette. He dropped it to the ground and crushed it underfoot. And as he did, the thing standing right in the middle of the blue raced up and smacked him.

Anita Calderón was a control freak. Then one day Hector Archuleta had simply, finally, had enough.

How long ago had Moses said that was? About ten years ago. Based on what he'd just heard, and based on his own experiences, there were definitely some parallels. Enough for Max to worry. Same house, similar sounding relationship, Max found another level of fear — that what was going on with his wife, with Alejandro and Alton, Wayne and Ivan, With Joe Ortiz and the story of the ghostly dog, what was going on with Sueño Roto and *la casa asesina de Ortiz*, the cries and whimpers, the screams and barks and knocks and scratches. Fear that it was all possibly build-up for a similar event to take place in that house. Fear that it was all training for Max to simply snap.

But whatever it was, whatever that amounted to, it was still only one piece of what was happening. There were people hunting him now. In one fashion or another, he was being hunted, he was prey, like the deer in that photo up in Shiloh's. The one with Alejandro's uncle. The one with everyone so proud and the animal so dead. A dead animal corpse on display in the hands of hunters, only this time, Max was the deer.

Maybe they'd wind up taking pictures of him. Maybe they'd wanna do Before and After pics, like those hair club for men commercials, except instead of putting them on TV, they'd put them up on the walls of Shiloh's, so the next idiot who came to town could see Max instead of the deer. He'd replace the deer; he'd be the deer.

And don't forget Armando, he reminded himself. You killed Armando, or you were there when he died. You took his body and hid him. That's breaking the law. You tampered. You ran. You hid. Any way you slice it, you've got guilt in your flesh and swathing your brain.

Max stepped to the Toyota, unlocked it. The sunlight intensified and became hot needles on his skin. He got into the car and started it. The engine made a brief scraping sound.

So what do you do? There's too much, it's all too much. It's all going round and round in a big whirlpool. A dream—no, nightmares... nightmares ready to swirl down into a monotonous black hell.

Time lost its meaning. It might have been an hour since he'd climbed behind the wheel, and, suddenly, an intense, almost insane sense of urgency took hold of him. He wanted to run. Run as hard and as fast as he could. Drive up Main Street and get the hell out, but the two streets that intersected were a thick black maze and at every turn was a dreary dead end, as though the town knew what he wanted, and cordoned off every possible route.

His shoulders slumped a little. He looked at the front of the store. The sun lit up in sheets and blades and he put on his sunglasses. He heard the soft and raspy sleep-like rhythm of his breathing. There was something artificial about it, an unreality that comes with fatigue. He put his hand up to the back of his neck and kneaded the flesh. He winced at the pain of his stiffness. Needles lanced down into his shoulders, then out his arms, to the tips of his fingers. He was still wound up tighter than a clock spring.

A sour fluid welled up in his throat. He gulped it down, sighed. Then his heart slammed and he jumped when knuckles suddenly rapped against the window.

He nearly threw the car into reverse without even looking, then caught both himself and his breath when he saw Selena standing there, on the other side of the glass.

"I'm sorry," she said as he lowered the window. "I did not mean to scare you." She smiled as she said it. It was an empathetic and sweet smile, endearing as hell.

"Good morning," he said. His voice was hoarse, something from the *café Colombiano*, maybe. Or maybe he was coming down with a sore throat. He hoped not. That would just cap it off.

"Did you crash your car?"

"Huh?"

"I don't remember seeing that damage there."

She indicated the Camry's front.

"Little accident last night. No big deal."

A moody silence fluttered down, cascading from somewhere unseen, pooling between them and then engulfing them.

Then, "I just saw you sitting there, staring blankly," she said. "For a moment I thought you were stoned."

The moodiness evaporated. She smiled, and so did he.

She looked good. Wearing jeans and a gray, tight-fitting UNM T-shirt, her dark hair gilded by sunlight, she looked incredible.

Even though he smiled, he felt hunger pangs, and his aches were not unlike a bad hangover. He was very thirsty. Dehydration. Too much caffeine. Water would hopefully help temper the shakes, and possibly rid of the scratchiness in his throat. He also needed food; his stomach called him an absent-minded son of a bitch.

"So, what are you doing here?" he asked.

"*Irrigación vaginal y tampones*," she said, then raised her shoulders and dropped them. "Just getting a couple of womanly essentials."

Max stared at her; he didn't know what to say to that.

A car blazed down Main Street with its stereo cranked.

"What about you?" she said.

"Hungry. Think I need to eat something." He kneaded the muscles in his neck again. "You wanna — you wanna join me?"

"Are you asking me on a date?"

"No, I'm asking you on a eat." He paused, shook his head. "That was stupid."

"Yes, it was. And yes, I'd like to."

"Yeah?"

"Yeah. Just let me run in and get my *productos de higiene femenina*."

***

There was a small restaurant down Calle de la Basura that Max hadn't been aware of. It was called *El Tecolote*, and was run by an old man and woman who hardly spoke any English. There were pictures of owls all over the walls, from photos to children's drawings, and the incandescent lighting made it feel more like a living room with several tables rather than an actual restaurant.

"I didn't even know this place was here."

"It's a secret little gem tucked away in Sueño Roto," she told him. "You need to be a real local to know about it."

The tables were metal and so were the chairs. There were a couple of oscillating fans set upon the short dining counter, behind which the old man sat with a crossword puzzle, and the old woman sat with nothing but her thoughts.

"Anything else in town I don't know about?"

"There's a Laundromat."

"Think I saw that."

"Then you know Sueño Roto." She smiled, lifted and drank her coffee. "There used to be a video rental store here, that empty building at the intersection, but the digital age pretty much killed all of those." She stirred her coffee without adding anything, then said, "Best pancakes in town."

"Doesn't the Silver Moon do pancakes?"

"Yes, but these are better."

"Quite a boast. I mean, with so many pancake places around here to choose from."

"I know," she said. "With all the variety, you'd think it would be hard to choose just one. Not easy, believe me, but I guarantee you, you won't find a better pancake in all of Sueño Roto."

A moment later, two plates of the best pancakes in town showed up at their table. Max couldn't deny it. They were pretty damn good. For a time they sat, saying nothing, just eating. The sun sliced through crooked window blinds. The tiny restaurant, with its steam and smoke and light sprinkle of customers, was even hotter than the world outside.

"So," she said after a time. "You doing any better than when I last saw you?"

"I guess that depends."

"On what?"

"On nothing. The scales of justice can be a bitch."

"By bitch, do you mean who I think you mean?"

"Probably, but that would only be a part of it."

"*Mierda*." She took a bite of pancake, chewed, then talked with her mouth full. "I'm sorry. Sounds like nothing has been going well for you since you got to this ball of shit town."

"Oh, it's not the town," Max told her. "Things

have been a ball of shit for a while."

"But this town is a ball of shit, too."

"Yes," he said. "I won't argue that. But like the saying goes, wherever you go, there you are."

"Where you are has something to do with it, though," she said. "Life has been just as hard for me other places, but, in some of them, I've been happier."

"Yeah, but, you know, it's that whole grass is always greener crap."

"Of course it's greener if you live *here*. It's the fucking desert. There *is* no grass."

"Touché."

Silence captured them again. For a time, it encapsulated them. There was music playing, very soft, from somewhere unseen. Max only just noticed it. It sounded like jazz, old jazz, Benny Goodman or Count Basie or someone, but it might not have been. It was too faint and tinny sounding for him to be sure. It might not have even been jazz at all.

"Should you be doing this?" she asked.

"Doing what?"

"Eating out with another woman?"

"I dunno. Probably not."

"So, then, why are you?"

Max drank his water. He had a cup of coffee too, but was mostly drinking water.

"Honestly?"

"Yes, honestly."

"Because you talk to me," he said. "You don't talk down to me. You don't belittle me. You don't make me feel inferior, impotent, useless. You don't shit on me with your words. You just talk to me, one person to another."

Selena looked down at the table, head bobbing in the slightest nod. She drank some coffee. "Sometimes all we need is someone to talk to us. Or someone to talk to."

"Amazing how hard it can actually be to come by."

She nodded again, wadded up her napkin and put it on her plate. "Yeah," she said. "Especially in such a small ball of shit." She couldn't keep herself from giggling as she said it.

He didn't expect the chuckle that rumbled inside him. It was fleeting, however. Almost immediately loneliness consumed him again.

"How is your wife?"

"What do you mean?"

"I mean, how is your wife?"

He shrugged. "Same as always."

"That bad, huh?"

"I don't wanna talk about it."

She leaned back in her chair. It made a metal squeaking sound. "Amazing how hard it can actually be, huh?"

"What's that?"

"Talking about it."

The cyclone of rage that now torpedoed through him was intense, but like the chuckle, it was also fleeting. He drank his water, emptied the glass. He drank his coffee, too.

"You don't have to talk about it, Max. You just seem to carry a lot. A young Atlas with the world on his shoulders." She paused, then continued.

"Have you ever read Ayn Rand?"

"No."

"Me neither, but I wonder if maybe you would relax a little if you tried doing one of her book titles."

"The hell does that mean?"

"*Atlas Shrugged*." She reached out and took his left hand in both of hers.

"You're shaking."

"I have tremors."

"So you always shake?"

"A little, yeah."

"You need to get out of this place," she said. "You need to get out before it swallows you whole."

"It's not that simple."

"It can be."

"No, it can't. Much as I would love for it to be, it just isn't."

"Why?"

"Why? Because I can't just pick up and leave."

"What do you have going for you here?"

Now it was frustration that crawled like a swarm of insects inside him.

"Seems to me you can't see a single thing, Max. I know I'm speaking out of line. I know I do not even really know you. But from what I've seen, I don't think you know who the hell you are."

"Who I am? I'm a lonely loser, a pussy-whipped asshole who gets no pussy. A scapegoat for the insecurities of others. I'm a goddamned joke. I'm a joke to my wife. I'm a joke to her family, to her fucking uncle, and to her pompous, snob-ass friends. I'm a fucking joke, a fucking punch line that gets no laughs at all."

Selena appeared taken aback, but only for as long as it takes for an eyelid to blink. She looked one way then the other, then looked back at him. "So, obviously, you think rather highly of yourself."

"It's simple math, really," he said. "I add up my experiences, I add up what I've done, I total it all up, total up my life, and no matter how I try to cheat it, the answer still comes up zero."

"You don't mean that."

"Sure I do. Why wouldn't I?"

"I don't think you really believe that. I know you're not playing the pity game, but I know, deep down, you don't believe what you're saying."

"You know what I have to show for my life? A nasty, controlling bitch of a wife, a stillborn daughter, a brother lost somewhere, either dead, in a nut house or on the street, and a new sweet dog that my wife despises."

"Why does your wife despise Granger?"

"Because she doesn't want me to have anything that might bring me joy, and she doesn't want anything liking me."

"So, if I may ask, why are you with this person?"

"That's a question I've been asking since nearly Day One."

"Any answers?"

"Zilch."

"All the more reason to leave."

"And do what?"

She shrugged. "Something other than what you have been doing." She finished her coffee.

Max crumpled his own napkin, tossed it onto his plate. "Maybe that's the real problem," he said. "I can't think of anything."

"So you would rather just sit around and be Milquetoast Man."

"No. I don't want that either."

"Then what do you want?" She flagged down the old lady for more coffee.

Max thought about it. It was hard to think. He shook his head. "I don't know."

What he did know was that she was right. He didn't have to like it, he didn't have to hate it, but she was right. Maybe he didn't know what he wanted, but what he did know was that he couldn't spend his life this way. Milquetoast Man seemed to sum him up pretty well. Did he really think, did *either* of them think they could go on the way they'd been going? Go on this way forever? Till Death do them part? All that had happened here, even if you put it all aside, what Max and Camille had—if they'd ever had anything—had crashed long ago, and the two of them were now just going through the motions, as all of it slowly burned. They were both so damn tired of the whole goddamn business.

Then, surprised he actually said it, he asked her: "Why does it matter where the Mondrian hangs?"

"What?"

"A painting I have. Piet Mondrian, a Dutch

painter. I have a print of *Broadway Boogie Woogie*, one of his more famous paintings. I love it. Camille hates it. She doesn't like it hung in the house."

"She won't let you hang a painting in the house?"

"Not anywhere where somebody might see it."

"Why would something like that be such a big deal to her?"

"I've been thinking about that." Suddenly he wanted to smoke again. "I think it's just like the deal with Granger. If it makes me happy in any way, it needs to be expunged."

"What does that mean, expunged?"

"To wipe something out, or destroy it. Get rid of it entirely."

"Oh."

"I'm not a person. She wants an automaton, a robot that will do whatever she wants and not complain."

"Do you remember what I told you the other day?" she said.

"You told me not to trust her." He picked up his coffee. "Why did you say that?"

Selena squirmed a little. Then she seemed to squirm without moving. "It's just something I saw in her. But one thing you might want to consider in what you've said, I think her self-esteem is even lower than yours, if you're willing to believe that. Based on what you've said, I think she is so insecure, but, unlike you, who turns it all inside, she does it the opposite way, and has to know she is in charge. If she wasn't, I bet you, I bet if she lost her control, even for just a few minutes, you would see somebody ten times worse than what I imagine you see when you look in the mirror every day."

Max didn't want to believe it, but it didn't matter if he wanted to or not. Something inside him told him that was exactly how it was. Again, simple math. Add up all she had done, and while he felt himself to be a zero, he also knew, deep down, that Camille likely went just slightly down into the negative. The realization he'd had not long ago: she needed him more than he needed her. The rattlesnake incident had been a good example.

Then it came without thinking. He said, "I want out," and became aware that his skull had a heartbeat. It was not very pleasant, but there was a mental heartbeat thumping in his head.

The old lady refilled their coffee, then went away without a word.

"Well," Selena said, "that's a start." She paused, then said, "You said stillborn daughter?"

Max gave her the rundown. He was a bit surprised at how easy it was to talk to this woman. She was the first person he'd felt comfortable around since he'd been in Portland. Never being one to open up too much in the first place, an introvert by nature, it was interesting at how quickly his guard had dropped, and how he could just be himself, both the good and the bad. He tried not to question it, but this knowledge remained in the back of his mind.

"What about you?" he said.

"What about me?"

"What about you and getting out of here?"

"I will be soon," she said. "I've been here much too long. Never wanted to be here in the first place. I'm going to get out, and I'm going to get out soon." Another pause. She drank some of her coffee, then looked him in the eye. "You should come with me."

"You kidding?"

"Why would I kid about that?"

"Because it's ludicrous."

"I have over ten thousand dollars saved," she told him. "I know that's not a lot of money, but it's more than enough to get out of this *bola de mierda*." She paused again, and seemed to put on a sweater of self-consciousness. "I do think you should come with me."

"Why?"

"Because I think you'll die here, if you don't get out soon."

"That's dramatic."

"What part of this breakfast *hasn't* been dramatic?"

He couldn't argue that. He drank his coffee, even though he didn't really want it. A part of him wanted to get up and leave. A sense of wasting time was sewing into his nerves.

Instead he said, "How well do you know Alejandro and those guys?"

The question seemed to throw her for a loop. "Why?"

"I'm just curious."

She squirmed again without moving.

"Armando seems to be missing," she said.

"Which one is Armando?"

"The little one that hangs out with them. The one who was grabbing me that night."

Fear replaced the waste-of-time feeling. It wove through his nervous system and punctured his bones, lacing deep into his marrow.

"You sure he's missing?"

She lifted her shoulders, dropped them. "No one has seen him in a couple days, and his car has been parked at the bar since…" She shifted. Her eyes narrowed. "Since the night he, how do you say it, man-handled me." She looked at him. There was a speck of scrutiny in her eyes. It was a tiny speck, but it was there. Her corneas became question marks, then shifted back to corneas and she shook her head. "I don't know them, other than from the bar. Why?"

"They just seem to enjoy giving me a hard time. Wondering if there's something you knew that I didn't."

"*Borrachos*. They are just drunk assholes. They drink so much I think it has damaged their brains."

"Seems like they'd singled me out, is all."

"If that is true, it is only because you are new to town. But don't you see? It is just all the more reason for you to get out of here."

"That makes it sound like I should just be running away."

"You make it sound like every card in the deck is stacked against you, and if that's really true, then the only way to win a hand is to break the rules."

"By running away?"

She shook her head. "By breaking the rules, whatever that might mean to you."

"Seems like you really want me out of here."

"I just want you out of what I can see is killing you, that is all." She looked at the old lady again, made a check mark in the air. "And you said it yourself," she went on. "You want out."

"I just wish it was that simple."

"It is."

"No, it isn't."

"It is. You're just afraid."

That struck a chord inside him. A deep, sustained, booming chord. The bass of it vibrated and rattled him into his childhood bedroom, where he sat on the floor, clutching his stomach, door locked, tears in his eyes and running down his face. He was afraid to unlock the door. He was afraid to go outside. Afraid of going out, but also afraid to stay locked up in the cell he had constructed for himself. Damned if you do, damned if you don't.

"Okay," he said. "What if I am afraid?"

"Then maybe you should do something about it. I've offered to help you. I assume with you not working and your wife working at the diner, you do not have a lot of money."

"You assume correctly."

"We could go somewhere that has life. Somewhere that has more than two streets. Somewhere with more than three restaurants, and maybe has a movie theater, or a gym. Somewhere

where, even if there is loneliness, at least it isn't so empty."

"And what about us?"

Her brow furrowed. "What do you mean?"

"I mean, what would you and I be doing?"

"Oh, you mean, like, are we now married?"

"Not quite how I would put it, but yeah."

The old lady dropped the check on the table and went away. Selena insisted on paying.

"I guess I didn't really think about that too much."

"Have you ever been married?"

She shook her head.

"Because the fact remains, even though it's its own ball of shit, I *am* married."

"Yes, I know. Like I said, I did not really think about that. Not with you and me. I know you are married. But forgive me if I come off like a *pinche puta*, but I sense it is your wife who is killing you most of all."

Max shrugged. There was little else to do. She was right and he knew it. He'd known it for a long time.

He inched back his chair. "I should probably get going," he said, and rose. "Thank you for breakfast."

"What are you going to do?"

That was a good question. A million thoughts raced around at once. He didn't *know* what to do. Maybe her offer was really worth considering. A ticket out of this place. Maybe a chance to start over, to pick up just a couple of pieces but mostly start from scratch. That's what he'd been wanting.

That's what he'd been wanting more than anything else. There was very little of his life that he wanted to retain. But the old adage crossed his mind: *If it sounds too good to be true, it probably is.*

"Why me?" he asked.

"What do you mean, why you?"

"I mean, why on earth would you wanna help me, of all people?"

Still sitting down, she finished her coffee. "Honestly?"

"Yeah, honestly."

"Because you're different. I can tell inside you are a real person. And you are just about the only person since I've lived here in this shit-ball who has treated me like an actual human being." She stood up. "I'm pretty sure you know what I mean by that." She took the check to the old man, who set down his crossword and rang them up.

Outside, parked side by side, they stood at their respective vehicles. The sun glared with scorching scrutiny, and the air had a dust flavor to it.

"Armando," she said.

"What?"

"Armando. The little man. You know something, don't you?"

Max felt a lump swell in his throat. He took a very deep breath, through his nose. Then he opened his mouth but all that came out was air. He cleared his throat, then managed to say, "What would I know, and why would I know it?"

A flock of birds passed by overhead.

Selena sighed. "Let me see your phone."

"Huh?"

"Your phone. Your cell phone. Let me see it." She held out her hand.

The tremors in his hands increased. His tension cranked up a notch. Icicles brushed his neck and melted down his back as he remembered Wayne in the parking lot last night. Wayne in his serpentine stance, telling Max to give him his phone.

But unlike last night, Max found himself reaching into his pocket. He took out the phone and slowly passed it over.

"Why do you want my phone?"

She flipped it open, pressed buttons, then pressed some more. The phone made soft beeping sounds. After a minute she flipped it closed and passed it back.

"Now you have my number," she said. "Call me, and then I'll have yours."

Reluctant at first, Max opened his phone. He scrolled through the numbers in his phonebook and found Selena Delgado. He called. Her phone rang—a digital rendition of "Für Elise." She didn't answer. Just smiled. He hung up.

"Now we are connected," she said.

"You working today?"

"No. My day off."

It was going on noon. The sun had not quite hit its peak.

"You asked me about Armando," he said. "So I'll ask you. My house. The Ortiz place. Do you know anything about it?"

"What do you mean?"

"I mean, what do you know about it?"

She looked at the sky, then at the ground. "Only what I've heard from drunks in the bar."

"And what would that be?"

She shuffled her feet, pluming up dust. "The story about Joe's dog. The rest stupid things. *Loco* things. Campfire stories, from what I can tell."

"But you know about what happened there."

"The murder? Yes, I know that a murder happened there. I've heard many different versions. Drunks are not usually the most reliable. Are you being afraid of the dark?" There was no humor on her face or in her tone.

"Maybe a little," he said.

There was a strange pause, as though timekeepers of eternity chose to dine in the moment.

Max took out a cigarette, lit it. It was better than the previous one but still unappealing. He dropped it and crushed it into the ground.

There was a heaviness in his throat. He tried to swallow it. Then he opened his mouth to speak but nothing came out. He tried again and the same thing happened. When it happened a third time, he checked it, as he realized that he was trying to tell her something he didn't want to tell her.

"What are you thinking?"

"Nothing," he said. But even as he said it, a cyclone of desperation roared inside him. He wanted to tell her, *Yes, take me away from all of this. Let's just get in your car and go. I don't care where, so long as it's far away from Sueño Roto and Ivan and Wayne and Alejandro and Alton. So long as it's far away from Armando and what happened that night. So long as it's far away from Camille. Especially far away from Camille. I'll go anywhere as long as it's far away from all this crap.*

"You appear to work overtime when you think about nothing."

He had no words for her, only his thoughts, and his thoughts wouldn't translate. They wouldn't manifest into actual words. Accents in the mind that were not on the tongue. Just the idea of going back to the house, or going to the diner, or to Shiloh's or the grocery store, the very thought of any of these things made him want to scream and flail and throw a tantrum, smash things, destroy anything and everything he could. Everything except for Granger and Selena, whose eyes he looked directly into.

"Sometimes my brain is like a swarm of flies," he said. "Buzzing and buzzing but not accomplishing much."

She laughed, but it wasn't a funny laugh. There was no humor in it. It dripped with discomfort, and oozed with related understanding. "*Trastorno mental*," she said. "Too much stress. I think it calls up extra voices to talk in your head."

"Maybe."

"Sometimes I hear random voices," she told him. "I know they are in my head. Not like a thought, but actual voices. It seems to happen out of nowhere, but I've noticed they only come about when the stress is so much that I'm afraid I'll explode."

"So, what, you think running away helps?"

"No. I don't think the voices go away just because you try to run away. But your environment can play a big role, I think. It can stir the voices, or it can adjust their volume." She waved her hand flippantly at the desert. "I think this place is stirring your voices. It stirs mine. Like I said, I've been just as bad off other places, but I was happier. I'm ready to get out of here and turn down the volume, and I think you need to do the same thing, that's all."

She'd opened a door. She was giving him a chance, an opportunity to get out. She was offering to help him. And he needed help. The trick of it was, Max was not used to help. Not genuine help. He didn't honestly know what actual help felt like, and so he didn't know for sure whether he could trust it or not. Max had always been trusting, but not in the right ways. Too much trust and too many burns. The blood in the panties of a pregnant woman, for example. It's nothing, he'd been told, and for some reason — for some naïve, inexplicable reason — he'd trusted that. Then the next thing he knew, Kimberly was dead....

This girl standing before him wanted to help. And he wanted to trust her. She seemed genuine, more than genuine, but that word was a badly blurred line. It was a word smudged and streaked with every conceivable shade of gray. There was no definition in a word like that.

"Maybe I'll call you later," he said.

She looked at him a moment, then nodded. "Do that. I'm going to go home and pack."

"You're really ready to leave, aren't you?"

"I guess so. Yes. I've made up my mind."

"Seems kind of sudden," he said. "I mean, since I've known you."

She unlocked her car. "There's nothing sudden about it, Max. I can wait a short while, but you really should call me. Think. Please. Think hard, think fast. But think. Then call me." She got into her car, closed the door and started the engine. A moment later she was driving away.

Max looked up at the sky, saw a flock of birds. Were these different birds, or the same flock coming round and round?

They're different, he told himself. You're the one going round and round. You're the one who rides the carousel, then gets off on the inside where nothing moves. You're mad at being stationary. So you get on the ride again, go around a few times and see the same old stuff. Then again you get off in the middle, and the same old stuff circles round and round but you still haven't gotten anywhere. You're still just standing there. Stationary. You ought to know by now that the carousel isn't gonna take you anywhere other than where you've already been.

He unlocked the Camry.

"So basically," he said, "I've been on a road to nowhere."

He got behind the wheel, slid the key into the ignition, turned it. A brief metal on metal scraping sound, then the engine came to life. He reversed out of his parking space. Dirt crunched under the tires. He pulled onto the road, headed for Main

Street. He hardly touched the accelerator. The car moved forward, slow but sure, like a turtle on wheels. The road ahead was deserted. It was a little over a mile to the intersection. He listened to the rhythmic sound of the tires rolling on asphalt, and thought about what was waiting for him back in town.

A couple of zeros and a couple of negatives. And Granger. Sweet dog. Granger was the positive. Granger and Selena.

He tripped and caught himself in that thought. Granger and Selena. The thought was crystalline as it passed through his mind. It had the same equivalency as one plus one being two. But still, he questioned it. He told himself to screw his head on right, and to make sure his heart wasn't just being deceptive.

The road passed beneath him in slow motion. The sun spat sparkles on reflective surfaces. He depressed the accelerator and picked up speed, as though he was suddenly in a hurry to get nowhere.

He reached the red light of the intersection. He looked at the Amigo Mart and the Dairy Queen, at the building that used to be a video store. Then he looked at the Silver Moon. Camille was in there, doing what she did. Maintaining control. He knew the types of things going through her head. She was sick of it all. She was sick and tired of the garish decor that was the quintessence of the Silver Moon. She was sick and tired of the people. Mostly it was the same people, day in and day out, and the majority of them were simple-minded cretins with a limited scope of the world. A bunch of brain-dead turkeys who couldn't see the world beyond their noses, complaining about problems, mostly of their own making.

The light turned green. He turned onto Main Street. The idea of seeing his wife ever again brought about intense nausea. He knew that when next he saw her, she'd have her ways of putting him down, then more ways still to make him apologize for being who he was. She'd use her words to antagonize him and batter him down.

In some ways, they *were* a perfect match. She was so goddamn insecure that she needed someone to control, while he was so insecure it seemed he needed someone to control him. A big problem with being controlled so long, however, is when the submissive knows they're really somebody else, but they can't be who they are, and when they find themselves apologizing twenty-four hours a day, both for being who they are and for being who they aren't, it becomes a conundrum. A complete knuckle-fuckery. The kind of thing that sends a man to the top of a tower with a rifle.

The driveway was just up ahead.

"She's not home now," he said, then said without sound: You could get the few things you really want. Get Granger and a couple of other things, maybe the Mondrian. You could get it all together and while you do it call Selena. Tell her yes. Tell her let's go; let's get the hell out of here. Hell, you can even leave the car. Take Selena's car. Let Camille keep the fucking car. Let her keep everything, to hell with it, to hell with her. That's what you should do. Call Selena and just get the fuck out.

He turned into the driveway. He was almost to the house when he slammed on the brakes.

TWENTY-NINE

Shallow breaths came very fast as tears danced in the corners of his eyes. A charge of paraesthesia skittered his flesh. Intangible things crawled on and under his skin. He left the engine running but got out of the car as his heart punched his chest with boxer-like precision.

There were pieces all over the ground. Puzzle pieces that would never fit together. Red and black and smashed, with glittering hairs of gold. One leg was erect, pointing to the sky. The parts still connected cranked every which way, and with eyes protruding, tongue blood red and draping over teeth, Granger still seemed to smile. Parts of him were mashed flat and rammed into the ground. Must have been run over a dozen times. But still the dog had a smile for him.

The dismal air was silent. His tears poured freely now. Then Max's stomach felt as though it was rupturing. He turned away and dropped to his knees and threw up in a scatter of dry weeds.

He saw the best pancakes in town again. They burned like acid as they gushed through his throat. Then he made fists in the dirt, drew a deep breath, and screamed.

THIRTY

The front windows were broken. There was glass all over the floor, dishes and glasses and mugs smashed in the kitchen. Strewn through the living room were ripped-apart books. Mystery novels. Science fiction novels. Horror novels. All kinds of novels. All of them destroyed. All of them reduced to garbage. Same with the DVDs. They'd been popped from their cases and snapped, or thrown.

Yet the furniture was intact. The television hadn't been damaged or stolen. The entertainment center, the credenza, the armoire, whatever the fuck you wanted to call it, was unharmed. The couch didn't even look sat in.

Max wandered the bottom level in a daze. He was still crying, but the tears were distant now, almost absent-minded. Everything he had to hold on to, everything that kept him going, all of it was gone. Granger was gone. For the love of God, he should have taken the dog with him this morning, goddammit. It wouldn't have hurt to take the pooch with him.

But he hadn't. He'd left him behind. He'd abandoned him. Deserted him. He'd left him all alone in this godforsaken house, and because he didn't take him with, somebody had murdered him. Mutilated him. *Look at the end result of not taking him with you. You goddamn son of a bitch. It's your fault. You killed Granger.*

As he crossed over to the stairway he grabbed that thought by the throat. He wouldn't, he couldn't blame himself for what happened. What had happened had been completely out of his control. Most everything that had happened had been out of his control. Would've, should've, could've, it all added up to a big fat nothing, and the Blame Game wasn't gonna help anything at all.

He went upstairs, legs wobbly.

Clothes were strewn about in the bedroom. Everything in the closet had been pulled out, though it didn't look much different than normal. A thorough search showed him nothing was broken, and nothing appeared to be missing. He wiped his face. Out the window he could see Granger's remains in the driveway. Looking down at them, he remembered what Wayne had said outside the grocery store. *Do you think we don't know where you live, scrote? Everybody knows where you live, man.*

Still crying, though less than before, his tears were now tears of abject sadness, mixed with a smidgen of humiliation, and dabs of vulnerability.

There was no one here now; he was certain. This had all taken place while he was talking with Moses, or while he was dining at *El Tecolote* with Selena Delgado. He was currently all alone. His impulse was to flop onto the bed and bury his face in a pillow. To wrap himself up in blankets and try to hide from the world around him. To cry until the pillow and blankets were drenched.

Instead, he left the bedroom, walked a few steps and entered the guestroom. There he stopped dead in his tracks. The closet had been ransacked. There was junk all over the floor. This part he'd pretty much expected. What he hadn't expected was the sight on the bed. *Broadway Boogie Woogie*, the Mondrian print, lay face up on the mattress. Several holes had been punched into the print, all the same size. In the middle of the picture, punched through the small white rectangle that was the center of the painting, was a pink vibrator.

THIRTY-ONE

Max put one hand under the dog's head and lifted it. Granger's open eyes, now dull and lifeless, stared off into nothing. Max lifted up what he could of the animal. The leg that had been erect now dangled by skin and tendons like an entangled yo-yo. Instantly, Max's pants and shirt were ruined. He eased the carcass into the mouth of the large garbage bag he'd brought outside with him, twisted the bag shut and knotted it.

Never safe, he thought. As long as I'm here, I'll never be safe.

His imagination conjured thoughts of what might have happened had he been home when they came here. Ivan, Wayne, and others rushing into house, dragging Granger along with them. Or maybe it wasn't those guys. Maybe it was Alejandro and Alton. Or maybe it was all of them. Max envisioned being kicked in the face and going down, being clubbed with a stick. Being kicked. Being forced to watch them cut and tear at

Camille's clothes and then drive into her…

He slammed the mental door on that thought. He shook his head, coughed with sickness, then shook it again. With each shake, the ache in his brain intensified.

He walked slowly, over dirt and rock and brush. He wondered if there was any percentage in calling the sheriff's department. Based on today, they hadn't been much use last night. Here he was, just a guy trying to get along and keep out of the way of others, and so far he'd been smacked, threatened, harassed, chased. He'd had to deal with the dead body of a violent drunk. He'd questioned his sanity multiple times, and now his home was trashed, the things he loved destroyed, and now he was walking in the desert with his dead dog wrapped in a garbage bag.

Tears came again. Tears of defeat, but his legs kept moving. He passed the shack, kept walking, then up-sloped the hill. He stood at the top and looked down, blinked several times, then blinked some more.

A single chuckle escaped him, but that was all.

"Curiouser and curiouser," he said, not sure why.

He walked down the slope, the garbage bag gripped in his arms. He set the bag down on the stone-studded ground and closed his eyes. His mind became a thousand whirlpools, and every swirl had its own perplexing current. A shiver rippled up one side of his spine and then down the other.

Exhaustion. Stress. Imagination. Either nothing

had changed or nothing had ever happened. Which was it? He was afraid to open his eyes. He was afraid of the answer, whichever one it was, or that the answer might be c) Neither of the above. Where would that leave him?

But everything that had happened *had* happened. He had a good, vivid imagination, but it wasn't *that* good. This wasn't like those movies where it all turns out to be in the guy's head. The whole *It was all a dream* bullshit. He could feel the gentle weight of Granger's body at the tip of his foot.

He thought about Armando down there. Armando's corpse.

Maybe it wasn't state-certified, but it seemed that he was now building his own private cemetery.

Your wife's dildo was stabbed through your favorite painting.

Everything paused. All was still but far from peaceful. The whirlpools became electric shadows that spread into one another, and a cleanse of cool sweat purged from his pores.

His eyes opened and the sun was still bright, blasting the earth. And the opening was there, roughly four feet high, three feet wide. He stepped around the bag that contained his dog and stood at the hole. He crouched down, got on hands and knees, and looked inside.

Blackness. Almost opaque. But the weathered ladder rungs were there.

When was the last time the God of Articulation graced you with a visit?

Whispers. Closemouthed words. His thoughts, but not the thoughts he was thinking. At the moment all he was thinking was void. The hole. The black hole in which he could see something. In which he saw useless ladder rungs.

Camille is fucking her boss.

Tears filled his eyes again, streamed down his cheeks.

Camille is fucking Pete Parsons.

It was a susurrated utterance, information expressed in a soft voice that wasn't his own. Thoughts he wasn't thinking, a foreign voice, but one very much in his head. The timbre was different, light and dainty, bordering effeminate, and it was unsympathetic. It merely said what it said.

Dry, beaten boards attached haphazardly across a decrepit vertical beam. Armando was down there. The cross boards were useless. The hole was useless. Everything out here was useless now. The desert was exactly what it had always been. A wasteland.

Not his thoughts, not his words, though he knew them from somewhere:

The Almighty, who gave the dog to be companion of our pleasures and our toils, hath invested him with a nature noble and incapable of deceit.

Max got back to his feet. He stared down at the bag. Frenetic tension wound up again, the kinetic wiring of his nervous system kicking back into gear. Electric frenzy. Fatigue charged a stampede of anxiety through him.

There are mysteries which men can only guess at,

which age by age they may solve only in part.

He knew those words. They were Bram Stoker's words. Immortal words from the immortal classic, *Dracula*.

There had once been a dead cat in a gutter in Portland. No one had ever bothered to remove it. Max had walked by it almost daily. He saw the slow progress of the animal's decomposition, and the stench was something he'd never forgotten. He smelled that same odor now, though from where, he couldn't pinpoint. It was all around him. It was Granger, it was the hole, it was the sun and the sky and the earth.

...Mysteries which men can only guess at.

The tension wheel in his sternum cranked. He acted without thinking. If he allowed himself thought he would slip into freeze mode. He stepped to the garbage bag, grabbed hold of the knot he had tied, and lifted.

Granger. Lovable, well mannered, intelligent and charming. Patient and gentle, devoted dog, filled with nothing but unconditional love. Acquaintances only a few short days, yet stronger trust than Max had ever known. Granger, the golden ray of light that had come out of Sueño Roto, now dead, killed, mutilated, by the ignorant malice of malevolent sons of bitches. Dead, smashed, destroyed.

"You got a fucking dog? You got a dog and didn't check with me? You can't even take care of yourself, no way you can take care of a dog."

"Fuck you, Camille," he said to the desert, then put one foot in front of the other, climbed up the slope, and headed back toward the house, carrying the bag that held his dead dog.

He looked around the scorched wasteland as he walked. It was littered with rock and brush and trees, and the jagged slant of both near and distant hills. Above was a flock of birds, ominous black specks pendant against the sky. Then the sun draped a blanket of fire over him. It had been there the whole time; he'd only just become aware of it. He wanted to move faster and get out of the heat, but he kept a steady pace.

Never safe, he thought. As long as I'm here I'll never be safe.

He thought about Granger's smile as he walked through chaos and around to the front of the house, where his breathing grew steady.

He loaded the dog's carcass into the car.

THIRTY-TWO

The first thing he saw when he stepped inside was the hunting photo across the room. The dead deer, its head held up by two brave warriors, foreground littered with beer cans. Gene Autry sang "Be Honest with Me" on the stereo, as smoke rose and whirled through the ceiling fans.

His gaze shifted to the left and he saw Carl behind the counter, whose stare silently asked a million questions at once. Max gave him a nod, then stepped deeper into the bar.

Conversations dropped and the Singing Cowboy's wrangler style voice became an audible wash so full of echo and resonance that it merely became a disagreeable whisper. No feeling like an outlaw barging into a saloon this time, nothing like a rabbit encountering a pack of wolves, his eyes ticked off every person in the room, one by one.

Ivan was there.

Wayne and his silent buddy were there with

him.

Alejandro and Alton sat at a table only a few feet away. With them was Mike, the cable guy who'd been to his house. The man who had found Armando's keys. The keys to the car still parked outside.

No one was smiling. Nobody's eyes emitted a clue. No face gave off any signs of guilt, or remorse, nor did they display contrary pride, smugness, or humor — they were all what Max assumed his own face was. Expressionless.

About six feet away from the men, Max stopped before them, between their respective tables, the bulky garbage bag held in his arms.

Ivan poured himself a shot of rye, his liquor-red eyes never straying from Max and the bundle he held.

All eyes were on Max; and in turn, Max's eyes were on all of them. The unusual country music silence, along with the fog of cigarette smoke, became an almost palpable thing in and of itself. A tangible wailing, rushing sound, which shook the smoke and made the rising tendrils of it quiver.

Then, for a moment, nothing existed in Max's sight except for six men. For a moment they were all there was in the world.

He cleared his throat:

"I don't know which of you committed the atrocities at my house," he said. "But I *do* know that it was one of you — if not all of you."

The bar remained quiet. The resounding susurration of Gene Autry continued on the stereo.

Max moved his hands along and around the bag until his fingertips touched, then he slowly dug his fingernails into the plastic bag.

"But whether it was one of you, a few of you, or all of you — whoever it was, you forgot the thing you always want to make sure you get when you go out and have a good time. Especially like the good time you had at my house."

Fingers deep into the plastic now, he pulled his arms apart, ripping open the bag, and said, "You forgot to take a fucking souvenir."

Granger's mutilated corpse fell to the floor. The sound it made when it landed was a cross between a thud and a plop and a splash.

There were gasps. Unseen people gagged, made terrified appeals to a deity. Somewhere a woman screamed.

The six men stared down at the dog, brows furrowed, expressions otherwise unchanged.

Blood and meat and dirt continued to rain down from the bag. Fleshy fur drifted like dandelion florets. Little bits of bone bounced.

"The fuck is wrong with you?" Carl shouted from behind the counter.

Max ignored him. He looked at the men individually again, then took them in as a whole, hoping they'd be shaken by a show of confidence.

"So there you go," he said. "Enjoy. Goodbye, and hello, as always."

He turned and walked out of Shiloh's, just as Gene Autry finished his song.

THIRTY-THREE

It was almost four o'clock. Camille would be expecting him to pick her up. He wasn't going to.

After getting back home he'd talked with Selena, then gone upstairs and taken a quick shower. He'd put on clean clothes, leaving the stained and ruined ones on the bedroom floor. He'd filled an ancient black JanSport backpack with his laptop, toiletries, a couple of shirts, some socks, and underwear. That was it. As far as he was concerned, there wasn't anything else he wanted or needed. Anything he would have wanted to take with him had been destroyed. It was a miracle his laptop was still intact.

He'd decided not to tell Selena about Granger.

The plan was to leave the Camry and take Selena's car. They'd drive about five-or-so-hours to Flagstaff, spend the night in a motel, and then get the metal scraping and all the sputtering and coughing her Subaru was doing fixed up in the morning. From there they'd head north, up through Utah, then west across Idaho and into Oregon. They'd spend a few days in Portland, and then figure out if they wanted to stick together or go their separate ways.

He was gonna leave the house in the state it was in; a way of telling her "fuck you" while at the same time making her wonder just what had happened. Maybe—just maybe—it would cause her to worry, even if only a little.

He didn't even want the Camry. Fuck the Camry. Everything, he wanted to leave it all behind.

Camille would call. No question she would call before she ever even saw the house. She would call and wonder where the hell he was. She would leave a dozen voicemails before four-thirty. Max would need to turn off his phone. Her incessant calling might be enough, even at this point, to break him. Maybe not, probably not, almost certainly not, but maybe, and he didn't want to take that risk. If he didn't get out now, he was never gonna get out. But it was enough to scare him, though. Just the thought of hearing her on his voicemail twisted a knife in his chest and clenched his stomach.

It baffled him that he had found this inner strength, while at the same time he was still as weak as a kitten. Everything that had happened, everything that had taken place since moving to Sueño Roto, and his overall opinion of himself, was still that of a pussy-whipped asshole.

And so you're running away, he thought. Well, you've tried. You've done what you've done, and all the numbers have added up to pretty much nothing. So now it's time to run. Seems you've been running your whole life but you've never really run. Kind of absurd, don't you think? But then again, everything is absurd, isn't it? Everything you've ever experienced has been absurd. But there's a simple adage you should really remember: Nobody runs forever.

Selena knew where the Ortiz place was. Everybody knew. She'd told him to give her an hour, and that was about a half-hour ago. He set the backpack by the front door and took out his cell phone. He was going to turn it off but then decided to wait until Selena showed up, in case something happened and she needed to call him. He put it back in his pocket...

Then he took it out again. There'd been a thought in his mind that he hadn't been acknowledging, but the card had just flipped over and shown its face, and a ball of thunder bounced around inside him, an internal lightning set him ablaze.

He called Frank Albertson.

It rang three times.

"Hello?"

"Frank?"

"Hi, Max."

"Tell me about Ivan."

A crackling phone-connection pause.

Then Frank sighed. "I told you before, Max..."

"And you were lying," Max told him. "I know you were lying. You wanna know how I know?"

"Jesus, what the fuck, Max?"

"Because the entire house is destroyed."

There was a sigh and nothing more. Seemed Frank was waiting for him to continue.

"My stuff. Camille's stuff. Someone broke in and just fucking destroyed everything. We got a dog and they fucking killed the dog, goddammit. We're both in danger, so quit the bullshit lying and tell me what's up."

"Sorry, Max," Frank said. "I don't know what you're talking about."

"You sure you wanna fucking do that, Frank?"

"Now you listen to me, Max—"

"How about you shut the fuck up, Frank? Unless you're gonna be honest, just shut the fuck up."

"I gave you guys a home."

"I said shut the fuck up!"

Another sighing silence, this one fused with melancholic strain.

"Yeah," Max said. "Yeah, you gave us a home. But you stepped in shit here, didn't you? Yes, you did. You stepped in a big mound of shit, and you didn't even clean off your goddamn shoes. You just took them off and left them here. Did you mean to give me your shit-covered shoes, Frank?"

"Listen, you little bitch—!"

"*Did* you *mean* to give me your *shit-covered shoes*, Frank?"

"You're a prick, Max. A real fucking little prick."

"So you don't care that your niece is in trouble?"

"She's not in trouble."

"She's not? You really believe that?"

"I really believe that, Max. She's not in trouble, and neither are you." Frank coughed, then, "Listen, Max. Will you listen now? Are you willing to listen?" His tone was condescending and beyond demeaning. "I know you're having a rough time there. You and Camille both, I'm sure. But don't call me and cuss me out with your goddamn NPD just because you're—"

"My what?"

"—having a rough time of things."

"My what?"

"What do you mean, your what?"

"What the hell is NPD?"

"You know what it is, Max. Just calm down and think about it for a minute."

"All I've been doing is thinking." He narrowed his eyes at the phone. "What's Camille been telling you?"

"Nothing I couldn't have figured out on my own eventually, Max, had we ever had the chance to spend more time together."

"And what's that? What's she said? What's NPD? What the *fuck* has she told you?"

"It's not like it's anything new, Max." His voice was calmer now, but still patronizing. "I don't know. Maybe you and I should've talked about it ourselves, just you and me. Maybe I have some of it wrong. Crap. Forget I said anything, but trust me when I say no one's out to get you, and certainly no one's after you because of me."

"One more time, Frank. *What* the *fuck* is NPD?"

"Shit," Frank said. "If you really need me to

tell you, Max, Narcissistic Personality Disorder. I know it's never officially been diagnosed, but traits of it are there for sure... Or maybe you're just delusional."

"Narci-whah the what?"

"Camille confirmed my assumptions sometime back, that you belittle and discourage her and others."

Max froze, his tongue a dead fish sitting in his mouth. His nerves crackled electric. Slow but hard, the tension wheel in his sternum cranked even tighter.

"I'm sorry if that sounds harsh, Max, but maybe you simply needed to hear it that way. Straight from the horse, as it were, you know? There haven't been on any medications that have worked for you, and..."

Max closed his phone as a whole new level of disquiet pumped from his heart, spread through his veins as the back of his mouth began choking. A heavy pulse beat in his brain as the disquiet made his insides cold.

Where in the world had *that* come from? And how long had Camille been telling people this, this—falsity? Belittling and discouraging her and others? The harmful ways he validated his self-worth? Bullshit. A pronoun exchange while Camille simultaneously chatted and looked into a mirror. *That's* what it was. Narcissistic Personality Disorder. Max felt himself morphing into one part rage and two parts hysteria.

Then one loud laugh escaped him. Probably the loudest laugh he'd ever projected in his entire life. It echoed throughout the house.

"Fuck her," he said, and took the car keys from his pocket, looked at them. There was absolutely no way in hell that the bitch deserved his car. Fuck her. Fuck her, fuck her, fuck her.

He stuffed the keys back into his pocket.

When Selena got here he would tell her about the change of plans, that they were going to C.W. McCall it to Oregon. Roll a truckin' convoy 'cross the USA — or at least up to Portland. His car was in much better shape than hers was, anyway, even with the front of it smashed up. He could follow her, make sure nothing happened on the way. And, if once in Portland, they decided to go in separate directions, nobody would wind up being left behind, screwed, without a car.

He looked around at all the chaos again. So many things broken. Life preservers destroyed, passions annihilated, dreams... broken.

The idea that he'd actually ever planned on the leaving the car for Camille at all now seemed pretty high up on the dumbest choices he'd made since arriving in Sueño Roto.

In give or take twenty minutes, he would be on the road, following Selena, on his way out of godforsaken Sueño Roto. On his escape route from Alton and Alejandro, from Ivan and Wayne, on his escape from where he was battered and belittled and nobody cared, and from where people killed innocent dogs. He'd be heading away from the dead man he'd dumped into the pit — the crazy drunk man who'd been ready to kill him — and, most importantly, finally on his escape from Camille.

He looked out through one of the broken windows. The sun thwacked its hot brightness upon everything. The air was dust dry and imploring him to leave Sueño Roto right away, to get out of the murderous house of Ortiz, where haunting sounds enjoyed tormenting him at night, where rattlesnakes made themselves comfy on the couch.

Pushing that all aside, he thought about "Uncle" Frank Albertson, the officious asshole, ready, willing, able, and *wanting* to lie, even with the knowledge that his niece could be in danger as a result of things he did — or didn't do, as the case may be. Clearly something had happened while the man lived here, and whether or not he believed that Max and Camille were in danger, it didn't change the facts, even if the facts were unspoken. There was proof that there were facts — Max had experienced their backlash first-hand — whether the man admitted to them or not. But not talking about them didn't erase them. Sticking your head in the sand or covering yourself in blankets didn't simply make all of the problems go away. It only made you ignorant to your own knowledge, and that could very well be the worst ignorance there was in the world.

Max wanted to laugh again but couldn't. It was all ridiculous, but it wasn't funny. Nothing was funny. Not a single moment of anything that had happened over the course of — what? — only a few days; none of it was funny. Most of it was nauseating.

He went back upstairs, hardly moving by himself, it seemed, hardly able, like a baby only recently learning to walk, and trying out steps for the first time, holding onto the side rail, legs quivering. At the top he turned and looked back down. His mind's eye turned the stairs into a deep black pit where Armando's body lay, wrapped in a blue sleeping bag with a knife in his throat. The fact that the little fucker was down there now almost seemed inconsequential. Except there *were* consequences. If not the law, then at least Alejandro and Alton and their cable guy buddy were consequences.

A humorless cackle popped out of him. He turned away and went into the guestroom, where the Mondrian still sat with holes punched in it, sat with the pink vibrator stabbed through its middle. Impossible, but Max could almost believe it was something Camille would do.

He went into the bedroom and looked around, solely to make sure there wasn't anything else he wanted to take with him. Having both cars meant there would be more room for stuff, but there was nothing he saw that he felt any need to take. One of the biggest appeals about this whole thing, about having just a backpack with a few essential items, was the notion of completely starting from scratch. More than anything, that's what he wanted out of this escapade. To strip everything down to complete and utter basics, and start all over again.

He crossed into the bathroom and took a leak, then went back downstairs and waited for Selena.

A few minutes later he heard tires crunching on dirt.

He got up, hefted his backpack over one shoulder then opened the door.

The car that pulled up wasn't Selena's Subaru.

THIRTY-FOUR

Max slammed the door and bolted it, spun and pressed his back against it. His breathing quickened to fast, shallow gasps, as his eyes helplessly scanned the trashed house, took in all the litter, all the bits and pieces of his life that had been destroyed, while clear sound in his left ear reminded him that the windows were broken, and locking the door had been pointless.

He let the backpack slip from his shoulder as he heard tires crunching, other cars pulling up in the driveway.

Squeezing his eyes shut, a single tear slid from one of them. Back at Shiloh's, plopping Granger's corpse on the floor for all to see, he'd hoped they'd be shaken by a show of confidence from him. Based on the number of cars now parked outside—three, maybe four—apparently all he'd shaken in them was an animalistic impulse, a want to expedite something Max had sensed to be an inevitable occurrence.

Outside he'd seen the gold Grand Marquis with the heavily tinted windows. In Max's mind that meant no other than Ivan, and there was no doubt that the second car, though he hadn't seen it, was an army green Bronco. Wayne. The third car, he was willing to bet, was Alejandro's Chrysler. And if there was indeed a fourth car, it made no difference whose it was, because the question in his mind had been answered. Whether true or not before, the answer to his question as to whom had been revealed. Now, anyway, it was all of them.

In full-blown panic, his mind scrolled through a list of items in the house. Things he might be able to use as weapons. They didn't own a gun. That was one thing Max and Camille had actually agreed on. No guns. The mental scroll continued to unravel, most everything scrawled upon it in his own poor penmanship, useless.

The only thing worth a damn would maybe be some of the knives in the kitchen, which was just off to his right. Leaving the pointless backpack where it lay, Max rushed into the kitchen, pulled open the proper drawer, and removed the eight-inch chef's knife. It felt light in his hand, insubstantial and timorous, about as useful as a trap door in a lifeboat.

But there was nothing else. Not a single damned thing, and there wasn't time to go on a scavenger hunt. As he held the knife, his mind flashed him an image of Armando's hand holding the butterfly knife in the night light, hard to tell exactly what movements were being made. The image jumbled and became the image of Armando on the ground, moon winking off the blade lodged in his throat. Car doors opened and closed outside and the kitchen reappeared, along with the chef's knife in his hand.

No time or desire to test the blade's sharpness, no time to search for something better, he moved swiftly from the kitchen to the foyer and then into the living room. The voices outside were unintelligible. Other than that some were English and some were Spanish, nothing else could be deciphered.

Max himself remained voiceless. The knife wobbled in his quivering hand and his knuckles whitened from the tight grip on it. Any second they'd be popping up in those glassless windows across the way. At that point there would be nowhere to run, if it wasn't already too late.

If he went upstairs he'd be hidden briefly, safe for maybe five minutes, tops. But he would also be boxed in; a rabbit cornered by wolves. The best option was the back door, out onto the patio. Quick as he could, he went to the door, opened it, slid outside, and closed it as quietly as possible.

Moving away from the glass door and the large windowpanes, some but not all of them cracked and smashed, he leaned against the stone and stucco wall. His first impulse was to run, but he stopped, and with a shuddering breath he pulled out his cell phone, already knowing how unreliable Southwest Mobile was. The only cellular service with good coverage in Sueño Roto—yeah, it had helped so damn much last night.

He called Selena.

She answered on the second ring.

"Hi, Max. Sorry I'm running a little late. I was just about to call —"

"Don't come to the house, Selena. You hear me? Do *not* come to the house."

"What's going on?"

"Call the police, please, call the police. But do *not* come here. Don't come here, under any circumstances, unless I call you. Understand?"

A brief moment of tense silence in the phone, while on the other side of the house the voices got louder.

Then, "What's going on, Max? What's happening?"

"…They're gonna kill me."

"What?"

"Just call the police, and don't come here, no matter what, unless I call you."

He snapped the phone closed, set it to silent and stuffed it back into his pocket as a single thought ran consistently through his mind, over and over again like a skipping record: *I'm fucked.*

Looking at the patio, at the desert landscape, the near and distant mountains, it seemed there was nowhere to run. There were trees nearby, aspen, ponderosa pine, piñon and juniper, many good for hiding behind, but these men, at least a couple of them, he knew, were hunters. These men, at least some but probably all, would be armed with much better than a hand-me-down kitchen knife…

And at least a couple of these men, right now, were likely making their way around the outside of the house. Any second he might come face to face with one of them — maybe more than one.

He looked back out to the desert, crouched, then ran, veering to his left, somehow thinking that keeping low would help him to go undetected.

If he made it to a safe spot, he'd call 911 himself, if indeed reception remained with his phone. If he made it to a safe spot and his phone still had reception, he also had no doubt there would be at least one voicemail from Camille.

He traipsed over a scatter of rocks, nearly lost his balance but kept it and continued.

There were voices behind him, but based on their volume through the crunching of his footsteps, they hadn't yet spotted him. He *hoped* they hadn't spotted him. Likely they'd search the house first, but if his figuring was correct, there were at least six of them, and the size of the house did not require six people to search for one man. At least a couple would go immediately around the house, and the large windows in the living room gave a nice view to anyone who happened to be inside.

Six against one. Six strong against one weak. And it was still daylight. There would still be daylight for at least a couple of hours. Heat waves still shimmered and rose from the desert floor. The whole earth brimmed sunshine.

Topping a small rise, Max crouched in the shade of a juniper tree and scanned the landscape around the house. He hadn't run more than maybe two hundred yards, and now he sucked air as he watched a couple of men wander around on the back patio. The wavering heat diluted detail. Having just seen these men only a short while ago, he couldn't recall what any of them was wearing. One of the men now, he saw, held a rifle. The other, if armed, wasn't so obvious about it.

Max remained as still as he could. Just because his vision was blurred, that didn't mean theirs was. He hoped the hard sun made the tree's shadow impenetrable. One jilt, one slip up and he might be seen, and while Max had spent a fair amount of time out here since they'd first arrived, he didn't know the area to save his life.

Funny thought, that.

Slowly, he moved backwards, out from the shade of the juniper and back into the sunlight. He took a few cautious steps, keeping his eyes on the patio, then tucked himself behind a large jagged rock, sat down with his back against it and gnashed his teeth.

Why had he veered left? What little of the area he *did* know was the other way, where the mineshaft was. But running to his right in that moment would have caused him to run straight past the living room's wall of windows, as well as past the driveway, and the likelihood of him being spotted and captured, or simply gunned down, would have been without question. Also, even if he'd managed to succeed getting past that way, other than the mineshaft and a minimal circumference around it, that direction was just as foreign to him as where he was now.

He looked up at the sky. It was cloudless and blue with faint streaks of gold smeared through it. Flecks of brightness darted into everything. Max set down the knife and reached for his phone, wondering if he was far enough away to talk without being heard by anyone at the house.

Flipping the phone open, he saw it had a signal, though already it wasn't as strong as it had been. He also saw the little icon in the corner that indicated he had a voicemail. Camille, no doubt, wanting to know just where the hell he was. The sun glinted off the screen and pierced his eyes. He snapped the phone shut and stuffed it back into his pocket as he heard voices, clearly closer than the patio.

The search team. Or part of the search team.

Slowly, he rolled up and over, onto his knees, and chanced a look over the top of the rock.

They were maybe thirty or forty feet away. Alton, wearing a red baseball cap and a white T-shirt and jeans, and Mike, the cable guy, jeans, T-shirt and a hat as well. Neither of them appeared armed, but the old adage *Looks can be deceiving* etched deep into his mind and it took him a moment to realize he was holding his breath.

Keeping his eyes on them, his hand moved along the ground until he found the handle of the knife at his side.

The men were heading across, from right to left. Max lowered himself back behind the rock, got off his knees and into a crouch, knife gripped tight in his left hand, and listened. Their footsteps came to him in soft crunches, though no matter how hard he strained his ears to home in on them, he couldn't tell if they were advancing toward him or receding away.

Right to left. Hopefully they weren't veering left as well.

The mineshaft flashed through his mind, but it made no difference if they found it or not — at least that's what he told himself. It certainly made no difference this very second.

Max closed his eyes and focused on his breathing, tried to keep his tremors under control. The sun scorched his back; his throat scratched with every dry swallow. He kept listening to the footsteps. In his mind it was as though they were walking in place. At the moment, neither man was talking.

Off to his right came a sudden, hard crash, the sound slightly hollowed by distance. Something in the house was just destroyed. Something bigger than dishes or books. The television, maybe, possibly the armoire, credenza... the fucking entertainment center.

Max found himself fearfully turning away from the sound, and as he did he suddenly became aware of how close the footsteps had gotten. The men *had* been veering left, or they'd caught sight of him and cut a sharp left. Though he presently couldn't see them, it was obvious they were pretty much within spitting distance.

He switched the knife from his left hand to his right, silently praying to someone or something he'd never believed in. He didn't want to kill anybody. He didn't even want to hurt anybody, or at least he was trying to convince himself of this. Beneath all of the fear and panic, the despair and tension, there was a clear, well-defined, underlying anger.

More than anger—rage. Rage at these men, at what had happened to Granger, what had happened to the house, to his stuff, to his life. Rage at all that had happened to him, what had happened and was still happening. Rage at his parents, at his brother, at the world in general, and at his wife, so much rage at his wife, at all of it, everything. But the one that trumped it all, the thing that really capped it off, that caused the rage to detonate thunder throughout him with maniacally rabid madness upon madness, was the rage that he carried for himself.

Rage for being an inadequate human being. For his timidity, for being a pussy, a namby-pamby, for letting others push him around, for allowing the world to control him, both as a whole and on a one-on-one basis. For being unable to speak up, to stand up for himself. For being so afraid, goddammit! So fucking afraid of everything!

There is no living thing that is not afraid when it faces danger, the Great Oz had said to the Cowardly Lion. Max had always focused on that little snippet from L. Frank Baum, disregarding or not remembering the very next line that followed, which came to him now, as though the Great and Powerful Oz was shouting in his ear: *The true courage is in facing danger when you are afraid*.

He remembered the rattlesnake. The unblinking eyes, the flickering tongue, the malevolently static-like noise of its rattle… How his arm had become like a rattlesnake, striking faster than the human eye could follow, snatching Armando's keys.

It had been the fear of the snake. Fear and fear alone. But he'd stood up to the poisonous viper, stood up to it in spite of his fear — and in doing so, something inside him had transformed. And it hadn't been a temporary transformation, even if at one point it had seemed that way. Something inside him had shifted. A rock had turned over and released an unnamable something, and now that something was back again, slithering through his blood and hissing in his heart.

Pathetic, inadequate Max Pendleton was just as dangerous, just as deadly as all of the things in the world that he feared.

Remaining crouched where he was, knife gripped firmly, he trained his ears on the two sets of footsteps, which startled him by abruptly coming to a stop.

Max's heart thumped. His body tried to jackknife out of its crouch. Neither man was in sight, but they were standing right there, just to his right and behind him.

What were the chances that they could see him while he couldn't see them? Pretty good, he surmised. Perhaps just a bit of shadow, the tip of a shoe, the top of his head might be standing out just over or beyond the rock. That's all it would take. In this very moment they might be silently scheming.

The quiet became absolute but electric. Max hastily went over his options: pop up and surprise them, hope his rage and the eight-inch knife were enough to... he didn't know — or wait, and let them surprise him and do things he didn't want to think about.

He stiffened as he heard slight movement in the parched underbrush.

Anything can go to hell if you wait long enough.

Then, "So, what'd you think?" It was Mike's voice that said this.

"Fuck if I know. You wanna search around here? I'll go on up a ways and see what's what."

"All right."

One set of footsteps began to retreat, but unless Mike stood right where he was for a while, or went looking in a different spot and spent some time there, the odds would still be two against one. If Max was spotted, or tried something now, it would take no time flat for Alton to return. Again, Max found himself in a silent, cryptic prayer.

Possibly a stray cloud, or a slight shift of the sun, the light turned the earth every color from crimson to black at once, blinding bright gold still stabbing at everything.

Max heard the click of a lighter, then a long sigh, and smelled the aroma of cigarette smoke. It felt as though twenty minutes had passed, but likely it hadn't even been twenty seconds since Alton and Mike's brief conversation. Alton's footsteps, however, had faded off into nothing.

A ruse, or was he really already that far away?

Portland felt like a lost dream now.

THIRTY-FIVE

Max stayed out of sight behind the rock, breathing occasional whiffs of smoke that puffed by him. The two of them were so close to each other, it was almost comical. Max's feet were starting to fall asleep as a result of his crouching stance, tingling with forthcoming numbness. If they completely fell asleep, Max would be that much more useless. He was going to have to move, at least figure out how to get his feet working properly. He did his best to slowly curl and uncurl his toes, as all the while Mike stood no more than six or seven feet away, smoking his cigarette.

Looking straight ahead, something new presented itself. Max hadn't seen it before, or had been too occupied with other things to comprehend the sight of it; and it was so close, too. It was bound to be the first place Mike inspected, if he ever finished his smoke break.

Piñon trees stood like a scattering of pinball

bumpers, while rocks in varying sizes stood unmoving and emotionless in the dirt and underbrush. Through it all, no more than twenty feet away from where he crouched, he saw the edge of a ravine. Crouched where he was, knees starting to ache, worried about being attacked within the blink of an eye, Max couldn't tell how deep it was—only that it was there. His eyes traced over the precipice, sketched it in pencil then went over it in ink.

Mike exhaled a final puff of smoke, then there were grinding crunches; Mike crushing the cigarette with his foot, no doubt.

Max crouched lower, his feet and knees protesting, as the nearby feet began moving again.

Not just the knuckles, Max's entire right hand had essentially gone white from gripping the handle of the kitchen knife, as the lone procession of a single shadow tangled itself with his body, then passed over it, and Max saw the back left side of Mike, followed by Mike's entire backside. The man hadn't bothered to glance to his left. A fifty-to-one chance, but the guy hadn't seen him.

Slowly uncrouching and standing upright, his knees immediately thanking him as the tingling in his feet at first intensified, then gradually settled as blood seeped back into them, Max drew a slow, deep breath, still wriggling his toes, and let up on the tight grip he had on the knife's handle, allowing circulation back into his hand as well.

He looked briefly over his shoulder, but didn't see Alton anywhere.

Mike stood no more than five feet away, his

back to Max. In the belt at his back was a pistol. Max knew little about guns, had never fired one in his life, but he knew the difference between an automatic and a revolver, and it was clearly an automatic tucked at the small of Mike's back.

Max forced depth and slowness into his breaths. He glanced at the ground as he lifted his foot and moved it forward. Gentle as he could, he placed his foot down. He knew that most animals will give some kind of warning if someone is getting too close for their comfort. Grunts, moving its weight from one foot to the other, often making full or half circles in a small area. Max had to currently view Mike as something other than human, because he knew that all of the men had taken on an animalistic persona; had all, on one level or another, tapped into their most primitive impulses. Yet animals, like people, have personalities. What Max had to do was not speak to him—not speak unless he absolutely had to, and by no means allow his enemy to speak. Speaking to him would mean he still thought of the man as a fellow human being, and he couldn't do that. Not if he wanted to live, if he wanted any chance of survival. Words would be too intimate. Words would dissolve any fight that Max had running through his veins.

Mike had given no reaction to the step whatsoever.

His other foot now, another slow, gentle movement. He raised the knife up and held it out in front of him. It continued to tremble but was steadier than before.

Remaining in place, Mike reached into his pocket. For a brief moment Max's heart made an attempt to quit, then his eyes saw the package of cigarettes.

It was now or never.

Max bent into a slight crouch, then hopped, swinging his knife hand around. He landed directly behind his adversary, and in an instant had his hand around the gun in Mike's belt, and the blade of the chef's knife pressed against the man's throat.

The cigarette pack fell to the ground. It made more noise than Max's footsteps had made.

"Don't make a sound," Max whispered, removing Mike's gun and stuffing it into the back of his own pants. His voice quivered but he didn't care. "One sound and I'll slit your throat. You'll never give farewell words before you depart."

So much for not speaking to him, but what could he do? He had to let Mike understand the situation. He didn't want to kill the man, but if it came down to it, the less they spoke, the less Max knew about Mike the Cable Guy, the easier it would be to view him as something inanimate, something easy to kill, rather than as a human being. And yet, still, even though at this point the man might be willing to kill him without a second thought, Max tried hard to maintain the fact that he had scruples, a conscience, morals, inhibitions. He couldn't simply kill somebody — maybe not even if it came to kill or be killed.

Regardless of any of that, however, at the moment he very much had to fight.

Mike didn't move. He stood like a statue with twitchy fingers.

"Keep your hands down, and walk slowly, straight ahead."

Mike started to say something but cut the first word short, causing it to be only a tiny sputter. Maybe he was afraid of Max and maybe he wasn't, but he was clearly smart enough to know there was a knife held to his throat.

Together, they moved toward the precipice. The closer they got, the deeper the arroyo appeared to be, and the harder Max's heart thumped. He didn't know what he was doing. He didn't have any kind of plan. All he knew for sure was that he had to keep control. Keep the situation in control. Keep everything in control.

About two feet from the edge, Max whispered to stop. For a moment, the two of them stood there looking down into the gorge, a thirty-foot drop, give or take. Certain areas at the bottom carried soft looking sand, while other spots held rocks that varied in shape and size.

An eternity came and went. Max continued to stare down into the gully, lacking a plan, feeling at a loss. They couldn't stand like this forever. A glance over his shoulder to make sure they still hadn't been spotted, and without warning Mike's feet suddenly slid forward from under him. He snap-kicked, trying to keep his balance on pebbles and loosened earth, trying to back away from the ground that crumbled beneath him.

The sky flashed a dazzle of sunlight as Mike's body fell back against Max. The knife fell from

Max's hand, clacked on a rock and was gone as he staggered back and saw Mike's arms flailing and clouds of dust puffing up around him. Mike spun and their eyes met for a split second, then the ground seemed to explode beneath him and he dropped out of sight.

The sound a second later was a cross between a thud and a crack. Max blinked dust from his eyes, and again became aware that he was holding his breath. A spasm twitched and then lurched in his shoulder as he slowly stepped forward and to the right, avoiding the spot where the earth had given way. He leaned as far as he dared and looked down.

Mike was on his back, arms straight out to each side. His torso and head were on sand, but the lower half of his body was skewed somewhat sideways on a cluster of jagged rocks. From where Max stood, there was no telling whether or not the man was alive. What was clear, however, was that the man was not moving. Dead or unconscious, he didn't know, but from the looks of it, if the man was alive, walking was going to be impossible, maybe forever.

Still looking down at the man, the next thought to cross Max's mind unsettled him.

One down.

THIRTY-SIX

Camille sat at the counter in the Silver Moon sipping her third cup of coffee since she'd come back inside, sick and tired of waiting for Max's no-show ass out in the parking lot. She didn't know how many messages she'd left him at this point, but it was certainly more than enough for his slow-assimilating brain to connect the dots and realize that he should have picked her up nearly an hour ago.

She thought about last night. She couldn't *help* but think about it. The car harassment, the car chase, the cold fear that had chilled her, their discussion up in the hills. Incidents like that don't simply vanish from one's mind. It had all been real enough. She'd been there, witnessed it first hand. And yet, still, even having experienced it, she was still having a hard time accepting the things that Max had said. Not because they weren't real, but because they'd come from Max's mouth. Max, who'd never outgrown being an adolescent pantywaist with an overactive imagination. With what had happened, it should have been easy to accept, but it wasn't.

Who's got the slow-assimilating brain now?

Absently, she added cream to her coffee.

"Still nothing, huh?"

She looked up at Peter, who stood on the other side of the counter. No matter what her mood, she never got tired of looking at him, into those gray-green eyes of his, like slightly tarnished jade. She shook her head, then sipped her coffee.

"You try calling again?"

"About ten minutes ago."

Peter sighed. Somehow, to Camille, the sigh seemed emotionless...

Well, why not? What in the world would Peter gain from Max picking her up? Less time with her—*that's* what he would get, and she knew that wasn't something he wanted. She didn't want it either; but at the moment it was the way things were, and the way they had to be. Ipso facto until papers were signed; and currently those papers didn't even exist.

She finished her coffee, flipped open her phone and looked at it, then closed it and put it away and asked Peter for a glass of water. Being such a heavy coffee drinker, she had overdone it, and couldn't stave off the jitters that began to assault her. She slid the empty coffee cup away, took a sip of ice water, and for the first time wondered if something had happened to Max. With everything that had happened last night, wasn't it possible that he'd gotten himself into some kind of trouble?

She nearly laughed at the thought.

Nearly, but didn't.

"You want a ride home?"

"Huh?" She looked up again at Peter.

"A ride home. You want me to drive you?"

Camille thought for a second. "What about the restaurant?"

"What about it? Danielle can handle it for, what, twenty minutes, half hour." He looked out to Danielle, in the process of wiping down a table. "You can keep things in control for half an hour or so, can't you, Danielle?"

"Sure, no problem. Gonna take Camille home?"

"You don't have to do that, Pete," Camille told him.

"Of course I don't. But if you're here too much longer I'm either gonna put you back to work or start charging you rent." He smiled, made a little head gesture. "C'mon. It's no skin off my hide."

Camille lifted her glass of water, looked at Peter and then at Danielle, then back at Peter. She gulped a mouthful of water, set the glass down and nodded.

"All right," she said. "Sounds good, thank you."

"Like I said, no skin off my hide."

She stepped off of her stool as Peter stepped out from behind the counter. He held the door open for her and called out over his shoulder, "Be back soon," then the door was closed and they were outside in the parking lot, walking around to the back of the building, where Peter parked his blue Saturn Astra. He unlocked the passenger door and opened it for her, closed it once she was settled, then went around to the driver's side and climbed in behind the wheel. He started the car and Otis Redding came on, halfway through "A Change is Gonna Come."

Camille buckled her seatbelt, then stared down at her hands in her lap. While she felt she should be, she was having trouble taking comfort in Peter driving her home. There was no reason for the discomposure, far as she could tell, but it was there all the same.

Guilt? Maybe, or at least not out of the realm of possibility. But it wasn't as though it would look awkward, getting a ride home from her boss — not after an hour of waiting on Max. If anything, she should be angry at the halfwit for neglecting to pick her up at the designated time. And she was. She was angry. Max knew damn well to be there at four.

And yet, it didn't feel right. Since they'd moved here nothing had felt right. They'd felt wrong in Portland, but felt increasingly wrong since they'd come to Sueño Roto. Max had changed. Good or bad change, she didn't want to give him any credit for his ability to do so, but he had become a different person since returning to New Mexico. No credit, because she didn't want him walking around acting even moreso like he was somehow King Shit of the world. Max was a lazy, spoiled lamebrain, and she had to remember that. She had to.

"You okay?" Peter asked.

She looked at him briefly, then out the window before returning her gaze to her lap. She nodded, unsure if Peter had seen it or not.

"I'm fine," she said, then returned her attention to the desert landscape passing by through the window. "I'm just thinking."

"Anything I should maybe know about?"

She laced her fingers together and nervously bounced them in her lap. "I'm wondering if maybe we should call it quits."

"What?"

"You heard me."

"Really? Are you serious?"

"Or maybe at least just take a break."

Peter grimaced; his knuckles whitened on the wheel. "Are you sure that's something you really wanna do?"

"I don't know. No… maybe."

"Is there something I've done?"

"No. No, Peter, it's not you."

"So, then, what is it?"

"If anything, it's me."

"Or maybe Max?" he offered.

"He *is* my husband."

Peter nodded once, cleared his throat, said, "A husband you've talked about divorcing since we'd known each other for less than an hour. A man you can't stand, whom you've constantly called a fool, and constantly said lacks backbone."

"Peter, please don't do this."

"Okay, well, what am I supposed to do?"

"Not this."

A thick, tense silence filled the car, so thick it

slightly muffled Redding, who was now singing "Don't Mess With Cupid."

The driveway was just up ahead.

Peter sighed. There was emotion in it this time. Camille looked at him, saw that he was grinding his teeth.

"I *did* say maybe just take a break."

"Maybe just take a break," he muttered. "That's the same thing as calling it quits in my book."

"So, what, have you had a lot of experience doing this kind of thing?

The car stopped on the road, about twenty feet from the turn into the driveway. Peter turned and looked at her with those amazing gray-green eyes of his, which were a little shinier than usual. The shine was a glaze of tears he was holding back.

"Is this really what you want?" he asked.

"I don't know what I want, Pete. I honestly don't." She leaned over and kissed him gently, then eased away. "But one thing I know I *don't* want, is for everything to turn into a complete and utter knuckle-fuckery. It's all so screwed up. I just need to try and make some sense of it all. Make some sense out of everything—or at least of something."

Peter looked at her, thumbed at the corner of his eye, then nodded. The nod was a reluctant one, but something about it, about the way he looked at her, let her know that she had control of the situation.

She reached across and gently squeezed his thigh. "You all right?"

More reluctant nodding. "I will be, yeah." He looked at her for a moment, then showed her a halfhearted smile, turned his attention back to the road and got the car moving again. After only a few seconds they turned into the driveway, and when they did, Camille's heart began pounding—hard.

Peter narrowed his eyes at the sight of all the cars parked in front of the house, but kept driving, slowly. A Saturn Astra at a snail's pace.

"Well, what's going on here?" Peter said to no one in particular, and stopped the car behind a Chrysler. "That looks like Ivan's Grand Marquis up there at the front."

As Camille's heart beat faster, sweat began popping out of her pores. Her throat constricted and her tongue knotted when she tried to tell Peter to back up and back up fast, get them the hell away from here. All that came out was a pathetic whimper.

For a moment the entire world was one big smudging blur. Then she heard the Saturn's engine turn off, and when it did her focus returned to the sight of two men flanking the car, one aiming a gun at Peter, the other aiming a gun at her.

THIRTY-SEVEN

Max didn't know anything about guns. Holding it pointed away from himself, making sure to keep his finger off the trigger, he studied the weapon in haste, trying to figure out if he could make sense of it. What he thought might be the safety turned out to be the magazine release button. The loaded magazine dropped out of the pistol but Max's reaction time was sharp, and he managed to catch it. He stuffed the magazine into his back pocket and then pulled back the pistol's slide. A bullet ejected out of what he knew to be the chamber. He didn't attempt to catch it.

For another minute or so he looked it over. He'd read enough books and seen enough movies to piece things together rather quickly, even if it was only on a very basic level. He retrieved and slid the magazine back into the handle, gave it a hard tap, then pulled back the slide, let go and watched it snap back into place. At this point, he concluded, all he needed to do was pull the trigger.

He also concluded that Alton was out here, possibly close by, and there were at least four other people, all of whom, likely, were capable of shooting him dead. If he was correct in his examination of the weapon he now held, though, at least he now had the ability to fire back—as long as the thing had bullets in it, anyway. He had no idea how many it contained, but he'd ejected one, which, to him, meant either one less chance of survival, or one less murder on his hands.

Watching Mike fall had brought back recent memories. Armando falling to the ground, drunk. Armando falling to the ground with a knife lodged in his throat. Armando falling down a hole, wrapped in a sleeping bag.

He forced the images away, tucked himself behind a tree, and let his eyes roam over the desert. He looked up at the tree branches jammed at strange angles above him, silhouetted against the sky. Looking back down, he strained his eyes and ears. No sign of Alton, or of anyone else. In the distance he could vaguely make out voices, over in the direction of the house, but the space between them made the voices empty and expressionless.

He stood there, practically hugging the tree, scanning the land in all directions. There was nothing else out here, and the vast expanse of the world constricted. It was like Selena had said about how the whole town being like a small room made entirely out of unbreakable windows, and the windows always closing in. How you could see the world, but the windows were always moving closer, never quite touching you, but always there, only touched when forgotten, and the contact only lasting long enough to remind you that you're trapped, that you're suffocating.

He looked down at the gun in his hand. The weight, the feel of it was uncomfortable in his grip, but with it also came a sense of power. Max couldn't tell if they were separate feelings, or if his discomfort was because of the power. Over the years he'd learned a bit about guns, simple things friends had passed along, such as you always treat a gun as if it's loaded, you never aim a gun at anyone unless you intend to kill them, never place your finger on the trigger unless, likewise, you intent to shoot your target. Max didn't want to kill anybody, yet he wasn't sure that he could follow those basic rules. He did not want to kill anyone, and yet at this moment Mike was not far away, at the bottom of a ravine, if not dead then certainly injured enough to possibly wish he was.

But that had been an accident. Max hadn't made the ground give out beneath Mike's feet. He hadn't pushed him over the edge. He'd had a knife, though no plan to use it, but even if he'd had a plan, the knife had fallen from his grip, unused, untarnished from violence. The knife was more innocent than Max, and time and again in the back of his mind, Max did his best to convince himself that he was innocent, too.

It had been kill or be killed, and nature had intervened; the Earth itself had been the referee and made the final decision. And now Max stood here, hidden behind a tree, the victor of Round One, though victorious by default, and in a contest where there are no winners.

The voices far off to his right momentarily grew louder. Whether their volume had merely increased or they were getting closer, he couldn't tell. From where he stood, the house itself was out of sight.

He gripped the gun tighter, making sure not to place his finger on the trigger, and listened. Put everything he had into listening, his eyes seeing the desert without taking it in.

The voices quieted again. For a moment the world was silent. The sun sighed out a blast of heat, then darkened just a shade.

If he could simply wait here and avoid detection, maybe they would eventually get bored and leave. But that was a big *if—a very big if—*and when Mike didn't return, whether they believed Max to be the reason for his disappearance or not, they would search for their missing comrade.

Pulling out his cell phone, he flipped it open, saw the signal indicator bars flickering between one and zero. He snapped it shut and put it back in his pocket, then scanned the landscape. No Alton. Nobody at all.

Waiting.

For all he knew he could be waiting for hours, simply prolonging the inevitable. And the longer he waited the more he ran the risk of losing his nerve. He was sure that Selena had called the police, but that really didn't mean a damn thing. They could and probably would take their time coming out here, if they bothered to come at all. He couldn't rely on them. He couldn't rely on anyone but himself, and the thought was more frightening than expected. The rage, the inner strength inside him, like a fuse on a firecracker, and there was no way to predetermine, when the fuse reached its detonation point, whether it would explode or be a dud.

But he couldn't simply wait. He certainly couldn't wait here forever.

One down. Six against one and one down, improving his odds to five against one. But regardless of the odds, his triumph in the altercation with Mike had been the result of luck, pure and simple. There was no way in hell he could luck out like that five more times. The odds were still heavily stacked against him.

Cautiously, he moved away from the tree and sought refuge behind another. From here he could see the roof of the house but not much more. He desperately wanted a drink of water. Every time he swallowed, it was the dry swallow of a dying man.

A quick survey of the area and he pulled out his cell phone again, flipped it open. The signal indicators were the same as before. He snapped it shut, and heard footsteps.

THIRTY-EIGHT

The car's doors were opened and Camille and Peter were instructed to get out.

"*Cómo estás*, Peter?" a third man said. He wore a faded blue plaid shirt with the sleeves rolled up. He looked vaguely familiar, but Camille couldn't place from where. Probably a customer at the diner. "What brings you out this way?" he said, and looked at Camille with a pair of unsettling eyes.

A rinse of cold fear distended within her veins and chilled her.

"You come out to give this lovely lady a ride home?"

"What's going on here, Alé?"

"*Nada*. We were just, you know, having a look around."

"With guns?" Peter said. "What's with all the artillery?"

"Wayne," the man named Alé said to one of the two armed men. "Go out back and call Alton and Mike."

The man named Wayne, wearing a black T-shirt and holding what looked like a highly illegal firearm, gave an emotionless nod and wandered into the house. Camille watched him go, and saw that several of the house's windows were smashed out. Already chilled with fear, another torrent of cold gushed and streamed through her veins.

Somehow, she managed to speak. "Where's my husband?" When she looked back at Alé, she saw he now held a revolver in his hand. Casually, as if playing with a set of keys.

"Who, Max?" He made grimacing duck-like lips and shook his head a little. "I don't know. We don't know where he is." His provoking eyes met hers. "Do you?" He took a step closer to Peter, now that Wayne was gone. "His car is here, but Max *no está aquí.*"

"What's Ivan doing here?" Peter asked. His tone proved his throat to have a dry lump in it.

"He's inside."

"Doing what?"

"I don't know, Pete. Would you like to go and see him?"

Some of the color drained out of Peter's face. "No, not especially."

Then it came out before Camille realized she was speaking. "Why are you all here?"

"Missus Max, I take it you're not aware of what your husband did today."

374 | Trent Zelazny

Camille knew that whatever the man said, it would be a lie, but she shook her head, anyway.

"He came into Shiloh's earlier. You know Shiloh's? The bar?" He snickered a little as he added, "That was great when you threw that beer in his face." The snicker quickly diminished, and he returned to frowning. "What he did is inexcusable."

"I'm sure whatever's going on, Alé, it's a misunderstand—"

"He came into Shiloh's earlier. He found myself, my friends, and also made sure to include Ivan and Wayne and Dante." He looked at the ground and shook his head. "He battered and tortured a dog, Missus Max. Mutilated it. A Golden Retriever. A beautiful dog and he tore it to pieces. Yes, he came into Shiloh's, made sure that he had all of our attention, then he dumped the poor thing right on to the floor, in front of us all." He looked at Camille again. "Your husband is an animal killer, Missus Max. On behalf of the dog, and on behalf of our friend Armando, we are here to serve justice."

"Who's Armando?"

"So you're a lynch mob," Peter said.

"No lynch mob, Pete. No, no. *Por el amor de Dios*, Max is not black."

"A lynch mob doesn't mean—"

"But he *is* a murderer. A murderer and an animal killer."

"Bullshit," Camille said, unable to refrain. "What do mean, he's a murderer?"

"We believe he killed our good friend, Armando Gutierrez."

"That's crazy! You believe but you don't have any proof?"

"Not so crazy as it sounds, Missus Max. He was one of the last people seen around Armando, and he is the only one without an alibi. You don't need to be a detective to know that the numbers add up."

"That's insane, that is truly insane."

Alé looked at her, and then to the man she assumed was Dante. Then, quietly, he laughed, and as he did a heavy-set man stepped out of the house, wearing a tattered baseball shirt. Alé took a couple of steps back as the large man approached, and took a stance near Peter. He looked Camille up and down, his face one half lascivious and one half hatred.

"You're Albertson's niece," he said.

THIRTY-NINE

Alton; it had to be Alton. The footsteps were nearby, off to his left. The man's feet took no care where they stepped or what they went through, which stirred up plenty of noise.

Max gripped the gun in both hands and aimed it in the direction of the sound. Slowly, he eased his finger into the trigger guard and onto the trigger, his heartbeat quickening. Sweat poured from his brow.

Kill or be killed. He hated it, but it was a current fact.

"Mike!" Alton's voice called out.

Max blinked perspiration from his eyes, tried to keep his breathing quiet and his hands steady as he aimed the gun in the vicinity of the voice. The ravine was maybe thirty or forty feet back behind him.

Lucky once. Chances were he wouldn't be lucky twice.

The footsteps closed in. They were no more

than a dozen feet away and Max saw the man's shadow, saw the shadow stop, heard the footsteps stop. There was a metallic click, like that of a gun hammer being pulled back.

"Mike," he said again, not as loud as before.

Max pointed the gun at the shadow, blinked more sweat from his eyes.

Far off, from the direction of the house, a voice called out. It could have been Alejandro, though Max wouldn't have put money on it. From the distance the words were unintelligible. He heard Alton's footsteps turn and walk a few paces away.

Then Alton shouted, "Coming!" and his footsteps picked up speed, away from where Max hid, as he hollered one more time, "Mike, c'mon!"

Something must be going on at the house, but for the moment, Max was safe—as safe as safe could be, given the circumstances.

Lucky once, now lucky twice. Each time he lucked out, the odds of his luck disappearing increased. No one stays lucky forever, and nobody runs forever. Max couldn't really run—not in this unknown wasteland—and he absolutely could not rely on luck. Luck was a fool's game, the kind of thing that keeps people trapped in casinos. Running was out, his luck might be out, which meant he had to take action, take some damned initiative, as Camille had told him the day the movers had come.

He peeked out from behind the tree, saw Alton heading in the direction of the house.

Whether he liked it or not, that's where Max needed to head, too. Waiting was simply not an option.

The sun used some kind of trickery and darkened a shade.

Max counted quietly back from ten, then eased out from his hiding place behind the tree.

He managed to sneak and slither his way without being detected, and now he tucked himself behind another large rock, a little over a hundred feet from the back patio. There was nobody currently in the courtyard but the back door was open, and he could just make out shapes moving around inside the house. He still heard voices, too, but they were just as unintelligible as when he'd been a couple hundred yards out.

What he needed was a plan, but Max had never been good at making plans, and for all he knew someone was creeping up behind him this very moment.

Still holding the gun, he debated stuffing it into his belt, but was incapable of letting it leave his hand.

The idea of being a sniper crossed his mind. But a gun like this would be no good as far as sniper tactics go. If he even wanted to attempt playing sniper, then he'd need something like the rifle he'd seen the one man carrying, and he had no clue whatsoever as to whether that particular rifle would be any better than the gun he currently held. And, having never fired a gun before in his life, he was by no means a marksman. Other than what he'd read and seen in movies, he didn't know the first thing about sniping. He never thought he'd ever actually need to use a gun.

No, if he wanted to take these guys out, he'd need to do it at close range. The thing was, he didn't really want to take them out; he just wanted them to go away. But that wasn't going to happen. This wasn't a matter of hiding under blankets or squeezing eyes shut tight and having the monsters disappear. This was real — a nightmare as real as they come.

Varying forms of utterances plumed from the house, yet still no definition, no cohesive words. At least there was no more clattering or crashing. For the moment, anyway, they weren't trashing anything else — of course, how much was there left for them to trash?

Max remained concealed behind the rock. Fortunately, at least as far as he knew, nobody had seen him. The ravine with the broken, possibly dead Mike now seemed miles and years away.

Action. He had to take action. Take some damned initiative.

But how? He couldn't simply charge in with his gun blazing. He'd be lucky to squeeze off one round before they shot him dead.

Then came a sudden loud crack. It echoed throughout the wasteland, and a split second later he heard a woman screaming. A scream he knew well. The hysterical and terrified scream of his wife. There was no doubt that the cracking sound had been the firing of a gun.

How the fuck did she get here?

Peter Parsons. He'd been fucking her, and now he'd given her a ride.

Camille continued screaming, wailing, and

there was no doubt in Max's mind that the gunshot had transitioned Peter Parsons from alive to dead. Jesus Christ, these guys were cold-blooded killers. And they were also relentless. But why him? Far as he knew they'd never gone after Camille at all. If they had, she would have told him last night, in one of their very rare open and honest conversations. She would have told him, but she'd said nothing. Because they had chosen him. For whatever reason they had chosen him. He, Max Pendleton, was the target, the means by which to get to Frank, unless....

Unless that was bullshit. In spite of his conversations with Frank, in spite of what had been said about the man, the sum of it all, really, seemed a lot more like a group of people picking someone out at random—or maybe simply the new guy—and harassing him, tormenting him. But to what end, and why?

That was the most frightening of all. There didn't have to be a why. At the house right now, Peter Parsons, or somebody else, was likely dead, more than likely. And the reasoning behind it all might truly be as simple as *there was no reason*.

He looked at the house again, and as he did gears started moving in his head. An idea came to him, one not much better than charging five armed men, but the only other option he could currently come up with. Looking as far as he could toward the driveway, he didn't see any approaching cars. The police weren't coming. Nobody was coming. Camille was trapped with those maniacs. And Max, he was all alone, and anywhere he went, there was a high risk of danger.

If he was going to hide and wait, or figure out any kind of plan at all, he needed a safer place. They might very well hurt Camille, but they wouldn't kill her. If they were killing solely for the purpose of killing, Camille would have been shot dead immediately after Peter, or whoever it was that brought her home. No, if they killed Camille, it would be in his presence. They'd killed Granger while he was away, yes, but now they'd kicked everything up a notch. They might hurt her, but they wouldn't kill her. Somehow, deep inside, he knew this was true.

Slowly, cautiously, he moved away from the rock. He went from tree to tree, rock to rock, sometimes having to double back a bit in order to keep himself out of sight. When he got close he put the gun in his belt at the back, lowered himself down onto his belly, and army-crawled until he reached the down slope of the stony earthen path. He brought his feet up under him, and, in a crouch, hurried over to the mineshaft, the corner of his eye catching the tennis ball, still sitting comfortably between rocks

His blood ran cold as he looked down into the dark opening. The ladder was barely a ladder, but his rage, his need for action, for concealment and protection, trumped his fear.

"Down the rabbit hole," he whispered to himself.

Carefully, feet first, he eased himself into the hole. With one foot he tested the first cross plank.

Not even half of his weight on it, the plank splintered, then snapped. He almost lost hold completely, "Shit!" but managed to get one foot on either side of the narrow pit. He remained in place but it didn't feel right. The stance was already straining the muscles in his legs. There was no way he could climb all the way down like this, especially when he didn't know how far down it went. At least the earthen walls were solid. If he fell, it would likely be due to his own carelessness rather than nature playing a joke.

Then something came to him. A documentary he'd seen on spelunking. Maybe it wasn't specifically spelunking but it was certainly something like that, rock climbing and canyons and caves and such. He remembered watching a man go down a narrow canyon, not dissimilar to the hole Max had now placed himself in. The man had set both feet against one wall and pressed his back into the wall opposing it. He'd used his legs, his back and natural body weight to body walk down the towering walls.

With his legs still out to either side, Max used his left hand for balance on the wall in front of him, just beneath the opening, where the desert stared indifferently, and with his right hand he withdrew the pistol from the small of his back. The circuitry of his nerves crackled at the idea of stuffing the gun into the front of his pants, but it was the only option, unless he wanted to drop the gun and forget about it completely, which he did not.

Once the gun was secure in front with the

barrel pointed far enough away from his johnson, he pressed his right hand against the wall behind him, put more force on the left in front of him, briefly contorting his body into an X. He took a deep breath, then swung his left leg over, alongside his right, and when it was solid he slowly eased his body backward, until the small of his back all the way up to his shoulder blades set firmly against the wall. He was terrified to let his hands go, but one at a time he did it, brought them closer to him, then sat there a moment, suspended by nothing but his own body weight, the rotted wood that at one time had been a makeshift ladder on his right.

His legs were bent at the knees, giving him more stability and leverage to work with. With caution, he released his right foot and eased it down about eight inches, pressed it back against the wall, then repeated the action with his left foot. Hands pressed out firmly on either side of him, he eased his body down to match up parallel with his feet, then brought his hands down, one at a time. He looked at the rickety ladder on his right. Had he actually tried using it, he'd likely be dead by now. From what he could tell in the gathering darkness, the wood looked worse than the cross board he'd chopped the day he found the hole.

The opening was about three feet above him now. Eventually one of these men would find it, and they would be able to see him only three feet down.

He repeated the same actions in the same sequence, bringing himself down another eight or ten inches. It was much easier than he had actually expected it to be. Climbing down was becoming less and less of an issue for him, not that it was a joy ride. What worried him most at the moment was getting back out.

Again, he went through the whole sequence, then again, again, and with each step down, the light above him faded, and new layers of darkness consumed his tiny claustrophobic world. Maybe, when he reached the bottom, he'd be able to find the flashlight he'd knocked over the edge when he'd been talking to the rabbit; and maybe, just maybe, with a little luck, the thing would still work. He hoped he could find it and he prayed that it wasn't in a million pieces, because the light kept fading and the darkness kept growing.

Right foot, left foot, ease the body down, then right hand, left hand. The barrel of the pistol poked his thigh with every step.

Eventually the light above became a tiny dot. Below him was absolute blackness. But he knew of a couple of things within the absolute blackness. Things he wanted to forget about. Things he wished he'd never known and had never experienced. Things he definitely didn't want to be approaching. Escaping the terror up above, he was lowering himself into genuine nightmares, a few inches at a time.

At least it was cooler in here. The black world around him smelled slightly of damp earth, with an occasional whiff of something fetid, and as the stench grew more pungent, Max knew the closer he was getting to Armando.

Every so often his feet and/or back pressed against something solid. To his hands it felt like touching a sidewalk.

The tiny dot of light above was completely gone now. His whole world was dark, and he couldn't help wondering if he'd ever see again. Despite the cool, the very mild, almost nonexistent dampness, he sweated profusely, kept blinking it away from his eyes, even though, on a practical level, it didn't really matter.

With his next step downward his legs extended a bit further, and another fear consumed him. The shaft widening, opening up too far for his body, with no idea how far the fall would be. To climb all this way down only to suddenly drop away and fall, fall through a world of blackness, with no idea of if or when he would ever hit the ground. He remembered the day he found the shaft, how he'd dropped a rock down it and never heard it land.

He thought of unstable rock, minimal ventilation and airflow, of things crumbling or caving in, the Cherry Mine disaster of 1909, Pennsylvania's 1959 Knox Mine disaster. Even though the walls around him broadened, the world felt smaller and smaller. The air became mustier, but with each sequenced maneuver downward, with each breath, every sound he made echoed up from below.

No question about it. The walls were opening up.

He was exhausted. He was weak. He was scared. Beyond scared. But his only choice now was to continue down. Right foot, left foot, ease the body down, right hand, left hand, then repeat. The breadth of the shaft opened another inch or two. When it did, his tremors increased; his skin burned while hundreds of needles pricked at the base of his skull and his breathing quickened. His heart pounded and he became lightheaded and dizzy, as thoughts of pending danger, some namable, some not, raced through his mind with stroboscopic quickness. It became difficult to breathe and the tingling at the base of his skull shivered down his spine.

Impressed that he hadn't actually had one until now, this was still possibly the worst of all times to enter into a full-blown panic attack. He stopped climbing and focused on his breathing, knees still bent but not like when he'd started. He added a bit more pressure on his legs to be sure he was wedged solidly in place, and shook out his hands, drew slow and deep breaths of the stuffy air. Diaphragmatic breathing, directly from his diaphragm. He was no stranger to panic attacks, and this was definitely a nerve-upsetting situation. No medications had ever really helped, but he'd learned tricks along the way, if not to get rid of them completely, to at least modulate it to the point where he could continue to function.

He sat there, suspended in darkness, and breathed.

How much deeper could the damn thing be? How far down had he actually climbed?

Far enough to eliminate the light that poured in from the opening.

Sitting there, resting, he wondered if he could climb back up the same way he came down. Maybe, but he was so tired, and going up would be more strenuous than down.

Then he remembered something. It was a little surprising it hadn't occurred to him before. Carefully, he wedged his left hand into his front pocket. His fingers touched and then took hold of the cigarette lighter he'd purchased the day he'd temporarily taken up smoking. No floodlight, but it was something.

Holding it in both tremulous hands, he pressed his thumb down along the spark wheel and a tiny flame danced up, swayed gently, then jittered in his hands. All around him was rock and hard packed dirt, rings of concrete, which he guessed had once upon a time been some kind of reinforcement. About ten feet above him, the haphazard ladder ended with a series of splintered wood. He didn't know whether this was a good or bad sign until he looked down. Just a couple of feet below him two of the walls ended, while the walls at his sides continued down about another eight feet or so, and he could just make out solid ground, some splintered wood, as well as part of what he knew to be Armando's sleeping bag.

Had he continued down pell-mell, he would have lost his footing and fallen. Eight feet might not be far, but when unexpected, it could have easily been enough to kill him.

He clicked off the lighter and stuffed it back into his pocket, feeling even blinder than before.

He put all of his strength into his arms, let his left foot drop and swung it to the side, got a foothold, then did the same with his right foot. He scaled down the rest of the way with only hands and feet, and when he reached the bottom he sat down, then fell to his back and let the strain in his body moan in agony, then slowly dissipate.

If he could have, he may have allowed himself to fall asleep, but that wasn't an option, even if he wanted it to be. There were still five people up above, looking for him, hunting him, and more than likely they knew this land better than he did. And there was also Camille, a prisoner of the madmen above.

But that was only one concern, because now he was trapped down here. Even if he had the strength to climb up the way he'd come down, the airshaft, or whatever the hell it was, was too high for him to reach. Hopefully there was another way out, because there was no way he was going out the same way he came in.

He took out the cigarette lighter and struck it.

FORTY

Camille couldn't stop seeing blood spouting out of Peter's head. Spouting, and then leaking, his eyes wide as if curious about something astoundingly meaningless, then rolling upward into his skull just before his body collapsed. She kept seeing it, over and over again, as she sat on the couch, which had been pushed and moved, the right side of it blocking the fireplace. Nearly all of her things were destroyed, scattered around like garbage.

"Where's Mike?" Alé said to another familiar guy, who wore a white T-shirt and a red baseball cap.

"I don't know," the man said. "We split up to try and find Maxi Pad. That was the last time I saw or heard from him. When I tried to rendezvous with him, I looked but couldn't find him, and he didn't answer when I called out." He saw Camille, sitting on the couch. "I see you've found the old ball and chain, though," he added with a snicker.

The big man, the man who shot Peter — Ivan — entered the room, still holding his very large handgun. His face appeared fixed in a permanent grimace. He looked at the lanky man in the baseball cap. "So let me get this straight," he said. "Not only do you *not* find who we're looking for, you manage to *lose* Mike in the process." It was not a question.

"Maybe he was just out of range. Hell, maybe he's on his way back with Maxi Pad right now."

"Unless Max got to him first."

The man in the baseball cap laughed and shook his head. "I seriously doubt that. If they came face to face, Max would shrivel up into a ball and crumble to ash."

"You're pretty confident, Alton," Ivan said. "Don't you remember what happened just a few hours ago?"

"What, at the bar?"

"Yes, at the bar."

"Of course I do."

"So why do you think the man would simply shrivel up at the sight of Mike?"

"Well," Alton said, "it just seems —"

"You're overly confident," Ivan said. "Only fools are overly confident."

Alé placed a hand on Ivan's shoulder. "Relax, *amigo*."

Ivan stepped away. "And don't talk to me in bean speak!" His voice reverberated off the walls, then charged the air with a kinetic silence.

Camille found that she herself had curled up into a ball, on the couch. It seemed that her heart was going to pound hard forever. She hadn't realized that there were five men in the room with her. Five men, plus Mike, who was still somewhere out there—and Max.

She thought about what Alé had said, about Max being an animal killer. Killer of a Golden Retriever. Granger. That Max had killed Granger. Bullshit. *She* was much more likely to hurt the dog than Max ever would've been, and there was no way on earth she would ever harm an animal. Even that rattlesnake, poisonous and deadly, had been handled without any harm.

If Granger was gone, one of these men—or all of them—had done it.

Bastards. Dirty no good bastards.

Ivan pinched between his eyes, then looked at the men and said, "Dante, Wayne, you and Alton go out and take another look. Alejandro and I will wait here with Miss Ball and Chain."

Camille watched the three men leave through the back door, then found her heart beating even harder as Alejandro and Ivan sat down on either side of her.

"Now, little girl," Ivan said. "You are going to call your Uncle Frank."

"W-why? What'd you want me to say to him?"

"I'll script it for you, don't worry. But just be sure. Be sure that you stick to the script." He paused, then, "Do you know what will happen if you don't stick to the script? What will happen if you try anything other than what is on the script?"

Here thumping heart sank. "You—you'll kill me."

Ivan smiled. "No," he said. His gun rested on his lap, aimed at Camille. "I'll let Alé here rape you, however he pleases, for as long as he likes. *Then* I'll kill you." He looked at Alejandro. "Find us some paper and a pen."

FORTY-ONE

Thank God Armando's body had remained wrapped. A fall down a shaft like that could have easily unraveled him, and while a part of Max had become anesthetized to such things, there was still only so much he could take. He had no interest in seeing what Armando's corpse had transformed into over the last couple of days. Other than the smell, the only real issue he had with the scene was the multitude of bugs that scurried in and out of the sleeping bag.

"I'm sorry, *hermano*," he said to the bundle, then clicked the lighter off for a moment to keep from burning his fingers.

Standing in the darkness, the first thing he did was move the gun from the front of his pants and return it to the back, as a million thoughts raced through his mind at once. He relived the night with Armando at rapid speed and in vivid detail. With the occurrence that night, as well as all of the other things that had happened since, there were no more questions about it. This was a lawless town. No sheriff, no deputy, nothing. Sueño Roto was just as bad as the old Wild West—maybe worse. Funny that he would only realize it now, as he stood in darkness at the bottom of a deep hole, next to a dead body.

Then again he remembered the flashlight. The green Economy flashlight that he'd just replaced the batteries in and had knocked down here when he'd been talking to the rabbit. He remembered that it had made a reverberating clack or two, and had apparently landed hard. He remembered that much, but struck the lighter again, turned away from the sight of Armando's wrapped body. He saw the car keys and the blue sleeping bag sack, dark, inanimate and uncaring. Then, to his left, a couple of feet within the passage, he saw it. It was in one piece.

Stepping over to it, he clicked off the lighter, fumbled his hand in the dirt, then took hold of it, and turned it on. The lens was fractured with a series of spidering cracks, but the bulb had remained intact, and there was light shining on the ground before him. He drew a deep breath of musty air mixed with the fetid stench of death, then let out a sigh of relief, and stuffed the cigarette lighter back into his pocket.

Musty air, the stench of death. The smells linked his mind to a new paranoia of mining accidents. It had been a while, but he'd read a couple of books on such things, and some of the words now came to him as though he'd read them only seconds before. Hydrogen sulfide or explosive natural gases. Methane. Dust explosions. Collapses. Escaping one hell only to enter another; and still, he had no idea whatsoever if there was even a way out of here. The place had been abandoned, maybe for exactly one or all of the reasons scrolling through his head. He knew that mining ventilation was a significant safety concern for miners. Poor ventilation of mines can cause exposure to harmful gases, heat and dust, which can cause injury, illness and death. He aimed the light upward. If that passage was for ventilation, it was half-assed at best. A useless damn hole with a useless damn tunnel.

He shined the light down the left passageway, which, if his assumption was correct, led somewhere alongside the house up above. The passageway to his right would then lead out toward the desert and nearby mountains. He could see no light at the end of either tunnel. There were no tracks, no evidence at all of any sort of mine railway.

Mountains. Mountains made a lot more sense for the start of a mine. Whatever people had been mining here, it seemed logical that the mountains would be richer with whatever it was.

He headed down the passage to his right.

FORTY-TWO

Alton, Dante and Wayne walked once around the entire house, and found nothing of interest. They then headed toward the mountains in the back, gradually fanning out as they did. Alton was in the middle, Dante to his left and Wayne to his right. The sun was setting. It stood in the distance as a pale tint of orange. He'd seen it all before but hadn't paid such close attention like he did now. The aspens, the ponderosa pines, the piñons and junipers, the lovely layers of rock and earth and sagebrush, chamisa — to some an allergenic nightmare, but gorgeous nonetheless. Far more beautiful than he typically realized. Beauty taken for granted.

Why had he not noticed it before, and why was he noticing it now? Maybe he'd been too amped up on finding Maxi Pad the first time out, but more likely he'd simply been taking the beauty of the desert for granted. He'd been a desert rat his whole life, born and raised in Gallup, never going farther west than Arizona, never farther east than Portales. A desert rat through and through. What was the word? Desensitized, yeah, that was it. Around anything too long and you become indifferent, unaware, uncaring. Desensitized.

So why was it now all of a sudden so stunning?

"Hey guys!"

It was Wayne, off to his right, about fifty yards away, standing on a mound. He waved his arms above his head as if trying to get the attention of a passing airplane.

Alton turned and made his way over, hearing Dante's footsteps coming up behind him.

"You find something?"

"Think you guys should see this."

Alton and Dante joined Wayne on the mound, just as Wayne headed down the slope, where the ground had a short and seemingly ancient stone path, which led to a square hole punched into the side of an earthen wall. An imperfect black square framed by dried, cracked wood, worn by weather and time, no more than a few feet high and wide.

"It doesn't go across, it goes down," Wayne said, on hands and knees, after sticking his head into it. He felt around at his pockets. "I don't got nothing. Either of you got a light?"

"I've got a lighter," Alton said, he and Dante now at the bottom, flanking Wayne, who rose to his feet and patted Alton on the shoulder.

"Tell us what you see, boss."

Alton got down on his hands and knees. He struck the lighter and reached it into the opening.

"Looks like a tunnel," he said. "A straight down tunnel. Maybe a well or something?"

"Why would a well be opened up sideways?" Wayne asked.

Alton got flat on his chest, head and both arms inside now, left hand bracing the side, right hand holding the lighter, extending it downward. On the far wall he saw a wooden beam a few feet down, dead wooden planks crossing it, like an ancient, useless ladder. The cross plank closest to the top was broken, only half of it hanging — or maybe dangling was a better word for it.

"There's some kind of ladder in here, but I don't think anyone could possibly use it successfuh—!"

A pair of hands grabbed each of his ankles and lifted them from the ground.

"What are you doing?"

His feet went up, higher and higher, and before he could let out the scream he so desperately wanted to emit, the lighter clicked off and fell out of his hand, and he was falling right after it, through the darkness. The narrow, torturous darkness.

The scream never came out of him, but something inside him, a thing that fell with his body, let him know that this was why the desert had become so beautiful again. Somehow, inside, he'd known it was the last time he'd ever see it.

There was a simultaneous crack and a crunch. Then the curtains drew closed forever.

***

"That was easy," Wayne said.

Dante agreed.

The two of them made their way back up and headed toward a clearing surrounded by trees. They lit cigarettes and stood there for a while, smoking in silence.

Then, "You think he's still out there?"

Wayne thought about it, shook his head a little.

"I dunno," he said. "I dunno, and I'm not sure that I care."

They continued smoking their cigarettes.

FORTY-THREE

For only give or take about a minute, the ground sloped down, then it briefly evened out before it started heading upward. The air was still musty but it no longer carried with it the stench of death.

It wasn't long, only a couple of minutes, his legs exhausted from a workout they hadn't gotten in a very long time, his back aching for the same reasons, as well as from crouching due to the tunnel's height. Max figured this whole area was part of a mining operation that had never been completed. Everything about it was too half-assed. Nothing about it said "mine" — only "hole" and "tunnels."

Behind him, somewhere far away in this tunnel, there came a thump. It echoed, reverberated around him. He worried about the tunnel collapsing and it continued to reverberate, to vibrate subtly, rattling new chains of fear inside him.

Then, just as the sound and the oscillation settled, his light showed him an opening up ahead. Not an opening to the outside world, but rather to an underground creation. The closer he got, the more he saw that it was a large cave, and in a semi state of awe, he staggered, then stepped into it.

Here and there were short stalagmites, while up above, rather than an upside down ocean of bats, were very short stalactites.

He'd been here before. Maybe not exactly here, but quite close to exact. He'd been here more than once, in a sense, one time with a famous country singer, a professional ball player, and a couple of people he didn't know, and another time alone with a phone ringing somewhere and no one to answer it.

It was the cave from his dreams. Not an exact replica, for there was another tunnel across the way and there was no writing anywhere on the walls and it lacked the touch of a Hanna-Barbera cartoon; but it was close enough for him to know it was the same place.

Why had he dreamed it? More than once? Thoughts and ideas ran through his mind like someone constantly scrolling through radio stations.

In the dreams there had been no way out, and with both dreams he'd been awakened by Camille, once in person and once on the phone.

There had been no way out. There had been no passage across the way, but in here, in reality, there was. A passage right across the way from him. Maybe, possibly, a way to get out. Reality trumped his dreams. He almost laughed, yet there was nothing funny about any of it.

He was still underground, still in a cave, and that passage across the way might very well lead to nowhere. Still, it was an option he hadn't had when he'd dreamed. It was an option he'd only just begun to see over the last couple days of his life. The option being that there were options.

Not entirely sure why, he took out his cell phone, flipped it open and checked it. No bars, of course. Not a single bar of reception. British Yogi Bear had lied.

Slowly, knowing that by no means was he out of harm's way, his throat aching from thirst, his muscles and bones ablaze with torment, he crossed the cave to the new passage. The first thing he saw when he stepped into it were dust covered railway tracks, and the passageway was higher and wider than the one he'd come in from. He aimed his light and looked out into the darkness before him, then started to walk.

FORTY-FOUR

Speakerphone.

Third ring:

"Hello?"

"Hi... Uncle Frank?"

"Camille, hi! How're you doing, Sweetie? How's Max?"

She swallowed down a gulp of dryness, stared down at the piece of paper in her lap, nervousness and fear blurring her vision, removing her ability to read.

"I'm fine, Max is fine," she said, and fought to get her eyes in focus. They had to focus. They had to see the letters, the words; they had to see them so she could take them into her brain and let the proper sayings come out of her mouth, and she had to make sure that things came out fluid, not like she was reading from a script.

"What's going on?" Frank asked.

"Oh, not a—not a whole lot, really. I understand that Max had called you a couple of times."

"He told you that?"

"Yeah."

"Did he tell you the ludicrous reason why he'd called me?"

Her eyes focused just then, and she read the proper line from the script. "I'm here with Max now. And Ivan."

Silence; dead air inside the phone.

"Ivan has a gun on us, Frank. It's a big gun and I'm really scared."

"Shit," Frank said, then cleared his throat, said, "Let me talk to Ivan."

"I'm the voice of Ivan, Frank. You have to talk to me and only to me."

"So what the fuck is this all about?"

"Money."

"What?"

"Money. He wants his money. You're on speakerphone, Frank. We can all hear everything you say."

"You mean to tell me this is real? That this really has nothing to do with Max's NPD?"

"NPD?"

Alejandro and Ivan both narrowed their eyes at her.

"His Narcissism. His personality disorder."

"No," she said. "I'm looking at a gun right now. This is very, very real, Frank."

More dead air.

Then, "Ivan?"

"I'm the voice of Ivan, Frank," Camille said.

"Ivan, whatever it is between us, leave my

niece and nephew out of it."

Ivan quickly scribbled something on the paper.

Camille read it. "It's too late for that."

Ivan's finger pointed at another line.

"I want my money," she said.

"Ivan, listen. I'll get you your money. I swear it."

The large man scribbled a single word at the end of the line she'd just read.

"I want my money, bitch."

"I can't—I can't give you what I currently don't have."

Ivan shrugged, stretched his arm across Camille's face, and shot Alejandro in the side of the head.

As Camille screamed she watched Alejandro collapse off the couch and drop to the floor, his head gushing blood and his body twitching. His gun had come free of his hand. Ivan kicked it away and stood up.

Camille couldn't stop screaming. Inside the speakerphone Frank was shouting, but in the midst of all the craziness it was nothing but mumbo jumbo.

Gun still trained on Camille, Ivan crouched down and patted Alejandro's pockets, reached deep into one and pulled out a cell phone. He pressed a button and the screen lit up. He looked at it briefly, then turned the lighted screen to Camille and whispered, "Number."

Her screams having diminished to wailing cries, she read off the number on the face of the phone.

"What?" Frank said.

She read the number again, a little bit slower, as slow as she could while caught in hysteria. Then Ivan stuffed Alejandro's phone into his pocket, grabbed Camille's cell and smashed it to bits.

FORTY-FIVE

There were two points of light just up ahead. Dim, golden light, one straight ahead, the second dimmer and slightly upward, to the right. The last fifty steps or so were the worst of them all. With every step toward freedom, claustrophobia closed in on him more and more. The closer the lights got the darker it got. Heart racing, his breathing wrecked, his mind thought of nothing except an appalling sense of dread as he moved through a cage within a cage within a cage, desperate to escape.

Almost there. His eyes caught sight of something that, in his haste, he ignored, and just as he felt completely and utterly smothered, as though he'd never get out, as the walls advanced closer and closer, suddenly he found himself standing upright, with the darkening sky above him. He reached his arms up to embrace it, the air, fresh air, life. Had he been physically capable, tears would have poured from his eyes.

He turned off the flashlight and dropped to his knees, then dropped forward and splayed himself in the dirt. He'd done it. He was free. He was out. He'd gone in and found his way out. Thank God, thank Heaven, thank whatever it was. Reality trumped his dreams.

Reality…

Reality was that nothing had changed since he'd first decided to climb down the long, dark passage. Someone — presumably Peter — had been shot. If Camille was still alive, and he suspected she was, she was at the house, held against her will by one, possibly five men, and only God knew what five animalistic men might do with a single woman captive.

But five was unlikely. At least two, maybe three, or even four of the men were out here looking for him, hunting him. Mike the cable guy was out of commission, but that still left five — assuming his math had been correct at the start.

Once again, the Ortiz property was covered with death.

Max rolled onto his back and stared at the sky. He watched the stars come out, one by one in the indigo-iris dark blue pigment that was not quite ready to switch to nighttime, yet thinking about it, getting there. It was dark but the world was still visible. He lifted his head and looked past his feet at the black passageway he'd emerged from. Ten, maybe fifteen feet of rock above it, and then he saw the sky and the stars again.

He sat up, turned his body left and then right, heard a couple of tiny pops. To what was now his left had been another passageway, smaller and slanted.

Max got to his feet, legs rubbery but still cooperating, and made his way leftward. The ground was flat where he stood, but slanted up about twenty-five feet away. He had no idea how far he was from the house.

At the bottom of the slant he stopped. It was an easy slope and he knew he'd have no trouble climbing it. But something else jumped into his head, or rather something had jumped *back* into his head. At the time he'd been at the mercy of claustrophobia, but thankfully that was gone now. He wasn't smothered, nor was he smothering. He was still Max Pendleton, standing *on* the Earth, rather than *in* it, and at the moment he could go in or out as he pleased. Now he wanted to go back in, because he remembered, but in his hysteria he'd paid no attention, to the thing he'd passed that said *Danger: High Explosive.*

FORTY-SIX

A few seconds later Alejandro's cell phone rang. Ivan removed it from his pocket, pressed a button and held it to the side of his head.

"One down," he said.

Camille wanted to shout that it wasn't Max he had killed, but that he *had* in fact just killed a man. She wanted to shout all kinds of things from clever cuss words to boggling gibberish.

She just wanted to scream. She wasn't finished screaming and wanted to continue, but the barrel of Ivan's gun stared her down and kept her silent.

"Now listen closely, you fucking kike," Ivan said into the phone. "Noon tomorrow, you hear me? Not one o'clock, not twelve fifteen. *Noon*. Mountain time noon, meaning noon here where I am. Where I am… and where your niece is." A pause, then, "Isn't this about the time you say *meshuggeneh* or some half-dick bullshit like that?" He cleared his throat, then, "Noon tomorrow I have my money. You know how to get it, so *get it*.

If I don't have it at noon, then at twelve-oh-one, your beloved niece will lose a finger."

It took everything Camille had to keep from screaming. Every ounce of strength and courage. God, how she wanted to scream! But she couldn't, she couldn't, so she simply cried. There was nothing else to do but cry.

"At one o'clock she'll lose another finger, then at two o'clock another, and so on and so on. You get the idea. Your niece pays in agony for every hour that you're late, understand? ...I said *do you understand*?"

There was a short break, a break in which the only thing that existed was terror.

"I don't care how you get it."

Ivan's gun hand dropped to his side as he began pacing, no longer bothering to look at Camille. He must have been certain that he had her paralyzed. That his intimidating machismo had completely and utterly filled her with fear, and that the fear was a neurotoxin, administering unresponsiveness.

What had he told the guy in the baseball cap earlier? *You're overly confident. Only fools are overly confident.*

Camille wasn't going to kid herself. Her chances were slim to nil. But if he was going to be overly confident, then she sure as shit wasn't going to simply sit here and wait for him to make good on the threats he was making.

She looked at Alejandro's gun, on the floor, maybe fifteen feet away. The problem was that big-ass Ivan kept on pacing right through its path.

"Jews get money!" Ivan shouted into the phone. "That's what they do!"

Allowing her eyes to roam over the room, to scan over the torn and broken items, with her heart trying to jackknife up her throat and out of her mouth, she saw it, only about a yard to the right from where she sat.

A board—a broken and splintered board that had, until recently, been a piece of the entertainment center. It was narrow, but she knew it had weight to it. The damn thing had always been so heavy. Not a baseball bat, but it should be heavy enough.

She adjusted her sitting position, moved about a foot along the couch. The lighting caught the board differently now. The whole thing was only a couple of feet long. The end nearest to her was jagged with splinters, but now she saw the other end more clearly. Stuck through the other end, the far end, were two, maybe three nails.

"I don't have to see your hebe-ass face," Ivan said, "so long as I see the money. Just show me the money."

She extended her right leg, felt the sharp splinters scratch along her ankle.

She moved another inch—

"Just show me the fucking money."

Then another inch.

FORTY-SEVEN

Books are wonderful things. They're even better if you read them. Had Max not read certain books in his time — even if it was all hazy now — he wouldn't have had a single clue about what he was doing. He wouldn't have known that, as it gets older, dynamite can become very unstable, having something to do with the nitroglycerin pooling if it's not stored properly, or even if it has been, but too much time had passed. He wouldn't have known about the sensitivity of explosives. He wouldn't have known how stupid it would be to even try moving it from where he found it, but that was fine; it was already exactly where he wanted it. If it hadn't been for reading certain books, he wouldn't have known a damn thing about exploding-bridgewire detonators, or that they use an electric current. He wouldn't have known about velocity of detonation or anything else.

Camille constantly remarked how what he

read was garbage, and how she wished he would spend less time reading fiction and more time reading non-fiction. As if non-fiction was strictly fact, one hundred percent truth. The fact was, however, Camille didn't really know a damn thing about what books he read and didn't read. But it had ruled over him, in one way or another, and as the saying goes, the most common form of despair is not being who you are.

He blocked the oncoming rant from his mind, and focused on what he was doing. It didn't take very long, but that was only because everything in the world was moving at warp speed.

The sky had shifted into night now. Prussian blue, the moon rising, necklaces of star-like jewelry suspended all about. Silent grandeur dropped from the vast space above, down all around him. The power, the quiet majesty of the night, the potency and existence between the essence, the descent of shadows, and deeper within the shadows where more shadows lurked, there lurked still more shadows.

"This is the way the world ends," he said.

FORTY-EIGHT

Ivan had just beeped off the phone when Camille slammed the board down hard across his wrists. The phone clacked away, but he held on to his gun, and brought it up. But Camille was already swinging again. He blocked the blow with the forearm of his free hand and simultaneously tried to shoot. The bullet punched a hole in the couch as she swung at him again, and he cried out and dropped the gun as the nails tore through the flesh of his hand.

She screamed. The scream she'd been holding back, been fighting with all of her strength and courage to keep from exploding out of her. Having no mouth and needing to scream, but now she had her mouth and the screams she released bordered on insanity, not out of fear but out of intense anger.

She swung the board again. But this time Ivan was ready. He caught the board and tried to jerk it away, but Camille held on. Splinters bit into her fingers and palms but she wouldn't to let go. Even when she saw blood coming from her grip she refused to let go. Right now, this board was her lifeline.

They played a game of tug of war and splinters continued to tear at her hands, and for the first time, their eyes connected. The look she saw in Ivan's eyes was terrifying enough to know that everything he'd said to Frank was true. He would slowly mutilate her, once every hour. Her fingers, her hands, her arms, her legs. He would mutilate her, and he would enjoy every minute of it.

In addition, Ivan was twice her size, and when he changed tactics and jammed the board forward as she pulled, sharp jagged wood tore through her shirt and ripped across her breast. Somehow she had managed to turn. If she hadn't, she would have likely been impaled. But Ivan's maneuver had worked. She lost her bloody grip on the board, and fell into the couch, wincing at her stabbing pain.

Ivan dropped the board to the floor and came at her barehanded. She struggled and tried to fight back, but the moment his fist connected with her face, she lost hope.

"You fucking bitch!"

He back-handed her.

"Fucking bitch!"

He hit her again.

Both on the couch now, Ivan on top, he got both hands around her neck and squeezed. For a second Camille's vision went pure white, then darkened and Ivan's face reappeared. Then another whiteout, then darkness, steady as a pulse.

Ivan's own words entered her mind again. *Only fools are overly confident.*

Gasping for air and failing, she dredged up something deep inside her. Some unknown strength that she couldn't account for, just enough to shoot her knee straight up between the large man's legs.

The grip on her throat loosened, then was gone, and she blinked and sucked in air as Ivan stumbled back, both hands clamped on his family jewels. His mouth hung agape as Camille gathered her wits and stood up from the couch. She couldn't see either gun now and she didn't have time to search. She kicked him right in the hands, which went straight through to his gnads. At her feet was a hardcover copy of a book called *A Splendid Chaos*. She swooped down, picked it up, and slammed it as hard as she could into his face.

His legs wobbled but he didn't fall. She stepped toward him and swung a right hand, but he dodged it. She tried a left but he dodged that, too. Then *his* right hand left his crotch and whirled a hard and heavy upward backhand.

Her head felt like a tilt-o-whirl. She tripped over some of her broken things and crashed hard on the floor.

"You fucking bitch," he said again, but the strength had gone out of his voice, his breathing now labored.

He stepped over, grabbed her arm and yanked her up like she was nothing more than a rag doll.

His other hand slammed into her crotch, and then she was up in the air, over his head. He threw her across the room. She landed hard on stone and rolled a couple of times.

As quick as she could, she sat up. Dizzy, the whole world swimming in double takes, she forced herself to focus.

She saw both guns now, but no way to get to either one. She scrambled to her feet, hardly able to hold herself up, and found herself standing right at the foot of the stairs. Without hesitation, she half raced, half hobbled up them, then turned left into the very first room and slammed the door. She engaged a lock that may as well have been a toothpick, then switched on the light and looked around the guestroom in horror. Trashed, like everywhere else... but the picture. The awful painting that Max liked so much, destroyed, punched full of holes by a very private thing of hers. If she'd had the time, she would have been sick. But there was no time for that. Not now. She could let herself be sick later, if necessary, but not right now.

She raced to the bed and pulled the pink vibrator from the center of the painting. There was nothing in this room that could help her. Nothing.

Still holding the vibrator, she went to the window and unlatched it. It was a horizontal window and it opened upward. There was no bug screen, only dark night air.

She heard heavy footsteps climbing the stairs.

Sticking her head through the window, it was too dark to see just how far the drop was, or if there was anything she needed to avoid landing on at all costs. She couldn't see; she didn't know.

An angry fist pounded at the door. Any harder and the lock would snap. The door would shoot right open.

Another quick glance out the window...

Why blindly jump to her death when she could attempt to take advantage? At the moment she had the element of surprise on her side.

Leaving the window open, she hastened back to the door, switched off the light, and stood at the side the knob and the lock were on. She clenched the vibrator in both hands, tried to draw a deep breath just as the latch broke. The door smashed open. She saw him before he saw her, and it resulted in a pink vibrator slammed hard into Ivan's throat. The sex toy dropped to the floor as Ivan collapsed, eyes wide as saucers, both hands at his neck.

Camille hopped out of the room toward the stairs. At the very top of them, momentum already moving her, one of Ivan's hard legs kicked her feet out from under her.

Another tilt-o-whirl, down, down, down the stairs.

FORTY-NINE

Wayne and Dante had been walking around for a good while now. If everything had gone as discussed, Alejandro was dead. Alton, Alejandro, Mike missing and Armando gone for days. Finally the sons of bitches gone, giving them full control in Sueño Roto.

There was such little doubt as to be nonexistent that Ivan had properly taken care of Alé. If Mike magically showed up somehow, he would be incredibly easy to take care of. The only one whose whereabouts were still unknown was Max. The one they'd had the most fun with... until tonight. Shit, Wayne had given the dude opportunities to leave, but the punk simply didn't listen. What was a consequence for not listening? Round robin gang-banging his bitch of a wife. *That's* what he'd get for not taking good advice.

Wayne lit another cigarette. Dante did, too. It was dark now. Time to head back. To hell with little old Max. Chicken shit bastard had probably run off, scared out of his mind. Out of everyone, he was the easiest to take, but he'd vanished, probably fallen off a cliff or gotten bit by a rattler or something. Maybe he'd simply dropped dead from a heart attack, and would soon be a feast for coyotes.

Whatever. Who gave a fuck? He wasn't coming back, and even if he did, so what? He could watch as everyone took turns on his wife. He could watch them kill her. His last show before his own demise: watching them rape his wife, again and again until everyone was satisfied, then watch her die. In some ways, it seemed perfect.

That was the real reason for wanting to head back. Wayne felt it and Dante felt it, too. The itch, the urge, the need to fuck some pussy. Missus Max was no supermodel, but all of them had agreed that they would be more than happy to stretch their meat inside her.

They'd been walking pretty much in a straight line, so even in the dark it was easy enough to turn around and walk a straight line back. Simple nighttime navigation.

It was turning out to be a beautiful and productive night. The stars glimmered in the perfect just-after-twilight sky, the moon aglow with comfort, with joy, and with conquering. They had conquered. They were men, and now they were the bosses. Alé, Alton and Armando had been pussies. Mike was a pussy. But they'd been in the way. Just strong enough and just enough in the way to make their own plans a total cactus fuck.

But it was okay now. Fucking A, *yeah it was okay*. Ha! Everything was working out beautifully, fucking vroom-vroom Monster Truck Jam Show beautifully!

Then, all of a sudden, they both stopped. It was faint but they both heard it. A voice. A whiny voice. Max's voice. Maxi Pad's whiny voice, crying for help.

With an almost childlike glee, they quickened their pace, then stopped at the edge of a drop-off. They'd come farther than they'd thought. Below was the opening to the old mine. The mine that had never been much more than a shit-hole to begin with. It wasn't even fucking worth partying out here. Neither Wayne nor Dante could ever remember partying out here. And little pussy Max...

Ha! They were right. The little namby-pamby had gone chicken shit and run away. The moron had run away and gotten stuck in the old goddamn mine! What an idiot! Ha! The fucktard! This was fucking hilarious, really. If he was lost and stayed down there, maybe he'd eventually find Alton.

Still standing up top, above the entrance, Wayne cleared the giggles out of his voice, and called down, "Can you hear us, scrote?"

"Yeah," Max called back, voice echoing. "Wayne? That you, Wayne?"

"Yeah, scrote, it's me."

"Thank God!"

"What happened, scrote?"

"I'm in the mine."

"Yeah," Wayne said, "I've gathered that much, dude. What happened?"

"A bit of the mine. It collapsed. My leg is crushed!"

"You all right?"

"No, goddammit! My leg is crushed!"

"All right, all right. Hang on, we'll be right there."

Wayne turned to Dante. They couldn't help it. Fuck, they just couldn't help it. They both giggled like children. This — *this* was even better than they'd hoped. How long had the pansy been down in there now? Fuck it, who cared? –didn't matter. What mattered, really, was that it was fucking funny as hell. Almost piss-your-pants funny. Hell, maybe if he was really trapped, they'd piss on him first. Give him a straight-in-the-face golden shower, force him to open his mouth.

There was a slope nearby on their left. Like kids being let out for recess, they hurried down it, turned right at the bottom, and found themselves at the mine's opening. A couple of steps in and they stopped.

"It's dark in here, scrote. Where you at?"

No answer. It was so quiet, as though they'd both just walked into the world of the deaf.

Both Wayne and Dante took out their cigarette lighters. They pressed their fingers along the spark wheels, and the cave became illuminated with a faint brownish orange. In the dim light they could just make out some wire or something, going off to the left.

Suddenly something was very wrong.

Something was very much amiss. At first neither of them could pinpoint it. But then they looked to their right, and saw the box, and they knew exactly what was wrong. They both knew, without a shadow of a doubt, that the detonator had been triggered.

Before either of them could scream, Dante and Wayne were each ripped apart into a thousand pieces.

***

Max had gotten far away in a short amount of time but dust and bits of debris still rained down upon him.

"Fuck you, scrote," he said, then let out a breath and turned to walk back toward the house. His night vision was good this evening, and the moon, in all her gentle glory, was growing brighter.

Thank God. There had been so many probabilities for things to go wrong. So many risks. So many variables But it had worked. Goddammit, it had worked.

"Three down," he said, his breathing now constant sighs of exhaustion.

That left Alton, Ivan, and, likely the worst of all, Alejandro.

Fuck it. He didn't care anymore. He was too tired to care. He was sick and tired of it all. Tired of the whole damn business. Slowly, he turned to walk away.

A human being is spirit, and spirit is the self,

while the self is a relation which relates to itself. Whatever the hell that meant, and why it crossed his mind now, he didn't know and he couldn't have cared less. If he got back to the house and it was a world of shit... well, at least he'd cut their number in half. At least he'd given them a fight. He was still alive, and therefore he was proof. He wasn't the pussy they all wanted him to be.

God creates out of nothing... isn't that what they say? He creates out of nothing and yet He makes saints out of sinners, while conversely making sinners out of saints. But then again, it's all out of nothing, right? Nothing. Zero. Zip. Something out of nothing. Is that even possible? Or did that mean that nothing actually existed? That all that had happened — everything — was nonexistent? Or did that merely make everything in the world a big misunderstanding?

What was suddenly up with all the philosophical jibber-jabber?

Because you just killed people, a secondary voice inside him said.

Again, fuck it.

He began to walk.

After only a few steps he heard cracking noises. Quiet at first, but the volume escalating quickly. By the light of the moon, he watched the ground move. It trembled, then shifted, then slowly began to cave in.

Like drawing a line on the earth with a pen of destruction, Max watched the tunnel collapse in on itself, spreading to each side at jagged angles. He felt the ground giving way beneath his feet, and jumped back just in time to not go down with it.

He watched it crumple and disintegrate, mostly forming a line, a straight line; a stripe of havoc heading back toward the house. Whether or not it would change anything happening there, he didn't know, but at least it would likely give everybody a good scare.

He laughed just a little, and continued his trek back to *La casa asesina de Ortiz*, the Murderous House of Ortiz, the Insane Asylum of Pendleton. How the hell would you say that in Spanish?

Another laugh escaped him. He couldn't help himself, and it didn't surprise him at all when he started whistling, nor was he surprised at *what* he whistled. The theme to *The Andy Griffith Show* had a hilarious sense of irony to it, even if it didn't make any sense and he wasn't sure why.

Regardless of what happened, and of anything else that might happen, it was indeed a lovely night.

FIFTY

The left side of the house was sunken and slanted. The rest of it, while still intact, looked weaker, as though a wrecking crew had taunted it, laughed and pointed and called it names. There were lights on inside and from where he stood all of the windows looked broken. Max stood at the far edge of the back patio. He listened. Not a sound. All quiet on the eastern front. This side did face east, right?

Whatever.

The closer he'd gotten to the house, the more caution had begun to set in. He was still tired of it all, and within the realm of uncaring, but as he got away from what he had just done at the entrance of the mine and moved closer to what still might be waiting for him, he couldn't help the return of caution, like a terrible sequel. It took hold of him again, though even the caution was tired. His wits were dulled, his adrenaline scant to nonexistent, and now he stood on the back patio, where only a few days ago he'd sat reading a book while Camille commanded movers, where his wife had come out and taken the book away from him, exercising her power and control.

Only a few days ago.

It felt like a lifetime.

Slowly, he resumed walking across the patio, toward the wall of now completely shattered windows. When he reached them he stepped through one, and the first thing he saw was Alejandro splayed on the crooked floor, a pool of blood around his head. The lighting in the house seemed off somehow, like dim stage light.

He turned away from the sight of Alejandro, whose death had little affect on him. Not much was going to affect him right now, it seemed. He wasn't affected when he saw the banister of the stairway gone, likely rattled and broken away from the underground collapse. He wasn't affected by the sight of Ivan, skull practically split in two, body bent in such a way as to imply that he had fallen.

There was little affect when he heard a woman sobbing, when he saw Camille on the floor, back against the wall, hugging herself. When she heard him, she looked up with a lost face, a face devoid of purpose or strength. Their eyes met, and for what seemed a long time nothing in the world existed except the two of them.

Sniffling, she finally said, "Max?"

A very slow nod. "Yeah. It's me."

He saw that her palms were ravaged as he watched her struggle and then get to her feet.

Then she moved fast, raced to him, bloody arms open, and hugged him, and when she did the sobs became all out cries.

"Max," she said again. "Oh-Max-oh-Max-oh-Max! Thank God."

He hugged her back. "You okay?"

She cried harder. "They're dead. They're all dead."

"I guess they are, huh?"

"Oh-Max-oh-Max-oh-Max."

"What about Peter?" he said. "Is he dead, too?"

She squeezed him tighter. "Yes. Oh God, yes."

He brought a hand up and stroked the back of her head. "Shame," he said, then stopped brushing her hair and held her at arm's length. "And you? Are you okay?"

He watched her close her eyes. Then she nodded, slow, then fast. "I hurt, but, yeah, I'm all right, I think."

He nodded again, slowly. "Good." He looked at the front door. "You know what you need to do, Cammy?"

She stared at him with teary eyes.

"You need to call nine-one-one."

"Ivan. He—he broke my phone."

"There are other phones."

"Why can't you just call them? Did you lose your phone, too?"

He shook his head. "No. I have it."

"So then call them. Why don't you call them?"

He let go of her. "Because I'm gonna go."

"What?"

"Yeah. I think it's time. I think it's time for me

to go."

"Max? What do you mean? What are you talking about?"

"This isn't a playground," he said.

"W-what?"

"No, Camille. This isn't a playground and we're not on vacation." He patted her lightly on blood-spotted, tear-streaked cheek. "Welcome to the real world."

With that, he headed to the front door. His wife didn't say a word as he looked and saw that his backpack was still nearby. At a glance, anyway, it appeared undamaged. He bent down, picked it up, and slung one strap over his shoulder.

No farewell words. Max walked outside and went directly to the Camry. He tossed the backpack into the passenger seat, then climbed behind the wheel. Got the engine going, then spent a good few minutes maneuvering the car until he got around all the other cars parked in the driveway. He drove down to the end of it, looked both ways, then turned onto the road that would eventually connect him to the Interstate.

After a few minutes he took out his cell phone and dialed Selena.

"Max!"

"Hi."

"Are you okay?"

It took him a while to answer. "I don't know."

"What happened? Jesus Christ, Max, what happened?"

He shrugged. "I guess, in a way, I won."

Silence. If it was awkward silence, Max didn't notice.

"I'm leaving," he told her. "I'm on my way outta town right now."

"Are you going to Flagstaff?"

"I don't know."

"But... Portland, right? You're going to Portland?"

The laugh that escaped him was so faint as to be nonexistent. "I don't know," he said.

"What's going on, Max? What? Do you want to meet somewhere?"

He thought about it for a moment.

"Call me tomorrow," he said. "We'll see." Then he snapped the phone closed and tossed it onto the passenger seat, alongside his backpack. He looked at the night around him as he drove. It really was a beautiful evening. A tiny smile etched into his face as he focused his eyes on the road.

He really *didn't* know where he was going. He didn't have a clue. Not the faintest idea whatsoever.

The evaluation coin whirled and twirled, wobbling and teetering but with no current intentions of falling to one side or the other. Neither heads nor tails meant a damn thing. Nothing was known and nothing was decided. So the coin just spun and spun as Max drove down the road, having no idea where in the world he was going, and not caring in the least.

www.ingramcontent.com/pod-product-compliance
Lightning Source LLC
Chambersburg PA
CBHW031943260626
47157CB00017B/2115